Get Ready For War

D0368256

Also by Ni-Ni Simone

Shortie Like Mine

If I Was Your Girl

A Girl Like Me

Teenage Love Affair

Upgrade U

No Boyz Allowed

True Story

Also by Amir Abrams

Crazy Love

The Girl of His Dreams

Published by Kensington Publishing Corporation

Get Ready For War

Hollywood HIGH

NI-NI SIMONE
AMIR ABRAMS

Dafina KTeen Books
KENSINGTON PUBLISHING CORP.
http://www.kensingtonbooks.com

DAFINA KTEEN BOOKS are published by

Kensington Publishing Corp.
119 West 40th Street
New York, NY 10018

ISBN-13: 978-0-7582-7355-0
ISBN-10: 0-7582-7355-X

First Printing: April 2013

10 9 8 7 6 5 4 3 2 1

Printed in the United States of America

To Selena James for seeing the vision and believing that the mean girls of Hollywood High would set the literary world on fire!
Get ready for war!

Welcome to Hollywood High,
where socialites rule and popularity is
more of a drug than designer digs could ever be...

1

London

Who the hell needed enemies when you had hatin' media hoes and bloggers maliciously tearing you up every chance they got and a bunch of selfish, backstabbing whores as friends.

Oh no. My enemies weren't the ones I needed to keep my mink-lashed eyes on. It was the Pampered Princesses of Hollywood High Academy who kept me dragged into their shenanigans, along with the paparazzi that lived and breathed to destroy me. Hence why I was wearing a floppy hat and hiding behind a pair of ostrich-leather Moss Lipow sunglasses.

I was a trendsetter.

A shaker 'n' mover.

A fashionista extraordinaire.

I was London Phillips.

Not a joke!

And my name had no business being caught up in any of the most recent scandals with Heather's (aka Wu-Wu)

Skittles fest. If she wanted to overdose on her granny's heart medicine, then she needed to leave me out of it.

My reputation of being fine, fly, and eternally fabulous was etched on the pages of magazines and carved in the minds of many. And I was one of the most adored, envied, and hated for all of my divaliciousness. It came with the territory of being deliciously beautiful. And I embraced it.

But being on top didn't mean a thing if you didn't know how to stay there. Reputation was everything at Hollywood High. And up until three days ago, I was perched up on Mt. Everest in all of my fabulousness, looking down at any- and everyone who followed me or aspired to be me, but could (or would) *never* be me. Yeah, it had been a cold-blooded climb to the top. But so what? A diva did what she had to do to get what she wanted and needed. And I had made it.

But I wasn't in New York anymore, reigning alone. No. I was in Hollywood. And I had to share the mountaintop with three skanks who were supposed to be the "It Clique." And they had been. *And we had been.* But now we were about to lose our crowns as the Pampered Princesses of Hollywood High if Heather, Spencer, and Rich didn't get it together—quick, fast, and in a hurry. Their antics were destroying my reputation. And theirs!

The media and bloggers were having a field day tearing us up in the headlines. Kicking us in our crowns and branding us last week's hot trash. Not respecting that we were the daughters of high-profiled celebrities. Naming us this week's flops. They really thought we had fallen off our white-horsed carriages. And from the looks of things, we had. Here I was, again, in the midst of Rich, Spencer, and Heather's bullshit. But enough was enough.

I was determined to handle Rich first. I had to get her focused. But this wench, who I thought was easy and gullible, wasn't playing along the way I thought. No, she was too busy chasing behind some boy whom she seemed obsessed with and hell-bent on being with. And that was a problem—for *me!*

Shoot. Can I get my life?

As I walked through the school's café doors, pulling out my cell, it was eerily quiet, but I had no time to figure out why. I needed to get in touch with Rich. where r you?

A string-bean-thin girl with a pink-and-black Mohawk, black eyeliner, and black lipstick stepped up to me and handed me a FREE WU-WU T-shirt being distributed by Wu-Wu's many stalkers, gawkers, and fanatics. I stared the walking toothpick down. "Beanpole, who told you you could get up in my space?" I snapped, tossing the shirt in her face. "Go hang yourself with it. And make sure you get it right."

Her eyes popped open.

I was sooooo not in the mood. I needed to know where the hell Rich and Spencer were. I already knew where Heather's wretched self was. But Rich and Spencer were both unaccounted for. This made the fifteenth time I had pulled out my phone today to check for any messages or missed calls from Rich because I had been calling her and texting her and leaving her messages since seven o'clock this morning. Sweating her; something I don't do. And still there was nothing from her.

Zilch.

Nada.

Not a damn thing!

As I was walking and texting Rich another where-the-hell-are-you message, I couldn't help but notice the noise level in the café. Normally it was full of chatter and laughter and all types of music.

Not today.

Dead silence.

All I heard was a bunch of clicking from cameras. And a few comments like "Uh-oh, it's about to go down now" as I made my way farther into the center of the café. Suddenly I knew what all of the silence was about. There was a group of girls sitting at our table. You know. The one that has, or had, the pink tablecloth and a humungous RESERVED FOR THE PAMPERED PRINCESSES sign up on it. Yeah, that table.

Screech!

Everyone knew on this side of campus that the Pampered Princesses were the ruling clique. And no one sat at our table. No one!

I pulled up the rim of my hat, inched my shades down to the tip of my nose, and peered at them.

I blinked.

I couldn't believe what I was seeing. The group of girls had on uniforms. And judging by the colors, I knew they absolutely did not belong on this side of the campus.

This has to be a mistake.

I marched over toward them, then stood and stared at the group of chicks who had foolishly parked their behinds and taken up space at our table. These preemies had *our* table covered with a fuchsia tablecloth. And they had the nerve to have the table set with fine china and a candelabra in the center of the table, as if they were preparing for some kind of holiday feast. And they sat pretty as they pleased, as if they owned the room.

They all wore their hair pulled back into sleek, shiny ponytails with colorful jeweled clips. I ice-grilled them, expecting them to scatter like frightened roaches. Not! They didn't budge. Didn't even blink an eyelash. Nope, those munchkin critters defiantly stayed planted in their seats and continued on with their chatter as if I didn't exist. And at that very moment, I felt like the whole cafeteria had zoomed in on me. I quickly glanced around the room to assess the situation. They had. And it was turning into a nightmare. All eyes were clearly on me! Cameras clicked.

I cleared my throat.

They continued talking and laughing.

Did they come here to bring it?

If I wasn't so pissed at their disrespect, I would have been impressed. And truth is, they were adorable. But that was not the time, nor the place, to give props to a bunch of bratty Beanie Baby sluts trying to serve me drama. I had enough of that with my own clique, so I sure wasn't going to tolerate it from a bunch of ninth-grade peons in navy blazers, green-and-blue plaid pleated skirts, and black Nine West pumps.

I picked up a fork from the table and tapped one of the glasses with it. "Umm, excuse you. Excuse you, excuse you."

The chick sitting at the far end of the table craned her neck in my direction and stared me down. She had beautiful skin and an oversized forehead. "The name's Harlow. H-A-R-L-O-W. And whaaat? You want my autograph? 'Cause I don't do groupies."

Oh no, now I knew that them being at our table was not a mistake. Those tricklets had strutted over to this side of the campus purposely to bring it. All in the name of getting it crunked.

Now, along with the media, we had teenybopper freshmen trying to bring it to us!

Oh, hell no! They really don't want it. Apparently they don't know what they're asking for.

I took a deep breath. Determined to keep it cute, calm, and collected. I couldn't afford to dish out another hundred grand for tearing up the café, again. Daddy would kill me for sure. "Sweetie, I don't know who misplaced your lunch period, and I'm sure this is your nap time. But this right here"—I patted the table—"is not for you."

She smirked. "And you are?"

I tilted my head. "About to become your worst nightmare in a minute if you-all don't get up from this table."

The four of them stared at each other, then looked around as if they were searching for something. "Umm, excuse me, Starlets," the Harlow chick said to her little Cheerios crew. "Do any of you see a name tag with the name Buffalo Hips on it?"

"Creature from the wild...," the three others sang out.

"Is looking for someplace to sit," a golden-brown chick sitting next to Harlow added.

Stay calm.

Just relax.

Let me try this again.

"Umm, where's your babysitter? Because apparently there's been an escape from the nursery; toddlers gone wild..."

"Umm, excuse me, Miss London," one of the white-gloved servers said, coming to the table with two trays. I blinked. He set a platter of burgers and milk shakes in the center of the table, then walked off, eyeing me.

Then those little disrespectful chicks had the nerve to snap open their napkins and lay them neatly on their laps.

Oh, this had gone too far!

I placed a hand up on my hip and tossed my Fendi hobo bag in the center of the table, disrupting everything on it. They jumped.

"Eww..."

"Ohmygod..."

"Did someone dump their garbage here? How gross is that."

"Isn't that last year's bag?"

"Exaaaactly, Arabia," Miss Forehead said, tossing her ponytail. "Old head's tryna serve us. Now get your fashion right."

Wait. Did Forehead just call me an old head?

They waved their arms up in the air and snapped. "Mmmph, exaaaaactly."

The other two sitting across from Harlow and the Arabia chick snickered, like two cackling backup singers. They really didn't understand. I was trying to spare them from a beat-down. Truth is they reminded me of me, and my old clique back in New York when we were their age. But that was then. And this was now! Still, they had heart. And they were sassy. Their diamonds sparkled. And one of them I knew for sure had money. I could smell it all over her. But that had nothing to do with all four of them being totally out of line.

I leaned in and spoke real tight-lipped. "I don't know if you four little bimbos are trying to be cute, or intentionally trying to work me over, or if you simply banged your oversized foreheads on the monkey bars during recess, but obviously you all missed the memo on which clique reigned supreme here."

They burst out laughing all hard and crazy, then stopped abruptly. "Hmmm"—they snapped their fingers—"Not!"

The Harlow chick turned to me and said, "No, ma'am, we didn't miss the memo. We didn't miss the blogs either. Let's see. If we're not mistaken, they all say"—she glanced over at her posse—"drum roll, please..."

"Losers!" they shouted in unison.

The cafeteria erupted in laughter.

My face was cracked. I couldn't believe that a pack of toddlers in cheesy uniforms were trying to set it off and disrespect *me* to my face. Cute girls or not, this was a problem!

Cameras continued clicking.

The Harlow chick was clearly Miss Mouth Almighty— and the appointed ringleader. "Page twenty-seven in *Hot or Not* magazine"—she started flipping through the tabloid— "says that you gutter hoes have fallen apart." She eyed me, putting a hand up to her chest. "Oooh, look at Heather..."

"Junkie," they sang out.

Another said, "Aaah, Wu-Wu's in the house."

"Not!" they all said, snapping their fingers again.

Harlow continued. "Black beauties, baby..."

"Crushed and ready to go...," the backup singers sang out. "Got it on lock..."

The Arabia chick said. "Oooh-oooh...don't forget about the fakest of 'em all."

"Who, Rich?" Harlow smirked.

"Boom bop, make it drop," they all said in unison. "Pop pop, get it, get it…"

"Yeah, a baby," Harlow sneered.

"Clutching pearls, clutching pearls," her three cheerleaders mocked, placing a hand up to their necks.

The café went wild.

It was clear that these girls had been watching us hard. *Mmmph, even the young broads trying to jock our spots.*

Harlow rolled her eyes. "Oh, puhleeeeze. How tired is that? *Clutching pearls.* Who says that?"

"Has-beens," one of her giggling sidekicks snorted.

"Mmmm, exaaaaactly!" Harlow and the Arabia chick snapped.

"Oh, wait," Harlow stated excitedly, clapping her hands together. "Let's not forget Spencer…"

"The dizzy chick," they said. "Smells like cat piss… smells like cat piss…"

"Somewhere…"

"Down on her knees. Down on her knees," they all chimed in.

"Mopping the floor and making videos," Arabia added.

"Nine-one-one, this is an emergency…this is an emergency…"

I was hot! Rich was somewhere knocked up, Heather was somewhere drugged up or going through withdrawals, and Spencer was probably somewhere neck bobbing. And, once again, I was the one getting dragged—*alone!*

Harlow eyed me up and down, curling her lips up into a dirty sneer. "And you, London…"

Ohhhhkay, here we go!

"Freak!" they all yelled out in unison. "Caught up in the matrix…Caught up in the matrix…"

I blinked.

And before I could catch myself, before she could get the rest of her sentence finished, I backhanded her so hard she fell backward. And spit slung from her mouth. They all screamed as I swung that little Gerber baby around the café and gave her the beatdown of her life. Then, in the midst of all the cameras clicking and tables being tossed up, the other three Romper Room hookers jumped up on my back and tackled me to the floor. And the only thing I could think about was being stomped down by a bunch of Crenshaw Crippettes in cheap, pleather pumps. *This was a state of emergency!*

I was clearly behind enemy lines. And it was all Rich's, Spencer's, and Heather's fault because they didn't know how to handle their scandal.

2

Rich

12 A.M.

I couldn't sleep.
Couldn't eat.
All I could do was think...
And I didn't wanna think.

Thoughts, and memories, and maybes, and could've beens, would've beens, and should've beens were as useful as a pile of knockoff Louis V. bags. A bad attempt by my mind to redesign what I knew could never change. And no matter how hard I tried to hold back tears or swallow the ache in my throat, I knew that when the sun rose, my world would still be the same. Tumbling down.

I settled into the soft white Egyptian sheets that covered the hotel's king-size bed and did my all to outrun my thoughts...

2 A.M.

I prayed hard that I'd slept for more than two hours. But as usual my prayers failed me...

And now I was having another round with coulda, woulda, and shoulda wreckin' my flow. Ugh! Feeling sorry for myself was so thirteen hours ago!

4 A.M.

I was going stir-crazy. Insane. This was not where I was supposed to be. Not again. The first time maybe...but not this time. This time, I was supposed to toss everyone who didn't agree with me the peace sign, while telling them to kiss my...

Ugh!

I should leave...

I sat up in bed. Walked over to my hotel suite's Juliet balcony and looked out at the crimson-clay colored mountains. I was in the middle of nowhere...Population two hundred and eight. A three-hour plane ride away from civilization. The perfect place for affluent teenage girls—who didn't stick to their parents' scripts—to leave behind their most scandalous secrets on the town's only—and very well paid—ob-gyn's cold steel table.

Maybe...

Know what? Screw maybe.

6 A.M.

I couldn't sleep at all last night. My thoughts were haunting me. This was so not the plan.

The plan was designer diaper bags, matching pink diamonds, Swarovski baby baths. The plan was blistering love between me and my man. Pushing a baby carriage. Having my publicist—something we all had for no other reason than to keep us relevant in the news—flood the media with pictures of my blue-blooded offspring. Maybe a shot at reality TV. Oh, and somewhere in between droppin' it and poppin' it and making my last rounds through a club or two was to be the royal marriage of the billionaire music mogul's princess and the low-money-millionaire commoner.

And no, I wasn't settling.

And yeah, I knew it sounded crazy.

And no, there was no way for me to help who I loved. Trust. My mother tried to stop me from loving him. And all it did was make me want my man more. Heck, I even tried leaving him alone. Twice. But all it did was leave me with two missed periods and two secrets to keep. So there was no fighting it. Knox was the only one I wanted. I had to have him. Period. No negotiation. No waving a white flag. I loved every inch of his six-foot, athletic-built, sexy-caesar, paper-bag brown deliciousness. And yeah, umm hmm, he was all of that.

Snap. Snap.

And yeah, yeah, yeah, sure, I could have any man that I wanted—with way more money and surname prestige. Heck, I was astoundingly beautiful: skin like chocolate silk, a Chinese bob that lay flush against my sharp jawline. Perfectly straight teeth encased by seductive, pouty lips. And my body was hella crazy: D-sized melon cups; molded, exquisitely round and dimple-free black-girl booty; hourglass hips; thick thighs; and luscious long legs. I was the embodiment of sweetness. Candy come to life. Swizz chocolate in human form. So there was no mistake I had it going on. Nevertheless I didn't want anyone else. I wanted Knox.

Even if I was mad at him and was too stubborn to answer his calls and tell him that.

This was way too much drama to only be sixteen.

According to my mother, the Know-Ev-ver-ry-thing-Queen, by the time I was grown, only God knew what kind of fresh-azz skeezer I would be.

I resented that.

Apparently my mother missed the memo: there was no more time for me to be grown. I was already grown. And I wasn't a skeezer—I just wasn't a virgin. Clearly there was a difference.

But did she care? Hell no. All Logan Montgomery cared about was what she had planned for me, and what I wanted didn't matter. My mother was such a dirty bitc—

Know what, I won't even say it, because truth be told, my mother was way worse than any female dog in heat.

What kind of person blackmails their daughter to come to the middle of nowhere by placing a gun—loaded with two lawyers, a Tiffany pen, and a threat to donate my trust fund to the humane society (How inhumane was that?)—to my head, if I didn't do what she said?

She left me with no choice. I had to come here and wait for the doctor to call the hotel suite and tell us when it was time.

She had me by the throat...but after this I was done with her. Finished. Because apparently she had me messed up. I was born with the platinum spoon; she was the ex-groupie. And her husband, the high school dropout turned rapper, turned billionaire CEO, was even worse than his wife.

I was sick of these people. And I was tired of my decisions being tied to their money. My life was bigger than that.

I was Rich Montgomery. Socialite extraordinaire. I walked on diamonds. I was the chick who put the *It* in the It Clique. I was the reason the Pampered Princesses could be considered pampered. I was that chick... Now all I needed was to feel like it...

12:00 P.M.

White sheets, stirrups, blue scrubs, and bright lights...

"Close your eyes and count backward. By the time you get to three you will be asleep..."

Nine... seven... five... four... three...

2:30 P.M.

I ran my hands across the cool white sheets. My palms were in search of Knox's hard, brown body. My fingertips needed to cup his muscular pecs. I needed his heat. His passion. His kisses. His love. To make love and erase the pain I felt easing into my chest and settling there. I needed him, but my palms felt nothing. No heat. No passion. Nothing. He wasn't there. A steel fist balled in my throat.

I opened my eyes and tears lined the rims. They slipped down my cheeks. I wasn't with Knox.

I was at the exclusive doctor's office.

Seated across the room on the left side of my bed, with her legs crossed and her eyes scrolling the pages of *O* magazine, was my mother—the dirty...

Tears continued to run down my cheeks. I reached for a Kleenex and my mother looked over the magazine she leafed through. "Oh, Rich, please, not the tears."

If I could get out of this bed I would slap her face. I narrowed my eyes and swallowed the fist in my throat. "Do you know how hard this was for me?"

"Considering that this is the second time we're here, I thought for sure that this had gotten easier."

"You don't even care!"

"You have about two seconds to drop that tone at least two octaves."

"Why, Ma? Are you scared someone may hear me?!" Instead of dropping my voice two octaves I raised it by two. "I swear you are sooo confused!"

"Oh, really?"

"Yeah, really, and you know it. You think that my life belongs to you!"

"That's right. That's exactly what I think." She lowered her eyes back to the magazine and flipped a page. "I'm glad you realized that. Perhaps this'll be the last time we have to fly to this godforsaken place and pay way too much money because you refuse to use condoms and continue to sleep with the hired help's herd. You really need to stop acting like a spoiled, self-centered brat and appreciate how lucky you are. Now, enough. Get some rest because in a few hours we are out of here."

"Oh, I'm sorry, Mother. Forgive me for not appreciating how you keep making me get abortions. I really apologize for the inconvenience—surely you'd rather be at the spa spending Daddy's money."

My mother stared at me and closed the magazine. I knew I was teetering on the edge, but I didn't care. Everything was not about her and what she wanted. And she needed to know that. I was sick of this control freak. This was my life and from this moment I was going to live it. My way. So, I returned the same nasty look that she had given me and at this moment we were mirror images of one another...until she rose from her seat and I felt like a five-year-old about to get a spanking.

Don't be scared...you got this...

She crowded my personal space and hovered over me, nose practically to nose.

"What did you say?" my mother asked. Her coffee breath blew in the center of my face. I blinked and she leaned in even closer.

"With all due respect, Ma. I really need you to back up. Literally and figuratively." She arched a brow and I continued. "I don't need you sweatin' me right now."

"Sweatin' you?"

"Yeah, you're way too close. And another thing, since we're going there, I don't want to hear any lectures about what you think is best for me, especially since you've never asked me what I want."

"Because what you want doesn't matter. Yo' azz," she said with her Southern California drawl in full effect, "better want what da hell I tell you to want."

"Okay. Since that's how you'd like to have it. I tell you what: after today I'll be your little robot. Will that please you?" I folded my hands in a prayer position and said in a sweet, sarcastic whine, "I won't get into any trouble, Mommy. I'll stay off the blogs, go to an Ivy League university—"

"And they would never have you."

"Oh, you're right." I placed one of my manicured hands over my heart. "Forgive me for that, too. From this abortion on, I'll be the born-again angelic virgin. Your little princess. Who keeps her legs closed and gets good grades. As a matter of fact, I'll be more like you. I'll leave the hired help's herd alone and instead I'll head to dressing rooms and stalk rappers and NBA players."

Smack!

My mother's hand sailed across my face and burned my

cheek as it landed. I almost fell out the bed as my head jerked toward the guardrail.

I quickly collected myself and as I tried to sit up my mother's hand flew through the air to smack me again, but this time I caught her wrist, flung her hand away from my face, and gave her a look that dared her to bring it.

For the first time in my life I felt I could fight her. Like I could take her down.

My mother snatched her hand away and scanned my eyes. "Oh, you wanna fight me, huh? Okay. You think you can beat me now, is that it?" She took a step back, walked over to the door, and locked it. "Is that what they're doing in Hollywood High—little girls fighting their mothers?"

"That's the problem—I'm not a little girl. I'm a woman." All I could see was red. The voice of reason went out the window, and at that moment I didn't give a freak about the consequences. If she whopped my azz so be it, but one thing was for sure and two things were for certain: I would fight for what I wanted.

"A *woman?*" my mother said to me as she removed her wedding band and twenty-karat engagement ring.

"A woman." I swallowed any and all fear that crept its way up on me. She had raised me to be a lot of things, but a punk wasn't one of them. So the look I gave her all but told her to try me.

"A woman. Okay." My mother gathered the drapes and the light in the room dimmed.

It was on.

"A woman," she repeated.

I scooted to the edge of the bed. I was sore, but I was also willing to ignore the pain to prove my point.

My mother walked back over to me and said, "Let me

help you out a bit. *A woman* has her own money and pays for her own abortions—actually a woman doesn't get pregnant by every Tom, Dick, and Knox she lies down with. A woman uses a condom and doesn't have to hold her mother's hand to the doctor's office—"

"I didn't ask you to bring me to the doctor's office!"

"Then you shouldn't have come. You're grown. You got this."

"It's too late now."

"You're right. It is too late, because if you keep runnin' your mouth, I'ma kill you." She sounded as if she'd just stepped off the streets of Watts. "If I were you—"

"You may as well be; you're making all my decisions."

"Oh, okay." My mother removed her earrings. "I see I'ma have to go to jail again."

"What? Jail?"

"Oh, you didn't know that, did you?"

I swallowed.

"Don't get scared now, sweetie. You wanna buck, so let's do this, homie. 'Cause see, obviously I need to reintroduce you to who I used to be and am only two seconds from becoming again: Shakeesha Logan Gatling. Grape Street Crippette. I put bullets in chicks' heads for less than the ruckus you just brought me." She positioned her right hand like a gun, put it to my forehead, and as she mushed me in my forehead she pulled the trigger.

I felt a slight nervousness try to sneak up on me, but I swallowed.

"Too late now," my mother said as if she'd read my mind. "You better shake that off. What, you need some Vaseline? Take your earrings off." She quickly reached behind my ears and unfastened my hoops. She placed them on the table and said, "So you want babies, huh? You wanna be a woman. You wanna be with Knox. You're willing to get beat down for Knox? You love him that much—"

"Yes, I love him! And that's not going to change. I don't care how many times you want to fight me, your own daughter."

"Oh, now you're my daughter—was that before or after I told you I'd put a bullet in a chick's head and you realized that I wouldn't be afraid to put one in yours? You're right, you're my daughter, and before I let you beat me I'd walk away from all the diamonds and the dollars and I would kill you. I don't have a fear of prison. I already know what it's like. Four years. You better Google me."

Prison? She really went to prison?

"Hell yeah, I went to prison."

Prison? For what?

"For manslaughter," she continued as she paced the room, pounding her fist into her palm. "Because when I was sixteen I thought I had all the answers. I didn't have money, my mother was getting high, and I had no idea who my father was. And my brother wasn't in college like yours. He was doing life in prison for droppin' bodies, and I was following in his footsteps. There was no Hollywood High, private school. I was gettin' schooled in the streets. My family was the hood and my GED was courtesy of California State Prison. And the day I was released, I dropped Shakeesha, became Logan, reinvented myself, and yeah, I stalked basketball players, and I stalked rappers. Because I had beauty and I had a body and I wasn't going back to prison.

"I knew there was something bigger than tossing up gang signs, drive-bys, and bustin' caps. And all of that I had erased from my mind. I snagged my husband, gave birth to the perfect son who never gave me a problem. Never back-talked. Did exactly as he was told and what was asked of him. Now, RJ could get whatever he wanted because he knew how to listen and play by the rules."

"Oh yeah, perfect Prince RJ."

"He is perfect. But you. You wanna raise up. You wanna bring it." She stopped pacing and leaned into my face. "Go ahead and take your best shot. Just know that whatever decision you make you better be able to lie down by it, because that's what women do. Lie in the beds they made. Now let's go. But just know that if you hit me, I'ma murder you. And I will do my time in peace. Now buck."

Smack! Crack!

My mother threw the first hit and my face was on fire and sirens blared in my ears. My mother slapped me so hard that tears sprang from my eyes and my shoulders shook. All I could see were stars.

"You're moving too slow!" She gripped me by my neck and pinned me against the headboard. I couldn't breathe.

Bap!

My mother hit me again and I felt dizzy. "You're grown!" She slapped me again. "You want Knox. You'll disrespect me for him." Her elbow pressed into my throat and she clenched her teeth. "I will crush your windpipe and you will be in here for a collapsed lung."

"Ma—"

"This ain't no ma. This is a woman's battle. Aren't you a woman? Fighting for what you believe in?" My mother didn't even blink. "You wanna come for me, then you better be ready, 'cause I got bustin' heads on lock."

My mother's elbow sank deeper into my throat and I

knew then she would kill me. I'd pushed her many times, but I'd never seen this side of her. The only other time I'd seen Shakeesha come to life was when one of my father's mistresses showed up at the door demanding money.

"Ma, please." Tears flowed down my face and over her forearm. "Please let me go," I gasped. "I...can't...breathe..."

"That's the point. I will take your breath." Her eyes were black and cold as she looked at me. "You want Knox, then you can have him, because I'm done with you." She let me go, quickly turned, and I jumped, grabbing my neck.

"No, don't jump." My mother slid her jewelry back on. "Little too late for that. Next time just come correct and work on your reflex." She dusted invisible wrinkles off the front of her peach-colored slacks and white sleeveless Chanel blouse. "For now, I'm packing away Shakeesha." She tucked her Chloé clutch under her left arm. "Because the next time she comes out you'll be added to the body count. The plane leaves in two hours and it will take off with or without you."

"Ma—"

She didn't answer; instead she walked out of the room and the door closed behind her.

And all I could think was my mother had lost her mind. *Welcome to my life.*

3

Heather

I was desperate to slice my wrist. Or take a blade and run it across my throat.

End it all.

Suicide-bomb my way out of hell.

And pray to God to sever my veins and let me bleed to death.

This way I could stop the sharp jabs that tortured my stomach and forced me to grip the cold edges of this repulsive steel toilet and dry heave.

I needed something.

Anything.

That could murder this monkey who crept up my back and ghostly whispered in my ear that I needed a hit.

When I didn't *need it*.

I just *wanted it* bad as hell.

There was a difference.

Uncontrollable sweat dripped from the crown of my head, over my forehead, and rained down my temples as I rose from the toilet and dried my face with the sleeve of my oversized forest-green jumpsuit.

You gotta get up...

How?

I wiped my face again and stood up straight, only to stumble against the wall. I did what I could to play off my legs feeling like willow branches, especially since all eyes were on me.

Snickering.

Whispering.

Pointing.

There was no effen privacy. None. Everyone who passed by or sat in open view of the toilet was *all in my business*. And with all of the noise and the constant buzzing, I couldn't even hear myself think.

Sweat poured down my temples again and lightning roared in my belly. I had to get the hell out of here!

My nerves were shot.

My head hurt.

My chest felt like it was giving way to an asthma attack. Even though I wasn't asthmatic.

I wanted to scream *Let me out! Do you know who I am!* But I'd been here for three days and had already screamed *I'm Wu-Wu Tanner* for twenty-seven hours straight, and the only thing it did was give me a headache and a sore throat.

I was America's sweetheart. A role model. The star of *The Wu-Wu Tanner Show*. Nickelodeon Choice Awards pick for favorite actress. Sold more Wu-Wu dolls than Barbie. More kids were addicted to me than Miley Cyrus. And none of that meant anything in here. What mattered were my charges and whatever the judge decided my fate would be.

I had to get it together so when I appeared before the judge sometime this morning, he wouldn't think I was a junkie mess. Because I wasn't a junkie. I just needed one hit and I would be straight. But thanks to the Los Angeles County juvenile detention center, holding me against my will, and Spencer, who made it her business to be all up in mine by calling the police on me after she crashed my party and disrupted my get right, I hadn't had a hit in three days, was sick, and going crazy.

Relax.

I can't relax!

Breathe.

I can't do that either!

I needed to sit down or I would pass out. The rubber soles of my tan plastic slip-ons squeaked as I walked into the dayroom and was greeted with, "Wu-Wu's in the house!"

I didn't respond. Instead I walked over to the chair closest to the corner of the room and sat down. A few girls snickered as I walked by. This place was the worst. I was surrounded by death—a bunch of hardened, nasty, low-budget girl-beasts who talked about me to my face, accused me of thinking I was hot, and had absolutely no regard for my celebrity status.

I'd been in this stinking hellhole for three days and only managed to eat half of a taco shell. After that, a posse of manly looking hood rats snatched away my tray of slop, tossed it in the garbage, and demanded to know where my clique, the Pampered Princesses, were now.

And what did the corrections officers do? They smiled.

Bastards.

God, I need a black beauty and a Frappuccino.

Although I'd bitten my fingernails down to raw bits I nervously tapped my sore fingertips on the sides of the chair, doing my best not to rock back and forth. When that didn't work I wrapped my arms around my knees but soon found myself swaying from side to side.

I couldn't sit still.

Couldn't stop sweating.

I was a mess.

I closed my eyes and leaned my head back.

"Wu-Wu, getyoass outta my seat!" I opened my eyes and there stood a king-size chick who, judging by the short haircut and mustache, must've thought she was a boy.

Dear God...

"Wu-Wu, I said getyoass up!"

I shook my head and rolled my eyes. God only knew how much I didn't want to fight, but I had to, so I said, "I don't know what show you think I star in, but it ain't the Punk Wu-Wu show, okay."

"What you say?"

"You heard me. And the only name I see on this seat is the property of Los Angeles County—"

WHAP!!!!

Oh, hell no! This beast reared her hand back and blazed her palm against my cheek. "Now getyoass up!"

I jumped from my seat ready to rumble when the CO, who I knew had watched this whole scene unfold but didn't get off her lazy behind, yelled, "Cummings, Johnson, what's going on over there?"

I held the side of my face and it took everything in me not to toss it all to the wind and wrestle this big-fat-nasty whore down to the floor. I wanted to take my fist and pound her. But I couldn't. I couldn't risk having a fight right before my court hearing and being tossed into isolation. There was no way in hell I could spend another night on the devil's playground. But...I couldn't let this sleaze punk me either. Because if I did that and I didn't get out of here today, I'd pretty much have given the okay for these beasts to do whatever they wanted to do to me...

And that wasn't an option.

"Johnson!" the lazy CO yelled, at the exact moment I decided to be a murderess. "You're up. Court's in conference room two."

Whew...

Johnson eyed me coldly and I returned the stare.

"Johnson!" the CO called again. "Let's go!"

"Trick," Johnson spat as she turned on her heels and headed over to the only way out of here, the locked electric door, where the CO cuffed, shackled, and escorted her to the conference room.

Hatin' ho.

I sat back down, somewhat relieved but mostly on edge.

I need a black beauty...

No, I don't!

Yes, you do!

Maybe I do...

I hopped up from the chair and walked over to another lazy CO who sat behind the counter. "How much longer?"

She never answered my question; instead she said, "Gosityoass down. And don't get yo' azz up again unless I tell you, or I will write you up."

I returned to the same chair I'd just hopped out of and

did everything I could not to bang my head into the concrete wall.

I looked around the room, and on the other side of the Plexiglas partition were boys making lewd gestures with their faces pressed against the glass, flipping their tongues and grabbing their crotches.

Twenty minutes later the CO called out, "Cummings!" from behind the desk. "Conference room two."

I anxiously stood up, walked over to the locked electric door, and one of the female correction officers handcuffed, shackled, and escorted me to the conference room where I would appear before the judge via teleconference.

The conference room looked nothing like the nightmare I'd just left a hallway behind. It was clean, had white painted walls, clear windows, and the glowing California sun shone brightly. The guard stood at the door. There was a television on the wall, a table with two chairs, and another chair that was already occupied by my mother, Camille, forcing me to do a double take. Surely someone was playing a game.

Camille sat wiping tears, as her flawless porcelain skin, compliments of her Swedish background, radiated as if she'd had a polished facial. Her golden blond hair was pulled back into a sleek French roll. Her makeup was MAC perfect and her thin frame was draped in a black, tailored Armani skirt suit, and on her feet were a pair of six-inch Jimmy Choos.

Jimmy Choos? The last pair of Jimmy Choos Camille owned had a hole in the bottom. These were brand-new.

When did this transformation take place? Last I remembered, Camille was in her standard nightgown, slumped over and being pushed into a paddy wagon.

Looking at her, no one would ever know her way of saying good morning was with a brown Virginia Slims in one hand and a cocktail in the other.

What the . . . is going on here?

"Heather, baby. Mommy's here," she said, sobbing as she rose from her chair and rushed over toward me. "I love you so much. I've been so worried. Mommy's going to get you out of here. Look at you—this garbage green is terrible." She flicked my collar. "So not your color. And these handcuffs, my God. And your hair, have you even washed it? Are they feeding you? My God, you look horrid." She stroked my cheek. "But that's all right, because Mommy is here and I'm going to get you together. Get you right where we need you to be. On top."

Camille pulled me tightly into her chest, hugging me close for a few moments before she slyly dug her nails into my back and said in a tight whisper, "As soon as we get out of here I'm going to kick your azz for drugging me. You, my dear, have crossed the line." *Yeah, I drugged you 'cause I didn't want you to disrupt my get right. And the quickest way to get rid of you was to put you into a nice sleep.* The vision of Camille slumped over with her mouth open and drool seeping out of her mouth made me want to giggle. She released me from her embrace and said, loud enough for everyone in the room to hear, "Everything will be okay, baby."

I stared at her and for a moment I wondered what was worse—this place, or at home with this witch.

I sat down in the chair and suddenly the handcuffs felt as if they were squeezing me.

I'll take the witch . . .

But one thing was for sure and two things were for certain. If Camille thought she would easily take me down, then obviously she needed more than a drugging. She needed to be handled for good. Mother or not.

"All rise. Court is now in session." The sheriff officer and the judge appeared on the television screen. The judge walked over to the bench and took his seat.

"You may be seated." The judge nodded.

We sat down and the judge said, "We're here on the matter of Heather Cummings. The charges are: underage drinking and possession of narcotics. Is there counsel present?"

"Yes, Your Honor." A tall brunette woman rushed into the room and said, "Michelle MacAndrew here for the defendant, and I apologize to the court for being late."

I blinked not once, but three times. And then I almost fell out of my chair. How in the heck did Camille secure one of the top criminal attorneys in California to represent me? I thought for sure Camille would do me dirty and make me target practice for the Public Pretenders.

But she didn't.

She came through with a six-foot-tall powerhouse, dressed sharply in a navy-blue pantsuit, white blouse, pumps, and a leather briefcase. Diva Esquire was well put together. She smiled at me, touched my shoulder, and suddenly I felt relieved.

"Counselor," the judge said, "this case was set for ten A.M."

"I'm aware of that, Your Honor, and I sincerely apologize."

"Apology accepted. Please state your position."

My attorney pointed toward Camille. "Your Honor, we ask the court to release Heather Cummings into the custody of her mother, Camille Cummings."

Yeah, get me the hell outta here, please!

My attorney continued, "We have secured a bed at Hope Always, a twenty-eight-day treatment center for adolescents."

Screech...Hold up, wait a minute...Treatment? What did she say? I'm not doing twenty-eight days with a bunch of junkies. Do I look like Lindsay Lohan? This chick has bumped her head.

I turned toward Camille and before I could protest and demand to know what kind of dumbness was she pulling, my attorney said, "Also, Your Honor, Ms. Camille Cummings would like to address the court."

"And me, too," I said to my attorney, and I could've been mistaken, but I could've sworn that she ignored me.

Camille sniffed and dabbed a Kleenex from the corner of one eye to the other and rose from her chair. "Judge"— she sniffed again—"Heather is my only child and I love her so much..."

Psst, please. She loved her cocktails more than she ever loved me. *Drunk beyotch.* If I didn't want to get out of here so bad I would have slapped her face for that lie alone.

Camille continued, "My daughter has opportunities that most can only dream about and I don't want to see her messing that up."

I struggled not to roll my eyes. Outside of using me for a comeback, what did she care about my opportunities? I couldn't believe Camille. If I didn't know better I would think she meant every word she said. But Queen Faux Pas was a washed-up Oscar-winning actress, and if no one else knew, I knew that she'd said more lines in this courtroom than she had in years. Nobody in Hollywood would touch her. She couldn't even breathe on a script and she had the audacity to talk about messing up opportunities. It was all I could do not to laugh. Camille was out of control.

She carried on, "So please, Your Honor, I'm asking the court to please release her to me. I truly believe that if Heather were to enter Always Hope, it would truly make a difference."

Hmph. Oh, now Always Hope was the answer? Isn't that amusing. Shifting responsibility again, Camille. Now Always Hope should do your job. Never mind that I spent half of my childhood crying, begging you to act like a mother and let me meet my mysterious black father. Never mind that you just told me his first name a few months ago, in the same breath that you announced I was a mistake.

Never mind that I always hoped I could stop looking like a mixed-raced mutt and could look like one race or the other. I didn't care which one—black or white—I just hated the lonely middle. I wanted to feel connected to something. Someone. Somewhere. But never mind that. All that ever mattered is what you wanted. And now you wanted Always Hope to change me . . .

Hmph, Always Hope.

Problem was, it was my only way out of here . . .

I swallowed. Gave the court a small smile, and held a look that made it appear like I'd agreed with the slickness Camille was pulling here.

Camille looked at me and I could tell she was doing her all not to laugh. She dabbed her eyes and continued, "I don't want to see my daughter in any more trouble, so I'm also asking the court to please help me to keep Heather on the right path by extending her probation until she turns eighteen."

"What?!" I spat. "Have you lost your mind?!" I tried to stand up but the shackles on my feet halted me.

"Heather," my attorney said sternly, "sit back and be quiet."

Oh, these two are playing me.

Eighteen?

Camille continued. "She's a precious little girl, Your Honor. She just needs more guidance. More structure. And with the court's help I believe with all my heart that my daughter will make it."

I wanted nothing more than to take my fist and lay Camille down. Now I wished I'd slipped a deadly Mickey in her drink. Then doing time would be sweet.

My attorney must've read my mind because she squeezed my shoulder. "Your Honor," my attorney said, "I have submitted to the court a letter from Heather's probation officer, Officer Sampson. He is also in agreement with the treatment program and with her remaining on probation until she turns eighteen as opposed to being sentenced to time in a juvenile correctional facility."

I could've choked. This was a setup. It had to be. They were all in cahoots.

The court's clerk handed the judge a letter. The judge scanned the letter and then looked at me. "Heather, you're a lucky young lady with a world of opportunity. Don't blow it. Twenty-eight-day treatment at Always Hope and probation until the age of eighteen." He banged his gavel. "Court is dismissed."

The correction officer uncuffed and unshackled me and I prayed my knees wouldn't buckle.

"Thank you, Your Honor." Camille smiled and I felt like all the air was being siphoned out of my body. "Thank the judge, Heather."

I swallowed. Quickly thought about granting Camille a beat-down, and then just as quickly changed my mind. "Thank you," I said, stiff lipped.

"Let's go, Cummings," the officer said, practically spinning me around and pointing me toward the door. I didn't even look back. I simply walked out of the room and I could feel Camille's eyes burning through me as I disappeared from her sight.

Forty-five minutes later I was dressed in the same outfit I'd arrived here wearing: a sequined bra top and a neon-pink ultra-miniskirt, except now the hem of my skirt was tattered. I stepped from behind the locked electric doors that led to the outside. Immediately the Los Angeles heat and paparazzi swept over me. Bulbs flashed in my face from the cameras all around me. There were fans shouting my name and reporters shooting questions like bullets. "Get back!" the guards yelled at the reporters, who kept firing away:

"What happened inside?"

"Sources say you were slapped by an inmate this morning?"

"Is it true that you were on a hunger strike?"

"Were you shouting that your name was Wu-Wu?"

"Were you going through withdrawals?"

I didn't know which way to turn; all I knew is that I had to get out of there.

"This way, Heather!" Camille said, and I felt one of the guard's muscular arms wrap around me, creating a clear path to a brand-new black Mercedes-Benz stretch limo.

The muscular arm softly pushed me into the limo and Camille quickly followed. The door shut hurriedly and a few seconds later we were flying up the freeway.

"Well, well, well, what a circus that was."

I jumped, that voice scaring the heck out of me.

"Oh, I didn't mean to frighten you, dear."

I looked at the seat directly in front of me and I couldn't believe this...

Was that...?

That's not...

Oh...my...God...

Oh. My. God.

"Kitty Ellington," I said in complete disbelief. Not only was she queen of America's number-one talk show, *Dish the Dirt*, she was my arch-nemesis's mother.

What the hell is she doing here? "What are you doing here?" I asked.

Kitty handed me a glass of champagne. "Heather, dear." She smiled. "I'm here because you invited me." She winked. "Thanks for giving me the exclusive."

"Exclusive?" I said, pissed. "I haven't given you a thing!"

"Heather!" Camille snapped. "Mind your manners! Now I know you didn't think your powerhouse attorney was free. And you have to know that you didn't have enough money to afford her, so in exchange for an exclusive, Ms. Kitty was gracious enough to ensure that you would be released."

Kitty smiled. "You talk to no one else for the next six months. Now come, let's chat."

"I'm not doing this!" I screamed. "Stop the car right now!" I reached for the lever and just as I opened the door, the driver swerved to the shoulder and said through the intercom, "Is everything all right back there?"

"NO!" I screamed, hopping out and charging away. I didn't know where I was going. All I knew was that I'd been set up and there was no way I'd be going through with this!

I could hear Camille's heels clicking behind me. Once she was a few inches away she reached for my arm and yanked me by my elbow.

"Get off of me!" I snatched my arm away.

Camille snatched my arm back and twisted it. "Do you want me to march you back to jail with those rough-ridin' hoes?" She shook me. "Do you, Heather? Because I have no problem marching your simple, weak, and pathetic little tail back in there and making sure you stay locked down. Now the choice is yours."

"Oh, now I have choice? I didn't have a choice when you sold my soul to the devil!"

"Oh, spare me the melodrama, would you! Kitty is no more a devil than that black beauty you're a slave to. Difference is, she pays nicely."

"Oh, she paid you. I see. Now you're prostituting me— real motherly, Camille. Real freakin' maternal!"

"Don't you look down your nose at me, missy! And no, she didn't pay me. She paid you in attorney fees. Unless of course that means nothing to you, because you'd rather be locked up twenty-four hours a day like a common criminal. All while your frenemies have their asses wiped by their maids. Is that what you want? To continue to be nothing? You know and I know that being Wu-Wu Tanner doesn't fulfill you; being a Pampered Princess does. Being accepted by them, belonging to the It Clique is where you've always wanted to be. But you can't seem to make the cut!"

"Shut up!"

"Oh what, did I hit a nerve, darling? Well, I certainly hope so because while you're standing here trying to decide if you want to give Kitty an exclusive, those snotty little Pampered Princesses are somewhere in their lush entertainment rooms, watching a report on you and laughing." She pointed ahead to the paparazzi who'd pulled along the side of the road and were headed our way. "And do you know why they're laughing? They're laughing because you have allowed them to make a fool out of you. Now when are you going to get tired of being on the bottom of the barrel, scraping and begging for scraps? If you want to be on top, then you need to know that being on top goes beyond being on the Wu-Wu show, hanging with your fan club president, and throwing Skittles parties!"

"You don't tell me what to do!"

"Like hell I don't! You owe me big-time. You drugged me, Heather. I've had more reports written about me in the past few days than I've had in years. And they haven't been good. I've been dragged through the mud and branded a washed-up actress and an even worse mother. And I'm pissed off about that. Help me God, if you don't do what I say I have no problem making sure your probation is violated. You understand? Now the choice is yours! You want to be a loser and keep those little skanks laughing at you, or do you have enough guts to stand up and fight for yourself?"

Silence.

"Answer me! I know you understand exactly what I'm saying!"

I didn't respond. And it's not that I didn't understand. I understood well. Better than I ever had. And what was perfectly clear to me was that it was time for war.

Load. And reload.

Assume position.

Click. Click.

For once Camille was right.

How long was I going to stand by and let the Pampered Tricks do whatever they wanted to do to me?

Bully me.

Talk about me.

Say all kinds of snide things about me and to me.

While I swallowed it.

Snorted my miseries away.

No more.

Those days were done.

And the old Heather Cummings was dead.

Born again was the new me.

Armed and dangerous.

I was leaving bodies behind. Starting with Spencer and ending with Rich and London. And if my mother didn't watch herself, she'd be a casualty, too. After all, Camille knew the rules.

Well, *she* had arrived. *And as soon as I get out of rehab, the sixteen-year-old devil rocks: six-inch stilettos, designer clutches, and diamonds.*

"What. Are. You. Going to do?" Camille spat.

I didn't answer her. Instead I watched the paparazzi gain position, aim, and shoot. Then I turned, walked back toward the limo, and slid in. Camille grinned as she slid in behind me.

"What do you want to know?" I said as the limo pulled back onto the highway.

"Oh, no rush," Kitty assured me. "I tell you what—you seem so stressed, why don't you relax." She looked over at Camille.

Camille nodded and Kitty slid me a blue silk pouch. I opened it and inside were two black beauties. I fought like hell not to smile, but I only succeeded halfway.

"If you'd like to relax before we do the exclusive, you can sit over there, press that button, and the center partition will rise and give you all the privacy you need to collect your thoughts."

I couldn't believe this. It felt so right and so wrong all at the same time. But I knew I needed this hit. I needed it, and in order for the new Heather to take her rightful position, I would need to get myself together.

I moved to the other side of the stretch limo, pressed the button, and as I sent the center partition up, Camille said, "Welcome to the battlefield, sweetheart."

4

Spencer

Revenge was like sipping a steamy cup of bittersweet chocolate. In order to enjoy it, it had to be served at just the right moment. It had to go down slowly. It had to be savored one sip at a time. And right at that moment, I was enjoying every bit of it. Heather had bound and gagged me, leaving me with no choice. She had to go down. And, yeah, that hurt me down to my cute polished pinky-toe because out of the three so-called Pampered Princesses, I had liked Heather the most. She wasn't as materialistic and loud and over-the-top as Rich Montgomery, who was nothing more than a spoiled, snotty, oversized brat. And she wasn't as pretentious and snooty as that ex-runway, I'll-never-get-another-modeling-job-because-I'm-a-fifty-foot-beached-whale, London Phillips. No. Heather was different. Yeah, she was a low-money wench living in a rented bungalow. And, yeah, her fashion statements were a bit cheesy and cheap. But so what? She had my back, and

I had hers. Or so I thought! Instead she bent over and practically told me to kiss her flat-as-a-rice-paddy butt!

That hurt! And, yes, I had to swallow back my tears. I really thought that we were friends. But I was sooooooo wrong. What a fool I was! That trick made it clear that we weren't friends. That we had never been friends.

"Friends? Friends?" she had spat at me. "You thought? We were never friends and never will be! I don't like you. You're a sneaky, dirty, conniving little ho. Oh no, excuse me, big ho. Who loves to snatch and sneak other people's boyfriends. Now gather your heels, walk back out the way you came in here...Now get out of here before we all stomp you down!"

I couldn't believe she had threatened me. That she had treated me like I was some thunder-thighs poophead.

But who was there for that walking cuckoo-clock when she couldn't remember her lines on the set of her television show and was on the verge of having a dang nervous breakdown?

I was!

Who took up for that wretched donkey hole anytime Rich and London made fun of her or talked down to her like she was smelly trash?

I did!

And how did she repay me?

By turning on a mic and humiliating me in front of all of her pill-popping butt lickers. Ooooooh, Heather Cummings was a dirty, rotten douche bag for that! And the moment she hopped her smelly tail up on that little raggedy makeshift stage in her backyard and rapped—or whatever the hell that howling and screeching was—about how she took one shot and dropped me upside the head, was the day she showed me just how messy she could be. What that cracked-out Barbie did to me was despicable! She ambushed me and opened fire. She tried to degrade and destroy me! But what she didn't know was I was armed, loaded, and ready to toss a grenade in her sandbox.

And the Gucci clique was clearly not ready for war!

So the ho thought.

I was a majorette. Not a dang Girl Scout. So Heather had better tighten up her corset and paste down her booty bags because if inmate Cummings wanted a fight, then goshdarnit, I was going to high-kick her across the minefield. And let me tell you one rickety-crickety thing: the one thing you didn't do was mess with me. Not Spencer Ellington, you didn't. I wasn't the one, two, or the four.

Now I couldn't speak for Rich and her big-faced Labradoodle friend, London. But Heather didn't want it with me. Oh no. That Skittles bandit had crossed into enemy territory. Wait. Why was I calling her a Skittles bandit? She hadn't stolen any candy. Actually I didn't see one dang Skittles in any of those glass bowls she had filled with pills. Oh, whatever!

Point is, that Cabbage Patch ho pulled out a rusty blade and shanked me! Now she was about to get a firsthand lesson in combat. In every war, there had to be an enemy. She declared it. She demanded it. Unfortunately, the beyotch didn't do her homework because if she had, she'd have known that whenever a ho declared war on a so-called friend, she had better know the rules of engagement.

The most important rule being: Never declare war on your enemies, then let them catch you sleeping. Oh no. You're supposed to be refreshed, rejuvenated, and ready to bring it. But instead I caught Heather snoring behind the wheel of her armored tank, looking a mess. And now Miss Turkey Tits was mine.

I glanced down at the latest issue of *Diva Girlz Weekly* with a picture of Heather's drunken mother, Camille, plastered on the cover. The headline read:

FROM THE SILVER SCREEN TO JAIL CELL, WASHED UP STARLET CAMILLE CUMMINGS ARRESTED!

On the cover of *Glamdalous*—the magazine for the glamorous and the scandalous—the caption read:

FROM TENNIS BRACELETS TO HANDCUFFS, ONE OF HOLLYWOOD HIGH'S VERY OWN PAMPERED PRINCESSES ARRESTED AND CHARGED WITH UNDERAGE DRINKING AND POSSESSION OF NARCOTICS

I smirked, picking up another article, and stared at a full-page photo of Heather wearing that god-awful fashion wreckage—a neon-green bra top and neon-pink mini. Her ponytail extension was hanging down past her butt crack. She looked like a real live rodeo pony. I read the caption:

PAMPERED PRINCESS GONE WILD! BOOZE, PILLS & HOT SCANDAL

I reached over and grabbed the scissors and started cutting out an article from the pages of *Teen Gossip*. The caption read:

TEEN STAR DRUGS MOTHER AND GETS IT CRUNKED!

Yeah, she might have been the one who sent that video of me down on my knees giving one of Rich's many boyfriends a special treat to the media. But she definitely hadn't brought me down. Talking about she brought down the Gucci clique. Ha! Goes to show you how much she knew. I only wore Gucci on Tuesdays. What a dumb ducky!

Now click-click on that, you two-faced skank!

I finished cutting out all of the news and magazine articles on Heather and her mother, then stood up from the kitchen table and walked over to the huge wall of glass that overlooked L.A. and allowed tons of sunlight in the room, wondering why Heather had turned on me.

Anderson, the new boo in my life, walked up behind me. He wrapped his strong arms around my waist and kissed the top of my head. "What's going on in that pretty little head of yours?"

I sighed, craning my neck and looking up at him. "Heather."

He raised a brow. "What about her?"

"I feel bad that it had to come down to this between me and her. I was good to her. But it's obvious she didn't give a damn about me or my kindness. I thought she would have learned her lesson when I Maced her in school a few months ago. But she didn't. I guess I'm going to have to take my nail file and gouge out her dang eyeballs next time."

"You're not regretting calling the cops on her, or sending those pictures of her and her mother passed out on the sofa to the media, are you?"

I shook my head, leaning back against his chest. "No. Heather started this."

"Good. And now you need to demolish her. No one hurts my sweet, sexy gum drop and gets away with it."

I smiled.

Anderson and I had been seeing each other on the low-low for over a month. And as bad as I wanted to swing upside down from a chandelier and lap up every inch of his dark-chocolate body, he wanted to take things slow. Toooooooooooo slooooooooooow, if you asked me! He was a gentleman. And he was thoughtful and sooo sooo attentive. But, goshdangit, his chivalrous ways were killing my libido. I wanted him to throw me down on the bed, rip off my La Perla undergarments and beat up the mattress. But no, not Anderson! My boo bear wanted to make sure we were more than sex. He said he didn't want to rush into anything sexual. That we had our whole lives to enjoy nights of passionate lovemaking. Okay, it sounded good. But I needed to feel it, too!

And yeah, he was London's boyfriend. But so what? The fact is, he wanted *me*. And he was breaking it off with her—the sooner the better. It served her right since she didn't know how to appreciate a real man. And she definitely didn't know the first thing about keeping a man like Anderson from straying, because if she did, he wouldn't have asked me out, and we wouldn't still be seeing each other.

"Spencer." Anderson turned me around and stared into my eyes. "However you want to bring her down, I'm with you every step of the way." He took my hand into his and placed it up to his lips. He kissed each fingertip, then slipped them into his mouth, teasing me.

I pouted. "I don't know why you keep teasing me like this, boo bear. Don't I turn you on?"

He pressed himself into me. "What you think?"

I felt the heat from his excitement and firecrackers started popping off inside of me. "I think we need to finish breakfast naked in bed."

He grinned. "All in time, my beautiful gum drop." He kissed me lightly on the lips. "Now how about—"

"Well, well, well... what do we have here?"

I gasped. It was Kitty, leaning up against the door frame, twirling a lock of hair around her slender, manicured finger. She looked fabulous in a peach Chanel knit crepe dress with buttons and a pearl belt. *What in the heck is she doing here?* I quickly stepped out of Anderson's embrace. "Mother, what are you doing here?"

She smiled. "Spencer, darling, I live here. Or have you forgotten?"

I rolled my eyes. "No, Mother. Actually I thought maybe *you* did." I hadn't seen her in almost three weeks. Aside from the occasional call here and there throughout the week, Kitty Ellington was pretty much invisible. And her role as a mother was nonexistent. No, she was too busy making her billions to be bothered with a sixteen-year-old. Let alone a daughter who I was convinced she was jealous of.

"I just dropped off that pathetic Camille and that rude little brat of hers and thought I'd swing by to pick up a few things before I head back to New York. My flight leaves in two hours. You know...duty calls. By the way, thanks for all those lovely photos. The exclusive is signed and sealed."

I stared at her as she sashayed into the kitchen, her Manolos clicking against the tile as she made her way over to me, locking eyes on Anderson and slyly licking her painted lips.

Strumpet!

She air-kissed me.

"And who is this fine chocolate-drop hunk of a man?" she inquired, practically drooling as if he were prime beef being tossed to a hungry lioness. She circled him, ready to attack, before extending her hand.

"Hello, Mrs. Ellington," Anderson politely said, taking her hand into his. "My mother watches your talk show religiously."

"Oh, that's wonderful. I'll have to be sure she gets tickets for the next ten shows."

"She'd love that. It's a pleasure meeting you."

"Oh no," Kitty purred, touching his arm then squeezing his biceps. "The pleasure is allllll mine. Oh my. Do you work out?"

He smiled. "Yes, ma'am. Three times a week."

She licked her lips. "Mmmph. And it shows."

"Missus Ellington, you're even more beautiful in person. Now I see where Spencer gets her looks and charm from."

Gag me!

"Oooh," she cooed as she unbuttoned the first three buttons of her dress, exposing her cleavage. "It's gotten awful hot in here all of a sudden. Spencer, sweetheart, be a dear and go grab mother something cool to drink. I'm parched."

Kitty giggled like some lovesick schoolgirl and made all kinds of silly-assed faces as if she had just peed in her panties from all the attention. I had to get her away from my man, fast, before he ended up on her long "Men to do" list.

I stepped in between her and Anderson. "And you'll stay parched if you think I'm playing *The Help*. Now, Mother, what *really* brings you home? There's nothing you have here you need. You have tons of clothes and other things back at your penthouse in New York."

She placed a hand up to her chest. "I've missed you, darling. And I wanted to see how you were doing, but obviously"—she eyed Anderson—"judging by the company you're keeping, it looks like you're in *very* good, strrrrrrrong hands."

I cleared my throat. "Mother, this is An—"

"Spencer, darling, I know exactly who he is. Anderson

Ford. Son of billionaire oil tycoon Freeman Ford." She tilted her head. "And the handsome beau of Jade Phillips's daughter—" She snapped her fingers. "Oh dear. Spencer, what's that child's name?"

I huffed. "London."

"Yes, yes. London Phillips. You *are* still dating her, aren't you?"

Her eyes flicked to Anderson, then back to me. Before he could open his mouth to speak, I grabbed Kitty by the arm. "Um, excuse us for one minute, Anderson. My mother and I have a few things to discuss."

He smiled. "I'll be right here."

I ushered Kitty out of the kitchen and into the solarium, shutting the glass door behind us. "Spencer, Spencer, Spencer," she said, wagging an accusatory finger at me. "You sneaky little harlot. Oooh, I love, love, love, love it. Anderson Ford, mmmph...nice catch, darling. That boy has more money than he'll ever know what to do with in this lifetime. Let's hope you know how to hold on to him. But just in case you let him slip through your fingers, I might need to taste, uh, test drive him myself."

"You even try it," I snapped, stepping up in her face, "and I will slice your throat. He is off-limits. Do you understand? You've slept with all of my other boyfriends, but you will not have this one."

"Well, technically, dear, he's not your boyfriend. He's still involved with that London girl, isn't he? And if my memory serves me correctly, he is over eighteen, isn't he. And you do know how I like them young."

I frowned. Kitty was disgusting. She was married to a man who was old enough to be her father, yet ran around chasing boys who were practically young enough to be her sons. I was convinced she was having some kind of midlife identity crisis or something. "Yes, Mother. I know exactly how much you enjoy staking out the boys' locker rooms. Tell me something I don't already know."

"Sooooo," she continued, seemingly unfazed by my remark, "have the two of you...you know, had sex yet?"

I huffed. "You wait one dang minute, you nasty snotrag. That's none of your business. You have really crossed the line now, Mother. Bottom line, you keep your horny paws away from him or I will declaw you. Where's your little boy toy, Rico? Wait, Lennox? Or was he last month's freak of the moment for you? Don't tell me they've tired of you already."

She waved me on. "Oh, Spencer, darling, unclench your booty cheeks. Don't be so constipated. I'm only having a little fun with you."

I sneered. "No. You unclench yours. Better yet, keep your sticky thongs on and stay the hell away from Anderson."

"My, my, my...awful possessive, aren't we? What does your friend London have to say about all of this? Or does she even know that you're up to your whorish ways, sneaking around with her boyfriend while smiling in her face. Oh, sweet-sweet Spencer. You. Are. Scandalous."

I rolled my eyes, placing a hand up on my hip. "And you are disrupting my morning, being here."

"Let me tell you something, Spencer dear. And you had better listen up good. All is fair in men, money, and war. If you want to drop down in the trenches and get dirty, then you had better strap up and be ready to fight for what you believe in. And that includes fighting for a man that isn't yours, but is good for you. But in the meantime, you had better keep a close eye on that Heather Cummings."

I blinked. "I'm not worried about her. Heather can't hurt me any more than she already has."

"Spencer, toughen up. There is no time to be getting all wrapped up in your hurt feelings. That little two-dollar trollop disrespected you. She called you out and declared war on you. And you need to handle her. You have twenty-eight days to prepare, since she's stuck in rehab. But by the time she's released, you had better be armed, loaded, and ready for battle."

She leaned her head back and twisted her hair up into a diamond clip. "Well, I have to get going." She kissed me on the cheek, then headed toward the door. She turned back to face me. "Oh, by the way, your father and I are getting divorced. And you're going to South Africa to live with him."

I narrowed my eyes. "What? South Africa? Oh, no the hell I'm not. I'm not going any-dang-where. You go. I'm staying right here."

"Spencer. You heard what I said. You're going to live with your father. It's time he started acting like a parent instead of running off into the wilderness. He's the one who wanted you in the first place. I've done my part. I gave birth to you. Now it's time for me to start living my life."

Before she could get all the way out the door, I stormed over to her and yanked her by the arm. "You want to live your life? Go live it. But you must not have gotten the memo, Mother. I said. I'm. Not. Going. Any. Where. *Now mess with me if you want*. And you won't be the only one dishing the dirt around here. I will drag you through the gutters of hell and set you on fire for the world to see. I mean it. I gave you those photos of Heather and her mother and you're getting your precious interviews. Now

I expect you to make good on your promise. Pay me my money. I want it transferred into my personal account by four o'clock today, or I will be giving my own exclusives."

She blinked. "You wouldn't dare."

I let go of her arm. "Fight for what I believe in, right? All is fair in men, money, and war. Isn't that what you said, Mother? Now try me."

She grinned. "Now that's the no-nonsense spitfire I expect to see from here on out. Take no prisoners, Spencer, darling. Aim your barrel, shoot, and ask questions later. I'll make the call to the accountant now and have your money transferred."

I leered at her. Kitty was useless. I was so over the days of wanting her around. I was so done with the idea of her being a mother. I was convinced some women should never, ever, have children. And Kitty was one of them. Her insides needed to be pulled out and tossed in a meat grinder to ensure she never got pregnant again. The only thing she was good for was her money. And even that I didn't need. I had millions of dollars sitting in a trust fund set up for me by my father, waiting to be collected on my eighteenth birthday. And there was nothing Kitty could do to stop it. But in the meantime, I was going to take her for everything she was worth. Oh yes . . . there was a new sheriff in town. Spencer Ellington. And I was kicking off my stilettos, taking off my diamonds, sharpening up my nails, and getting ready to claw up anyone who got up in my face. And make no mistake. I would handle Heather, Rich, and London as needed, one by one. Whoever drew their weapons first would be taken down.

5

London

Everything in my diamond-glistening, designer-clad world seemed to be falling apart...no, spiraling out of control...right before my big, brown, dreamy eyes. And I hated it. Hated that uncontrollable feeling of not having my manicured fingertips on the beating pulse of my own life; hated not being in control of everything around me. And I despised, even more, the frightening thought of not having the ability to snap my fingers and have others around me bend to my every whim and follow my orders.

And this...this feeling of losing myself had me stressing the hell out.

My life was a shattered mess!

Daddy was disgusted with me and decided that giving me the silent treatment for the last three days was a much better choice than wringing my neck or beating me senseless for smacking up those snot-nosed, too-hot-in-the-box, slick-mouthed, pygmy look-alikes who thought they could bring it to me. And the end result? I'm the one who ended up with a sprained ankle and had three of the four Powerpuff rejects jumping up on my back and pulling my hair, all because I was stuck at school defending the reputation and honor of being one of the goddamn Pampered Princesses all by myself. I swear. There was no honor among catty, conniving hoes. But, whatever! It is what it is. Still . . . Daddy saw what I did as disgraceful. So I had become invisible to him. And that ate up my nerves!

Then my darling, domineering mother—who couldn't stay home longer than a week—was back in Paris floating on some runway or hosting some star-studded charity event while monitoring my caloric intake via our morning FaceTime chats, compliments of MAC. She was ecstatic when she witnessed the electronic scale register that I had lost six pounds. "Oh, my darling London!" she exclaimed at five thirty this morning. "Vous serez sur la piste en peu de temps." She was excited that I'd finally be back on the runway in no time. That's all she cared about. Being runway ready! "I am so proud of you, sweetheart. I knew you could do it."

Then there was the issue of Rich—who up until thirty-seven seconds ago, I still hadn't heard from—being MIA. Yes, *poof!* Gone! Absent from all communication! She had literally fallen off the face of the earth and left me no forwarding address. Like, really, who the hell did that?

To add to my already miserable existence, I had a boyfriend—who I really didn't want, but needed for appearance's sake. He was good for me. Or at least that was what my parents were brainwashing me to believe. He was articulate and polished. Cultivated and educated. He was who I was expected to one day marry and have bouncing bundles of joy with—heirs to his family's multi-billion-dollar empire. Blah, blah, blah.

But I hadn't been able to reach him for the last week, despite leaving him several messages. That was soooo not like him. He was a well-trained puppy who wagged his tail and did what I wanted. Well, that's not entirely true. There was the one time when he called himself checking me and laying down ground rules a few weeks ago in his car, but that didn't last long. I quickly yanked him by his leash and got him back in line. And I had him worshipping the ground I walked on, eating out of the palm of my hand and adorning me with beautiful, expensive trinkets. Up until now...

Then there was the issue of my guiltiest pleasure—my boo, my whole entire world—who I still wasn't talking to. But that was fine as long as he kept calling me and kept sweating me, because at least I was in control. But once his "Pick-up-baby-I-miss-you" calls had stopped, I was a panicky mess! And little did my mother know. *He* was the reason I had lost those six pounds. I couldn't eat. I couldn't sleep. I couldn't think straight. I was too consumed with him calling me. Incessantly staring at the screen of my cell, checking for texts and willing it to ring just so that I could see his name and face flash across my screen. But it hadn't rung or beeped since Sunday night.

And that was driving me insane. I felt like I was on a one-way train ride to Looney-ville.

Cuckoo-cuckoo!

That's how this was making me feel, like I was two scoops from crazy.

How could he do this to me? To us?

He was everything my boyfriend wasn't. He was a bad boy. He was hood bred. He was rough and rugged and as gritty as the streets he came from. He was sooo dang wrong in all the right ways. And he was the love of my life. Still, I couldn't allow him to play me.

And—finally, after all of this nail-biting and torturous waiting—my man had been calling me all morning. And the only reason I hadn't answered the phone was because I had to make him pay. Problem was, I didn't know how long I could hold out. The truth was, I loved him. But my heart ached. I knew he had done me dirty. But that didn't matter. I wanted him. I needed him. And I didn't want to be alone in this world without him. Why couldn't he just love me back? I wanted love and peace. And all he wanted was drama.

You don't love me...you love yaself. You too effen self-ish to love anyone other than ya'self...

How could he say that to me when I'd given him every part of me, emotionally, mentally, *and* sexually since I was thirteen?

...I'm tryna make moves and you tryna play games. I ain't got time for that. I need a grown woman...Every-thing's what's best for London. First I thought it was ya parents. But now I realize it's you. You're the problem here. Not them..."

I sighed, wiping tears from my face. I was starting to feel like he was using me.

And all I ever did was love him. And want the best for him. Yet that hadn't been good enough. I knew we had a plan. And I promised to see it through. But sometimes bad things happen and plans have to change. But that didn't change my feelings for him.

And I thought he would love me anyway, but I was wrong because he didn't.

Still, this was the twenty-seventh time he had called this

morning. And yes, it had relieved a lot of my stress. It let me know that he still cared. And now that he was back sweating me, it showed me he still wanted me. That maybe he still loved me. And that I was in control. It was a shame you had to treat a man like a dog for him to come to his senses.

I smiled, slowly feeling back on top. *I knew my boo would finally get his mind right.*

"What, Justice?" I abruptly answered, feigning annoyance in spite of my heart defying my tone and leaping with joy.

"Oh, so that's how you speak to ya man now?" he coolly asked. His voice was hot and husky like sweet, dark, melted chocolate. I swallowed, hard.

Stand your ground, girl. Don't fall for the okey-doke!

But he sounds so dang delicious.

"I'm not playin' with you, London...I've already wasted too many years effen around with ya dumb behind..."

"So you're breaking up with me?"

"You figure it out..."

I blinked back the sting of that night when he stood right here in my bedroom and cursed me out. Told me he was sick of me and wanted nothing else to do with me.

"Last I checked I didn't have a man. Remember?"

"Yeah, a'ight. Whatever, yo. You know that was just my ego talkin'. You got me buggin', yo. You know I ain't lettin' you go, baby. It's me and you, like we always said it would be. I got too much love for you." He lowered his voice. "Wit' ya sexy self. I miss you like crazy."

I rolled my eyes and grinned at the same time. His intoxicating voice made me dizzy. He had such an overpowering effect on me. On my sanity. And I hated him...for that.

Stay strong!

"Yeah, okay. If you say. Now how can I help you?"

"Yo, go 'head wit' all that. You miss me?"

You have no idea how much. I sucked my teeth.

"No," I lied, closing my eyes, his eyes, his lips, his chin, his muscular body, all taking shape in my mind's eye.

"Baby...I wanna make love to you. You miss how I make you feel?"

Heat shot through my body. My breath quickened.

"Give me a kiss, yo."

I shifted the phone from one ear to the other, walking into the adjoining sitting room. I picked up my crystal butterfly and stared at it. My wishes, my hopes and dreams, were all wrapped up in this boy. And so far nothing had worked out the way I had planned.

"Justice, please. You think you can curse me out, then storm out of my house, not call me for four days, then all of a sudden call and whisper a bunch of sweet nothings and everything's supposed to be good? I can't keep doing this with you."

"I know, baby. I was dead wrong for that. But you know how I get when you start ya BS, yo. But check it. I'm over it now."

I frowned. *Well, good for you. I'm not!*

"I wrote a song for you."

Ohmygod. How sweet. Maybe he really is sorry, this time.

Keep it cute, girl. Don't get gassed. "Oh, for real?"

"Yeah. It's called 'I Love You and I Miss You.'" He started humming, then sang a verse. And I couldn't help but grin. His voice was like heaven. "Yo, what you think? I was up all night writing it."

"It's beautiful. But..."

"Look, London, baby. I know I said some effed-up stuff to you last week, but you hurt me, for real for real, yo."

I stared at the phone. I had hurt him? Was he serious? Had he lost all touch with reality? I frowned. "Justice, you cursed me out. But you know what? I can't get into it right now. I gotta go."

"What?"

"You heard me. I don't have time to play with you. Rich is supposed to be coming over. Spencer is coming over. You know, the people who care about me."

He snorted. "Oh, the media hoes? So you gonna dis me for them?"

"Yes, I am."

"Yeah, a'ight. That's real effed up, yo. But you know what? All y'all hoes deserve each other. So do you."

I gasped. "Ohmygod, I can't believe you said that."

"You started it. You and ya slick mouth. It's all about you. Eff me, right? You still on that. Oh, what y'all wanna do, huddle to get y'alls whoring together. I get the message. I ain't nothin', right? It's all about you and Rich. And Spencer. And the little crackhead."

"She isn't a crackhead. And we happen to be friends by default. So get it right."

"Yeah, whatever."

"Exactly."

"Yo, you know what, London? You sound stupid. I see you still a little girl. Here I am tryna love you, tryna tell you how I feel about you. I'm sittin' up all night, cryin' over you, writin' love songs to yo' ungrateful behind, wonderin' if you still gonna be my wife, but you ain't ready for me. Eff Rich,

Spencer, and *you*. All four of you snakes can suck a big one."

Click!

My knees buckled.

My heart started sinking.

He hung up on me. Why didn't I shut up and listen?

I was on the verge of tears. I wanted to collapse right in the middle of the floor and have a full-fledged tantrum with lots of spit, drool, and tears. But before I could, my housekeeper Genevieve's voice cut through on the intercom. "Miss London. Miss Rich is here."

Oh, so she is alive. Mmmph. I just chased my man away. And right now I am not in the mood for Rich and her theatrics.

"Miss London?"

I sniffed, wiping my face. "Yeah? I'm here."

"Should I send her up?"

I stood and stared at myself in the mirror as I grabbed a tissue and dabbed at the corners of my eyes. *I don't know why I keep letting him do this to me. Hurting me.*

I don't deserve to be treated like that.

This is not about me and Justice. Justice doesn't care about me. So I'm done with caring about him. He's right. I am so stupid. I have to get my life back together and focus on what's important. No scheming, no planning. No stress, no worries, and no Justice. It was time to get back to something I could control, like getting the It Clique back on top where we belonged.

I wiped my eyes dry. "Yeah, send her up."

I placed a hand up on my hip, eyeing Rich as she walked through the door. "Oh, so you just gonna show up after I've been texting and calling you for the last five days.

You done took me waaaay out of my comfort zone. Because I don't do that. I call you once—if you don't call me back, you're written off. So you had better have a good reason as to why I haven't heard from you, in like forever. Have me worried sick about you. And I don't do worry. So was silent treatment a result of morning sickness, 'cause I don't appreciate not hearing from you."

She waved me on, smacking her lips. "London, please. What's the crisis? I didn't come all the way over here to be lectured to. I coulda stayed home for that." She patted her chest. "Rich needs attention. She needs attending to. So I didn't come over here for you to be sweating me." She flopped down on my chaise and lay back on it, placing a hand up over her forehead. "I have one last cry left for the morning and I didn't get a chance to use it because I was interrupted by you and your ranting and raving." She let out a disgusted sigh. "Ah, you are soooo selfish, London. You don't give a damn about anyone but yourself."

I stared at her in disbelief as she stretched out on my chaise as if she were in a doctor's office waiting for therapy. And here I was in pain. Yet she had the audacity to call me selfish. "Selfish? Are you kidding me?"

She lifted her head up off the chaise. "And there you go thinking I'm a joke. What part of 'Rich needs attention' did you not understand? Maybe we need to switch positions, 'cause you're buggin'."

I sighed, walking over to her. "You know what, Rich. Let me see if you have a fever, 'cause you have lost your mind." I sat down on the chaise alongside her and pressed my palm up against her forehead.

Rich eyed me. "It is nothing wrong with me. Obviously, there's something wrong with you."

"Yeah, being worried about you."

"Wrong answer. That's not it. Spill it."

I quickly shifted my eyes. "There's nothing to spill."

Rich sat up. "Now, along with you being inconsiderate of my misery, you're lying."

I frowned and hopped off the chaise, feeling defensive. "I don't have any reason to lie to you."

But I did. Still, I wanted nothing more than to confide in her. I had grown to love Rich like the sister I've always wanted, but I was still hesitant to share with her this fog of confusion I was in. I was torn. I was conflicted. And I was deeply hurt, knowing that I loved a boy who didn't love me back. But Rich wasn't exactly the most understanding. And she could be harshly judgmental. And the last thing I wanted, or needed, was her looking at me like I was stupid.

Rich got up from off the chaise and walked over to me, placing a hand up on her hip. She snapped her fingers. "Uhhh, hello? Did I miss something here? Let me tell you something, London. I was home dealing with my own misery. My mother has taken my Bugatti. I've been saddled with a three-series Mercedes..."

"Eww..."

"Exactly. My Parisian stylist has been laid off because Logan has an attitude. And now you. I don't need this right now."

I shook my head. "Okay, Rich. Let's talk about you."

"No. Let's talk about you. I'm not selfish like that, London. Now hurry up and tell me because I can only push my own problems aside for five, maybe ten minutes tops."

I felt like tears were about to explode from my eyes any minute if I didn't change the subject. "We need to do something about this media mess. You, Spencer, and Heath—"

"Uh-uh. Not today, boo. I'm not doing this with you. I already told you before that all press is good press. And as long as they're keeping my name in their mouths I'm still on their minds. Boom. Now next up is you and your drama. Not what's up, and don't tell me about that dizzy Spencer, or the crack whore. Just talk you. London. So just tell me what's going on because I've been depressed for the last four days. I mean, really. How many times do I have to keep telling you this? I'm looking for a reason to boom-bop and drop it. I've been on a drought. Whaaaat? I'm ready to water my well. The only people off-limits are your mother and father. Anybody else can get it-get it. From the house manager to the gardener. Mmmph. From eight to eighty. Now, who done messed with my bestie-boo? And I'm not gonna ask you again. So might as well tell me who did it, where they're at, and when we are going to look for 'em. Be—"

"Rich, now you know I like to keep it calm and keep it cute."

Rich bucked her eyes and put a hand up on her hip. "Lies. Because I heard that you molly-whopped a tableful of five-year-olds. And then got jumped. Now you know if I was there it wouldn't have gone down like that."

"But you weren't there," I snapped. "And that's the problem. And, once again, I had to pay out a hundred grand to the headmaster. And, once again, I'm in trouble with my dad. He's furious."

"He really needs to stop sweating you and let you live. What's a hundred grand? Unless y'all are broke or something." She tilted her head.

I frowned. "You know what? Let's talk about your pregnancy. How's that working out for you? Do I see *Teen Mom* in your future? I hear they're having a casting call."

She gasped. "Ohmygod. How insensitive. I don't believe you just said that to me. You got jumped and now you wanna attack me. That really hurt my feelings, London."

"I didn't mean to hurt your feelings. But that still doesn't answer my question."

"Listen. I haven't heard from Knox. He isn't answering my calls. My mother is sweating me hard. And this pregnancy, most of the time I want to pretend that it doesn't exist."

Tears welled up in her eyes. But they were also welling up in mine. I walked over to her and draped my arm around her shoulder. "How long do think that's going to last? You can't pretend forever."

Rich sniffed. "Until I lie down in the bathtub and give birth or wake up from this nightmare."

I swallowed back an avalanche of my own tears. All of what she had said stabbed at me, puncturing holes in my past. "*I want you to have my baby...we're gonna be a family...I love you...*"

"Stop it!"

Rich looked at me. "Stop what?"

I blinked, catching myself. "Um, stop crying. It doesn't change anything. You can't cry over spilled milk, or babies that come before their time."

Rich sighed. "You're right. 'Cause I've had enough tears to last both of us a lifetime. We both can't be broke down. And your stuff is easier to fix."

So you think.

Tears finally fell from my eyes. "He broke up with me," I blurted out. "He hates me."

"What? All this is because he broke up with you? I had one more touching line to say and now you're back on yourself. Who does that? Girl, you better stop wearing your feelings like a sapphire bangle"—she snapped her fingers—"and get over it. Boys are not like diamonds; they're not rare. And they're barely a girl's best friend. They're dogs. They're nothing. They're more like cubic zirconia. You can pick them up anywhere. All they do is get you pregnant, then turn on you. And if you're lucky, they don't leave you with the coochie cooties. Or have you sitting up in a clinic wearing a wig, praying that nobody notices you."

"Why can't men just get it together?"

"Girl, you know why. Because we keep making excuses for them. And keep taking them back. And keep loving them even when we know they don't deserve to be loved. And we confide in them..."

"Wait a minute. Is all this about me, or you?"

She huffed. "London, are you paying attention here? This is about you."

"Oh, because for a moment there, I thought we were back on you. So glad you cleared that up."

Rich continued, dismissing me. "The point is, I'm tired of being stressed out. And being in love with them. I swear, I'ma turn to Internet dating, and then when I get tired of them I can cut the computer off. Now why did he break up with you?"

I hesitated, trying to get my story together. I couldn't tell her the real deal, but I could give her a half-truth. "Because he's trying to make me choose between him and my friends and I think it's so unfair that I can't have both."

Her eyes popped out. "Whaaaaaat? Is he crazy? What kinda mess is that? The way he was all up in the club poppin' and droppin' it with Corey? Please, he did you a favor. I don't know why you're with his corny behind anyway. I don't care how much money he has. Whack dot com. London, you cannot be this weak or pathetic, girl. This is a new day. Don't no boys tell us who we can be friends with. You don't let no man run your life. Unless he's *your* father and we already know he needs to calm down a little bit because he gets out of hand."

"All right now, Rich. You're going too far with the daddy stuff."

She put her hands up. "I'm just sayin'...that is soooo two-thousand-and-seven. He needs to relax. But anyway, back to me...no, I mean you and your drama. You have got to stop having so much drama in your life. Get it together, bestie boo 'cause you are a mess. I mean, really. How much more of this do you think I can take?"

I ignored her ramblings and shook back my own feelings of guilt. The guilt of not being able to be completely honest with my girl, my best friend—the one person who I had grown the closest to, ever. Being stuck in this crazy dilemma of not knowing how to be a friend and still keep my man was what hurt me the most. But this wasn't about me. I had to get my man back; had to get our situation straight.

I swallowed back my emotions. "Well, now that you've said all that and we've run through my diary of drama, let's flip through a few pages of yours, starting with where you've been the last four days. And ending with what are you going to do about this pregnancy? I've called you over a hundred times..."

"No, a hundred and forty-seven times, but who's counting. I never imagined you'd be sweating me like that, London."

I rolled my eyes. "Screw you, girlfriend. Sweating you hell, I've been worried sick about you. I didn't know what was going on. Now you spill it. Bring me up-to-date, and spare no details."

"Girl, please. Like you said, I don't even like kids."

"Okay, soooo what does that mean?"

"It means from here on out, I'ma do what I want. I'm sick of my mother and her BS. My father is selfish. RJ is perfect. Knox wants me to be someone else. I'm so over this morning sickness. And after today, I don't want to talk about it."

I could see the pain in Rich's eyes. I reached over and grabbed her hand. "Why didn't you call me?"

"London, let's forget it."

"You know what, Rich? We don't have to talk about it. But whenever you're ready to talk, I'm here for you." I gave her a hug.

"I know. And I'm here for you, too. Now enough of *The Young and the Restless*. Talk to me about the playground jump. And how you let a buncha preschoolers do you in like that. That picture of you on the blogs was not pretty. Did you read that interview Co-Co Ming did? That troll is all over school flapping his gums about how you got dragged by a bunch of underclassmen."

I rolled my eyes. "No, I didn't read it. But I did read what everybody else has to say about all four of us, which is why I've been calling you. We need to talk about how we're going to get ourselves together. I invited Spencer over—"

"Oh noooo. I can't do the dizzy trick today."

"Look, I don't like her either. Matter of fact, I don't like her breathing the same air as me. But we have to deal with her. Like we talked about last Friday in the bathroom before Heather had all the rich kids in her backyard popping Xanax, that we needed to get it together. All this craziness between us has got to stop, now. You know. Let's just cut them off and start a new clique. I can't do snorting baby Tylenol. And Spencer works my nerves. She's stupid."

"Plain and simple. You can't get no dumber than that."

"Exactly. So let's cut our losses and get rid of them."

"We can't do that."

I huffed. "And why not? Are you serious?"

"They got too much dirt on us. They know too much."

"No, correction. They must have too much dirt on *you*. Not unless you've been running your mouth telling them hoes my business on the low."

"What are you trying to say, London? You've just insulted me. Your mouth is really off the hook right now. I just wiped your tears and consoled you and you trying to bring it to me."

"I'm just saying, bestie boo . . . your mouth is sometimes out of control."

"Don't bestie boo me. What business of yours you think I wanna tell? That you've been over here crying and stressing over Doctor Corny? That's no business. That's fact. Who does that? If anything, I'm embarrassed for you. Another thing to get added to my misery." She shifted in her seat, crossing her legs, and tooted her lips up. "Tryna do me. What kinda games you into? What, you invited Spencer over here so y'all two lollipop hoes can gang up on me? Well, then bring it. There's no church in the wild."

I blinked, confused and convinced that Rich had fallen off the deep end. "Along with your abortion, you must have gotten a lobotomy, too. I asked you a simple question and you lost your mind, for what? What do they have on you?"

"They know about my visit to the STD clinic in a blond afro wig."

"Clinic? Eww. When did this happen?"

"Freshman year. It was a one-night stand."

Ohmygod, yuck. This girl doesn't know a thing about condoms.

"And they know about the twins, Jason and Jonathon. Two shots of tequila, and I had them both in my bed. And then there was the time with the whips and chains and spiked heels, and Zachary's..."

I immediately cut her off. "Umm, Rich. Forget it. I've heard enough."

"And the only thing I ever told them about you was when you ran up in the club and bust Anderson over the head with a bottle. And the time you were in jail crying like a baby."

I rolled my eyes. "Girl, it didn't even go down like that. But anyway, why did you tell them my business?"

"Girl, please. Because I had a moment of weakness and felt like I had to spread the wealth. I couldn't just let them have something on me. Well, I'm sorry. Maybe I shouldn't have told them that. But, garden gnomes or not, we can't stop being their friends."

I shook my head. "Fine. Then we all need to figure out how to get this media mess in order. Have you even seen the headlines?"

"Yes, I have, Miss Keep It Cute. That's how I know you beat up a table of five-year-olds."

"It wasn't just any table. It was *our* table, which is part of the problem. It isn't just the media after us. We have haters all around us, trying to snatch our spot. And the question is, what are we going to do about it? Are you no longer fierce, fly, and fabulous?"

Rich eyed me. "London, there you go, insulting me again."

"Rich, shut. Up. Please. This is not about you. This is about the Pampered Princesses who have been knocked down off of our thrones. Our reputations are real Humpty Dumpty right now and we're the only ones who can put it back together again."

"Well, that's what I have a publicist for."

"Newsflash, boo. She can only work with what you give her. And at the moment, that hasn't been much. All of our reputations are on the line. And I'm tired of it. I don't like being in the press like that."

"All press is good press."

"No, it's not."

"Yes, it is."

"You know what, Rich. Forget it. I'm not gonna keep doing this with you. When Spencer gets here, I'm going to send her on her way. And whatever is said about us will just keep being said about us. But I am not going to be a part of any of it. This isn't even my crew. This is your crew. You invited me into this. Made me believe y'all had it on lock." I shook my head. "I thought we were best friends."

"Yeah, we are best friends. And we do have it on lock. And don't ever question if I think I'm fabulous again. And you're right. We need to get it together. Now I see why you called me over here, because you couldn't do it without me. You should have just said that. We coulda got right to the point. But, whatever. I've already been inconvenienced. So here's what we're going to do." She paused as if she was giving it some thought. "Okay. We're going to tell Heather that crack is whack. Then we're going to tell Spencer to stay off her knees in bathrooms. We're going to let them know that we run this. And they need to learn how to behave."

"Uhhh, excuse you. Aren't you forgetting something— or someone, I should say?"

"Oh yeah. And you, Miss Happy Hands, you can't go around tearing up the café every time someone says something you don't like. How immature is that? We're going to have to start jumping whores after school."

"Uhhh, ohhhkaaay, Miss Fix It. And what about you?"

She gave me a look of astonishment, placing a hand up to her neck as if she were clutching jewels. "What about me? I'm going to make sure the three of you stay in line."

Before I could check her, Genevieve's voice blared through the intercom, announcing that Spencer had arrived.

Showtime...

6

Spencer

So this is what the inside of low money looks like, I thought as the door opened and I was greeted by a dark-chocolate woman who was in desperate need of a makeover. She had thick, woolly hair that was twisted up in a knotted bun that needed the immediate attention of a hot oil treatment, hacksaw, hot comb, or a combination of the three. And her uniform, although neatly pressed, was buttoned up to her neck like she was a missionary or on her way to a religious camp. All she needed was a Bible and white gloves and her look would be complete. Aunt Jemima was late, wrong, and so not it. I took her in as she stepped back and welcomed me in.

"Hello, Miss Spencer. Miss London is expecting you."

"Well, she just ought to be," I said, shifting my chocolate crocodile tote bag from one hand to the other, "since she was the one inviting me over here. I could be on my way home right now instead of wasting gas coming here.

This better be important because I'm in no mood for any of her foolery."

I took in how lumber-jack tall she was as she towered over me. I gasped. Her shoulders were wide and it made me wonder if she were a man, or had been one in another life. But she had a womanly face. Oooh, she was a big country biscuit. I tilted my head. "Umm, did you play football in school?"

She smoothed out the front of her dress and straightened her shoulders. "No, ma'am. I most certainly did not. Why?"

I smiled. "You look like someone I saw on the cover of *Sports Weekly* once, that's all. But maybe it was your son or something. Do you have a son?"

"No, ma'am. I have a daughter."

"Does she play sports?"

"No, she's two. Now if that's all, I have to get back to work." She paused, pointing to the staircase. "Miss London is upstairs. Her bedroom is to the right down the west wing hall."

Ewwww, yuck. How rude was that? *Damn linebacker! Wait...she's a quarterback!*

I climbed the elegant curved staircase, heading toward London's room. Although the last place I wanted to spend my afternoon was here, the thought of being all up in London's pie face, knowing I was going to be leaving here then going straight home to cuddle with her man, was worth the torture I'd have to endure by being in her company.

I freakin' despised her knick-knack-paddy-whack-give-a-dog-a-bone self.

She was despicable.

And I would gladly spit nails in her face and set fire to her hair if opportunity rang my buzzer. I took a deep breath as I made my way down the long hallway. If I didn't hate her so much I would have been able to appreciate how lovely their home was. But, whatever! She was the enemy I needed to keep close.

I knocked on the door. And a few seconds later, it swung open.

"Hey," London said dryly.

I knitted my neatly arched brows together, stepping into her bedroom. I spotted Rich stretched out on a chaise. I gawked at her, then back at London. "'Hey'? Is that the code word for an apology? Because the last I checked that's exactly what you owed me. Or did you forget how you stepped your hot breath up in my face and threatened to crack my face just moments before we stepped out on the red carpet last week?"

"What? Apology? Girlie, you had better lay off the gas fumes, 'cause you got me confused. I don't owe you nothing but a moment of my time."

Rich grunted, crossing her feet at the ankles. "See. I told you. And she done came up in your house tryna get it crunked already. Girl ain't even been here a minute and she's already at it. Mmmph. Couldn't be me."

I placed a hand on my hip and tilted my head. "What couldn't be you? A virgin? Anti-easy? Save it. Talk to the hand. I have no time for your trampy foolishness today, Rich. Now back to you, London. You invited me over here, for what? I didn't come here to be greeted by Hannibal Lecter's twin sister, The Man-eater."

Rich sat up in her seat. "What? I'ma show you a man-eater all right when I beat your face in, 'cause I done had enough of you and your games. London invited you here trying to be decent to you. I knew you weren't worthy of our time." She looked over at London. "Please. She needs to go find herself the nearest train to jump in front of so we can be done with her."

I felt myself about to go off. "You know what, Beef Patty? Obviously you have a problem with me. But guess what? You two muskrats are irrelevant. So how about *you* go find a bridge to hop off of—headfirst."

Rich leaped up. "Oh, no this silly-willy dingbat didn't. London, I'ma have to write you a check later because we're about to tear this room up. I know she's not tryna bring it to me today, or any other day. This ho's the reason we're in all this mess in the first place."

I slammed my purse against my leg. "*I'm* the reason we're in this mess? Trampalina, please! Are you kidding me? Has your brain been hanging outside all day? I didn't do a hee-haw thing to you donkeys."

"Donkeys?" London snapped. "Now wait a minute. I—"

"No," I huffed. "You wait a minute. I didn't come here to be attacked by no wildebeest. I did not see *Wild Kingdom* posted up on the gate when I pulled up. But"—I shot a look over at Rich—"I did see a low-budget C-class Benz parked at the bottom of the hill."

Rich shifted in her seat. "Don't look at me."

"Well, then why does the tag say 'Rich' on it? You forgot I was with you when you got that C-class. That was what you used to learn how to drive. My guess is you've been reduced from the Bugatti back to the basics. Now what, London?"

"Uh-uh," Rich snapped. "No, you didn't."

"Uhhh, yes, I did," I shot back.

Rich stood up. "I suggest you shut your mouth and let's get to the issue at hand. Apparently you don't understand the rules of the game. Rule number one: we don't keep secrets. And obviously you are still performing tricks."

I blinked. "Trick? You wait one ding-dong-the-witch-is-gone minute. I don't do tricks, booga-boo. That's your department, Miss Trixie." I shot London a look. "Get your pet armadillo before I skin her."

I eyed Rich as she stepped out of her heels. "You just don't learn, do you? I thought you'd get it when London and I boom-bopped, dropped it on your head when you were upside-down in that ditch. But obviously that wasn't enough. What's left to do to you, Spencer? Peel your skin back and drag you? Is that what you want, Spencer? 'Cause you know I'll bring it to you."

I raised a brow. "Bring it then, Crotch Rot."

"Damn it!" London yelped. "Will the both of you stop it?!"

Rich rolled her eyes. "Well, she started it." She eyed me. "I hope you're satisfied. Now—thanks to you and your junkie girlfriend—we're in the paper, again. I don't do Gucci. Maybe a bag or two, but not enough to be called some Gucci clique. That low-rank skank could have at least said Chanel. Like Gucci, for real? How dare she?"

"Well, how dare *you*!" I snapped. "Accuse me of being the cause of all this mess."

Rich stepped up in my face. "Well, she's *your* friend. I don't give a damn if she went to jail or not. She was up on some dingy makeshift stage in a funky neon-green skirt rapping about me. She must have lost her mind. And you stood there and allowed it. And don't think her calling you dizzy is going to make us think you weren't in on this. Because we all know that's a term of endearment for you."

I tilted my head. "Oh, really? I didn't *allow* Heather to do a thing. So let's get that straight. And yeah. You're right. Heather *was* my friend until she did what she did. And so were you at one point."

"Look, you two," London interjected. "I didn't call both of you over here for this."

I rolled my eyes. "And who are you, again?"

London blinked. "Oh no, girlie. Don't do it."

Rich grunted. "Mmmph. See. I knew it. I don't know why you even wasted your time inviting this space cadet over here, any—"

"I didn't ask to be invited over here."

London snapped her fingers. "Hello! Hello! Public service announcement. This is a live broadcast! Both of you are here because we have a mess to clean up. And bickering back and forth about it isn't gonna do anything to change it."

"And who are you, Oprah? You need to get your own crap right."

London blinked. "Oh, no this hooker didn't."

"Oh, yes she did," Rich instigated. "She just called you a fat know-it-all in your own house. How disrespectful is that?" She turned to me. "Surely I must be in the twilight zone because the only two caught up in the matrix are you and Heather. If I'm gonna rock a headline, then I need to put it there. But that stunt you pulled was unacceptable. Sic her, London. Let this wench know."

WTF? Sic her?

London's eyes almost popped out of their sockets.

I smirked. "Oh yes. Here, London. Here, London, girl.

Yeah, bring it, Fido. Sic me. Bite me. I gotta special treat for you."

I looked over at Rich and knew her well enough to know she was holding back a laugh. A mess.

London shot Rich a nasty look as if she was two seconds from leapfrogging up on her. "I know you're not getting ready to laugh, Rich. I'm not an effen dog."

Rich held up her hands in mock surrender. "Look, let's not get off track. Spencer came up in here and tried to divide and conquer."

I huffed. "Rich, please. You're delusional. The only thing that divides you are them ham-hock legs and the STD-positive scallywags you let run up in you. But you're right. You are definitely in the twilight zone because I didn't do a thing to either one of you."

"Ding-ding-ding," Rich said sarcastically. "Over in this corner we have the dumb blonde who finally gets it. That she did absolutely *nothing* to stop Heather from dragging us."

"Look, girl. I didn't know she was going to hop up on that raggedy stage and say all that stuff. I was shocked. And hurt."

Rich huffed. "Whatever. Nobody cares about you being hurt. You hurt me. We used to be AFs."

I frowned. "AFs?"

"Yeah, AFs. Almost friends, then you turned on me."

"Well, almost doesn't count. Obviously we were never anything."

Rich clapped. "Exactly. Now you get it. That's why I'm going to whip you and be happy about it. The point is, you knew she had said all that mess and you came back to the school and said nothing. You coulda said something while we were in the bathroom, but nooo. You didn't. Why, Spencer? You open your mouth for everything else, don't you? Or is the only time you know how to open your mouth is when you have some boy's boxers dropped around his ankles?"

I blinked.

"Then you wonder why I don't like you or your rock star girlfriend. Please. Both of you trifling slut-buckets are beneath me."

"Beneath you?" I screeched. "How dare you! Is that before or after you've rolled yourself out of some boy's stained sheets? The only thing *beneath* you is a towel to sop up all of your nastiness."

"See," Rich said, bumping her chest up into me. "You didn't hear a word I said to you in the bathroom last week." She put her finger in my face. "I told you—no, warned you—to play nice. But you still wanna get it crunked. I don't know why you stay trying me when you know you don't want it with me."

"Make my day, Big Bird," I said, patting my bag. "And I will scatter your brain like chicken feed all up in here."

Rich pushed me, causing me to stumble backward. "Well, get to scattering. 'Cause you're a punk without your Mace."

"I didn't bring any Mace today. I brought something sharp and shiny just for you. I'ma end this once and for all. So say your prayers." I whipped out my blade and started waving it in the air. "'Cause I'm gonna rock, sock, and slice you to sleep."

Rich screamed, "Ohmygod! London, call the cops, now! I want her arrested! I want her off this property! And I want her sent to jail!"

London stepped in between us. "Both of you are crazy. Rich, I am not calling the police. And Spencer, there is no need for weapons, so put that blade away. And both of you stop."

"That's right, London. Tell her, girl. Let her know how we don't appreciate what she did to us. And then she pulls a machete out on me. Who does that?"

"This is not a machete," I said, pointing my knife at her. "It's a Sebenza. Strong and rugged and able to gut and fillet you in a blink of an eye. So get it right."

"Well, that's what's going to be in the police report when I'm done with you. London, we should bring it straight to her head for that."

"Rich, please. Let's keep it calm and cute."

I laughed. "Oh, right. Keep it real cute; just like you did when you attacked them little girls in school Monday." I looked her up and down. "What, you're about six feet tall? And you're the one stomping down on little peewee lightweights. Yeah, that was real *cute* all right. And you're the one worrying about the media. Please. What a two-faced bully. You invite me over here for this?"

London took a deep breath. "Spencer," she said slowly. "I'm only going to say this once. Please don't go there. The three of us are stuck with each other. And the three of us need to figure out a way to get along long enough for the media and everyone at Hollywood High who is laughing and talking trash about us to know that we are still holding it down. We already discussed this last week. I thought we were all clear on this. Rich is right. You knew what was about to go down. You stood in front of the cameras last week and said you were sure Heather would make the front pages the next day, so how did you know that?"

I set my bag down on her table. "How do you think I knew? I went to her house. I saw the bowls of pills and the fountains overflowing with booze. I saw her mother passed out on the sofa, drooling. I was the one who stood there, humiliated as she danced and popped and rapped in front of all her druggie friends..." I felt my eyes starting to burn with tears. I fought to keep them in check. I loved that girl. She was the second best-friend that had betrayed me and turned her back on me. And the first one was standing right in my face. "...Talking about how she did us all in. But guess what? The rules were clear. Or did you both forget? Selective amnesia, is it? I was told that we play nice in public, but behind closed doors we don't deal with each other. So why would I tell either one of you anything? Y'all don't like her. And you don't like me, for no good reason other than to be mean and nasty. But it was all good last year when you were talking to me about London behind her back, about how much you hated that she was moving to L.A. And now that she's here, you're busy smiling up in her face; the best of friends. How phony is that?"

"And, ohhhhhkay. But I like her now. And my problem now is with you. So stick to the matter at hand," Rich said.

"And what exactly is your problem with me? Since I've never gotten a clear answer on that."

She huffed. "Oh, Spencer. Get over yourself. Don't stand here and try to act like you don't know what my problem is with you. RJ, RJ, RJ...'til the end of effen time. You were my friend. But you had to go run off with him. Our friendship wasn't enough for your sleazy behind. You had to sleep with my brother—the golden child. And then I get blamed for that."

"Are you serious? Rich, you're the one who went back and told your parents."

"Yeah, I did because I warned you that I didn't like you messing with him from the pickup. I let you slide the first time I caught you letting him hump you."

"Please, Rich. That happened like how many years ago? And you're still on that?"

"Yeah, but it happened more than once."

"If you're talking about what happened over the summer, you need to get over it. RJ is grown. He slept with me because he wanted to. He didn't need you to babysit him or monitor who or what he was doing. You were busy being desperate trying to get the attention you've always wanted. You thought telling on us was going to get RJ in trouble. Jealousy got you cock-blocking. Who does that? I didn't run off telling your parents about you and Knox, but you all up in my business."

"Ho, you were my friend. And you turned around and screwed my brother, after I told you I didn't want you messing with him. Then what do you do? You start dating him behind my back, being the sneaky little skeezer that you are. You were all up in my house. And I didn't even know it. And my mother didn't care that he had you all locked up in his bedroom 'cause she trusted you. Mmmph. Sweet, sweet Spencer and perfect RJ. She thought you were a nice little virgin girl and her pride and joy was Mister Innocent, so yeah I told."

I fought back my tears. I really cared about RJ, and I really cared about Rich. But I couldn't understand what the problem was. "He was my first love. And you broke us up."

"And you ruined a friendship. Your own mother didn't want you around for the holidays, but I did. My family embraced you. We loved you. I loved you like a sister. And you stabbed me in the back by sleeping with my brother. You put him before me. Before our friendship."

I twisted my lips. "Well, it's too late to be crying over spilled cookies. What's done is done. I slept with him. I dated him. And I cared about him. But he's moved on. He's in Oxford. And you and I are standing here. Now what?"

"Good question," London said. "How about we start with a truce."

I folded my arms, eyeing Rich, who was eyeing me back. And we both had tears in our eyes. "You know what, Rich? Even though you make my panties ruffle, I miss that. I miss what we had. But I know we'll never have that again. I don't trust you."

"Exactly," London said. "And Rich doesn't trust you, either. How could she, after what you did to her? So enough of the memories. You all have new best friends. I'm Rich's best friend. And Heather's yours."

Rich smirked. "Well, she was until she turned on you."

"Yeah," London agreed. "And that's not our fault. But we still need to figure out a way to get along. Now do the two of you wanna reign at the top again, or be down at the bottom looking up at some other hoes sitting up on our thrones? I'm not gonna let you two keep dragging me. If y'all wanna argue about brothers and who's screwing who, then do you. But I'm not going to be bothered with it. Before I let myself get defamed I will hop on the next jet to the UK and go to boarding school and never think of any of you again. Enough's enough. So, what's it going to be? The truth is, neither one of you can stand to be in the media because they will chew you up, spit you out, and never let you go. You tryna be Kim Kardashian, Nicole Richie. Paris Hilton can't get a kind word if she paid for it. Is that what the two of you wanna be, defamed hoes? The friendship is over. I get that."

Mmmph. I could have sworn London said that with a smile. I eyed her, raising a brow.

Rich rolled her eyes.

I sucked my teeth.

"Look, the two of you can stand here looking silly if you want. But we need a truce. And we need it now. So, Spencer, you better—"

Nothing unnerved me more than the word *better*. I didn't take orders from some king-size Whopper queen. "I don't think so," I snapped, walking toward the door. I turned to face them. "As Rich said: The only commitment I have to the word *better*, is that I *better* stay rich and I *better* stay beautiful. Anything other than that is optional. I'm out."

I snatched open the door and there stood this six-foot-tall cat daddy dripping with chocolate. I didn't know who he belonged to, but he was definitely somebody's sin. And if I didn't have my mind set on getting home to London's boyfriend, I would have forgotten my manners and had her houseguest, too. I pushed him to the side, no excuse me, no nothing, and swayed my hips. I could feel his eyes on me as I popped my sock-it-to-me out the door. And all I could think was, *Eat it up, baby! Maybe I'll come back for you next.*

7

Rich

It was a good thing that I worshipped in the Church of
Stay Fly and Be a Lady at All Times; otherwise I would
have taken my diamonds off, yoked Spencer by the nape
of her ultrabony neck and choked every ounce of super-
duper dumb out of her. Just who did she think she was!
And did she really just try to shank me? Like really? Really?
She'd better be thankful that I didn't believe in throwing
the first punch or I would've torn her up.

Straight got it crunked.

Word.

Hood was already blueprinted in my genes so it would've
been as simple as filing a nail for me to take it to the streets.
And not Rodeo Drive either. Crenshaw.

Thing was, I didn't do ghetto.

Straight classy.

And besides, I didn't feel like tearing up London's house.
I'd much rather ensure that Spencer's Twitter account was
hacked and the secret freak-nasty video of her in black

leather and RJ with whips and chains, tweeted its way to her darling followers.

Hmph, I knew how to behave. Even revenge had proper etiquette.

But *if I hadn't* exercised control over my manners— psycho-freak would've brought the worst out in me.

Truthfully, I felt sorry for her. Like, she had to be either high or crazy...and judging by the way she carried on I'd take door number one. After all, she and Heather were besties for a reason.

Bing! A lightbulb went off—Heather and Spencer: fraternal twins from the planet of Stoopidcrackwhores.com.

Clutching pearls.

I swear I really needed to get back to my appointment. The standing one I'd had with misery. Feeling sorry for myself took precedence over this nonsense. If anything, I needed some spa time to recuperate, because the last thing I expected on my way over here was a gang fight with my AF-turned-archenemy.

Puhlease.

Spare me.

Spencer was so selfish. She'd rather fight with me than look in my eyes and see that I was in pain.

"What are you doing here?" London's voice drifted into my ears and interrupted my me-time. I looked over at her and that's when I realized I was standing center stage and in my audience was a sweet piece of chocolate—a hottie. A sweet-like-apple-cider cutie. A boo-drop so fine that the only thing on my mind was where'd he been all my life.

Snap-snap, baby.

Now this was what I called the antidote to misery. "Awwl," I said, walking over to him and boldly locking my right arm into his left. "Did London invite you over here to make me feel better?" I gave an innocent schoolgirl giggle, while placing his free hand around my waist. I winked my eye at London and gave her a thumbs-up.

Yank!

Oh…my…did this heifer just rip me from this Zulu warrior's arms? I looked London over like she had lost every bit of her mind. She had to know better than to touch me when I was being consoled by a cutie. "Oh, hell no!" I snapped. "London—"

"Are you serious right now?" She rolled her eyes at me. Real hard and real stank. "You need to calm your freak meter down!"

Freak meter? Is she trying to play me?

Before I could say anything she looked at my future baby-daddy and said, "I asked you a question."

He smiled and I swear that sexy smile lit up the room. "I can't get no love?" he asked London.

She hesitated, so I stepped up—lip gloss poppin' and cleavage show-stoppin'.

Snap. Snap.

"What, you want a hug, FBD?" I smiled at him.

He blushed. "FBD?"

"Future baby-daddy."

"You don't need any more baby-daddies," London said, pissed. But I didn't care, I was too busy blowing an air kiss at FBD and watching him return my affection with a soft wink. Hmph, as far as I was concerned we could skip the formalities, leave here, and go and get married. Meow. I'm certain that being Mrs. Sexy would look hella good on me.

Just as I went to tell boo-boo my life story about being

hurt and looking for a man who would treat me right, it hit me that I was being selfish.

OMG.

And selfish was soooo not me.

Here I had used my thickalicious body and stunning good looks to seduce this dude and I had no idea what he may have been to London. Suppose he was her way of getting over the king of corny—Anderson?

I took a step back and just as I started to ask London who he was, he drank me in, in full view, and said, "Yo, L-Boogie, what's good? Who is this sexy thing?" He licked his lips and flicked my chin. "Can we get an introduction?"

Immediately my temperature rose. I swear if somebody had checked me right then I'd have had a fever. I fanned my face and made sure that my D cups bounced as I slid my arms around his neck and said, "It's okay, L-Boogie, I got the introductions and the condoms." I paused. *I don't believe I just said that*. I fought back my blush. "I'm just playing—"

"Yeah, right." He smirked as he reached out and touched the tip of one of my curls and twirled it. "I betchu was just playin'."

Whew!

And to think that when I arrived here I was down in the dumps, but now I was clearly on the mountaintop. Yes, yes, Mt. Everest. Miz Thang's swag was back.

Boom!

But before I could decide if I wanted to take him home or arrange a short stay, I needed to know his name. Nameless boys weren't my forte. That was for hoes. "Yeah, L-Boogie, introductions, please."

For the second time in a matter of minutes London hesitated and I had to take charge—again. "The name's Rich," I said. "Rich. Like an overflowing of cash. I'm sixteen, newly single, and two hours and fifteen minutes ago I had issues, but as of right now, I'm stress-free. Now give me your stats, lil daddy."

"His name," London said with a razor-sharp edge, "is Justice." She slid in front of me and blocked him from my view. How rude.

"Oh, this is Justice?" I said, bumping her out the way and now resuming my place in his face. "Why didn't you tell me he was so delicious? I mean, such a nice and fine, chocolate, strapping young man." I brazenly touched his right bicep and ran my index finger up the protruding vein. If I were fresh, and easy, by the end of the night I would change his name from Justice to Give-It-To-Me-Daddy. It took everything in me not to purr. I quickly grabbed my purse, scribbled my number down on a piece of paper, and as I went to hand it to my FBD, I let the paper slip and land right on top of my breasts—my fleshy hilltop. Then I took my hand and pushed the piece of paper into my valley. "OMG. Would you look at that?" I pointed to the edge of the paper in my cleavage. "I only wanted to give you my number and it seems I lost it." I pointed. "Down there."

London looked at me as if I were some dirty hot trollop. "You can calm down and tuck your horns back in. This is not the week for freaks or an STD lottery."

Screech!

Oh, no she did'eent!

Can you say mad hater? And umm, wasn't she just crying over Anderson this afternoon? And umm, just a couple of months ago—the same night we stormed into the club and broke bottles over my ex-boyfriend Corey's and Anderson's heads—she insisted that I get with her friend *Justice*. The same *Justice* standing here, and now she was throwing shade? Like what was good with that? Who does that? Or had she reneged on the invitation?

I looked at her and said, "London, what's up with you turning into Shady-Old-Lady-Grady. I'm tryin' to drop my boom-bop and you're putting me on pause. Did something change, 'cause last time I checked you were trying to hook me up with Justice? Remember? Or was I dreaming?"

Justice shot London a nasty look as he removed my phone number from my fleshy valley.

London's eyes turned dead red as their gazes clashed. "No, you weren't dreaming," Justice said. "London told me a lot about you, sweetness."

"Yeah, I did," London snapped. "But that was right before she told me that she wasn't interested in meeting you. That she was hung up and strung out over Knox." She squinted her eyes at me. "Yeah, remember Knox, Rich? And remember those nine months you came over here mourning about him?"

I don't believe she said that. And Knox? I know she didn't bring up Knox. The mere mention of Knox's name at this moment was a declaration of war and I know London didn't want it. So I shot her the same nasty look she gave me, but before I could cuss her out and instruct her to watch her mouth, my phone rang. For a moment I thought about taking my ringing phone and slamming London in the head with it. Then I looked at the caller ID: *Knox*. And my heart dropped.

She'd conjured him up. And now the flood of emotions

that I'd been able to push to the side had crept back into my chest and hung out there. I could feel tears beating in the back of my eyes, but there was no way I was going to cry. No way in hell. At least not while I was standing here.

Instead I gathered my purse and slid it on my shoulder.

Justice looked me over and said, "Lil Sexy, you bouncing already? What's good? When can I call you?"

I shot London a slow, nasty look that rose from her toes to her head and said, "Maybe you should ask L-Boogie for permission." I walked over to London's bedroom door and slammed it behind me.

Trick-ass! I can't believe she played me like that.

Knox's call rolled into voice mail. Once I was at my car I leaned against the driver's-side door and sucked in a deep breath. *Don't cry... don't cry...*

Memories of Knox pained the hell out of me. It had been a week since we'd broken up, and although he'd been calling me every day—sometimes three or four times a day—I refused to answer the phone. He'd hurt me and he would have to deal with that.

I whipped into my driveway and almost crashed into the garage.

What...in...the...hell...is Knox's car doing here?

Is he crazy?

I swallowed and slowly walked up the stairs. I opened the front door and there in the foyer was my baby. The only man I'd ever loved with my whole heart. The only man who'd ever loved me—and not just for my body, but simply because...he just did.

I looked at Knox and almost smiled. But then I quickly reminded myself why we were in this situation in the first place. "What are you doing here?" I asked him snidely. "Last I heard from you we weren't doing this anymore. And who let you in here?"

"I did." My mother's words cut across our conversation and she stared at me without blinking. Disgust was written all over her face. I could tell she wanted nothing more than to bring it to my throat again...but she didn't. Instead she said, "Make this quick."

"Really?" My eyes brightened. "You're going to let him stay?"

"Don't get it confused," my mother said sternly. "I'm still not pleased with you. And you do not have my blessing. But since you're a grown woman, I'ma let you handle this. But just know that you will not be bringing your men up here in my home. Get your own spot. Now, like I said, make this quick." She turned on her heels and left us standing there, her wrath lingering behind her.

"Now why are you here?" I turned back to Knox.

"Wassup with the attitude?" He looked at me with his eyebrows furrowed.

"Don't worry about that. Now why are you here?"

"I didn't come here to argue with you, so watch your attitude and take it down." He took two steps toward me. "We need to talk."

"We don't need to do a thing but part. You go home and live your life, resurrect Nikki, and I'ma go on and do me."

"Here we go with this bull! You're back on that again? Things don't go your way and you throw a tantrum! I don't have time to be playing with you—"

"You're right you don't have time to be playing with me, or to be sneaking and creeping with me at eleven thirty, twelve o'clock. You don't have time to be driving fifty and sixty miles just so I can duck and dodge cameras. The only thing you have time for are condoms and lectures to tell me about how you can't do me. So cool. Since you don't have time then, what are you standing here for? Why don't you step? As a matter fact you're moving too slow." I walked over to the front door and swung it open.

Knox shook his head. "You're pathetic. Do you even hear how you sound? You are really buggin'. I've been calling you for five days straight, leaving four and five messages a day. And you would have four or five more if your inbox wasn't full. I came here because I was feeling like dirt, and bad—"

"Yeah right, Knox. Only reason you're here and the only thing you want to know is if I plan on ruining your lil precious life. Well, I don't, college boy, so you go run along and play with your frat brothers, 'cause I'm good. Now. Get. Out!"

He chuckled in disbelief. "You got some serious issues." He shook his head. "You don't have to tell me twice to get out. I'm not gon' sweat you. I told you what it was. I told you how I felt, but you only hear what you want to hear. Did you hear me when I said that I wanted to be with you all the time? That we had to take it slow because we had the rest of our lives to be together? But you didn't hear any of that. So skip it, you're right. You do you, and while you're doing that, grow up. Little girl!" He walked swiftly out the door and before I could think about what to do next, he was revving out of the driveway and reversing down the hill.

Immediately my heart shattered, pieces of it flying in different directions, pricking my skin and making me feel sick to my stomach. My head ached. My heart ached. My body ached. I was confused. I didn't know what to do. All I knew is that I was leaning back against the wall, sliding to the floor. Tears raced from my eyes.

"Now that's a shame," my mother said as she came in and stood over me. She shook her head. "Thought you were grown. At least that's how you brought it to me. But a grown woman knows how to handle her relationships and how to keep her man. Not chase him away." She rolled her eyes. "But. Then again. When you treat your mother like dirt you get what you get."

"Ma—"

"Oh please. We're on a first-name basis, remember? Now get up off my freshly waxed floor and go to your room—excuse me, *my* room, that I'm still kind enough to let you sleep in. I don't want to hear all this crying and carrying on for another moment." She snapped her fingers. "Now let's go. Take that to your bedroom, the one you need to start paying rent on. Because that's another thing grown women do—pay their own way."

I couldn't believe this was happening. This trick was at it again. All about Logan and nothing about Rich. Here I'd just lost my man, was throwing myself a pity party, and there she was adding piss to my punch. If I had the strength I'd kick her...

I wiped my eyes, stood up from the floor and regained my balance. Just as I'd gotten myself together enough to walk without my legs feeling like willow branches, I looked my mother over and headed straight to my room.

8

London

I watched as Rich snatched up her oversized Balenciaga bag and stormed toward the door in dramatic fashion. And for a hot second, I could have sworn she threw an extra shake in her thick hips just as she slammed the door. *Skank!*

What in the hell just happened here?

This is not how the meeting with the two of them was supposed to go down!

I blinked my eyes, totally dumbfounded at what had quickly unfolded in front of me. My best friend literally whoring herself out to my man! So what if she didn't exactly know that's who he was. The point is, she had no business doing it, especially when she was supposedly so "in love" with this Knox guy.

Then again, I shouldn't have been so surprised at what just happened. Miss Gasoline Drawers had always been a walking inferno. Put a fine boy in front of her and she went right up in flames, ready to rip off her clothes and drop, pop, and roll with him; no questions asked. Nasty ho!

And Justice...the nerve of him! He stood there and flat-out disrespected me, undressing Rich with his eyes, licking his lips, and practically screwing her *down* right there in the middle of the floor with no regard for me. How effen disrespectful was that?

Then he...he...refers to me as some L-Boogie, like I'm some washed-up wannabe Lauryn Hill! L-Boogie?!

What the hell?

My God! There were sparks between them!

That is not a part of the plan!

Yet, there was something in Justice's eyes that told me what my heart didn't want to accept. He wanted her!

Panic gripped my chest. The thought of the two of them going at it like two wild animals in heat made the blood drain from my head. Him touching her the way he touched me, making love to her the way he made love to me—it was all too much to bear. I felt light-headed. And sick!

When I finally mustered up the courage to shift my eyes away from the door over to Justice, he was glaring at me, his jaws clenching and unclenching. "Yo, on e'erything I love, yo. If you was a dude, I'd break ya jaw; for real, for real."

I gasped. "What? You must be joking."

He scowled. "Do I look like I'm effen jokin', yo? You lucky I don't put my hands on no chick, 'cause I'd check ya chin real quick, yo."

I blinked. *He can't be serious!*

"For what?" I asked incredulously.

"For bein' so effen stupid, yo. The broad was right here and you wanna be on some BS."

"First of all, I'm not stupid. Second of all, how did you get in this house?"

He sucked his teeth. "How ya dumb behind think I got in here?"

I swallowed. *Genevieve.* She'd always been the one to open the gates to the rear entrance of the house and sneak Justice in and out of here behind my parents' backs. She'd always maneuvered around the watchful eye of Daddy's surveillance system to sneak Justice out. And she was the one who'd sneak food up to my room for Justice or check in on him whenever I had to leave him here alone. Those were things she did when I asked—no, *told,* her to. But today she had no business letting him in without being directed to do so.

But how did he get in touch with her? How did she know to open the gates for him?

I swallowed, making a mental note to myself to confront Genevieve the first chance I got. "First of all, Justice, the last time I checked, you didn't want anything to do with me, remember that? You stood here and cursed me out and stormed out of here, telling me you weren't beat for me anymore."

"Yeah, 'cause you had me hot, yo. You always doin' and sayin' dumb ish."

I huffed. "Get real, Justice. You cursed me out, disrespected me, then didn't give a damn about whether or not my parents were home when you stormed out the front door. I've risked everything for you."

"Yo, you ain't risked a thing for me, yo. So save that bull. All you care about is yaself. I've been sweatin' you from the rip, tryna get you to see how much I love you, but all you wanna do is keep playin' me, yo. I called you to

apologize, to make up wit' you; to let you know how I
miss you, and ya dumb-azz brush me off for them birds,
like I'm some scab."

I pulled in my bottom lip. I missed him, too. More than
he could ever imagine. But I refused to tell him that. Not
after the way he played me in front of Rich.

"Well, what did you expect me to do, Justice? Be all
grins and giggles? Greet you with open arms? You broke
up with me, remember? Then you just show up here, like
everything's all wonderful. Then you turn around and
straight-up disrespect me by kicking it to Rich right in my
face. How nasty is that? That hurt me."

He clucked his tongue. "Umph. Ya silly behind don't
know the first thing about bein' hurt, yo. You hurt *me*. I
gave you my effen heart, yo. I ain't never give no broad my
all, 'cept ya silly behind. And what you do? You throw it all
back in my face. Playin' head games wit' me, talkin' about
how you had a connect out here. That you had a master
plan to get me put on, gettin' my hopes all up that I would
snatch up my own record deal. Actin' like you was all
'bout it, 'bout it. Then you come out here and turn 'round
and eff my whole world up, talkin' 'bout you don't wanna
go through wit' it 'cause you done had a change of heart."
He took a deep breath, palming the front of his face like
he was ready to lose it. He dropped his hand down to his
side, balling it into a fist, then pressed the back of his fist
to his mouth. "You hurt me, yo; real talk. How the eff you
think that made me feel, yo? Tellin' me to go independent,
like I ain't good for nothin' else. You tryna crush my
dreams."

I couldn't believe he would think that. His dream had
become my dream. Hell, it was all I thought about. The

last thing I would ever do was hurt Justice. I loved him too much. He had to know that. I reached for him, but he brushed my hand away.

"Don't touch me, yo."

Inside I was falling apart, bit by bit. I still tried to hold on to what little pieces of me I still had left, but they were slowly slipping through my fingers. I held back my tears.

"Justice, you mean everything to me. I love you."

He eyed me. "London, quit the bull, yo. I don't mean jack to you. And don't talk to me about *love*, 'cause you don't know the first thing about *love*. Love is about making sacrifices. You 'posed to have my back. Not be tryna block my flow. Not tryna throw hate all up on me. But that's how you roll, London." He twisted his lips up. "Talkin' 'bout you love me, yeah right. You don't even love yaself..."

Ouch! That cut me *deep!*

He didn't know what he was talking about. He couldn't. I *did* love me. I just loved *him* more.

"You have a lot of nerve, Justice. You claim you love me, but you stood"—I pointed to the spot where he and Rich had stood, flirting and lusting after each other—"right there and practically tongued down Rich. How do you think that made me feel?"

"Oh, here you go wit' the exaggerations now. Now you wanna be the victim. Poor lil London, done got her lil feelin's hurt. Yo, get outta here with all that. You should already know what it is. I was just spittin' game to that broad."

I folded my arms tightly across my chest. "Well, it looked like a whole lot more than game to me. It looked like you were really feeling her."

"See. Here you go again wit' the okey-doke. I don't give

an eff about that chunky broad. What I look like tryna eff wit' some piglet ho? Effen thighs rubbin' together like two drumsticks. That broad is only good for one thing…"

Yeah, sex!

I shook the thought from my head. "This isn't how it was supposed to go down; that's all."

He sucked his teeth. "Well, last time I checked, plans changed, remember that? So tell me. How was it *supposed* to go down?"

"Do you wanna sleep with her?"

He frowned. "What? Yo, are you effen listenin' to me? I just told you that bit—" He shook his head. "You know what, just forget the whole thing. Do you. And I'ma do me. I told you what it was wit' us and you still on the dumbness."

"Stop calling me dumb, Justice. I'm only asking a question. I saw the way you were looking at her, then you call me some *L-Boogie*, like I'm some around-the-way hooch. How hot trash is that?"

Justice gave me a disgusted look. "Well, uh, how 'bout this: if the trash bag fits, wear it. I'm done wit' goin' back and forth wit' you. You know what I'm tryna do, and you either wit' it or you not." He snapped his fingers. "Wait, I got the digits already. So, uh"—he flicked his fingers at me—"*poof!* Dismissed. Ya services are no longer needed, L-Boogie. So you can go take ya silly lil behind somewhere and lick ya wounds 'cause I'm handlin' mine, somethin' you shoulda been doin'."

Whoa. *Did I miss something?* All I could think at that very moment was *What did I do to make him so mad? When did this whole thing between us turn so ugly?* Clearly I couldn't have done anything to him that bad to warrant this level of...disrespect and loathing. Who was he?

My man hated me!

I ran a hand through my hair at the nape of my neck. Tension was coiling around us like a knotted rope, and it was becoming harder for me to breathe. I clutched my chest, trying not to hyperventilate.

He stared at me, then actually snorted out a laugh. "On some real ish. You're pathetic, London."

I was losing this fight. But I didn't want to throw in the towel. I didn't want to surrender to the fear of it being over. And I refused to give him the satisfaction of seeing me break down in front of him. No. As bad as I wanted to fall to my knees and wail at the top of my lungs, I wouldn't.

I squared my shoulders and steadied my shaky nerves. "Why are you being so mean and nasty to me? What did I do to deserve this?"

He walked up and glared down on me. "'Cause you real effen stupid, yo." Then added, "You make me sick, yo. Wit' ya ugly self. You insecure. Fat, nasty..."

Slash!

His words cut into me.

"Well, if I'm all of that, why were you with me?"

"'Cause I feel sorry for you. Look at you. Ya mother sweats you about ya weight 'cause you're two biscuits away from bein' a submarine. All you need is some lettuce and tomato and you'll be a full ham sandwich. And your mother, she was tellin' the truth. Face it, London. You can't even make ya way onto the runway."

Slash!

"Stop it! That's enough!"

"No, what's enough is you bein' a hater. I'm sick of you,

yo. If I woulda knew how silly you was I woulda never effed with you from the rip. Look at you, six-foot-tall, giraffe-neck self. Big-foot Amazon. Don't nobody want you. I was the best thing you'll ever have, and you couldn't even get that right. At least ya girl Chunky Monkey was ready to show me some love. At least she knows what a real man is all about. I can tell she knows what to do wit' a real man. And I bet you she'd appreciate havin' a real man by her side. You still a lil girl, L-Boogie."

"That's not my name, Justice!"

"It's ya name if I say it is, lil girl."

I blinked. I couldn't believe I let him do this to me. Stand here and say all these hurtful things to me, about me. He was right, I was so stupid. I thought he loved me— flaws and all—but now I see I'm on my own. My eyes burned with tears.

My lips quivered. "All of this because of Rich?"

He scowled at me. "No, all of this because of *you*." Then, as if my nightmare couldn't get any worse, he took his hand and mushed me in the face. "Stupid-azz trick!"

Dying...

Dying...

Dead!

Now I knew what death was.

I was in shock. I was hurt. My own father had never, ever put his hands on me. Yet the only man I'd ever loved had just hit me, and called me stupid and insecure and fat. He called me an Amazon. Everything in me crashed.

I didn't want to fight back. I didn't want to argue. I didn't even want to hate him. I wanted to love him. And all I wanted to do was pretend that this wasn't happening. That it didn't exist. I wanted to rewind the clock and make it all go away. To start over and make up. But it was getting worse by the second.

Girl, you need to go upside his head.

I can't!

You gotta fight him. Otherwise he's really gonna think you're stupid.

I'm not stupid!

I'm not fat!

I'm not ugly!

Then go upside his head, the voice inside my head egged on.

And in one swift motion I reared my fist back and punched him in the face. I jumped up and started swinging on him like I was possessed. And in some sense, I guess I was. I was crazed by love and hurt and disrespect and anger.

"Yo, what the fu—!" He lunged at me, grabbing me by the wrists. "Are you effen crazy, yo, puttin' ya hands on me like that?"

"Get off me!" I tried to break free from him. "I'm sick of you hurting me like this!" Tears started pouring out of my eyes as I kicked and clawed at him, trying to hurt him the way he had hurt me. "I do nothing but love you and you treat me like dirt!"

"Yo, c'mon, chill, baby, you wildin' out, for real."

"C'mon hell, punk. Don't 'baby' me. Get your dirty hands off me!" I started kicking his shins and stomping on his feet, causing him to shuffle around the room while trying to hold my arms.

"Yo, chill, London. I don't wanna hurt you, yo."

"You've already hurt me! There's nothing else you can

do to me that you haven't already done. Whyyyyy, Justice?! Why would you do this to me?"

He wrapped his arms around me, lifting me up from the floor while I continued kicking and screaming, and pinned me down on the bed. I tried to wiggle free of his grip, but he was too strong for me. "GET OFF OF ME, Justice!"

"No. Not until you calm down. Stop tryna fight me. I don't wanna fight wit' you, yo."

"You started it, punk! You put your hands on me first! You called me all kind of nasty names." I was crying loud and hard, almost choking.

"Chill, London..."

I wasn't hearing him. The only thing ringing in my ears were the mean, nasty things he had said.

You're stupid...I'm sick of you...effen Amazon... don't nobody want you...

"C'mon, London, stop it! I really don't wanna hurt you, yo."

"Do it then, punk!" I screamed, not caring who heard us. I tried to wrestle myself free.

He started laughing. "Yo, why you buggin'? Chill, chill, chill, London, yo. I'm sorry, baby. Stop wildin' out, yo. Calm down."

"Get off of me!"

I bit his arm.

"Oww!" he yelped, letting one of my wrists go. I slapped him. "See. Now you pushin' it, yo."

"Get off of me!"

"Not until you calm down."

I couldn't calm down. I was a hysterical mess!

"Calm down, hell! I want you out of my house! And out of my life, Justice! I can't keep doing this with you."

"C'mon, baby. You don't mean that."

"I do, I do, I do," I kept repeating, hoping I could convince myself that I really did. "I swear I do. Get off of me! I'm done with you."

"C'mon, baby, chill. Forget the plan. If it's gonna have us beefin' 'n' fightin' like this, then I ain't even beat, yo. You mean too much to me."

"Stop it! Just stop it with your lies, Justice. You already told me how you feel."

"That wasn't me, yo. I was mad, baby. You know when I get mad I say all kinda crazy ish. I'm sorry. I didn't mean to put my hands on you..." He kissed me on the lips. I tried to bite him. He laughed. "See. You still wildin', yo. I said I'm sorry, baby. So you need to chill, and let ya man love you."

I stared at him. Tears falling unchecked.

"You know I love you, girl. I can't wait to spend my life with you. Remember that night I asked you to marry me?"

I shut my eyes. I didn't want to look at him. Yeah, I remembered it. It was one of the happiest moments of my life. But I wasn't going to tell him that. I didn't want to think about that. I was still stuck on how he had played me in front of Rich. How he had told me off and put his hands on me. I was too heartbroken to think of anything else. He did me in.

"Yo, baby, on e'erything I love, when you said *yes*, that was the happiest night of my life."

I wanted to smile. But I couldn't. No matter what, I didn't want to lose him. But I didn't want to hurt anymore, either.

I missed his touch. God knows I did! I missed the way

his body felt on me. His hand started roaming my breast, traveling down to my waist, then to my butt. "Let me love you, baby. You want ya man to make you feel good, huh, baby? Let me make sweet love to you, London…"

My brain was screaming *NO!*

But my body was moaning *Yesssssss!*

"I love you, baby…"

"No, you don't," I sobbed.

He kissed me again. "Yes, I do. You're my world, baby." He kissed me again. "You're so beautiful. Ain't nobody ever gonna love you like me. You're all mine, London."

"Wh-wh-what about Rich? You want her?"

"Yo, eff that Pillsbury dough ho. I told you that broad ain't nobody. I want you, baby. I mean, she's a cutie and all, but she ain't got nothin' on you, baby." He used his free hand and slid it up under my shirt, cupping my breast. "I've missed you, yo. I don't know why you be frontin'." He whispered in my ear, "You turn me on, London. You always have."

He tried to kiss me on the lips again. I shook my head.

"No, Justice…"

He licked my neck. "You know you missed ya man, baby. Why you be takin' me through a buncha changes, yo?" He kissed my tears. "Let me make you feel good, baby."

"Stop, Justice. Get off me!"

"You know you don't want that. You just talkin', yo."

I needed him.

I wanted him.

And I was willing to do whatever I had to, to keep him.

9

Spencer

"**P**ose for the camera."
Click, click!

I looked up from my magazine and there was Co-Co Ming, staring at me with one manicured hand on his ultra-slim hip, holding a camera up in his other, smirking. *Sweetmercifuldragonslayer*...The enemy was every-where today, starting with this fire-eating buzzard.

I hadn't seen this Brokeback Betty since that awful inci-dent at Heather's pill party last week when he was up on the stage spinning around in his tight, white leather hooker shorts and black thigh-high six-inch boots, showing his bare chest and pierced nipples—dancing and prancing and high-kicking it like he was in the skid row Olympics. Mmph, he definitely earned the gold for head ho of the hoodrat pack.

He tooted his lips up. "If it isn't Miss Itsy Ditsy, the Lone Pampered Princess, left to defend the crumbling throne all by her dizzy self."

I frowned. "Don't worry about the Pampered Princesses or our throne, sugarbooty. But what you better do is get your collagen up first, before you bring your flat-faced self over here trying to serve me. The Pampered Princesses are just fine."

"Wishful thinking, boo." He laughed. "Face it. The Pampered Princesses have now become past tense; has-beens. All the blogs have stamped you-all as Poo-Poo in Pampers. *Get it?* Hot messes. Your crowns have been snatched and stomped on. And your reign as Hollywood High royalty is over, daaaahling. So you might as well pack up your little one-girl show and run on home, because it's curtains... lights-out for all of you stuck-up, snotty hoes."

I tilted my head, twirling a lock of my hair. "Ummm, you think?"

Click, click!

"Oh, I know, sweetie. Chop, chop! Who shotcha, boo?" he taunted, snapping another photo.

I glanced around the café, then down at my timepiece. *Where the hell is Rich?*

Probably somewhere wrapping her thunder thighs up over some boy's shoulders, I mused. *With her man-eating self.*

Today was her first day back to school. And since Queen Kong London was suspended for the rest of the week, I couldn't wait to see how Miss Boom Bop It-Drop It was going to act without her sideshow rodeo ho beside her. This morning, when I spotted Rich at her locker, I walked right up to her, tossed my hair to the side and said, "Café... twelve sharp. Be there or get shredded," then strutted off to homeroom without giving her a chance to respond.

I hated to admit it, but London was right. We needed to

get this media mess under control. Their shenanigans were destroying our reputation. And we needed to at least *act* like we had each other's backs, even if we couldn't stand each other. And, after talking to my boo bear, who helped me to see that storming out of London's house yesterday wasn't the way to play my hand, I decided being cordial to Judas's sister...uh, I mean London, wouldn't be that torturous considering I'd be snuggling with her boyfriend while smiling up in her face. So I texted Rich last night and told her that I agreed to get along with them—for the moment.

Anyway, Rich was already five minutes late. And now I had to deal with this little Pekinese look-alike. All I wanted to do was read the latest edition of *Ni-Ni Girlz*, drink my strawberry smoothie, and sext with my boo bear. He had already sent me two nude pictures of his...heehee, well. Let's just say, my most favorite part of the male anatomy. Speaking of which—if Anderson didn't start shaking out the chocolate goodies soon, I was going to end up collapsing from deprivation. It's bad enough I was starting to get the shakes every time I was around him. I needed my fix for something thick, dark, and chocolate. And I needed it NOW! But he was still holding out!

"What, cat gotcha tongue, Miss Cuckoo?"

I crossed my legs, trying to pinch back my frustration. "You know what? You keep standing here snapping pictures if you want. But I'm about three seconds from slopping gravy up on your biscuit, boy." He blinked, staring at me like he had no dang clue what I meant. "Oh, rice cakes, don't act like you're stuck in brown sauce. I *said* I will smack you upside your head. Now keep talking slippery and see what I slide you."

He wagged his finger. "Aaah, temper, temper."

Click, click!

I pulled in my bottom lip, trying to keep it classy and cute. I had on a new pair of strappy seven-inch Roger Vivier pumps and really didn't want to break a heel off in his face, but he was really, really asking for a stomp down. I glanced at my watch again. Now Rich was fifteen minutes late. This was ridiculous! I told that ho twelve sharp!

I jumped up from my seat. "You better ring the alarm, chopsticks, before you find yourself chopped in the got-dang throat. Don't think I won't. Now I asked you to high-step it on away from this table and you still wanna flap your egg roll at me. Well, guess what, Miss Ring-Ding-Dingaling? I'm not London. And I'm not Rich. You might toy with your little pierced nipples, boo. But you won't toy with mine. I will smash your shutters out."

He threw his manicured hands up in surrender. "Oooh, cranky, cranky, I see. What, no bathroom stalls today?"

I rolled up my sleeves. "I don't do stalls, so get your yippity-yap straight. But since you think you know so much, I got some 'One Time for Your Mind,' Miss Moo-Moo Peek-A-Boo. And I'ma give you to ten to back it up out of my face before I skin your scalp back."

I yanked open my handbag, keeping my eyes locked on him. "You've been real frisky, Co-Co. Ten...but WuWu ain't here today, boo. Eight...and I'm not serving up Skittles, sweetie. Six...you think you can prance over here and disrupt my day and not get skinned. Four...see, Heather with her ole junkie self might have escaped my wrath, but you will feel my fury." I pulled out a pair of Sundragon nunchucks, whipping them up over my shoulder as I walked around the table.

The café fell silent.

Co-Co started walking backward, real slow. "Now, now, Spencer. Let's not do anything rash."

"Oh no, stink-stink," I sneered, doing a figure eight, passing the nunchucks underarm, then striking left and right, then wrapping it around my waist. "You came over here tossing daggers." I repeated the motions. "And now I'm about to put a rash upside your egg noodle."

Co-Co spun on his heels and started running, flailing his arms in the air while everyone in the café started laughing.

I scanned the whole café, narrowing my eyes and pointing while doing another series of figure eights with my nunchucks. "And the rest of you can get it, too! This table is off-limits, period! Do you hear me? Off. Limits! Now try it. And see what I dish you. I will beat the sweet and sour out of your mouths."

A few people gasped. Everyone else went back to what they were doing. I walked back over to the table, tossing my nunchucks back into my bag, and took a seat.

Mmmph, these dang roosters tryna pluck the wrong hen. I will crack eggs, scramble 'em up, then fry 'em all real quick.

I finished flipping through my magazine. Rich finally showed up, tossing her Louis up on the table. I looked at my watch, then up at her. She made a face, twisting her glossed lips up. "What?"

I slammed the magazine shut. "Thanks to you taking your slow sweet time, I had to deal with that Chinatown piñata."

She frowned. "Who?"

"Dang, girl, are your ears clogged with wax or something? I just told you, Co-Co Ming. I had to get him right.

And you're all late and wrong. Seventeen minutes and thirty-six seconds, to be exact. I told you to meet me here at twelve sharp."

"You know what, hooker? Don't do it. You don't run me. And you're not running the show here, so take down that stank attitude before you get smacked down. I'm still seconds from beating your face in for pulling that machete out on me yesterday."

"Oh, puhleeease, Rich. Your imagination is so extra."

"And so is your mouth, so shut it before I put a fist in it. I'm soooo not in the mood for you." She pulled out her chair and sat.

"The feeling's mutual. Still, we made a truce to get along, so let's. Truth, dare, consequences, private, or repeat?"

She furrowed her arched brows together. "What?"

I repeated. "Truth, dare, consequences, private, or repeat? Remember when we used to play that game?"

"Yeah, *and*?"

"So we're playing it now. So pick one."

"I'm not playing no games with you, girl. What I look like? Didn't you just pull an axe out on me?"

I chuckled. "Oh, Rich, let's not dwell in the past. That was yesterday. And this is today. That's part of your problem. You don't know when to let stuff go. Now, truth, dare, consequences, private, or repeat?"

She huffed. "What is the point?"

I looked around the café, then back at Rich. "Look around you. Do you see anyone else sitting at this table besides you and me? Would you prefer that we sit and play Miss Mary Mack or some mess instead of staring at each other like two fools? And you know a) I'm not a fool and b) I don't do you, either." I jumped up from the table and snatched open my bag. "But you are starting to get on my doggone nerves."

Rich's eyes popped open as she placed a hand up to her chest. "Clutching pearls, clutching pearls. Whew, violence. This time I will call the cops on your Looney Tunes behind. Because if you think you gonna give it to me the way you did Lexi Matthews two years ago then you got me messed up."

"Wait one ding-dong minute. I was taking up for you. And you know I always had your back and never let anyone mess with you."

"I had yours, too. I cursed her out and then I ran to come and get you."

I smiled, sitting back down. "Exactly. And then we tore her up together."

"Yeah, and we gave it to her real, juicy, and good. With a lot of gravy on it."

"A whole lotta gravy. Boom, bop, and dropped her all up and down these halls."

"And being suspended and paying that hundred grand was well worth it."

"Like a shoe sale!"

"Freshman year, we had some good times back then."

Rich tilted her head and stared at me. "Yeah, but you've changed."

"No, I didn't change. You did. But I'm not gonna sit here and go on all night...I mean, all day with you about it. So, truth, dare, consequences, private, or repeat? And I'm not gonna say it again."

"And whatchu gon' do? Stab me? Get all low budget and hood on. You better be thankful I'm bougie. Now truth."

"Did you kiss Bobby Landers underneath the table when we were in eighth grade?"

"Yes. We were experimenting."

"Is that how you got that cut on your lip?"

She frowned. "Yeah, from his braces."

"Okay, another one. Truth, dare, consequences, private, or repeat?" Rich picked truth. I took a deep breath. "Do you miss our friendship?" Rich shifted in her seat, crossing her legs. "Just tell the truth. Nothing extra."

"Yeah. I miss it."

I reached over for her hand. "Me too."

"Truth, dare, consequences, private, or repeat?"

"Private," I said. Rich leaned up in her seat, waiting. "I was pregnant two summers ago."

Her eyes popped open. "Whaaaat, *you*? By who?"

"RJ," I confessed.

Rich's face went blank. "RJ, as in *my* brother, *RJ*?" I lowered my eyes and nodded. "Wait a minute. You mean to tell me you were messing with my brother two summers ago, too?"

I nodded again. "We kept it on the creep-creep."

"Did he know you were pregnant?"

I shook my head. "No."

"Why didn't you tell him?"

I shrugged. "What was the point? He went back to England. And I..." I took a deep breath. "Remember when I had to be rushed to the hospital from school?"

She nodded. "Yeah, I remember that. The same time you had that fight with Lexi."

"Yeah." I felt myself getting choked up. "I had a miscarriage that day. She hit me in my stomach." My eyes shifted away.

Rich blinked. "Oh, wow. Lexi made you lose your baby. She was the cause."

I nodded my head.

"Did you want to keep it?"

I couldn't speak. I just nodded.

"Why?" she whispered.

My eyes met hers. "Because all of my life the only thing I've ever wanted was unconditional love. And I really thought having RJ's baby would give me that."

I dabbed under my eyes with the backs of my fingers.

"Do you wish you didn't lose it?"

"Yeah, sort of. I mean, I know everything happens for a reason. And I definitely wasn't ready to be a mother. Shoot, I'm still not. The ugly thought of having my stomach stretched out, and my gorgeous shape ruined." I eyed her, tilting my head. "Having my waistline look like yours... mmmph, no thank you. I'd take death by lethal injection first."

She frowned. "Spencer, don't get it crunked up in here. We're doing good so far and I'm trying to feel sorry for you."

I giggled. "I'm just saying, Rich. I mean, who wants to have stretch marks and their stomach jiggling when they walk? I know I don't. So, in that sense, I'm glad I lost it. But it still hurt because I had lost a piece of..." I closed my eyes and took a deep breath, breathing in memories of RJ, trying not to cry. He's the only boy I ever gave my heart to. And no matter how many other boys I sexed or toyed with, RJ still had it.

Rich stared at me and tears welled up in her eyes. "Are you still in love with him?"

I lowered my eyes. "Sometimes I think I am. When he's home and I'm with him, I know I am. It's when he's not here that I'm not so sure. But there's always something missing when he's gone."

She took me in, considering my words, then she shook them off. "This is too much for me, girl. Let it go. RJ is over in Oxford. And I overheard my mother cursing him out because he's over there smoking weed. So don't hold your breath hoping for a Prince Charming because he's going to come home a shriveling weed head. He'd probably be better off with Heather."

"Eww, how nasty," I blurted out. "That would be illegal."

"What?"

I quickly shook my head. "Never mind. I'm just saying. That would be a real problem. I'd have to gut her, then end up in jail."

Rich chuckled, shaking her head. "Spencer, you need help, boo. I'm convinced you're crazy. But it would kinda serve you right if she did mess with my brother—not that I would approve of that trash-bag ho getting anywhere near him. But still—after what you did to me, sleeping with Corey behind my back, it would serve you right to get a dose of your own medicine."

"Uhhhh, hellooooo...for the zillionth time, I *never* slept with Corey. He never stuck his key inside my treasure chest to get my gold coins. You were the only fool to let him key up your Lucky Charms."

"Okay, Spencer. I'm tryna stay a lady because I know all eyes are zoomed in, but you are really trying it."

I waved her on. "Oh, Rich. Please, loosen your girdle, girlie. That's your problem. You're like loose change in some things, then tighter than a buffalo's butt hole in—"

The minute I spotted him walking into the café toward the jocks' table, my blood turned to cherry-colored icicles.

I narrowed my eyes and laser-beamed one of the enemies. Corey!

"Who are you shooting daggers at?" Rich asked, craning her neck and following the direction of my glare.

"That three-timing, fake daddy mack attack," I snarled. "That's who! I should go over there and claw his intestines out."

She quickly snapped her head back in my direction, rolling her eyes. "Have at it, girl. I want no part of that. I'm in enough trouble behind that boy."

"Oh, that's right. I forgot you're being sued for trying to peel his face back." I chuckled to myself. "What, for ten million?"

She flicked her wrist. "Yeah, something like that. And I told him I would peel his face *off*, not back. But, whatever. I don't wanna talk about that. I wouldn't be in any of that mess in the first place if it weren't for *you*."

I huffed. "Oh, hold up, wait one manicured minute. How dare you? Don't try to blame *me* for *you* not being able to keep a leash on your dog. Maybe you should have walked him more, and fed him treats, and petted him the right way and he wouldn't have strayed."

She slammed her hands down on the table, leaning up in my face. "Well, maybe if you woulda stayed up off your knees—"

"I wasn't always on my knees, Mack truck. Sometimes

I'd be bent over and he'd be on *his* knees snacking me from the back, so get it right."

"Ugh! Clutching pearls!" She cupped a hand over her mouth. "I think I just threw up in the back of my mouth."

I lowered my voice. "Umm, sweet potato, you might want to get your hot breath out of my face. We have an audience. And I think they think we're about to have a cat-fight."

She smacked her lips, then narrowed her eyes. "Well, they're right. I'm ready to boom-bop, drop-it, drop-it."

I slid my hand down in my bag, tilting my head and smirking. I had to be ready, just in case. "Well, this will look real cute on the front pages of all the blogs, won't it? 'Pampered Princesses at it again.'"

She stood straight, then brushed imaginary lint off the sleeve of her blazer. She plopped her dunkadunk back in her chair. "Count yourself lucky."

I tilted my head. "Your turn."

She huffed. "Truth, dare, consequences, private, or repeat?"

"Truth."

"Did your mother really sleep with your boyfriend Curtis?"

I shifted in my seat, rolling my eyes up in my head. "Yeah, that skank did. She waited until he turned eighteen; said it was a birthday gift, welcoming him into manhood."

"Mmmph, yuck. Why didn't you tell me that?"

"Because I was embarrassed. And hurt. And I didn't want you to know how screwed up Kitty is, when you have such a great mother."

Rich rolled her eyes. "Girl, please. If you only knew. Miss Kitty seems so cool. She doesn't sweat you. She lets you do you. You don't know how bad I wish my mother would get her late-night creep on. And stay outta my business. But you...you don't have to worry about having a mother constantly up on your neck sweating you. You can straight do you. Boom, bop, drop it-pop it and handle yours. Girl, you can have a boo up in your house and go for broke. Me, I got Logan sitting on my back and her husband threatening to make me disappear."

I gasped. "What, make you disappear? Oh my. I didn't know he was a magician. I thought he was a thug."

Rich blinked. "Spencer, let's just get back to the game."

"Truth, dare, consequences, private, or repeat?"

"Private," she said, pulling out her compact and checking her eyeliner. She pulled out her signature handkerchief, dabbing at her eyes. She snapped the compact shut. "I'm still in love with Knox."

"Since you were eight years old?"

She nodded. "It just won't go away. No matter how hard I keep trying to leave him alone, I—"

"Then be with him," I said, cutting her off. "You know he loves you."

"No, he doesn't. Last time we spoke, he pretty much told me he didn't wanna see me again."

"What? When was this?"

"The morning of our invitation party for our masquerade ball. You know. The one that's been postponed because of your little pill-popping friend."

"Heather's *not* my friend after what she did to me."

"Yeah, right. Whatever. Anyway, it was over between me and Knox right after he told me he wanted to use condoms because he wasn't ready to be a father."

"Sweetheavensinthemorning, so I was right! You're not

just fat. You really are pregnant. And here I felt bad for telling you to handle your waistline."

"Well, save it. I'm not anymore."

"You lost it?"

"No. It was taken from me."

I blinked. "What in the world? Who took it?"

"My mother."

"When? Where?"

"Monday. In the back hills of Arizona."

GreatwallsofPrada...how many times is this? "You had another a—"

She nodded, wiping tears. "Unlike you, I didn't have a fairy tale. I wasn't given a choice to keep my baby."

I gasped, reaching for her hand again. I squeezed it. "Oh no. Rich, I'm so sorry. See, this is why you need *your* real best friend because I would have gone to Arizona with you no matter what; right there by your side."

She gave me a faint smile. "Thanks."

"Was Knox with you?"

"No. He doesn't know. And I'm not gonna tell him."

"But he knows that you were pregnant, so how is he not going to know?"

"I'll tell him I miscarried or something. I don't know. I'll figure it out." She took a deep breath. "Can we pleeease close the confession box and talk about something else? I'm good. We've made up. Now let's move on. My turn. Truth, dare, consequences, private, or repeat?"

I giggled. "This time dare me, boo."

Rich chuckled. "Hey, now! That's what I wanna hear. Let's boom-bop it! 'Cause I'm ready to take it to the brain and—"

I gagged. "*Whaaaat?* You want brain? You dang freak. Are you asking *me* for oral sex?"

"Spencer, you dingbat. Hell no! Get your mind out of the gutter, trick. You can't do a thing for me. So don't flatter yourself. I was *saaaaying*, I felt like taking it to the skulls of four skankadank lollipop-lickers. And I dare you to set it off with me."

I leaned up in my seat. "Well, why didn't you say that then? Who'd you have in mind?"

She grinned. "The Starlets."

"Ooooh, yessss, love it! Let's go serve those baby raccoons a hot dish of Ash Tuesday."

Rich gave me a blank stare. "What in the...you know what, forget it." She hopped up from her seat. "Let's go over there and get it-get it. Teach those wannabes that the Pampered Princesses still rule."

I got up and gathered my magazine and handbag. "Well, come on, honeeeeey. Momma is ready. But I need to stop at my locker first."

Rich raised an arched brow. "Stop at your locker for what?"

"Uhh, hello. We're about to go into battle. I need to suit up, pull out the artillery, and ammo up."

"Then let's go slaughter some hoes!"

10

Rich

"Hey, lil daddy!" I gave a soft wave and dropped my don't-stop-get-it-get-it booty switch into overdrive. Spencer and I had arrived on the freshman side of campus and the teakwood corridor was lined with sexy, sweet, and tender testosterone. Cuties. Young. Fresh. Tenderoni meat. Ev-er-y-where. All I needed were slow jams and a glass of Merlot and we could make it work. Usually I didn't do youngins, but the ones here, humph, inspired me to be the kind of cougar who worked in a day care and stalked the boys around the room.

Oh-kay!

'Cause it was about two. No, three. No—*five* who could get it-get it.

Snap. Snap.

I undid the top three buttons of my baby-blue Tory Burch sleeveless top and revealed sneak peeks of my ebony lace bra and plump come-get-'em-baby cleavage. For a moment

I couldn't remember why I was here. Was I boy shopping? Was I man-hunting? I wasn't sure. All I knew is that my future-baby-daddy radar was off the freakin' meter and I was seconds from drooling. Excitement perked up my busty jewels and it took everything in me not to bend down and shake my ta-tas loose. After all, these natural and plastic surgery–free double Ds were a magnet for bringing all the boys to the yard.

Whew! I felt like going in my purse, taking a few twenties out, and making it rain up in here. Do geezus! I fanned my face. I didn't know about Spencer, but a few minutes more and this diva, right here, was set to overdose on cutie crack.

I took a deep breath, slowly licked my luscious lips, and just as I pushed the right side of my hair behind my ear, I spotted him: Mr. Pretty-Daddy!

Mr. Compared-To-All-The-Other-Hotties-In-Here-Was-A-Grown-Man.

Mr. Broad Shoulders, Squared Off.

Mr. Smooth Honey-Colored Skin.

Mr. Hazel Eyes.

Thick brows.

Light mustache.

Sexy chin hairs.

"Oh my," Spencer purred. "Who is that?"

"There you go again," I said, cutting my eyes at Spencer with a tinge of attitude. "I spotted him first."

"Girl, we can go half with this one."

"There you go, still wanting to be on your knees." *Spencer was such a whore.*

"And there you go trying to get pregnant again. I should've known that breast-feeding wouldn't be good enough for you. You have to pour your claws on him and have him for dinner, man-eater. Now do you want to argue or are we over here to ho-hunt and handle the Starlets?"

I should slap her face... but then again she had a point. "You know what, Spencer, let's put the argument on pause. Because I'm here to do what we came to do."

"Hold up, Rich." She slammed her hand on her right hip. "Didn't I tell you about telling me to go on pause? For the hundredth time I am not a CD player—"

"Pause—"

"Didn't I just tell you—?"

"Would you just shut up! There goes one of the hoes right there!" I pointed and grabbed Spencer by the arm.

"And sweetheavenlyhoespimpin'ain'thard...There she is holding hands with your next sex victim."

Screech... My red bottoms came to a thunderous halt and there stood a medium brown girl with a sleek ponytail that hung to her shoulders and a bang that swept across her forehead. She smiled from ear to ear, looking all stupid and dreamy eyed. Real dumb and love struck. As if she could ever know what to do with a man like that.

This trick wore a nasty fuchsia varsity jacket with a tacky metallic gold star with the word *Starlet* written across it in sparkling silver letters. And beneath that hideous monstrosity was the green and navy blue plaid Hollywood High uniform.

All I could do was roll my eyes. I couldn't believe this nasty, gross, low-budget, financial-aid-havin' ho still rocked a uniform and attempted to come and serve us. Apparently she needed some assistance with getting her thoughts in order.

And London said one of them smelled like money. London had lost her mind. I sure hope that this wasn't the baby beast who stomped London down—or my view of that Amazon would never be the same.

I popped my lips, placed my hips in sugar-mama motion, parted this ho's love session and boldly stood in front of her. Then I took Dreamboat's hand from Miss Whack, placed one hand on my waist, and then smoothly completed boo's hold on me by placing the other hand on my waist and sliding my arms around his neck. His eyes revealed that he was pleasantly surprised. I snuggled deeper into our fostered embrace and Mr. Fine inched closer. I had it. Going. On. "Like what you feel?" I asked in between my innocent schoolgirl giggle.

"What the hell?!" Chickie had the nerve to interrupt our moment.

"Not a word," Spencer said with one rubber-gloved finger pressed to Chickie's lips.

Why does she have on gloves and when did she put those on?

"You are so fine." I ran my right hand through Dreamboat's curls and lightly licked my lips.

"Yes, he is fine, Rich," Spencer cooed, walking up behind him and running her index finger softly across the nape of his neck.

We sandwiched him and Spencer said, "Don't be shy."

"Why are you two washed-up broads over here?!" Chickie danced her neck from left to right and popped her eyes wide. She pointed her finger and continued on. "Should I call the rest of the Starlets and let them know to watch their men and be on bimbo alert? Obviously y'all came over here to get worse than what your resident Amazon got."

"Awwl, sweetie." I turned toward her. "Don't be mad

just because before we handle you, we'll be doin' your man." I turned back to lil daddy and winked. "I'm Rich."

"And I'm Spencer," Spencer whispered against his neck. "Now tell us your name, 'cause we're the dynamic duo."

"You two dirty bus-line gutter rats. The pimps are down the street if you're looking for a comeback. You two put the slut and the whore in slore. So scurry your heels back over to the other side of campus, with your old faces and run-down bodies. Tricks." She looked from me and Spencer over to boo-boo and said, "And you better not tell them your name!"

I guess he didn't follow instructions well because he said, "It's Xavier." He nervously grinned from ear to ear.

"Xavier! I can't believe you're over here smiling! You must want your face slapped!"

"Don't worry about it, baby," I said, stroking his cheek. "If she slaps your face I'll be there to kiss your bruises."

Spencer said, "That's right. And I'll be there to help take the rocks out of your pocket."

"Oh, I gotta trick for y'all slores!" Chickie sneered as she pulled out her cell phone. "Y'all are over here on our side of the campus and the Starlets run this. Okay, did you not see the blogs this morning? The Pampered Princesses are tired!"

"Girl, please. First of all I don't do Gerber teen magazines!" I snapped.

"And second of all," Spencer said as she walked from behind Cutie and snatched Chicka-doo's phone. "You're not running anything today and you will not be making any calls at this moment. We need to have a word with you in private!"

Chickie took a step toward Spencer. "You better give me back my phone before I spit in your face!"

No, she didn't!

"Oh, really?" Spencer reached in her oversized bag and pulled out a fly swatter and slapped Chickie dead in her mouth with it.

Whap!

"Oh snap." Dreamboat snickered.

"Now say something else," I dared Chickie as I arched one brow and snapped my fingers in her face. "We're not playing with you."

"Now let's try this again," Spencer continued. "I said, I need a word with you, you little gnat."

"Don't—"

Whap! "Shut your mouth," Spencer said, tight-lipped as she swatted her again.

"We'll come back for you later, boo," I said as I motioned my finger for him to lean near. I lightly brushed my lips against his and whispered my telephone number. Then I turned back to Spencer and this lil crack baby and said, "Now let's go."

Spencer pushed Chickie into the bathroom lounge and I locked the door.

11

Spencer

I slid behind the wheel of my McLaren, courtesy of Kitty—uh, my mother—then waited for the valet to shut my dang door. I tossed the furry-faced fellow a twenty, then sped off, leaving Hollywood High, with all of its palm trees, in the dust. After that little workout on them two cheese doodle-dos, aka the Starlets, I needed to get home, run me a long, hot bath and luxuriate. Nairing up a bunch of hoes was exhausting; especially when you had no dang help from the boom-bop-crunk-it-up drama queen herself. I was disgusted. That loud-mouthed Rich couldn't bust a window open if it slammed down on her pudgy neck. She's such a scaredy-crow.

I couldn't get over how she ran out of the bathroom with her boobies and booty bouncing up and down. Oh, it was awful seeing all that junk in her suitcase. I wanted to laugh. She sprinted down the hall like the fire in her cootie-shoot had returned with another disease. My. God! Blondwig.com strikes again. Mmmph. If Man-eater didn't watch where she dropped her thongs, she was going to end up back on the Ten Most Nasty Hoes list, again.

Rich is a mess!

I pressed a button and Nicki Minaj started jibber-jabbering, or whatever that is she does. "Roman's Revenge." I giggled, thinking how fitting the song was since I had just finished bringing it to two little itty-bitty piggy hoes trying to crisscross over into the wrong lane. Whoop, whoop. Beez in a trap! But I pulled out my bag of whip-azz and did it on them.

"Rah-rah, like a dungeon dragon," I sang and finger-popped, swinging around the corner. "Sing, Nicki! They don't want it with me. I get crazy!" I bounced up and down in my seat, swinging one arm in the air. "Rah-rah... whoop, whoop... Fly cutie like me... snatching out hoes' teeth, chopping off their feet... bringing them slutaroos to their knees... tryna bring it to me... please... Nair 'em up, Nair 'em up! Get your hair up!" I burst into laughter, swerving into the traffic. Horns blew.

What in the sneezusjezus is wrong with these fools out on the road today? I can't even get my sing on without some mess!

I flipped them a finger. "Oh, blow it out your gas pipes!" I yelled. "Y'all don't want it with me." I floored the pedal, and my Benz quickly shot up to eighty. I zoomed in and out of traffic. "Whoop, whoop... get out the way!" I went back to singing the rest of the Nicki song—well, my ver-sion of it—when the music was interrupted by the sound of my cell phone ringing over the music. I rolled my eyes, hitting a button on the steering wheel.

"What do you want? You low-down dirty Pillsbury pill

popper!" I snapped. "I'm singing and laughing and minding my own dang business so why are you calling me?"

"I-I," Heather stammered, "I want to apologize for saying all those mean, nasty things to you. I'm sorry for hurting you. I—"

"You're sorry for *hurting* me? Oh no, Miss Tylenol. Don't be sorry. You declared war! You tried to set it off in the kitchen and fried up the wrong sausages, girlie. And now I'm gonna gut you from the rooter to the cooter, then feed you to the wolves..."

"Spencer—"

"You crossed the wrong railroad tracks, trickie. And now your caboose is mine."

"Spencer—"

"Oh no, Miss Prescription Freak. You turned the gas on the wrong one. No, the right one! I'ma light your fire, girlie. You going up in smoke! Do you hear me, ho?!"

"Spencer, please let me—"

"How about I let you slurp my sewer, you gutter rat? Now I see why your ole drunk mother hates you, and your father never wanted you! You're evil and ugly, you...you... you wiggly-eyed albino python! You're a two-headed snake, Heather! I want nothing to do with you! And if you ever call me again I will spray-paint you a permanent suntan, paleface!"

I pressed the button, ending the call. The music eased its way back through the speakers. The nerve of her! She might have forgotten what she said to me that day at her little pill party. But I hadn't. *You are the dumbest ho I've ever come across. Your name is wedged in between dumb and dumber...Friends? We were never friends and never will be! I don't like you. You're a sneaky, dirty, conniving little ho. Oh no, excuse me, big ho...*

I wiped a lone tear as I raised the volume up. I was not about to sashay down Horror Lane, rehashing every nasty thing Heather said. Oh no. Heather Cummings was dead to me! All I needed to do was have her funeral, then toss the dirt on her.

I pulled up into my circular driveway, surprised to see Anderson's car parked in front of the estate. *Anderson! Oh no! OhGodohGodohGod!* I screeched on the brakes, rammed the car into park, then quickly jumped out of the car, leaving the door wide open. I ran up the four steps, then swung open the front door. I raced through the house, finding him sitting out on the terrace with Kitty hovering over him like a hungry vulture.

"Kitty!" I screamed as I was greeted with a back-shot view of Kitty's roadside. The side that most men rode on. I knew what trick she was up to. She was trying to get her booty rocked. She had on a white see-through camisole and black lace boy-shorts, and a pair of white mink stiletto slippers. All I could see were all my other boyfriends that Kitty had marched off with. She was the Pied Piper of Nasty. The ho-gram. But not this time. And not with Anderson!

"What in the hell do you think you're doing?! What in the heezysneezy are you wearing? And why are you back here? I thought you were in New York."

She straightened her body and faced me, grinning. "I was, dear. I flew in on the redeye to see my darling daughter. And to—"

"Swoop down on my man."

Kitty tossed her head back and laughed. "Oh, Spencer, darling, collect yourself. You and that overactive imagination of yours is going to get you committed to the nut ward sooner than not."

Anderson jumped up from his seat, walking over to me. "Gum drop, you're home from school early." He planted a kiss on my forehead. "Is everything all right?"

I eyed him, then shot Kitty a dirty look. "No, it's not. Apparently I'm just in time for the freak show."

I glanced down at his crotch and saw his goody bag. I gasped. It was stretching the fabric of his dress pants. He tried to place a hand over all his excitement. Dirty dog!

I fumed as Kitty licked her lips.

"Anderson, what are you doing here when you know I was in school?"

"Your mom invited me over. She was kind enough to get my mom season tickets to her show."

"As promised," Kitty purred, letting a sly grin slip over her painted lips as she slipped an arm through his. "I am always a woman of my word."

I pulled him from her. "Oh, please. And you couldn't overnight them?"

"Of course not, dear. What kind of woman do you think I am? I like to personally deliver *all* things Kitty."

What a slutasaurus! I rolled my eyes. "Oh, spare me the pig feet and pickle juice act. You don't really want me to answer that. The only thing it looks like you're ready to deliver is a platter of hot nastiness. But if you know what's good for you, you had better tuck your old dusty servers away before I cool-breeze your burners. And go put some clothes on. You should be ashamed of yourself."

Kitty pulled at her camisole. And one of her boobies popped out. She didn't even bother fixing herself. "Anderson, dear, please excuse me while I have a word with my darling, delusional daughter."

He nervously shifted his eyes from her chest and cleared his throat to say something, but I stopped him in his tracks. "Yes, Anderson, please excuse us. Go up to my room. I'll be there in a minute to pick up where my scandalous mother left off."

He kissed me on the cheek, then turned to Kitty. "Missus Ellington, thanks again for the tickets. My mom is going to be extremely thrilled."

Kitty waved him on, batting her eyes as she stuffed her breast back into her camisole. "Oh, no problem. I'll do *anything*—and I do mean any-thing—for a fan."

I smirked. "Don't you mean man?"

Anderson quickly excused himself, then walked toward the winding staircase that led upstairs to my suite. We both eyed him, waited for him to disappear, then pulled the claws out. "How dare you," Kitty snapped through clenched teeth, "embarrass me like that!"

"No," I shot back, slamming a hand up on my hip. "How dare *you* invite my man over here behind my back, flouncing around in that flimsy come-get-'em getup."

She laughed. "Last time I checked, he wasn't your man. Or have you forgotten that major detail? My God! I know I didn't give birth to a bimbo, so you can't possibly be standing here thinking that fine, sexy stallion is your man. Tell me that isn't the case. Or I will make a call to have you put away today."

"Put me away?" I asked incredulously. "How about, you're the one who needs to be put away for walking around in that slut suit. You're forty-one dang years old and it's time you started acting like it."

"How dare you! I'm thirty-six!"

"Yeah, right, Mother. In which dream?" Next thing I knew, I started screaming at her in French. She hated when I did that. I was so dang sick of her. *"J'en ai marre de vous! J'en ai marre de vos moyens sournois! Vous* don't give a damn about me, Kitty! *Vous vous occupez uniquement de Kitty. Vous savez que j'aime Anderson! Pourquoi ne pas vous rétracter vos griffes seule fois... Vous* are ridiculous—"

Kitty's eyes flared open. She shortened the distance between us, her heels clicking against the calamander wood floor. She yanked me by the arm. "Don't you use that tone with me, young lady! I am still your mother. And you will speak to me in English. Now repeat yourself or get every syllable slapped out of your mouth."

I yanked my arm back, pushing her. "I wish you would. And we will both be going out of here on stretchers. Now try it."

She blinked.

I narrowed my eyes, pointing a finger at her and zigzagging it in the air. "I saaaaaaaid I'm sick of you! I'm sick of you and your sneaky ways. I saaaaid, all you care about is Kitty. You know I like Anderson. So why can't you, just this once, keep your claws off. Now how's that for translation?"

She tucked her hair behind her ears. If I liked her, I would tell you how pretty I thought she was. But right about now, Kitty was simply just pretty dang sneaky! "A word of advice, Spencer dear: Get rid of the jealous act. It's so not becoming. Do you actually think Anderson is going to be with a girl like you? Ha! You're too unstable, dear. A man like Anderson needs a strong, powerful woman who knows how to follow rules and play the game the way it's supposed to be played. Then alters the rules when he least expects it. Not some dizzy little tart who gets her panties all up in a knot every time she gets knocked off base. Learn how to play your position, darling. And you won't ever have to worry about someone else coming along and taking your spot." She flipped her hair. "You have a lot to learn, Spencer. And you had better hope you look half as delicious as I do when you reach my age, dear."

"Don't try me, Kitty. I mean it. I already warned you once."

"Spencer, darling, save those idle threats for that little cartoon clique you play with. And you girls call yourselves the Pampered Princesses." She snorted out a laugh. "Ha! What a joke. That Heather's a junkie in rehab; probably getting high right now as we speak. Rich doesn't know whose bed she wants to be in next. London is keeping more secrets than a whore in heat. And you"—she shook her head—"my darling daughter...you're too busy chasing other girls' boyfriends and having ridiculous tantrums when you can't snag them for yourself. What a mess. All of you."

I blinked.

"Don't serve me, dear, 'cause I will slice you up on a platter. But since you are my only child and I am the loving mother that I am, I'm going to give you a reprieve. I will let you redeem yourself."

"*Loving mother?* You? Oh, spare me! Define *mother*, Mother. Is it somewhere between the nonexistent words *mom* and *mommy*? Because that's what you are, Mother— nonexistent. So don't *you* serve me any of your hot-trash talk about being anything to me other than a pain in my sweet, fluffy cheeks. So spare me. I don't have to redeem dipsy-doodle-doo with you. Now hopscotch your stank-self back on over to New York, and stay the hell out of my eyesight. I'm sick of seeing you here."

She stepped back into my space. I reached for the large crystal vase filled with white orchids, sitting atop the oval table, prepared to whop her upside the head with it. Kitty and I fought twice before over her sleeping with a boyfriend. And I would scramble her eggs again, if she tried to juice Anderson.

"Oh, sweet, darling Spencer, get a grip. There's no need for violence today, dear." She walked up and cupped my face in her hands. "You are so much like me when I was your age. Strong-willed and free-spirited. And as beautiful as they come. But you are still so very wet behind the ears, dear. When I was your age, I was luring men—filthy-rich men, not boys, into my bed. And now, I'm luring all the young studs. You don't know the first thing about being a woman, sweetie. Now you can do one of two things. You can take some motherly advice, or you can keep doing what you do. But from where I'm standing, the only thing you'll end up with, darling, is a set of chapped lips, a sore throat, and a nasty case of rug-burns for spending your life down on your knees, waiting for belt buckles to hit the floor."

I snatched her hands away from my face. "You're such a hater! You are so jealous of me, Mother. It's sinful. I'm everything you're not. Young, beautiful, and rich!"

She laughed, placing her hands up on her hips. "Yes, darling. You are definitely all of those things. But you won't be young forever and beauty fades over time if you're not careful. Then what? You end up a rich, lonely hag who's sucked down the whole city and has had multiple plastic surgeries desperately trying to hold on to her youth."

I frowned. "You wait one dang minute, Kitty! How dare you disrespect me! Who in the heezy-jeezy are you speaking of? Surely not me! And I will never be lonely. You better check my YouTube stats. I have fans who adore me. So, go suck on that! I'm done with this conversation because it's obvious you don't know a dang thing about me. So you can't tell me what to do, or how to do it."

She grabbed me by the arm again as I turned to walk out of the room. She swung me around to face her. "Let me tell you how a real diva does it, Little Miss Grownie. You snag an old, fatherless billionaire—with maybe a good ten to twenty years left on his life sentence. You sex him down real good. Make his eyes roll back in his head and have him begging to God to keep him alive long enough for another round. You pump out a baby. Then get your own TV show. You secure your future, darling. Then you take your fallopian tubes and donate them to science. That's what you do, dear. Not become some starry-eyed lunatic over a boy who will never be yours." She let out a disgusted grunt. "You're an embarrassment. And I will not have it. Do you hear me, Spencer? I will not stand for it. There are three things you don't ever do: You don't beg a man. You don't cry over a man. And you don't ever get desperate for a man. You get paid, darling. And you get even. And if you can't get even, then you find yourself a nice little boy toy, or two, to help you sleep at night."

I blinked.

"Now do I make myself clear?" She tilted her head, waiting. She tapped her high-heeled foot. "I said. Do. I. Make. My. Self. Clear?"

I blinked again. Sweetjigglybootyjuice! Kitty was…was… a heartless, conniving witch! I clenched my teeth. "Very. Now get your hand off of me."

She let go of my arm. "Perfect. Now go make yourself useful, dear, and track down some juicy dirt for me to dish. You know I have to keep my ratings up." Her cell rang. I eyed her as she pulled it from out of her pocket. "Kitty here. Oh, Camille, darrrrrling…yes, of course…Talk to me…"

I watched as she walked out onto the terrace, closing the glass doors. Whatever!

"I can't stand that woman." I sneered, storming into my bedroom. Anderson was stretched out across one of my pink leather chaises, talking to someone on his Black-Berry.

"Yes, sir…What time?…Okay, sounds good. Yes, yes… I can't wait. See you in a bit." He hung up.

He watched as I paced the room.

"Everything okay?"

"No, everything is not okay. I walk in here and find my mother practically in your lap. Then you stand up and I see your goody bag is stretched and ready to be had. If I hadn't walked in when I did, Kitty would have had a mouthful of…"

He chuckled.

Oh, he must want his face rearranged. I narrowed my eyes. "I don't see anything funny about that. That was downright disgusting what Miss Trick-A-Lot was trying to do. That woman has no shame."

"Gum drop, that's no way to talk about your mother. And you're blowing things way out of proportion. She was simply being a gracious hostess."

"Mmmph, graciously ho-ish is more like it."

He stood up and walked over to me. He pulled me into his arms. "Has anyone ever told you how sexy you are when you're having a tantrum?"

I poked my lips out, then pressed my body into his. "No. But why don't you tell me. No, show me."

He grinned, kissing me on the forehead. "I wish I could. I have to go over to London's."

"London's? What do you have to go over to that boar's house for?"

"She's not a boar, gum drop. She's my fiancée or have you forgotten that?"

I frowned. "Don't remind me. But why do you have to go over there now?"

"Because her father called and invited me over."

"And you have to go now, this very minute?"

"Yes. We're going to hit the court for a game of basketball. Then I'm having dinner with him, Missus Phillips, and London."

I blinked. "Dinner? Oh, a regular ole family affair. How cute."

Anderson cupped my chin and planted a sweet, juicy kiss on my neck, then my lips—no tongue though. Damn him! Then he took my hands and lifted them to his lips. He kissed them. I poked out my lips.

"Well, go be with your future wife and her family. Obviously you'd rather be with that ole big-hoofed slutasaurus than stay here with me."

"I don't like it when you call her names, gum drop. Actually, you shouldn't call anyone names; especially when it's someone who's never done anything to you."

Oh, no he didn't. I frowned. *I'll call her what the hell I want!* See. I was trying really, really hard to be nice, but... sweet joy oh joy, was Anderson really asking for me to skunk it up in here and take it right to his face? First Heather, then Kitty, and now him! But I knew one thing: if he called himself trying to wreck me for calling Trampalicious names, then he had another ding-dang thing coming. I was going to get down and funky on him. I counted to ten in my head. *Two...four...six...eight...eleven, I mean, ten...* I took a deep breath.

I folded my arms across my chest, narrowing my eyes. Then Kitty's voice floated in my head. *You don't ever beg a man...And you don't ever get desperate...*

"You know what, Anderson. Maybe we should leave each other alone. Let's just part the seas, now, before it gets flooded and one of us gets drowned."

Anderson pulled me closer. "Gum drop, stop talking foolish. That's not what you want, and neither do I."

I raised a brow, stepping out of his embrace. I turned my back to him, shutting my eyes. I took a deep breath. "I mean it, Anderson. Bow out gracefully or get plowed down."

He stepped in back of me and pulled me in by the waist, then pressed his thick, hard body into mine, stroking my hair, then nibbling on my ear. He lightly flicked his tongue into my ear, then whispered, "Cut it out. Stop acting jealous."

There goes that word again! He and Kitty both had me confused.

I turned to face him, hand up on my hip. Head tilted.

"Jealous? Oh no. I don't do jealous. I do revenge. I just want the truth, Anderson. Give me the truth and nobody gets hurt. Give me lies, and somebody's got to die."

He laughed, shaking his head. "What am I gonna do with you? Here you go again. Come here." He pulled me into him again, then cupped my booty-cheeks. And squeezed. And I felt my Duncan Hines get moist.

"If you take me right now, I'll let all of my aggression out."

He chuckled, kissing me on the lips again. "You're too much, gum drop."

I rolled my eyes. "Well, obviously not enough to keep you from running out on me. You must really wanna be with that bit...her."

He eyed me. "You have it all wrong, gum drop. Trust me. London doesn't want me. And I'm not interested in her. One, what we have is an arrangement, period. Two, she's not attracted to me. And three, she already has a boyfriend. But her parents don't approve of him so she uses me as her cover. And I'm cool with it. As long as I get my trust out of the deal, I don't care who she does."

"Shut. Up," I said, inching closer to him. Oooh, this was starting to sound juicy. Kitty would love this dirt! It was straight filth! I drooled, wanting more. "I mean, don't shut up. Keep talking, boo bear. So you mean to tell me Queen Kong—" Anderson raised his brow. "I mean...London has a secret boo?"

"Yeah."

"Well, I'll be spit-shined and polished. Isn't that something? Who is he? Wait—" I stopped, remembering the sexy drop of man-meat that showed up at her bedroom door a few weeks back. SweetAlmondJoy...London was an undercover hoodlum. I knew she was ghetto-trash. "I think I've seen him before."

"I'd be surprised if you had. London usually keeps him well hidden. The only one who even knows that she's still seeing him is her house manager. She keeps her dirty little secret well hidden."

"No, I'm certain that guy who showed up at her house is him."

"What'd he look like?"

I closed my eyes, picturing him in my mind. And how I wanted to eat him up, but was too dang busy rushing back to Anderson's sexless behind. "Like deep, delicious trouble," I pushed out absentmindedly.

"Justice is a user."

So Justice is that sexy chocolate-drop's name? How poetic.

I tilted my head. "Seems to me all of you are. You're using Ama...I mean London, to get your inheritance. She's using you to keep her parents off her back. And Mister Trouble is—"

"Bad news," he said, cutting me off. "That bum means her no good. All he does is hurt her and treat her like crap. She's never going to be happy with him. He doesn't deserve her."

I blinked. What in the world?! "Wait a minute. Why do you care how he treats her? Or whether or not she's going to be happy with him? If that's who she chooses to be with, then obviously she must like it. Obviously, she's happy with him. So what's it to you? Do you have feelings for her?"

I stared into his eyes. Ohsweetjuicyfruit...he had beautiful eyes. But I decided that I would gouge them out if I found out he was playing me like a spoiled shrimp dish. I was going to slice him three ways to Sunday, right down to the bare meat.

"Absolutely not. How many times do I have to keep telling you? It's an arrangement."

"So then why do you care about what happens to her so much?"

"Because I'm the one she calls on every time he makes her cry. I'm the one who's there to pick up the pieces every time that scumbag hurts her. That mofo is poison."

"Listen, I don't do sympathy. Let her get her dose of toxin. And if I'm lucky enough, it'll be something poison control can't treat. Good riddance. Now back to you. I'm gonna ask you again: Do you have feelings for her?"

"Listen, gum drop. I already told you, no. Now if you can't play your position the way I need you to, then maybe you're right. We shouldn't see each other. That's not what I want. But I'm not interested in being questioned either. And I'm definitely not interested in some insecure little girl. So can you handle this thing between us or not?"

In my mind's eye, I could see Kitty shaking her head, laughing at me. Oh no. I wasn't going to give her the satisfaction of being right. And I definitely wasn't going to let a good man like Anderson slip through my fingers. Oh no, Spencer Ellington was no dang fool. I was horny. I was determined. And I was going to have every inch of Anderson if it was the last thing I did. And if not, I would make his life a living hell!

I tilted my head, grabbed at his goody bag, then squeezed. "The question is, can you?"

12

London

So many emotions were running through my heart and mind. I was still hurt and angry at Justice for how he spoke to me yesterday, then put his hands on me. And I was disgusted at how he disrespected me with Rich. Still, I loved him deeply. Problem was I only felt closest to him when we were wrapped in each other's arms. I only really felt loved most by him when we were caught up in the throes of a hot, sweaty, sexathon. And I was still basking in the afterglow. And it was a feeling I didn't want to let go of. This thing between us—with him running hot and cold; his constant moodiness—kept me on edge. But it also kept me wanting to love him more. Wanting to prove to him that I was all he needed. All that he'd ever need. I couldn't let him go.

Still, snatches of our argument from yesterday nagged at my soul.

...Wit' ya ugly self. You insecure. Fat, nasty...

My head began to ache. I closed my eyes and put my

hands up to my face. I knew I wasn't ugly. My parents always told me how beautiful I was; passersby always did
double takes whenever I walked by. I was a cameraman's
dream. But Justice said I was ugly. Who could imagine one
word would have so much power over me...over anyone.
I was gorgeous, damn it! And the world should have been
mine to do whatever I wanted, yet I was stranded on a
four-letter island named *Ugly*.

Feeling emotionally shipwrecked and alone, I felt nau-
seated. It wasn't how Justice said it that hurt the most; it
was the way that he looked at me when he said it that
drove the nail into my self-confidence. And now I didn't
feel so beautiful anymore. I didn't feel desirable to him.
And that killed me. I opened my eyes and stared at myself
in the vanity mirror, struggling to keep my emotions in-
tact.

*...Look at you, six-foot tall, giraffe-neck self. Big-foot
Amazon. Don't nobody want you...*

But Justice had made love to me as if I were the only
girl on earth. And, most importantly, I felt loved.

Then why did he say all of those mean things to me?
Why did he have me questioning myself?

I opened my towel, then stood in front of the floor-
length mirror and stared at my nakedness. I studied my
appearance. I wasn't fat. Still I didn't like what I saw.

*You're my world, baby...You're so beautiful. Ain't no-
body ever gonna love you like me. You're all mine, London...*

Justice was all up in my head. I was consumed with
him. And soooo confused. I couldn't get enough of him.
But I didn't want the abuse, or the disrespect; I just wanted

him. And as long as we stayed rolled up in my sheets, I knew I'd have him.

You turn me on, London. You always have…

"Damn you, Justice," I whispered to myself as I applied a coat of lip gloss over my pouty lips, then dabbed Coco Mademoiselle behind both ears, over my wrists, then along the center of my breasts. I didn't want to think negative thoughts, didn't want to harp on yesterday. Today was a new day. And it had been great so far. I wasn't going to do or say anything to ruin it. No matter what, I was going to enjoy what was left of our day together.

I stared at my reflection one last time, tightly tucking my towel back around my body, then opened the bathroom door and walked back out into the bedroom. There he stood with his back toward me, fully dressed, talking on his cell and clearly in a hurry to be somewhere else. The question was, where and with whom?

I watched as he shifted from one socked foot to the other, then shoved his hand down into his baggy Gucci sweats.

I blinked.

"Yo…keep talkin' slick…Oh, word?…Yeah, that's was-sup…We'll see…yeah, a'ight, bet. I'll meet you there. Don't front."

He turned around. "Oh, snap," he said, seemingly surprised to see me standing there. "Don't be sneaking up on me like that, yo. How long you been standing there?"

"Where are you going?"

He walked over to the foot of the bed and sat, reaching for his Timbs and working his feet into them. "I gotta make a quick run."

"Now?" I asked, disappointed.

"Yeah," he replied dryly.

I eyed his cell lying on the bed beside him. I wanted to run over and snatch it so I could scroll through his call log. "Who were you talking to on the phone?"

He stood up, tucking his phone into his front pocket. "Yo, why you questioning me?"

Is he serious?

Am I missing something?

I blinked, placed a hand up on my hip, then took a deep breath. I didn't want to set him off, or give him any reason to run out the door. The truth was I wanted him to stay. I needed him to hold me in his arms a little while longer. "I don't want you to leave," I said . . . no, whined. "I thought we were going to lie around and cuddle the rest of the day."

He smirked. "Yo, you mad funny. You still on punishment, yo. I'm rationing out this good love. When you know how to act, then you'll get more. When you get your mind right, don't give me a buncha grief, and know how to respect me as your man, then you can get all I got—anytime you want it. Until then you get the bare minimum."

I couldn't believe what I was hearing. I looked around, hoping there was a punch line to follow. There was none. I was standing there letting let this boy play me, once again. I couldn't figure out what was wrong with me. Why wasn't I strong enough to be done with him? I didn't deserve to be treated the way he continued to treat me. Yet . . . there I stood, begging him to stay.

"Justice," I said with pleading eyes, dropping my towel to the floor and walking over to him. I reached for his hand, then placed it on my bare breast, cupping my hand over his. "Please don't leave me. Make love to me again."

He pulled his hand away and scowled at me. "Yo, London, you buggin' for real. Pick that towel up and go put some clothes on. Stop actin' all thirsty. You think sex is gonna change what you did? How you treated me?"

Treated him? How about how he treated me? I really wanted to confront him about it, but I didn't want to argue. So I let it go.

"I thought we had made up."

He tsked. "Well, you thought wrong. We ain't made up. I'm still pissed behind how you played me yesterday."

"But what about all the lovemaking we did?"

He sniggered. "All that was, was sex. So get over it. It didn't change a thing. And it definitely didn't change what you did."

"What?" I screeched. "Are you serious? You lay up all night with me, and allllll morning with me, and practically all afternoon, acting like everything was all good. Now all of a sudden, you get off the phone and are back to having a problem with me. How is me wanting you to stay and make love to me again, being thirsty? I call myself loving you and wanting to be with you. Now all of a sudden it's a problem."

"Well, yeah . . . and you're smothering me, too."

"How am I smothering you? I don't sweat you. Yesterday was the first time I saw or spoke to you in over a week. I'm not trying to smother you, or upset you. But I really want—no, need—to know what I've done. How can I make this work for us? How can we go back to the way we used to be?"

He twisted his face up. "We can't."

I felt my cheeks burn. My lips quivered. *Don't you dare cry, girl.*

"Why can't we?"

"You've changed," he said, looking at me disgustedly. "You're different. You're too needy. And it's a turnoff."

I gave him a confused look. "Needy? You're the one who's changed."

"You just are. And I'm tired of arguing with you about it. Always clingin' up on me. I ain't changed. I'm still me. Still the one making all the efforts, still the one putting my life on hold for you. Everything's still about London. It's like every time I turn around, it's something different with you, yo. You got too much going on for me. You got too much lip. And you're acting desperate. It's a headache, yo. I thought I could do this wit' you, but"—he shook his head—"yo, I don't know. I don't think I can. I need some space—a lot of it."

I felt my stomach drop to my feet. "What about the plan? What about everything we talked about last night? How we were going to get you on top, then get married."

He scoffed. "Plan? Screw the plan, yo. You the one who had a problem with it. Now all of a sudden you back on. Yo, I can't keep goin' back 'n' forth wit' you. This is what I'm talkin' 'bout. You confused, yo."

"You asked me if I would handle Rich, and I told you I would. How is that me being confused? Whatever you need me to do, Justice, I'll do it. I just can't do all of this arguing. It stresses me out."

"Stresses you out? What about me?" He beat his chest with the palm of his hand.

"Who is it, Justice? Who are you trying to be with? What skank-whore are you trying to run out of here to be with?"

"What?" he asked disbelievingly. "See. Here you go wit' the dumbness again. If I wanted to be with someone else I'd be with them."

"What about the plan? Like where is all this coming from? We just lay in bed and agreed with going forward with everything so you can become a superstar. We were supposed to elope and get married."

"After the performance you put on yesterday, chasin' ole girl up outta here, she ain't checkin' for me."

"Oh, so that's what this is about? Rich again."

"No, it's about you again. And if she ain't checkin' for me, we can't make nothin' happen, stupid."

"Don't call me stupid, Justice."

He scoffed. "Well, that's what you are. I'm tired of creepin' up the backstairs and sneakin' up in here, hidin' out like some fugitive. I'm ready to be free and do me. As a matter of fact, I see ya maid more than I see you. She seems to have my back better than you do. She looks out for me. But you"—he shook his head again—"nah...it's all about you. At first, yo, I did think it was gonna work wit' us, but...I just can't shake that every time the plan gets ready to go into effect, you flip on me. So what that says to me is, you frontin', London."

"Frontin'?" I questioned, shocked. *The nerve of him!* "I'm not frontin', Justice."

"Then what you call it, London, huh?" He stared at me, then started moving around as if he were dancing, waving his hands up and down. "Ohhhhh, Jusssssstice, I got this girl I'ma hook you uuuuuuup with," he mocked. "Ohhhhh, Jusssssstice, this is how we're gonna be able to run awaaaay and get maaaaarried. Allllll I need is the ring, Jussssstice. Well, you got the ring. But what did Justice get." He snapped his finger. "Oh, wait. I got it. Too many nights closed up with you. I don't have no gigs, no record deal, and no Rich. But here you got all of me. And I'm cold on all of that. No more.

"I'm done wit' you sellin' me a buncha pipe dreams, gettin' my hopes up, makin' a fool out of me. All you want me for is sex, like I'm some closet freak. You'll say anything to keep me down. I'm done." He shot me the peace sign. "Yo, you do you, 'cause you sure not doin' anything for me."

I stood in the middle of my bedroom in complete disbelief. This came out of left field. I didn't know what to say, or think. I really meant it this time that we could go ahead with the setup. Yeah, the other times I was scared, hesitant. But this time I really meant it. I was so serious. I would do whatever Justice needed, wanted me to do. I'd been without him, and I'd been with him. And I didn't want to be without him anymore.

"I understand why you're mad at me, Justice. And it might seem funny, but it's not really that way."

"I'm tired of figuring out what way it is. The girl was right here, and you blew it, yo. You yankin' on her, comin' at her all sideways. Yo, c'mon now." He shook his head. "You're too insecure."

Everything he was saying was true. I was insecure. I did blow it. I let my emotions get in the way of what I knew I had to do, what I was supposed to do—for my man. But, there was Rich. Really liking her wasn't supposed to be a part of the plan. But it was. I really cared about her. She was my friend. And knowing that Justice expected me to keep my end of the deal, I had to swallow the bitter pill of knowing that I could lose her friendship. But Justice was my man. So, eff Rich. The way she came at him all up in my face, popping and dropping her booty and pushing her breasts all up on him, like she was Miss Universe—that let me know, right there, that she'd do my man. She was a whore!

All those secrets she told me, especially the one about her doing Spencer all dirty, sleeping with her boyfriend Chris, then flipping out when Spencer did it to her with Corey. Fact was, Rich didn't care about anyone except Rich Montgomery. And she'd lie, cheat, and creep with whomever she had to, to get whatever she wanted.

Bottom line, Rich was scandalous.

So how could I choose a chick like that over my man?

Justice stared at me long and hard. "Do you love me, London?"

Tears started stinging my eyes, but I refused to let them fall. I had hurt him so much. "Yes, I love you. I hate that you have to question that."

"Then step off. If you love me, let me breathe for a minute. Can you do that? Back up off of me, and let me figure out if I really wanna keep goin' through all this extra wit' you. Let me deal wit' the hurt."

I was ready to hit the floor; ready to roll up and die.

"Yo, you—"

"Miss London," Genevieve said through the intercom, cutting Justice off. "Dinner is ready."

"I'm not hungry," I responded, keeping my eyes on Justice.

"Your father has requested your presence at the dinner table."

Justice smirked, then mouthed, "Go run to daddy, lil girl."

"Genevieve, please tell my father I'm not feeling well."

"Okay, Miss London."

"Yo, I want my ring back," Justice said, opening his hand.

My eyes popped open. "I'm not giving it back. You gave it to me. You asked me to marry you, and I told you I would."

He walked up on me. "Nah, I'm good. I ain't beat. Give me my ring, yo."

"No, Justice."

He grabbed me by the arm. "I'm not playing with you, London. I want that ring back."

"Ow, you're hurting me. Get off of me."

Why was he turning on me like this? He wasn't even acting like this until he got off the phone. *Is he seeing somebody else now?*

"London?" my father's voice blared through the intercom. Justice let me go.

"Yes, Daddy?" I answered, moving to the other side of the room.

"You need to get down here for dinner, now."

"Daddy, I'm not feeling well."

"London, I'm not trying to hear it. I let you stay up in your room last night, but tonight you need to get down here. Your mother's home and Anderson just got here. And the four of us are having dinner together, so you have five minutes to pull yourself together before I come up to bring you down."

I sighed, feeling defeated. "I'll be down in a minute."

"Make it quick," he replied, shutting the intercom off.

"Go on, be wit' ya lil perfect family," Justice said sarcastically, rolling his eyes up in his head. "And ya future baby daddy, Mister Billionaire wit' his whack-azz. As a matter of fact, get him to buy you a ring, Miss Desperate. I'm outta here."

I was feeling helpless and hopeless all in one. "Justice, pleeeease. Don't leave. Give me ten minutes, Justice. That's all I ask, ten...minutes. I'll be right back."

"Yeah, a'ight. Go do you."

I hurriedly stepped into my walk-in closet, pulled a Diane Von Furstenberg print dress off the hanger and slipped it over my head, then put on a pair of slides. "I really don't want us to argue and fight anymore. Baby, you have to know how much you mean to me. I don't want to give up on us, ever. And I hope you don't either. I really love you."

I smiled when I felt him behind me. He leaned in and wrapped his arms around me, pressing his lips up against the nape of my neck. I closed my eyes and pressed my booty into him, leaning my head back on his chest.

"I love you so much," I said, slightly grinding my backside into him. Something didn't feel right. I snapped my eyes open, looked down at the hands around my waist, then froze. It wasn't Justice. Those hands belonged to someone else. I jerked my body around. "What the hell are you doing in here?!" I yelled, pushing him away from me.

"Awww, how's that for a Hallmark card?" Anderson said snidely. "I love you, too."

I blinked.

"Don't look so disappointed. Who'd you think I was? Juuuuuustice?" He chortled.

I was in shock that Anderson was standing in front of me. And that Justice was nowhere around. He had really left. Something he had never done before. He'd always be down for camping out here, locked in my room for two and three days, waiting for me to return to him.

"What are you doing up here?" I asked tight-lipped.

"Your father sent me up to get you. No, actually... I volunteered to come up, hoping to catch you with your legs up in the air, doing what you do best. But judging by the rumpled sheets and"—he sniffed the air—"and the love funk still lingering, I must have just missed the performance."

I rolled my eyes, brushing past him, walking back into my room. "Screw you, Anderson."

"From where I'm standing, looks like you're already screwed, or been screwed—in more than one way." He shook his head. "Pathetic. Speaking of which, where's your little slimy boyfriend, Justice the YouTube king of scams. Don't tell me he's had a better offer and has found himself another fool to use."

I huffed. "Mind your business. Don't worry about Justice. Worry about your own self."

"Poor, pathetic London," he taunted. "Wasting her life away loving a wannabe celebrity."

"Shut. Up! What are you doing here, anyway? I called you-all last week and you didn't return any of my calls."

He flicked his wrist out, glancing at his watch. "I had more important things to do than to deal with the sickening musings of you. Besides, I don't need an invite from you. Your parents love me."

I scowled. "Well, I don't, so get the hell out."

"Yo," he said mockingly. "Don't flatter yourself, mama. Dig what I'm sayin', home fries?"

"You pompous, arrogant, egotistical sonofa—"

"Watch your mouth, London."

"You don't tell me what to do. I'm so tired of living this lie."

He straightened the sleeve of his Prada blazer. "Let me tell you something, London." He paused, flicking imaginary lint off his shoulder. "Your life of lies started long before I came into the picture. Every day you open your pretty little brown eyes, you're living a lie. So spare me your tired tirade."

"Whatever. I can't keep doing this. I'm so sick of playing this charade with you. I'm breaking this thing off, now."

He smirked. "Go 'head, end it. And your little ho-house of cards will come tumbling down. So do it. And let's see how far that gets you. My guess is straight to some skid row ho-trap where some dope-fiend pimp will trick you out for his next hit."

I wasn't hearing anything Anderson had to say. He was of no consequence to me.

Justice really walked out!

And I had no idea where he had gone, or who he was going to be with. I couldn't even pick up the phone to call or even text him, with Anderson standing right there in my face, my father downstairs at the dinner table—commanding my presence—and my mother somewhere with a scale and tape measure ready to measure my body fat and weigh me in. I couldn't even fall out and have a breakdown. This was too much to deal with.

I glanced around the room, then frantically walked into my bathroom, looking behind doors and into closets, searching for him, hoping he was hiding out. He wasn't.

I stepped back into my bedroom to find Anderson stretched out on my chaise, one big loafer-clad foot crossed over the other. His hands were behind his head. "You know, the two of you really deserve each other."

I eyed him, both hands on my hips. "I'm glad you've finally realized that."

He snorted. "Of course I have. Project gutter trash meets Upper East Side trash."

"You know what, Anderson? Kiss my a—oh, wait. I forgot. That's not your thing, is it, boo-boo?" I said snidely. "You like it when yours is being kissed instead."

His eyes narrowed. "Watch your step, London."

I snapped my fingers at him, smacking my lips and swiveling my neck. "No, you watch yours. And, as a matter of fact, get the hell out of my room. And stay the hell out of my life."

Out of the corner of my eye, I noticed the doors to my armoire were ajar. My stomach dropped. *OhGodno!*

I raced over and pulled open the doors. I pulled out the antique box filled with precious jewels, given to me by my great-grandmother. I searched through its contents, then dumped everything out onto my bed. I almost fainted. My engagement ring was gone! I shook the jewelry box upside down to be sure my eyes weren't deceiving me. They weren't.

OhGodohGodohGod...

My heart thumped like crazy. I started hyperventilating and choking. I started rummaging through my jewels again.

It has to be here!

I anxiously ran back over to my armoire, tearing open drawers and knocking things over. My chest tightened.

Please God...

No, no, no...

It's gone!

I'd been robbed! Justice stole my ring! I couldn't have hurt him that bad for him to take my engagement ring. With Justice gone and my ring along with him, I felt like I had lost everything. I had nothing! My life was over!

Whyyyyyyyyyyyyyyyyyyyyyy?!

What did I do for him to hate me like this?

How could he do this to me?!

Tears started falling from my eyes as I heaved in and out.

Anderson clapped, standing up. "Bravo! You get a standing ovation. I always said you should be an actress. You'll get your gold star on the walk of shame after all for your starring role in *Thugalicious*. Speaking of thugs, what'd he steal from you this time—another family heirloom? Don't expect me to replace it!"

I wanted to cry. And I wanted to slap that smug look off Anderson's face. "I hate you! I hate everything you stand for. Go find a bridge to jump off of."

"I hate you more. But I'm going to pretend that I like you to get what I want, and I suggest you do the same. We have a year and a half left until you turn eighteen. I marry you, I get my trust fund, you get yours, then I can be rid of you and you can run off into the ghetto with your bum boyfriend."

I sneered, hands flying and fingers snapping everywhere. "Marry *me*? Boyfriend, puhlease. How's that going to happen? I could never be your groom. Sissies don't get married...not to women. Or did you forget that?"

He glared at me, stone-faced. "You better watch yourself. We both have secrets to keep."

I flipped my hand in his face and switched my hips back

into my closet, then came out with my handbag. "Well, I'm not so sure how much longer I want to keep mine. Now get out of my face."

I headed for the door, flicking the light off on him.

"And where do you think you're going?"Anderson asked, following behind me.

I ignored him, taking the back stairway that led to the south side of our estate.

"London," Anderson hissed. "You can't just leave like this."

"Watch me," I said, turning to face him. "And there's nothing *you* or anyone else can do to stop me."

"And when you can't find him, don't call crying to me."

I threw my hand up in the air and flipped him the finger. I walked down the flight of stairs that led into the solarium, then slipped out the side door and into the garage where my car was. I had had enough. I was tired of bending over and letting everyone screw me up the rear. Justice, Anderson, Rich, my parents, eff 'em all!

13

Heather

"Hello, my name is Heather. And I'm a junkie." The very words that not even Jesus pointing an Uzi could force me to say.

Puhlease.

I was a lot of things—a drunk's kid, fatherless, a tiny bit of a fame whore, an estranged member of the Pampered Princesses—but one thing I wasn't, was a junkie.

Hmph, I didn't get high.

I didn't do dope.

Meth.

Crack.

Ecstasy.

I had parties.

Lotza fun.

I didn't nod out.

Beg for money on the street.

Drool at the mouth.

My lips weren't white, pasty, and cracked up.

I had all my teeth.

For all intents and purposes I checked all the boxes for being cute—more so for others than for myself—but still, I wasn't a junkie. And the only two things I needed to change were my mother and my location. Because I couldn't stand Camille...and this druggie jail, better known as rehab or hell. I needed to blaze my way outta here!

I'd been in this boring, sad, and pathetic place for four days too long and even The Blind Rapper could see that Always Hope *was not* the place for me.

I needed to cruise down Sunset Boulevard in a chauffeured drop-top Benz. Profilin' and freestylin' in Bumble-Bee Chanel's. Crushed black beauties in my hobo Hermès purse.

I needed the set of my sitcom.

The Wu-Wu Tanner Show.

I needed to live my starring role...

I needed to be free.

Not stuck in here and wondering why every waking moment was an evolving nightmare.

"Heather, are ya lissstenin' to me?" Camille shouted into the phone.

Hell no. As a matter of fact I forgot I was even holding the phone...

"Thass your ffffreakkin' problem, misseee. Ya don't lisssten."

Given the way Camille's voice slurred, I knew she was drunk off of vodka and not her usual scotch. Which meant one thing—it would be impossible to get her to shut up.

I could hear Camille toss back a gulp and then push cigarette smoke out through her thin lips. "And ya need to lisssten up. Because ya not coming back, coming back up in here until your thoughts are in order. I can't. And I won't live with a junkie. Now I don' mind a little drankin'. We can clink a glass or two. Maybe even do a little hash—"

"Hash?"

"You know, a lil weed. But I will not, and I mean it, I will not tol'rate a pill poppin'. Junkie. Up. In here. Next thing I know you'll be stealing and I'll wake up one morning screaming. And you know why I'll be screaming?!" She paused. "Answer me, Heather, do you know why I'll be screaming?"

I rolled my eyes toward the ceiling. "No, Camille, humor me. Tell me why."

" 'Cause you would've ripped off my Oscar and sold it on the street—"

"Oh, Camille—"

"And my furs. And my jewels. Oh no, M-Misseeee." She stammered and I swear I could see her wagging her long, thin finger. "Not up in here. Not today. Not next week. Not next year. Not ev-veeer. My mother didn't tol'rate it from me and I will not tol'rate it from you. So you better figure out a way, figure out a way, to fall in line with that, umm..." She paused. "That umm...umm..." She snapped her fingers in the background. "That, umm, yeah, treatment. Oh, and you better see to it that that counselor doesn't call me again. Claiming that I need treatment. And I *know* you put him up to that—"

"Camille—"

"All I do is drink, Heath-thooor!" Camille exaggerated my name the way she always did when she was attempting to beat me over the head with her point. "And I've never heard of anyone who drinks being a thief!"

"Camille—"

"And by the way this rent has to get paid. We are going on two months behind and there's no way I can be evicted."

"What did you do with that money Kitty gave you?"

"Heath-thooooor! How dare you bring that up!"

"Because you got a million dollars from that woman for interviews and exclusives that I didn't even want to do! And you mean to tell me that you didn't pay the rent? Really?"

"First of all, Heathooor, you're out of place. You don't count my mon-ney, hon-ney! I'm the parent here and if you would've listened to me you'd be at home getting your buzz on instead of being locked away like some caged animal who needs to be tranquilized! So don't bring drama to me because you didn't know how to act." She paused, blew a puff of smoke, and continued on. "And I still haven't forgotten about how you drugged me. I was 'sleep one moment and the next thing I knew I was being finger-printed in a paddy wagon—"

"Camille—"

"And now I'm being dragged through the media like some Kartrashian—"

"Would you. Shut. Up! It is not all about you!"

"So this is what you're learning up there in trea'ment? How to disrespect your mother?" She sniffed. "I'm the only one who likes you and will tol'rate you. No one else can stand ya. Just like Spencer, who you thought was your friend—just the other day you told me you called her and what did she do? Gave ya the dial tone. And what did you do? Cry. Like a baby! You bet-ter learn to appreciate peo-ple! Starting with me. Your mother, Heath-thooor." She sniffed again.

*Is she crying? Oh please. Here we go with the theatrics.
What movie is this from?*

She continued, "From the moment I gave birth to you
it's always been about you. I lost everything to keep you.
Had I known life would turn out like this I would've kept
my appoin'ment, but now I'm stuck. And I've made
lemonade out of sour lemons and no sugar. And still
found a way to make it sweet."

*What did she just say to me? Now I know for sure that
the only regret I have about drugging her is that she did-
n't keel over!*

Camille's rant carried on. "You did me proud until you
turned out to be a crackhead. We were almost back on top
and then you wanted to sniff glue and drink hand sani-
tizer. And give parties encouraging kids to rob their parents' medicine cabinets. I'm ashamed and I have never
been more humiliated in my life. Now I have to run from
the paparazzi. Run. Run. Run. I am under tremendous emotional distress. Your mission in life is to ruin me, *Heathooor*!
I had to see my psychiatrist to get some Xanax because of
this stress! And that's another thing—now I have to buy a
lock and chain for my booze and medication because I
might wake up one morning to find you stoned off of my
stuff! And I will not have that!"

"Camille—"

"Don't cut me off, *Heathooor*! What you need to do is
work on getting your job back, because your last check
just came here! And sixteen thousand—no, eighteen thousand—needs to come out of this check. Sixteen for rent
and two for my peace of mind. I am stressed, *Heathooor*.
It's bad enough I have to call that Kitty again to get a cou-

ple of dollars. And the last time I was on that show she called me an alcoholic!"

"Oh no, not you, Camille." I rolled my eyes toward the ceiling.

"Can you believe that? That Kitty has a filthy litter box. Nasteee! She plays dirty." She paused. Belched. "But she also pays good money."

"So in other words she's your welfare check. How anti-Hollywood. Selling your soul to the highest bidder. You have a problem, Camille."

"I don't have a problem! That's you with the is-sues! Now I have to go. You have insulted me. I have a headache and I have to refresh my glass. Now you be sure to tell that counselor not to call me. I'll get there for a session with him, when I feel like it. And not before. Now tell me you love me."

Click.

What did I do to deserve her...?

I held the pay-phone receiver in my hand as my thoughts trailed off to a thousand other things I'd rather be doing.

I shook my head and rattled the change in my pocket. I had three dollars in quarters left—since druggie jail didn't do cell phones.

How played was that?

God, I needed a picker-upper.

Camille had sucked all of my energy and I needed an escape or I was going to blow. My eyes skipped across the pale blue walls where anti-drug posters hung like works of art, blaring pathetic messages of JUST SAY NO and DRUGS KILL.

I was so over this!

Drugs didn't kill.

People killed.

They killed your kindness.

Killed your spirit.

And they killed my tolerance for bull, which is why I could barely stand people anymore.

Except Co-Co...

I lifted my eyes and smiled, only for them to land on this dumb poster that read SAY NO TO PRESCRIPTION DRUG ABUSE.

Shoot me! Who writes these things? Obviously some creep who doesn't know how to party...spare me. Drugs kill, yeah right. I can handle my pills. All they do for me is get me in my zone. Get my mind right. I ain't hurtin' nobody. I'm just doin' me...and everybody else is all up in mine. Which is why they can kiss my...

I dropped my money into the phone and waited for it to ring. Immediately Snoop Dog and Wiz Khalifa's "Young, Wild and Free" greeted me.

"Turn the music down," Co-Co screamed into the background. "My girl is on the phone! My Wu-Wu! What's doin', boo?"

"What's all that music in the background? Y'all are having a party without me? You couldn't wait for me?" I was two seconds from being full-fledged pissed.

"Wu-Wu, this is a campaign party to get you back on the set, babe. That rat-face-wannabe Hollyhood trick they replaced you with is horrible! Grotesque! Oh, girl. I ran up on her the other day and tossed my slushy in her face. Hollywood High is giving her no love. We have petitions all over the place! We have *Free Wu-Wu* posters, we have egged up the producer's car, staged marches. We are not playin'! We are doin' it for you! Who shotcha, baby! Wu-Wu's in the house!"

All I could do was smile. At least Co-Co was free enough to have his mind right. He continued. "Now let me tell you what's been going on at the ranch."

"What's that?"

"The farm animals are out of control! First of all security is on high alert because some freshmen claimed they were robbed and their hair was shaved off by two masked women."

"Are you serious?"

"As serious as your rehab sentence."

"Dead."

"Umm hmm. And oh, let me tell you about the Horse. She got beat down by a bunch of ninth-grade baby thugs!"

"What?"

"Yes, girl. Slaughtered! They dragged her all over that café. Don't worry, I have pics and all the uncut and raw video footage you need to see. As a matter of fact I just made a guap selling them to the blogs! That money went toward your campaign and a sweet bag of beauties."

"Word?"

"Thunderbird! And by the way, I'm in West Hollywood now."

"Serious?"

"As an STD. I could no longer deal with my father trying to give me straight-man fever. Obama set it off for me! I'm a queen all day and proud of it! I'ma always have a switch in my Asian hips and my father may as well get with it! Now what you been up?"

"I'm up here surrounded by junkies, high killers, and stupid anti-party posters!"

"What? We gotta bust you up out of there. What a mess!"

"Tell me about it. Anyway, I miss you so much, boy!"

"I miss you, too! And I have some champagne on ice waiting to celebrate the day you come back."

"I'ma need more than some champagne. I'ma need to be beautified."

"I gotcha, girl. I got that goodness that sent Lindsay Lohan crazy and made Brittany lose her mind that time. I got that fire, girl! Everybody that comes through here has to pay fifty dollars a pop, but for my Wu-Wu it's free all day. You'll be stockpiled."

Electricity shot through me and joy made my heart skip a beat.

"One time for your mind," Co-Co said as if he'd read my thoughts. "By the way, don't worry about Camille, girl. She called here drunk, but I handled her. I paid the rent for y'all!"

How embarrassing! How could Camille call my friend, drunk? "What? You paid the rent? When?"

"I paid it two days ago."

I can't believe Camille. Trying to steal from me.

"And with the money I'm bringing in I might even buy that house for you."

"It's like that, Co-Co?"

"It's like *that*. I'm killing it. I'm shuttin' corners down and bringing 'em to the living room. I'm not taking shorts anymore, I'm taking jackets! In a minute I'ma have half of Hollywood High gettin' high! One time for your mind!"

"And there you have it, Co-Co. And while you're taking jackets make sure you get the kitten heels to match."

"And you know it, boo. And you know it. Who loves ya, Wu-Wu?!"

"You do, baby!" I laid a big, juicy kiss on the receiver.

"And don't forget that. Now bye, darlin'. Stay strong, 'cause when you come home it's gon' be on!"

"Owwl," I squealed, and snapped my fingers as I dropped down low and snaked back up. I didn't have my booty pads on, but I felt Beyoncé-bootyfied. All that was missing was a pill or two. But that was okay because talking to Co-Co always got me juiced up. "One time for the mind!" I said for the hell of it as I hung up the phone.

I snapped my fingers and did another dance. I hadn't felt this good in weeks. I could almost feel the beauty juice rushing through me. Just the thought of it was orgasmic. "Whew!" I shook my shoulders as I glanced up at the clock.

Group started ten minutes ago.

Talk about a high-blower.

I gotta get out of here.

I turned toward the door and immediately my heart dropped. Leaning against the door frame as if he'd been there too long, and wearing a stupid smirk on his face, was my personal pain in the . . . my druggie jail correction officer. Shakeer Mills. Better known as my case manager.

Ugh!

I couldn't stand him.

And it didn't help me one bit that Mr. Nerve-Wrecker was fine. He stood about five-ten, five-eleven at most. His flawless skin was the color of smooth chocolate and his sexy eyes were the color of sweet ice tea. He rocked a wavy caesar with enough spin to make you dizzy. And his light mustache was neatly shaped around his luscious lips and melted into his faded beard. Now I knew what Co-Co meant when he said that a cutie was so fine you had to call him Mr. Goddamn.

I didn't know if my vision of him was because I'd been locked away for days, my hormones, or a combination of the two. All I knew was that there was fine and *fi-one*. And Mr. Panty-Rockin' Sweetness put the O in it.

For a moment I felt nervous and wondered if I had anything out of place. And then I remembered that everything about me was out of place.

I swallowed. Looked over Mr. Wreckin' My Flow And My Nerves and wondered how long he had been standing there. I shot him a look that clearly said *Why. The. Heck. Are. You. Bothering. Me?!*

"Don't you have somewhere to be?" He stood up straight, and I could've sworn that he was checking me out on the sly.

I rolled my eyes toward the ceiling and slowly brought them back down. "As a matter of fact I have several places to be. Like on the set of my sitcom. In the backseat of my limo. Rodeo Drive. Home."

"You have group."

I twisted my lips. *Whatever.* "I was on my way there."

"Before or after you dropped down and brought it back up on that last finger pop? Or before or after you said you wanted to be beautified?"

OMG, apparently he'd been standing there long enough to be all up in my conversation. Nosy. I took a deep breath and ignored his last statement.

He took a step closer to me and continued. "From what I just witnessed seems like you're right back at the place that got you here. Right back up on your stage in your backyard."

I batted my eyes and lowered my lashes. "Okay, Mr. Mind

Reader, I'm guilty as charged. And since you can read my thoughts, maybe you should have a nine-hundred number, sir."

His jaw tightened and a pulsating vein ran down the right side of his thick neck and beneath his lavender button-up. He slid a hand in his right dress pants pocket and *do Jesus*, his swag was making me sweat. I wiped my forehead and he said, his voice dropping to an annoyed octave, "Maybe you need to come to my office so we can finish this conversation."

"Oh wow, I'd really love to. But umm, I'm on my way to group."

"Not anymore you're not. You're on your way to an individual session. You'll catch the next group. Now let's go!"

Psst, please. I know he had me messed up. I don't take orders. This wasn't a drive-through. He had me twisted. "Seems you missed the star of *The Wu-Wu Tanner Show* announcement. And I know they handed out flyers before I came here." I snapped my fingers. "So I know you see that I'm a star and I need to be treated like one."

He frowned. "Oh really? A star? Well, here's what I see. A pill popper. A junkie. A little girl who throws Skittles parties and instead of facing her demons she snorts pills to chase them away. What I see standing before me is a mess."

"I know you didn't—"

"Look, one thing I'm not going to do is argue with you. You're not running any show here. Because the last show you ran had you terminated. So how about this, Your Majesty. You have two choices: you can either stand here with all that lip if you want to, or you can program." He turned toward the door. "And keep in mind," he said over his shoulder, "I'm the one who writes the reports on your progress and sends them to the judge. And right now there is no progress. So like *I said*, you need to come to my office." And he walked out and left me standing there, watching his fine behind get smaller in the distance.

I hesitated. It had crossed my mind to walk out the front door and blow this place. Until I remembered I had to be buzzed out.

WTF!

I gathered myself, tucked my attitude like it was a clutch beneath my arm, and made my way to Mr. Fine Distraction's office—where he sat behind his mahogany desk and looked through a chart.

I tapped on the door frame.

"Have a seat," he said, never looking up.

Ugh, I wanted to gut him!

I sucked my teeth and plopped down in the chair, my coils bouncing over my shoulders.

He picked up his pen and proceeded to write a note on the chart he'd been reviewing. A few minutes later he closed the chart and looked up at me slowly. "You know what? You need an attitude adjustment."

I rolled my eyes so hard it's a wonder they didn't fall out and slap his face. "My attitude is adjusted; I'm not giving you the heat that I usually bless people with."

"Oh really?" He paused. "You know what, Heather? You want out of here?"

Hell yes! Duh. "Like yesterday."

"Okay. You got it."

Finally God was in the prayer-answering business!

"Thank you for being so understanding," I said, but not meaning one word of it.

"Not a problem. Because one thing I can do for the resident star is make it happen."

"See, I knew you recognized me." I smiled. "Thank you soooo much! And just to show you how thankful I am, let me know if you have a daughter and I will be sure to send her a signed Wu-Wu doll."

He smiled, reached a muscular arm across his desk, and picked up the phone. He dialed a number and said into the receiver, "Hello, can I have Judge Raymond's chambers, please."

Stop the press!

Immediately my chest tightened and a sharp pain shot up my left arm. I thought I was having a heart attack. "Why-why-why are you calling the judge?" I stammered, panicked.

He covered the receiver. "To have him send someone dressed in blue for you."

I was about to piss on myself. Flashbacks of a king-size chick who thought she was a boy popped into my head. "Judge Raymond will send me back to jail. I can't do jail! I can't go back there! Please! I'd have to fight for my life!"

He eyed me.

"Please. I can't go back!" Tears dripped down my cheeks. I reached over and placed my hand on the hand he held the phone with and pleaded with my eyes. "I can't go back there! I'll work the program! I'll do whatever you want!" *I was desperate.*

He paused. Looked me over and asked, "You'll do what?"

"I'll work the program. I swear." Sweat dripped down

my temples and over my forehead. I felt like I was going through withdrawals all over again.

He hung up the phone and I leaned back in my chair, breathing a sigh of relief.

"Sit up," he commanded.

I did as I was told.

He leaned in toward me and said sternly, "I promise you, the next time you *will* be leaving here in handcuffs. Are we clear?"

I nodded. "Yes, sir."

"Now the first step in working the program is owning who you are. Now who are you?"

"My name is Heather..."

"And why are you here?"

"I'm a junkie."

14

London

...If you was a dude, I'd break ya jaw...for bein' so effen stupid...

...If I woulda knew how silly you was I woulda never effed with you from the rip. Look at you, six-foot tall, giraffe-neck self. Big-foot Amazon. Don't nobody want you...

Oh God, I felt sick. How could he talk to me like that? I lifted up my diamond-jeweled Dolce & Gabbana shades, then dabbed at the corners of my eyes. I dared not spill a tear.

...Stupid-azz trick!...

I shifted in my seat, pulling my shades back over my eyes. I felt like kids in class were staring and snickering at me as I sat in the back of my AP Latin class. This was too much! I wanted to bolt out the door and run out the front doors, but knew I couldn't afford any more write-ups for cutting class, or school.

Right now I didn't care about Cicero or neologisms, or

dactylic hexameters, or whether a subject or predicate was at the beginning or end of a sentence. Latin class was the last place I wanted to be. I wanted to be home in bed, wrapped beneath my exquisite sheets with my nails raking along the seam of Justice's back as he made magic stir deep inside me while whispering sweet nothings into my ear. But that wasn't about to happen, since I had no clue where the hell he was. So, yes, my mind was any-and-every-where except Hollywood High.

Miss Stein, my teacher, was talking, but her words slurred and she sounded like one of the Chipmunks. Her high-pitched voice faded in and out. All I could think about was Justice. Justice, Justice, Justice!

I hadn't seen or heard from him since he slipped out of my bedroom and snuck out of my house. Thursday night, to be exact! One of the worst nights of my entire teen life. He dodged out of my house—with no goodbye, no kiss on the lips, no "I'll see you later," no "I love you"—taking every piece of me with him.

London, you're pathetic.

Justice and Anderson had both called me that. Maybe they were right. Maybe I was pathetic. Or maybe I was simply a girl who wanted to love and be loved back. Maybe I believed in knights in shining armor and princesses and a happily-ever-after. Maybe I hoped and prayed and wanted like hell to be happy forever and ever...amen—with Justice. Or maybe I was just a fool for love. No, no, I wasn't any of those things. I was simply a fool!

A fool for thinking Justice would ever stop hurting me. A fool for thinking he and I could run off into the sunset, like they do in the movies, and live, laugh, and love each other until our dying days. I was a fool for thinking my parents would ever approve of him and welcome him with open arms. And I was a fool for still believing it could all come true.

...You make me sick, yo. Wit' ya ugly self. You insecure. Fat, nasty...

Justice had stolen from me. He stole my laughter. He stole my joy. He raided my thoughts. He robbed me of my life. And I had nothing; nothing but a truckload of insults, and a trash can of snotty tissues from crying for the last four nights and four days.

Oh, and I had—once again—a broken heart. No, scratch that. Not even a broken heart; I had *no* heart. No heart to stand up to him. No heart to walk away from him. No heart to stop loving him and being consumed by him. My heart had been broken so many times that I could no longer feel. I was paralyzed. And numb.

And maybe I did make him mad, but I did nothing to deserve what he'd dished out to me. The punishment did not fit the crime. I pissed him off for a moment and he sentenced me to a lifetime of misery. Where was the *justice* in that? Oh no, justice was unfair. It was cruel and un-kind. Justice was poison. And it, and he, were killing me slowly.

...don't talk to me about love *'cause you don't know the first thing about* love.

Justice was so wrong. I knew—well, I thought I knew—what love was with him. But I was tired of *love* putting me on punishment. I'm the one who'd been blindsided. It had taken my heart, my love, my body. It stripped me of everything. In one breath, I wanted to love him and leave him alone, then in another I felt like I would die to have him back. So here I was in the back of Latin class, texting him again, hoping love would find its way back to me.

Justice where r u?

I felt like I was I going insane. I felt schizophrenic. Voices were telling me to hate him one minute, then to love him the next. Then they'd turn around and tell me to hunt him down and kill him, then tell me to love him all over again. These voices were controlling me. Telling me he had to pay for taking my love and spitting on it. Telling me I had to keep on loving him and not give up on him. I felt stupid for wanting to cry. But I couldn't help but cry.

Then there were times when I felt like I had multiple personalities. That I had a starring role in a nutty sitcom called *The Forty Faces of Dumb London*. One minute I was the fly, fabulous, stiletto-wearing diva draped in diamonds and designer wears who loved her body and embraced her beauty and held the world in the palm of her soft, pampered hands. The It Chick who didn't care about boys or drama or bull crap. Then the next minute, I was the sniveling, needy, obsessively jealous chick who thought she was fat and ugly. And cried and begged and stalked her boyfriend. I was a spoiled brat who lied and defied her parents and kept dirty secrets all in the name of love.

It was all too much to keep up with.

Justice why r'nt u callin me back? Stop hurtin' me! This silence is killin' me! why r u doin' this 2 me?

A thousand whys raced through my mind: Why couldn't I just leave him alone? Why did I keep letting him hurt me like this? Why wasn't I good enough? Why couldn't I make him happy? Why did it hurt so bad, but feel so good? Why did I love so hard? Why, why, why? I was getting tired of holding my breath waiting on the answers.

I had everything: money, beauty, a banging body, good sex. Justice and I were supposed to be a family. It was supposed to be me and him against the world. But lately it had become me, myself, and I—alone. Once again, Justice had abandoned me. I tried and I tried and I tried. Kept crying and crying and crying. And it just kept getting worse. Loving him was a battle that slowly was turning into a war. Justice was the man I'd die for. But he turned out not to be concerned about me. Now I knew the sky could really fall. If I were a butterfly I'd fly away. Oh, wait...I couldn't even do that. Justice had my wings!

The fourth-period bell rang, temporarily pulling me out of my misery. I listlessly grabbed my handbag and notes, then slid out the door, pulling out my phone for the tenth time, checking it. I felt like I was walking in a thick fog as I glanced at the screen. *Ugh!* There was a text from Anderson. I rolled my eyes up in my head. He was not who I expected, or was hoping, to hear from.

U okay?

I ignored him. Granted, he had dropped me off at school this morning—because my father felt it was his duty to make my life even more miserable by taking my car away for the next two weeks—but still, that didn't give Anderson the right to think he could check up on me, like he was really my man. Please. I was tired of him and my parents being all up in my business. I knew my parents thought they had a right to be. But Anderson kept forgetting his place, dodging his lane, and crossing all up into mine. I didn't need him to be asking me how I was doing. Mmmph. He needed to worry about how *he* was *doooooooin'.*

Absentmindedly, I walked the hallway, texting Justice for the fiftieth time this morning. He still hadn't responded to the other text messages I had left. And I couldn't leave any more voice messages because his inbox was full.

I sent another text.

U kno what Justice, F U! I'm not gonna keep sweatin' U

I tossed the phone back into my bag and stabbed my heels into the marbled floor as I made way to Rich's locker and waited for her. Before I knew it, five minutes had passed and Rich was nowhere in sight. I was in a crisis, on the verge of an emotional meltdown, and that shallow, self-righteous strumpet was nowhere to be found. I was always there for her. But when I needed her, was she ever there for me? Nooooooo, of course not! She was the Princess of Selfish, the epitome of not giving a damn about anyone but herself. So you know what? Eff her, too!

I pulled out my phone one more time to check for messages, even though I hadn't heard my phone beep or felt it vibrate since the last time I had checked it. There were none. This was ridiculous! Who does that? *Oh God, I hope he's all right. I know we had that big fight. Oh God, nooooo! I hope he's not somewhere floating facedown in the Pacific. It'd be my fault. I'd never be able to live with myself.*

I sent him another text, asking him to please call me, telling him that I didn't mean what I had texted before. That I only wanted to hear his voice to know that he was okay. If he would just call me I could get through my day. I could express how I felt. Let bygones be bygones, then move on and keep on loving him. But he was making it difficult.

But you know what? I didn't need him. It was good while it lasted, but obviously it was over. So I was going to get myself together and keep it moving. And this time I meant it. I was done. I pulled out my cell, determined to make this the last time I texted him.

U kno what justice? screw u! I'm finished wit U. Thnx 4 showin me the man U r, or better yet, r not! Ur pathetic!

A few seconds later my cell rang and I immediately answered without looking at the screen. "Hello?" I said, hoping to hear my man's silky voice.

"I guess that means you still haven't heard from him," the deep voice said. I cringed.

"What do you want, Anderson? I've had enough of you for one day."

"Is that any way to talk to the guy who made sure you got to school safe and sound today? Don't get yourself all up in a huff. I only called to see how you were holding up your first day back, knowing how distressed you've been."

"Anderson, spare me. You only dropped me off to school out of obligation so you could look good. You don't care about me. I'm pathetic, remember? So let's stick with the program and stop frontin'."

He laughed. "Liking you is not even up for discussion. The fact is, I saved you from your father's wrath when you ran up out your house like some lovesick maniac, chasing behind a boy who won't even love you back. So you owe me a little respect and some kindness as gratitude."

"I don't owe you shi—"

"Ah-ah-ah, be nice."

"Anderson, let's get something clear. I. Don't. Like. You. Okay? So the sooner you get it through your head, the better."

"See. I should have let you drown. But, no, once again—I tossed you a lifeline and saved the day."

I sucked my teeth. "Please, *drown?* I don't think so. I

don't need saving, especially not by you. So you can take
your lifelines and shove 'em where I know you'd love
them to be. I didn't ask you to lie for me, so stop acting
like you did me some favor. I got this. I was ready to handle my own. I got me. Now you go get your life and stay
the hell out of mine! And stop worrying about who's loving me or not."

He laughed. And that only pissed me off more. "What
the hell is so funny?"

"Oh, London, London, London...actually, *you* are.
You're a beautiful mess. But your attitude makes you butt-
ugly. And it stinks..."

I blinked. *Beautiful? Wait, Anderson's giving* me *a compliment? Since when?*

Wait, did he just call me a mess?

Well, you are *a mess!*

"Whatever. And you're a pompous prick, but guess who
cares?"

"I know, I know. You don't. Yet you spend all of your
time caring about people who don't care about you. I'm
not your enemy, London. I know you're hurt. But I'm not
the one who keeps hurting you. You're always talking mess,
always coming at me sideways, but anytime your back's up
against the wall or that idiot disses you, who's the first person you call? I am. So, yeah, I might be a pompous prick,
as you say, but I've never given you my butt to kiss. And
right now, all I'm doing is calling to check on you. But
since I'm such a nuisance, I'ma let you go. You can wallow
in ya misery all by ya'self."

"You know what, Anderson? I don't effen need you to
call me. And you don't ever have to worry about *me* calling you a—"

"Yeah, right. Who you gonna call? Justice?" He laughed. "Picture that. Oh wait, let me guess. Rich. That's who you'll call. Hahahaha. That's even funnier than you thinking Justice is ever gonna change. Do you really think Rich is going to listen to you pour your broken heart out to her? Ha! All Rich cares about is Rich. And whose bed she's going to jump in next. And what designer she's going to wear from one day to the next. That self-absorbed girl has the attention span of a spider. So, yeah... go call Rich. And let me know how you make out with that. I'm done with you."

Click!

Did he hang up on me? I glanced at the screen. The word *Disconnected* confirmed what I already knew. Whatever! I shoved my phone down into my bag, as the glass doors of the café opened. I couldn't wait to get caught up with Rich. I hadn't spoken to her since that day she tried to breast-feed Justice. Ugh, I still couldn't get over that! But I wasn't going to hold that against her. Whores do what whores do—whore. So, it was to be expected.

As I walked into the café, I was immediately greeted by the music of the chatter. It was everything I was not. It was lively. It was like a finger-popping hip-hop song. Made you bounce to the rhythm. Made you want to shake and drop and pop right back up. It was definitely a totally different vibe from last Monday when I got jumped up in here by a bunch of *now* bald-headed hoes. I still wanted to thrash them, though. But oh well... karma snatched them and took their hair right along with her. Served them right!

"Bonjour, Miss London," the maitre d' said, greeting me with a smile. "Est-ce que vous aimeriez manger aujour-d'hui?"

"Good morning, François. I'll have grilled shrimp over a bed of crisp spinach, and a bottle of Bling." I really wasn't hungry, but a nice refreshing bottle of water would hopefully soothe the gnawing in my stomach caused by all the stress of not hearing from Justice. I hadn't really eaten much since last Thursday, and had dropped another four pounds, which absolutely made my mother jump with joy this morning.

"For the lovely lady," François said, winking at me, "coming right up. Good to have you back."

And for the first time all day, I smiled. François was the only person I truly liked at this school. "Merci," I replied in French.

But my smile was quickly snatched from my lips the minute I heard, "Heeeeeeeeeeey, Miss Lonnnndon." I glanced over at the table on the left side of me and there was Co-Co Ming, giving me a phony finger wave. He wore a purple and pink Versace print shirt and khaki men's dress pants with a pink tie. "Welcome back from that beat-down." I rolled my eyes. He continued, "Lonnnnnnnnndon, daaaaaaarling. Smile for the camera, click, click, click."

As he snapped a picture of me, I shot him a look that said *Not today. As a matter of fact, not ever!*

"Ooooops," he gasped theatrically. "Clutchin' pearls, clutchin' pearls." He tossed his pink Mohawk from side to side and he reminded me of a peacock. The whole table laughed at his antics. *What an effen cream puff!* I despised that boy, or whatever he was.

I kept on walking, passing the side-eyed glances as I made my way toward our table, daring anyone to say something slick. I stopped dead in my tracks. As if my day couldn't get any worse. *WTF?! Oh, hell no!*

I couldn't believe my eyes. Rich was posted up at our table with Spencer, cackling and giggling like they were reunited and had found their way back to being the best of friends again. They had already ordered and were eating—*without* me!

I blinked. This was not what I expected to walk up on; the two of them breaking bread and getting along! I know we were all *supposed* to pretend that we liked each other for appearance's sake, but the two of them were taking it too far. They looked like they were really enjoying each other's company—a little too much!

I walked over and tapped my foot. "Oh, so this is why you didn't meet me at the lockers?"

Rich huffed, placing her fork on her plate. She dabbed at her mouth with her napkin. "Meet you? Girlie, please. The last time I saw you, you put me out of your house because a cutie walked through the door; remember that?"

"Oh, Rich, please. You didn't meet me because you had a cackle and caw appointment with this dizzy—"

"No, no, no," Spencer said, wagging a lobster tail at me. "Don't go there, you giant panda. If you want to get poached, you got the right one. We were having a good time without you. And we don't need your fever up in here. So if you're tryna get it hot, you had better spin around on your padded paws and high-step it up on into the rubber room, and go release your crazy." She turned to Rich. "Because we're not what, Rich?"

"Havin' it," Rich answered, snapping her fingers.

They both fell out laughing.

I rapidly blinked my eyes. I felt like I was thrown into a time capsule and sent back to last Monday when I had to confront those little Starlet hoes. This couldn't be Rich turning on me; not like this. Oh no. This had to be an imposter.

I shifted my handbag from one hand to the other, then placed a hand on my hip. "You know what? If I have to walk out of here and come back, it's only to see if this situation is really real. 'Cause the last I checked, *Rich*"—I paused, then neck rolled it—"you said Spencer was a mouth-whore, blowing out mono like it was a breath mint."

"Oh, really?" Spencer snapped, neck-rolling it back at me. "Well, the last I checked, *London*, Rich said you were real quick to block somebody's bump 'n' grind. A jealous freak is what she called you. Mad 'cause you couldn't get any action. Had a cutie up in your room and you tried to boom-boom rock him for yourself, and he wasn't even stroking, I mean checking, for you, *L-Boogie*."

Rich giggled.

I felt weak at the knees.

"And like Rich said," Spencer continued, "your boyfriend Doctor Corny, the Mad Rapper, wannabe skankster... wiggy-wiggy whack! So don't come over here trying to do me 'cause you will be done, hon. You will be baked, fried, and boiled alive."

Co-Co walked by and snapped, "Owwwwl, who shotcha? Boom-boom, popped ya? Lonnnnnndon, pick your face up, boo."

Spencer continued on as if Co-Co were invisible. "Then she got the nerve to go by some *C-Smoove*. Ha, yeah, right. He can't be all that *smoove* romping around in the forest playing with endangered species."

I frowned. "Ditz-ball, who and what are you talking about?"

She huffed, raising her voice. "I'm talking about your

boyfriend, *C-Smoove*; and you, panda, aren't you and your relatives on the world's most endangered species list?"

Co-Co gasped. *"You're* C-Smoove's girlfriend? Oh. My. God. I think I'm going to be sick!"* Before I could ask him what the hell he meant by that, he quickly swished off in his purple kitten heels, leaning over and clutching his stomach as if he were about to toss up his lunch.

"What was that all about?" Rich asked no one in particular. And of course she didn't wait for anyone to answer. "Ummph, Co-Co has some serious issues. You know his father threw him out. Yup, tossed him and his kitten heels right on out into the streets. Ummph. I wish Richard Montgomery would. He knows I would turn it out. Boom-boom, bop him right upside his head."

"Oh, Rich," Spencer said, taking a sip of her kiwi smoothie. "The only thing you like to boom-bop up on is a boy's"—she giggled—"oh, never mind. But, ummm, excuse me," she said, looking me over, "and who are you?"

I was sick of that girl. Her mouth was too slick for my liking. I felt like tossing the table up. And before I knew it, I had lunged at her and cocked my hand in her face like it was a gun. I was ready to beat her upside the head. "Slut, I will beat your face in."

Spencer slid her hand down into her bag. And before I knew it, she had whipped out an Altoids tin, set it up on the table, then popped it open. She eyed me, then dumped the tin upside down. BB gun pellets rolled all over the table. "Do it, boo," she said, laying a BB gun next to the tin. "Make my day, panda." She patted the handle. "And I will stunt your growth. You will be picking pellets out of them big kneecaps of yours, Buffalo Billy."

Rich jumped up from the table. "Now wait. Y'all don't

need to be arguing over me. Spencer, put that away; there's no need for violence. Say no to guns, boo. See, this is why we can't stay out of the headlines for more than five seconds. Y'all don't know how to act. We need to get along. Both of you need to stop being so selfish. It's only one of me. Not even on my best day am I two people. Now, London...Sit down and rest your feet. We don't need all of this tension."

"Yeah," Spencer said, smirking. "Sit down and park them hoofs."

Rich sprawled out over the table, hollering and laughing at the top of her lungs. "Bwwaaaaaahahahaha. Ohmygod, ohmygod, ohmygod! I can't breathe! Bwwaaaaaahahahahaha! No you didn't tell her to park her hoofs, girl. Bwaaaaaahahahaha. You are crazy!"

I couldn't believe this. That ho had turned on me. Rich was a two-faced, backstabbing slut-bucket.

I set my bag on the table, folding my arms across my chest. Okay, I was pouting, so what! Rich had no right to laugh at me like that. "Haha, hell. I don't see anything funny."

Rich finally pulled herself together, then looked over at Spencer and said, "Now, Spencer, that wasn't nice. But for real, London, I am upset with you for how you treated me the other day. You didn't have to embarrass me like that in front of Sexy Chocolate."

I pulled out a chair and took a seat. Just the thought of her calling my man some Sexy Chocolate had knotted my stomach. This ho was relentless. She was a walking poster for an Easy Lay commercial. I mean really. She should have been a mattress, as easy as she was to lie on. Freak!

I needed damage control before this whole situation turned uglier than what it already was. Spencer was winning her back, and I couldn't have that. I sighed. "Rich, honestly, I didn't mean for it to happen like that. And I really don't need for you to be mad at me right now."

Rich eyed me, then pursed her lips. She pushed out a deep sigh. "Well, all right. I guess I can forgive you, *this* time. But don't let it happen again. The King Herman version of the Bible says—"

"Ugh," Spencer said, shaking her head. "Rich, everybody knows it's King Henry."

I rolled my eyes, disgusted. *They were both idiots.* "It's King James."

Rich rolled her eyes back at me. "Whatever. King Herman, King James, or whoever else he might be, says in the Bible to forgive like seven times"—she reached into her bag and pulled out a pink leather-bound notebook, then flipped through a few pages—"and right about now, London, you are working on forgiveness number four. See," she said, pointing to a page in her notebook. "Right here is where I'm going to add this one 'cause I gotta keep track of what you hoes do to me."

She pulled out a pen and started writing as she spoke. "Monday at twelve thirty-seven, London was forgiven, once again. And I really don't know why I keep forgiving her. I'm waaaaaaay too kind. And, although I really wanna get it crunked, I have to do right and stay true to what the Bible says." She snapped her book shut, then looked up at me. "I don't know why I have to keep telling you that I worship in the Church of Stay-Fly-And-Be-A-Lady-At-All-Times, so I don't know why you keep testing my religion. But, I tell you what. If you act right, London, for the next sixty days I'll knock off one of your violations."

Spencer giggled. "Well, since I won't be popping kneecaps and busting veins out the side of panda's neck today, I guess I should collect my bullets." She picked up all but one and placed them back in her tin. "This one's for you," she said, sliding it over to me. "As a souvenir to remind you what happens when you skid out of your lane. But, anyway, welcome back to school."

"Isn't this like your third suspension since the first day of school?" Rich asked, shaking her head as she cut into her crab cake. She rolled her eyes up in her head as if she were having an orgasm. "Oooooh, this is soooo delish. Mmmmph, makes me wanna slap somebody." She finished chewing, then said, "Giiiiiirl, I don't mean no harm. But looks to me like you have some behavioral issues."

Spencer agreed. "Uh-huh, straitjacket crazy."

Rich chuckled. "But for real, London, you really need to get it together." She opened her notebook again, pointing to the top of a page. She started reading from a list. "Number one, you have issues with your parents; two, can't keep your hands to yourself, constantly suspended; three, you keep having man problems; four, you're sexually backed up, can't get none; five, you're jealous of me. And I thought we were besties. Six, don't know how to treat your bestie; seven..."

I was stunned. I couldn't believe this delusional trick actually thought I was jealous of her. And then she had the audacity to be keeping tabs on me. Good thing I didn't throw away the notebook I kept on her. It was as thick as a phone book with all the shenanigans and stunts she pulled.

Spencer sighed. "Ohsweetcreamylovebiscuits, London, you're even more messed up than I thought."

"Wait a minute," I snapped. "This is not Pick on London Day."

Rich smacked her lips. "You're right. It's Forgive London for the Two Hundred and Sixty-Seventh Time Day, that's what this is. But, whatever." She slammed her book shut. "You finally get it. It's not all about you."

She eyed me as the waiter placed my food in front of me. I lifted the silver cover and stuck my fork into a shrimp, then slipped it into my mouth. "Anyway, what were the two of you over here laughing about before I walked over? I know y'all weren't laughing at me."

Spencer waved me on. "Oh, musty rabbit, please. You're not that funny for us to be laughing at you."

"Then what was so funny?" I picked at a piece of spinach with my fork, then placed it in my mouth. I forced it down, then took a sip of water. "Let me in on the joke 'cause from what I saw it looked like the two of you were having a grand ole time."

Rich clapped her hands. "See. There you go, acting all jealous again. This is what I'm talking about." She opened her book again. "Now I gotta add another—"

"Rich, shut that book and stop writing crap in it about me. Geesh."

"Mmmph, yeah, 'cause if she doesn't she's going to run out of numbers," Spencer said, clasping her manicured hands in front of her. She eyed me, then looked over at Rich. "Umm, Rich, can we trust her enough to keep a secret?"

I blinked.

Rich looked me over, then twisted her lips up. "Yeah, I guess we can. So you want me to tell her, or you?"

"No, girl, you can tell her," Spencer said, pulling out

her compact, then checking her face. Conceited ho! "She's your cheerleader. Pom-pom away." She applied a fresh coat of lip gloss, then snapped her compact shut.

Rich leaned in and looked over her shoulder to make sure no one else was around. "You know that masked woman that has security on high-alert around here?"

"Yeah. The one that attacked those two Starlets?"

Rich nodded. "Uh-huh. Here's your criminal right here." She pointed over at Spencer, who popped her collar.

"Whaaaaaat?!" I asked, shocked. "You two did *whaaaat?*"

"Girl, will you keep it down. Your mouth is too loud. That's why we didn't wanna tell you. That's another one of your problems. Your mouth's too big."

"Mmmhmm, Project Loud," Spencer added. "Write that down, Rich."

"Oh, you already know I'm on it," Rich said as she opened her book. "Loudmouth strikes again. Tried to tell London something and she got all—"

"Rich, please," I snapped. She was a split second from getting whopped upside her head. I was trying my damndest to be patient, but she was really wearing my nerves thin. It's bad enough I had to stomach watching her and Spencer laugh it up, acting all bestie-bestie. And now I had to put up with her and that notebook. "Will you get back to the story?"

"Don't rush me, London," she huffed. "Are you going to eat the rest of them shrimp?" I frowned, sliding my plate to her. She popped two shrimp into her mouth. "Oooh, yes. Next time I need to get these. Delish." She popped another one in her mouth. My God, she was a cow!

"Rich, the story, please . . ."

She took a sip of her drink, then wiped her mouth. "Are you going to keep it down so I can finish telling my story or am I"—Spencer pulled out duct tape and slid it over to Rich—"going to have to seal your trap shut?"

I rolled my eyes. "My lips are sealed. Cross my heart and hope to die, stick a needle in my eye."

Spencer tilted her head. "Is that a dare? Don't tempt me."

Rich snickered.

"You know what? I'm about tired of this little unexpected clique the two of you seem to have formed. Y'all acting like I'm not even here. And, Rich, you're really getting your Benedict Arnold on."

"Ummph. I see you passed your history test. Annnnnyway, as I was saaaaying, before you got all psycho and sensitive on me. We marched over to the other side of campus and snatched two of the Starlets up..."

"Wait," I said, surprised. "Y'all went over there to fight those hoes for me?"

Rich frowned. "For *you*? Girl, please. No. I went over there because they were popping trash about *me*. What I look like, tryna fight your battles? Ummph. I still can't understand how you let four little munchkin sluts beat you down in the first place. That makes no sense to me, but whatever. You're gon' have to wear that, boo."

"Yup," Spencer chimed in. "And wear it well. And aren't you like sixty feet tall? I mean, there's no reason they should have been able to climb up on your back like that. Even if they stood up on each other's shoulders to fight you, you still should have been able to handle them. I mean, really? What kind of giraffe are you?"

Rich shook her head, giving me a sad look. "Girl, it's a disgrace to the Pampered Princesses' code of ethics."

Spencer agreed. "Yup, it says: Thou shall not ever catch a beat-down by a bunch of underclass hoes."

"What the hell are the two of you talking about? It was four of them against me!"

"Anyyywaaaay," Rich continued, dismissing me with the flick of a hand. She reached for the rest of my shrimp and popped them into her mouth, two at a time. I frowned. "The whole thing was my idea, of course. 'Cause you know Spencer's limited. She has *real special* on lock, so you know she wasn't going to be the mastermind behind it."

"Wait a ding-dong minute," Spencer snapped, slamming a hand down on the table. "I know you're not trying to turn tricks up in here on me..."

"Clutching pearls," Rich said, grabbing her neck. "I don't turn tricks, I turn 'em out. Pow!" She jumped up and pumped her hips. "Get your facts right. The only trick in the room is you, boo. Now go suck on that." She snapped her fingers, then sat back in her seat.

I laughed, relieved that they were starting to turn on each other. Breaking their little party up was going to be easier than I thought.

Spencer waved her on, laughing. "See, if I wasn't in such good spirits, I would reach my hand down in your mouth and snatch out your black, rusty tongue, then yank out your tonsils and wear them like teardrop earrings. So be thankful I'm feeling good today. Now get back to telling the story before the next news headline is about you losing your mouth guts."

I had to bite down on my tongue to keep from laughing. That girl was a nut. Normally I would jump right on in and Rich and I would tag-team Spencer up one side and down the other. But today, like Rich told me, she was on her own. She'd have to wear whatever Spencer dished out to her.

She eyed me. "London, I know you're not over there laughing at me."

I sipped my water. "Nope, not at all," I said, smirking.

"Good," she snapped, twisting her lips up, then sliding her straw into her mouth. She took another slow sip of her drink. "So, anyway...Spencer and I masked up and went hood on them. I dragged and gagged that Arabia, well...um, not until after I dropped my number down into my bosom and told her boo to come get it. Bang-bang, baby."

"And when you finally woke from that dream," Spencer stated, rolling her eyes, "you were standing in your own puddle of piss while I was doing all of the work. So liar, liar, your feet are on fire. All you did was shake in your heels and scream, then you ran out like some scaredy cat. You probably tore your panty liner up, too."

I frowned. *Ugh, how gross! Some of the nastiest things come out of this guzzler's mouth.*

"That's going too far, Spencer. I wear thongs. Make it clap, baby. Booyah! Now get your facts straight. Now baaaaaaack to what I was saying..."

Thankfully, the lunch bell rang before she could finish her story of lies. And it's a good thing because a) I was getting sick of watching those two superhoes chopping it up like long lost besties; and b) I didn't believe one word coming out of Rich's hot, filthy mouth because she auto-tuned the truth, like she was Rihanna. But exaggerator and whore or not, she was still my best friend, and Spencer was the frenemy. So Rich stayed, but Spencer had to go.

I watched as the two of them stood up and air-kissed on both cheeks, then hugged. I wanted to gag. Then to add insult to injury, Rich had the nerve to say, "All right now, boo, martinis after school. Meet me at the Kit-Kat Lounge. London, I know you won't be going since you're on lockdown. So, we'll send you a postcard."

I blinked.

"Oooh, love it, boo," Spencer said, grabbing her bag, then tossing it up over her shoulder. She narrowed her eyes at me, then walked up on me and whispered real low, "I see the hate in your eyes, Trashy.com. But I'm warning you. Try to come between Rich and me again, and I'm going to Nair your lashes off. And you better hope that's all I do. Now toodles, Low Money. Don't get your hate up, get your cake up."

She strutted off, her curls bouncing and hips swinging as I stood there with my mouth dropped open. Okay, so I wasn't invited out to drinks with them—so what. Who cares?! I didn't want to go anyway. And so what if I was still on punishment! She could have still invited me. Eff her! They could go have their little night out on the town. Tricks! But, you best believe. If I didn't know anything else, I knew what I had to do. That friendship was coming to an end. I was shutting it down, quick!

"Rich," I called out, fast on her heels. "Wait up."

15

Spencer

Anderson had swooped me up in the air in his helicopter this afternoon, then gently landed on the helipad of his family's three-level yacht, *Buff Daddy*. Here it was two weeks since that godawful night in Santa Barbara and I was still having trouble shaking that nightmarish image of him with his tongue stuffed down London's gullet.

And every time I had to look at her big face at school, it made me want to slice off them sumptuous lips of hers and fling them to the crows.

God I hate that ratchet moose!

I still couldn't believe that I, in a moment of weakness—something I rarely ever had—became vulnerable and broke down in tears, telling Kitty the next morning everything I had seen the night before, and how it had devastated me.

Kitty's voice ricocheted up against my brain as I inhaled the ocean breeze. I gripped the railing, replaying our conversation in my head. A scowl had been painted on her face, her tone laced with disgust. *"Tears?* You have got to be kidding me! My God, Spencer, no! Please tell me you are *not* crying over some boy who was never going to be yours..."

Yeah, I knew his arrangement with Amazon. That her mother and his were sorority sisters and belonged to the same high society circles, that their mothers hatched the idea to play matchmaker a year ago, promising that he and Queen Kong would get married. And their fathers agreed that it's the only way either one of them will get their inheritances. Whatever! And, yeah, he told me what the rules of engagement were. That as long as I went along with the program, we'd spend time together. I was expected to not try to put claims on him. Well, guess what? Rules were made to be broken, goshdang it! And I wanted to break every one of them with him. London didn't deserve him. I did.

But Anderson was playing me. And I didn't take too kindly to anyone playing me like I was some old hand-me-down handbag.

Here I was on this magnificent yacht, standing by the railing out on the deck, glancing up at the sky, trying like heck to enjoy myself. This was supposed to be a romantic night alone with Anderson and all I kept thinking about was him pawing and gnawing all over that furry-faced llama.

I couldn't erase the image of the two of them out of my head.

I stared out at the Pacific Ocean. *How could he do this to me?*

I blinked back tears as Kitty's voice continued to invade my thoughts.

* * *

Stop this!" she had snapped, grabbing me by the cheeks with one hand. Her eyes turned dark and ugly. This was a side of Kitty I rarely ever saw. "I will not have this. Do you hear me? None of it! I don't give a hot damn if that boy kissed the inside of Oprah's thighs, you don't ever, ever, drop one ounce of saltwater, or ruin good eyeliner, over a man; especially one that you should have only been borrowing in the first place. You were supposed to toy with him, pleasure yourself, then discard him like last night's news, *not* catch feelings. Have you not learned anything from me? Someone hurts you, you don't drop tears, you drop bombs, darling. Blow 'em up on the spot, then toss their bleeding carcass out in the streets for the world to see. Do you understand?"

"But he kissed her..." I kept saying over and over.

Slap!

I grabbed my face in shock. Kitty had never slapped me before. She grabbed me by the shoulders and wildly shook me. "Spencer, pull yourself together here. Look at you. You're a sniveling, snot-nosed mess! And I am appalled. It's so unbecoming. And not anything Kitty Ellington would ever associate with. Tears are for the weak and incompetent. You're not weak. And you're not incompetent. And I will not have you carrying on as such. I will not have it, I say. We don't do tears, dear. We do terror. We wreak havoc and turn worlds upside down. That's what we do..."

She placed a hand to her chest. "This right here, seeing my only daughter crying, hurts me down to my core..." She paused, holding back what I thought was a set of her own tears.

At that moment, I felt like maybe Kitty really did care about me. Ha! Wishful thinking!

She let go of me. "I had no business leaving you with Vera, that ole backward coot—love her dearly, but she has ruined you. All she's ever really been good for is cooking and cleaning. And God only knows what hanging with them pampered messes you run with has done to you. I did this all wrong. I see now that letting you come back home was a big mistake. When you got expelled from Le Rosey I should have immediately shipped you off to Singapore or Bora Bora. Sweet heavens! I thought I could trust you to be responsible. How could I have let this happen? How could I have been so foolish?

"I'm trying to run an empire and crush the competition, but obviously I need to put all that on hold because you don't seem to know how to handle being a woman. My God! I thought I did right by you by giving you free rein of this house and letting you raise yourself. But I see now I made an awful mistake thinking I could trust you to handle your business. This is utterly absurd, and unacceptable, Spencer. You have literally lost your mind. And I will not stand for it!"

I blinked. I couldn't believe what had fallen from out of her mouth. I was distressed and all she gave a dang about was her precious empire.

Damn her!

And damn Anderson!

Her voice continued ringing in my head. "I'm going to tell you this only once, Spencer dear, so listen up. And listen up well. You are only as hot as your last headline. So you had better lace up your corset, don your stilettos, and seduce the enemy. Conceal your intentions with your cunning ways, get into their heads, learn their weaknesses, find out their deepest secrets, then when they least expect it, you strike full force! You bring them to their knees."

"But what if I can't? What if I am not able to uncover any of their dirty deeds?"

She tilted her head. "You're an Ellington. There are no what-ifs. But just in case you screw it up, you had better have your bags packed because I'm shipping you off to the wilds of Africa to roam the jungles with your father. Now, shut off them godawful tears and go get me a story so juicy and scandalous that it'll shut all of Hollywood down..."

I blinked.

Kitty's right! I need to get down and dirty and get my ammo up.

I touched the exquisite Cartier diamond necklace Anderson had given me at dinner and forced a smile. I had to play it cool. I needed to seize the moment. Then bring him to his knees. I needed to crush the enemy! But the dang truth was, although I was seething, I still wanted Anderson... naked and handcuffed to the bed!

He came up behind me and lifted my hair to kiss the back of my neck. I still hadn't had sex with him, which was another thing burning a hole in my love bucket and had me thinking he was up to no good with that London. "What are you out here thinking about, gum drop?"

Shutting your world down, you no-good grizzly!

"You," I said, smirking.

"You smell good," he murmured, nuzzling and cranking up the heat stirring inside of me.

This boy doesn't know, I will do a Rich on him and peel his face back, then sauté his eyeballs.

Feeling Anderson's body pressed in back of me slowly softened my angry heart a pinch. So before I pulled out my sharpened cutlery and rearranged his face, I decided I was going to give him one more chance to redeem himself. Then I'd try to forgive him for kissing that mongoose.

Anderson kissed me again, then his hands snaked around my waist. "You're my sexy gum drop, with your sweet, sassy self. You feel so good in my arms, Spencer."

Is that what you told Moose Face the night you were cleaning her tonsils?

"I could really fall for you, love. You're so beautiful."

Oh my...

Well, I know you didn't tell her she was beautiful...

"You don't know what you do to me, baby."

Ohhhh, Anderson. Show me, daddy. Show momma how much I mean to you.

I closed my eyes and silently prayed.

Oh, heavenlysexgoddess who swings so high...I beg of you...Please let this boy glide his big, warm hands down into my goodies.

Anderson removed his hands from around my waist. I couldn't believe it. What in the sneezy-jeezy was going on here?

Strike one!

Why was Anderson not pawing at me? What in the whoopty-do was this world coming to?

I took a deep breath. *Okay, calm down. Maybe he's a little shy*, my inner sex goddess suggested. *You know how some boys are. Slow to the start, but quick to the finish. Give him a moment to get his nerve up.*

He turned me to face him, then kissed me gently on the lips. He stared at me. "You're so beautiful, gum drop."

You already said that, idiot. Rip my clothes off!

I batted my lashes. He kissed me on the lips again. "And so sexy, baby." He pulled me closer into him. And I could feel…oh my! My mouth started watering and every nerve ending started tingling. And just that quick I almost forgot he had been caught sucking face with Amazon. Maybe I was going to get my strudel tossed and pulled apart after all.

"Come," he insisted, taking me by the hand and leading me toward the stairs that led back down into the cabin. "Let's call it a night. I want to take you to bed and hold you in my arms."

I grinned. *Ohhhhkay, daddy…Now we're cooking with grease!*

I swung my hips into seduction mode as we made our way through the living room, then down a hall. Anderson opened a door on the right, then flipped on a light. "This is the master quarters," he said, standing back to let me in. "Welcome."

I gasped, stepping into the cabin. It was huge, with a private balcony that gave you a spectacular private view of the ocean. All types of lusty, wanton thoughts fluttered through my head as I imagined us out on the balcony, naked.

There was a huge, fluffy four-poster bed without a canopy in the center of the cabin, a matching chest of drawers on one side of the room, and an ivory chaise lounge in the corner. Yes, there was plenty of room to play!

Still, I should have known some things were simply too good to be true when Anderson stated he was going to hop in the shower—alone—then wait for me in bed. But I ignored the warning that this was a misguided missile about to tear right through my fairy-tale ending.

We started going at it like wild beasts in heat. His hands went up my flyaway, then...his cell phone rang.

"Spencer, hold up," Anderson said breathlessly. "Wait, wait..."

"Noooo," I growled in between my kissing and pawing him. "I've waited long enough."

I smiled when he let it roll into voice mail. But then it rang again, and again, and again until he pushed me off of him, reaching for his cell on the nightstand and climbing out of bed.

"Uh, yeah...what? Are you okay? Calm down...you have to stop putting yourself through all this...I'm out of town...okay, I'll be there...give me thirty minutes..." He disconnected the call, then turned to me. "Look, get your clothes on. We have to go."

I blinked in disbelief. *"Go?"* I glanced over at the clock. It was 3:27 A.M. "Are you kidding me? At *this* time in the morning? Why? We have unfinished business."

He started shuffling around the room, getting dressed. "Nah, our business is done. London needs me."

London?

That beeeyotch!

Instantly, tears sprang from my eyes. I had never felt so humiliated in my entire teen life. No boy had ever turned me down. Not even the headmaster's nineteen-year-old son, Jacque, at Le Rosey—my old boarding school in Switzerland—was able to deny me. He soon fell for my seductive charm and quickly forgot that I was only thirteen. Yes, it had stirred up quite a scandal for the prestigious school, but it was well worth it. I had kept my eye on the prize and had gotten my mark. But Anderson had rejected me. He had shooed me away—like some crusty-lipped smack-whore in tore-up heels—for Miss Monkey Butt.

He frowned. "Why are you standing there crying?"

"Look at me, goshdangit!" I yelled, my arms flying everywhere in exasperation. I was a split second from spinning around and turning into the Nutty Princess and tearing his dang yacht up. "I'm pissed, that's why. I've been more than patient with you, Anderson. I've deleted all of my playoffs in my phone, for you..."

He gave me a quizzical look.

I threw a hand up on my hip. "Don't stand there with that blank look on your face, like you don't know what I'm talking about, Anderson. You're the only one I'm see-ing. I went through my phone and deleted all of my goody-bag calls because I want to be with you, and only you. You've been leading me on for weeks, using me. And I'm sick of it!"

"Now, hold on here. You're reaching way over the top now. I'm not after you for sex, and I have a ton of money. So using you is far from the truth. And I've never lied to you. You knew my situation from the beginning. I told you not to try to put claims on me. You knew I was involved with London. And you knew the reason why. Now you're standing here trying to flip the script." He reached for me. "You agreed to this, gum drop."

I pushed his hands away. I wasn't trying to hear any-thing he had to say. "Don't you 'gum drop' me, you...you dream snatcher! You...you lowdown, dirty, cooter-teaser. I should slash your dang wheels, split your sockets, run down your ankles..."

There must have been a crazed look in my eyes because he stepped back, holding his arms out. "Whoa, calm down, Spencer. There's no need to get all psycho on me."

I ripped open my flyaway baby-doll, exposing my naked melons. "Psycho? I'll show you psycho! Look at all of this goodness, Anderson! What boy wouldn't want me?" I turned around and smacked my come-get-'em and shook it, glancing over my shoulder. "What boy wouldn't want all of this bang-'em-up, huh?" I faced him, scowling, trying to keep my tears in check. But they were spouting like an angry faucet. I was falling apart. This boy didn't want me. And I didn't know how to handle that. It was all new to me. Not the feelings of rejection, because I had already experienced that from Kitty. And not the aching feeling of being unwanted, because Kitty had shown me what that was like, too. No. This feeling of desperation—desperate to be touched and loved and wanted—was cutting into my heart. And Anderson had taken the blade and twisted it. But I refused to go down without a fight.

Snapshots of him kissing down that walrus in her car flashed through my head and I felt myself about to spin into the Nutty Princess. No, this boy was really playing me. And I didn't appreciate it.

I'm such a fool! This boy doesn't even want me. He'd rather eat a sloppy Big Mac than have a sweet, juicy peach!

I was pissed. I was confused.

I snapped an arm up on my hip, narrowing my eyes. "Are you having sex with Amazon?"

"Who?"

I huffed. "London. Are you waxing her beaver? Rolling your hot dog in her buns?"

I held my breath again. I could possibly forgive him for kissing that beast on the mouth, but sleeping with that thing would be unforgiveable.

He glowered. "Not that it's really any of your business, but no. London and I haven't slept together."

I silently blew out a sigh of relief. "And Bigfoot hasn't tried to highjack your boxers, not once?"

He gave me a frustrated look. "I told you, no."

Well heehawthewitch's-seesaw, Queen Kong is wound up tighter than a corn husk.

I still don't trust you, Anderson Ford! "Mmmph, well, what in the world is wrong with Prudezilla? Is she a lipstick butcher?"

He bunched his brows together in confusion. I sucked my teeth. "Is Queen Kong a man? I mean, she's kinda strong and muscular like one. I bet she's on steroids, too." I paused for a beat, blinking my lashes. Then it hit me. She was a man! "I knew it! I knew she was a fraudulent whisker-having hyena with a jimmy bat and golf balls tucked between her legs."

He shot me an aggravated look. "Look, enough of this. I've told you more than once to not call London names, Spencer. It's juvenile and tasteless. Now get dressed. Or get left."

I blinked back the sting of his tone. My lips quivered. "Oh, so she calls and you go throwing on your big red cape to play Captain Trash Man? London calls you crying and you jump to her rescue. Well, go collect your trash, Mister Trash Saver!"

He threw my overnight bag on the bed. "Look, I'm not playing with you, Spencer. Get effen dressed. And I mean it."

I jumped, ready to attack him, then froze. The blood from my face started draining down into my gut. I clasped a hand over my mouth, feeling sick. I took several deep breaths to steady my nerves, glaring at him. It all made sense to me now. Why he really didn't want to end it with that walrus, why he had his tongue shoved down her throat, why he didn't want to have sex with me, why he was running off to rescue that bat...oh God! It had nothing to do with his trust.

"You're in love with *her*," I blurted out.

"*What?* In love with who?"

"That whore, London! You're in love with that pie-faced dragon. I know you are."

"Wait..." He paused, putting a hand up, then pulled in his bottom lip. He stared at me as if he was repulsed. "You know what? All this name calling is uncalled for. London isn't a whore. And she doesn't deserve that from you."

"London doesn't deserve that?!" I sneered. "What about *me*? I don't deserve being dismissed. What does she have that I don't?"

"Me," he said nastily. "And for you to think otherwise proves to me that you're crazier than I thought. Because the only thing you'll ever be is the sidepiece. And the sooner you realize that, the better."

My lips quivered. "But—"

He frowned at me. "Hurry up and get dressed before I forget I'm a gentleman and tell you to get home the best way you know how. The sight of you is making me sick." He walked out, slamming the door behind him.

Ohsweetmermaidflippersandfins...he's willing to toss me overboard like shark bait for that...that she-man!

I stood there in horror. He had turned on me! Tears flooded my eyes as I snatched my bag off the bed and stormed into the bathroom, slamming the door. I gritted my teeth. Come hell or high heavens, Anderson and his sixty-foot mammal-faced Amazon were about to be destroyed!

16

Rich

It was an honest mistake. Falling in love...and being in love...this long with Knox. We were meant to be a hit-it-'n'-quit-it type of thing.

Something to satisfy our puppy crushes and kick the playground game of Kiss-A-Girl-Get-A-Girl up a notch.

Upgrade to friends with midnight benefits who rode shotgun through the city, acting silly.

Then leave each other alone.

Quit the pursuit. And abandon it next to the monkey bars and the chalky game of hopscotch.

But we didn't...

He wouldn't let it go...

I couldn't let it go...

And somehow we got caught up in our kisses tasting like licorice. Our love tasting like smooth, rich, and addictive Sugar Babies. And somehow—in the midst of all of this—we formed this crazy desire to boo-love.

How sick.

And then we upped the pillow talk from sweet nothings to daily convos filled with laughter. Confessions. Secrets... We knew each other's favorite color.

Favorite food to eat.

Favorite thing to do.

What made the other smile...

Cry...

Lie...

Then we started ruling each other's thoughts and becoming a part of what the other dreamed.

Whack.org.

Knox was supposed to be my buddy. We were meant to be fly, not each other's valentines. This whole deal was played.

I mean, I did a lot of things, but one thing I didn't do was love. Why? Because Rich Montgomery was never-ever-ever supposed to get caught up.

Y.O.L.O. was my motto. And since I knew you only lived once, I was determined to do it up! Love 'em and leave 'em. Not get dumped.

Not cry every night before I cut the lights out.

This was some bull.

"Excuse me, Miss Rich, can I get you another drink?" Startled me. My eyes popped open wide and I remembered that I wasn't home curled up in the corner of my bed, crying my eyes out. I was in Santa Barbara at the exclusive Kit-Kat Lounge, sitting at the glass bar with my fake ID tucked in my purse, on the same bar stool where I'd been every night this week after school, drowning my misery in beer, hot wings, and blue cheese sauce. I was pretty much shuttin' the lounge down.

How anticlimactic was that?

I pushed my hair behind my ears and said, "Yeah, Johnnie. I'll have a pitcher of beer, off the tap. And, umm, another platter of hot wings. Extra sauce."

I watched Johnnie—a short, spray-tanned-orange man with bright red highlights in his hair—walk away. Half of the time he looked at me with loaded eyes, as if he had a million thoughts about me on his mind. But he didn't dare express an unsolicited thought to me. Because if he did, trust, that would give me just the psychotic reason I needed to lose it!

Johnnie disappeared from behind the illuminated glass bar and through the black leather double swinging doors, where the five-star kitchen was.

The Kit-Kat Lounge had become my favorite hideaway. A place where I could outrun everything and everyone—my friends, the media, my fans, my parents...

The one-room club was a sexy and elite atmosphere. Only the very wealthy and the politically connected were allowed in here. The walls were painted a sleek onyx and the ceiling was a starched, virgin white. The floors were made of albino bamboo and in the corners of the room were white leather couches and square glass tables. In the center of the room was a stage, where signed and unsigned artists performed. Along the sides of the stage were petite glass tables with black blown-glass chairs. And at the front of the room was the clear-glass bar with black leather high-back stools and me...drowning my misery.

This is crazy...

I have to get it together...

But I miss him...

But that doesn't mean I have to chase him...

True.

I took a gulp of my frosted pitcher of beer that Johnnie had set on the table next to my hot wings. *I don't chase boys...*

They chase me.

Yeah right...

In an effort to shut my miserable mind up I shoved a hot wing in my mouth and licked the excess sauce off my fingers.

This was so anti–Rich Montgomery.

Jazmine Sullivan's "Lions, Tigers, and Bears" filled the air and immediately a sore knot wedged its way into my throat.

I was a mess.

And all I could think was that God had to really have a problem with me.

I wish I could talk to my mother...but she hates me...

"Hey, girlie!" scared the hell outta me and almost caused me to fall off of my nightly bar stool.

OMG. It can't be.

"It's me!"

Jesus, please don't let this be...

"It's Spencer!"

Oh my God...what is she doing here...?

Spencer stood next to me, looked me over, and gave me her classic stupid, lost-in-space smile. Then she took her bony fingers and slid my platter of hot wings and blue cheese sauce down to the opposite end of the bar and away from me. "Ick." She frowned.

Deep breath in...

Deep breath out...

"Eww, who's doing hot wings?" She popped her glossy lips and grimaced. "All that cholesterol," she said like a controlling health nut. "And Rich," she carried on, oblivious to me looking at her like she was crazy as hell, "who dumped that fried-stroke-on-a-plate in front of you? And then they left their bones there? And I mean they are sucked down clean."

She would notice something being sucked down.

"Right down to the gristle." She tossed her hair over her shoulder. "Oh my. And that white snot—"

"Spencer—"

"Scandalous."

"Spencer—"

"Classless and inconsiderate. And why are you interrupting me? How rude is that?"

"Spencer!" I pounded my fist on the bar, shaking my empty pitcher of beer. "What. Are. You. Doing. Here? Who invited you here?" I was clearly confused. And pissed. Talk about an invasion!

"Who invited me here? Are you still trying to strike out and be a comedian, Rich? Because, umm, you invited me."

Duh! I knew I invited her here. But she had to know I didn't mean it. Like really, she knew we were making a fool out of London. I had no desire to see her face after school ended.

Spencer tapped on the bar, getting Johnnie's attention. "Bartender!" She snapped her fingers. "Come. And get these hot-nasty-heart-flamin'-wings and bring us a spinach salad and cottage cheese."

I almost threw up in my mouth. Spinach who? And cottage what? I didn't do spinach and the only cottage I did was in Aspen.

Johnnie picked up my wings and as he turned away

from the bar I snapped, "Johnnie, give me my wings back!"

Spencer gasped. "Your wings? Ohmygettin'jiggywit'it! Didn't you just overdose on Jenny Craig?"

I rolled my eyes toward the ceiling. "You know I'm supposed to be the teen spokesperson. And so what! Now is not the time to bring that up!"

"Gagging! You need to be ashamed of yourself. Unless of course they simply hired you for the before shots. Because there is no way you can be for after."

"Excuse you. *After* is written all over me."

"Correction. Bypass surgery and love handles are written all over you. Your stomach guts are on their way to being the size of a quarter. How gross. I can only imagine the headlines. SweetMarylovin'life, 'Pampered Princess Dead.' " She sat up on the bar stool to the right of me.

"Really, Spencer. You can't be serious right now."

"I'm just making a point. But hey, if you wanna die looking like the Kool-Aid man's wife then, Johnnie, let her have her wings. Because I'm not going to worry about you. I'll just have me a drink."

"Good. Now let me have my hot wing high and get my drink on in peace. This is probably where you and Heather went wrong. You don't know how to respect a girl's get-right."

Spencer raked her nails along the edge of my plate.

Screech! Oh no she didn't!

"You know what, Rich? I'm going to let that Heather comment go. But I'm warning you, don't bring her up again." She shot me a warning eye, as if I could give a damn.

"Gurl, bye!" I flicked my hand carelessly toward her face. "Chile, puhlease!" I reached for my frosted beer mug and took a long gulp, down to the last drop, plopped the mug on the counter and wiped the excess from my mouth with a finger.

Spencer gasped and stared at me. "SweetBiblestories I think I've seen a ghetto ghost."

A what?

"I need to clutch your pearls for you," she said in disbelief. "You are out of control! What's next—crack? When did you start drinking beer? You can't let Jenny Craig see you like this—"

"Eff Jenny Craig! I didn't like that nasty food anyway. I had my chef cook for me every night. He is the reason I lost weight. I stole him right from Oprah! So to hell with Jenny Craig. She can kiss my—"

"Rich, you know what? Having a dumpy behind is on you. What are you, like a size twenty-two anyway?"

I lowered the hot wing I'd just placed to my mouth. "I am a size twelve and I look good."

"Yeah." Spencer popped her lips. "Until you get up from that chair!"

"Anyway, Spencer, and why are you here?"

"I just told you that you invited me."

"I know I invited you. But I didn't really mean for you to come!"

Spencer batted her eyes as Johnnie handed her a drink. She took a sip, teased her stirrer, and said, "I don't know what has you confused—those hot wings or that jug of chilled piss. But I came here because last I checked, America was a free country. There was democracy, and I had enough money to get in here! And besides, I was hoping that you weren't here."

"Oops. Let me shut you down real quick. I'm here every night!"

"Looking at the imprint in your seat, I can tell!"

"Eff you, Spencer!"

"And D, E, F you, Rich! And all the rest of the alphabet. And besides, you know and I know that whenever you look pathetic like this you don't want to be alone."

I hate that she knows me so well! I swear I just want to slap her!

Spencer continued. "So you need to finish your wings, guzzle that beer, and be happy that someone wants to be here with you! Now anyway, let's just get to the good news before I have a serious problem with you."

I arched one brow and dipped the other. "And what's the good news?"

"My father just sent me a package and you know what was in it?"

No. And I really couldn't give a damn about what that old-behind, one-hundred-and-eight-year-old daddy of yours sent you.

"My daddy is so sweet."

No, he's not. That azz is old. Old enough to be my great-great-great-granddaddy and hers, too! He's old enough to be the original star in Roots. *He was probably Harriet Tubman's first husband. Mr. "Kumbaya"! I swear I* felt a Negro spiritual coming on, so I sang, "Swing Low, Sweet Chariot."

Spencer paused.

Set her drink on the counter. "What is wrong with you?! People are looking at you! Why are you singing grave-digging songs at the bar! You know I don't play with death! How dare you! And then you start singing that song after I mention my daddy. You always do that, Rich, and I don't talk about your drug-dealing daddy or his jailhouse ways! What you just did"—her voice trembled—"was hurtful. And I don't need you reminding me that my daddy's knocking at death's door. You're trying to kill my father!"

I tried not to, but I couldn't help but stretch across the counter in laughter. "Clutching pearls, Spencer," I said, collecting myself. "I wasn't talking about your father."

"You're such a liar! A hot-wing-eating, beer-drinking, fat, nasty liar! I should e-mail a picture of you to Jenny Craig right now."

I slid my middle finger into the air. "Like I said, eff Jenny Craig!"

Spencer quickly snapped a picture of me and immediately sent me to twenty. "Spencer, that's going too far now! Delete that."

"Apologize first. You just tried to bury my father and I didn't like that. Now apologize or meet your next headline." She flashed the picture in my face.

"Eww, apologies." I frowned. "I don't do apologies. I mean, if your feelings fell down your designer sleeves and landed on the table, then that's unfortunate. And I'll help you pick 'em up, but that's about as far as it goes."

"You know what, Sponge Bob Betty? Let's just forget it. As a matter of fact I feel sorry for you, sitting over there looking like Pooh. My heart goes out to you. So let's get back on track. I'm taking the diamonds my daddy sent me and having bangles made."

"Whew, fancy."

"I know, right. And wait a minute. Let me tell you I almost got my car torn up on the way over here. And Kitty just bought it for me a few days ago. There are such haters on the road, trying to crash my shine…"

I. Wish. This. Chick. Would. Shut. Up. She has been running her flytrap since she barged her way in here. And I really don't want to hear anything about her daddy. She knows he went to school with Jesus. That man is old and she knows he's old and knocking on death's door. "Knock-knock-knockin'…" I sang, and Spencer gave me the evil eye again.

"Don't be rude, Rich," Spencer said. "Don't cut me off. Now on to physics class…"

Who? What? Physics? Was she serious? Like really, did she actually think I went to school for anything more than a fashion show and a popularity contest?

What a blonde!

Spencer kept going and all I could hear was, "*Whomp, whomp, whomp…* and *whomp…whomp…whomp…* and *whomp…whomp…whomp…*"

"Rich, are you listening to me?"

"Uhmm hmm."

"Okay, now let me get to the goodness: Mr. Fine. The permanent substitute, Sanchez Velasquez."

"Who?"

"The teacher…"

Now she's on the verge of hoeing herself out to a teacher? Like, ill? Who does that?

I should've just made up with London. Yeah, she was selfish, but she didn't compare to this low-standards trick.

"Excuse you." Spencer snapped her fingers in my face. "Are you sleep-sitting? What's next, a snore? I've been talking to you about my new car, my bling, and how fine Mr.

Velasquez was, and you haven't complimented me or agreed with me yet. All you've done is break out into songs! How thoughtless is that? What could you be going through? And by the way, what are we going to do about this masquerade ball?"

"What?" I blinked in disbelief. "You should be asking your friend Miss Fiends Anonymous about that, since she ruined it for us."

Spencer twirled one of her curls. "You know what, Rich? If I wasn't being nice and we weren't getting along"—she patted my hand—"I would drop acid in my drink and douse you with it."

Immediately I started coughing. All I could see was my skin melting off.

"And like you told Corey, I will peel your face off! Now I would hate to mess up your pretty face because I have nothing but love for you, Rich. But don't call that girl my friend." She leaned in and whispered, "And by the way, you were right. She is on welfare. Because she wouldn't even be at Hollywood High if she didn't have a donor sponsoring her."

"A donor!"

"Yes!"

"How in the heck did she get a donor?!"

"I think she starred in a late-night infomercial for Save the Children."

"Whaaaaaat!" I rose from the bar and slammed my drink down. "I can't believe you are so selfish. Here I've been sitting and wallowing and drowning in my misery. Sad and practically depressed and you've been sitting on this juicy information! And you had to know it would cheer me up. And you wait an hour to tell me! You selfish beyotch!" I flopped back down on my stool. "You don't give a damn about me!" I pounded my fist on the glass bar, getting Johnnie's attention. "This time I need a double! Hennessy!"

"Now you're drinking Hennessy and mixing it with all that grease." She looked down at my plate. "When did you eat all of those wings? Did you breathe those in, dungeon dragon? You'll be in the emergency room by morning. Johnnie, I'll just have another cosmo and an ashtray."

An ashtray?

Spencer reached into her purse and pulled out a cigarette. And just as I thought she was about to light it up, she twisted the cigarette butt and smoke started rising.

OMG. Don't tell me that she was walking around with an electronic cigarette. This girl was crazy. She took a pull from the cigarette, tooted her lips and blew invisible smoke. She squinted her eyes as if nicotine really rushed down her throat. "Girl, you don't know the half of it!" She set the cigarette in the ashtray.

"What half don't I know?"

"Girl, this here is going to kill you."

"Shoot me then. Riddle me with bullets. Put the last nail in my coffin!" I said, excited, jumping up and down on the stool. "Give it to me, baby!"

"Camille's real name is Norma Marie."

I deflated. "That's life support information, Spencer. You already told me that." I picked up her electronic cigarette and took a pull.

"I bet you didn't know this then: Heather doesn't know who her father is. And Norma Marie won't tell her! How skanky is that?"

"Low-down, low-budget skanky."

"Umm hmm, Heather has a drunk for a mother and an invisible daddy. A statistic, which is why she probably gets high all the time. The only thing she knows about her daddy is that he's black!"

"Black!" I screamed. "OMG. I didn't know Heather was black. I thought she was Mexican. That explains why she didn't know Spanglish. Because when I said you need to stop being a hoey-oh, she didn't know what I was talking about."

Spencer gave me a blank stare. Then she turned to the bartender and said, "I'll take another one, please."

"Come on, Spencer, keep going, I'm dying now. I need you to take me all the way to code blue."

"Well, here's code blue for you—Norma Marie told Heather 'no pills, no drugs, no crack, and no more talk about your daddy; he has a daughter and he doesn't want you anyway!'"

I gasped. "I wonder if her daddy is Lil Wayne!"

"Lil Wayne?" Spencer looked confused. "Isn't he like twenty-something? Too young to be her father."

"Duh! A man is never too young, Spencer." I took another pull of the cigarette and blew invisible smoke in Spencer's face. "They start making babies at six. And by the age of ten they start looking like men. That's what had me fooled a few years ago when I was thirteen going out with Kaareem. He was just about six feet tall, and come to find out he'd just turned nine." I tossed a shot back and set my empty glass on the counter, signaling for another round.

Spencer looked stunned. "Nine? Rich. How desperate were you?"

"About as desperate as you were sleeping under that

cardboard box with Joey. That wasn't a science experiment; you knew he was homeless."

"I was being nice."

"No, you were being Captain Save-A-Ho. Ho for homeless!"

"Rich, don't you dare bring that up! You have called my daddy old, said Heather was my friend, and now Joey."

"Oh, stop being so sensitive! Anywho, back to Heather."

"Yeah, back to Heather before we get to rolling on the bar stools. Well, Camille is the one who found Heather's stash. And the day that I was at Heather's house she sailed all of Camille's bottles over the balcony. I thought I was going to be hit!"

"Dead. Buried and helping the devil out in hell. You have killed me, Spencer. Now reincarnate me. Do you know anything more?"

"Umm, no, I'm going to keep you dead. I like you dead better. Now kill me and tell me something juicy about Dogrilla! I can't stand that pound puppy!"

I couldn't help but stretch out laughing across the bar.

"Ruff! Ruff!" Spencer howled, causing me to laugh until tears fell from my eyes. At first they were tears of joy…at least until Jazmine Sullivan's "Need U Bad" eased through the speakers and she sang a line from the song. A vision of Knox danced before my eyes. Taking my tears of joy and turning them into tears of sorrow. And suddenly I could hear Knox's voice. Feel his touch. His scent floated beneath my nose. I needed him. I wanted him. I had to have him. But there was no way in hell I could get up from here and chase him. I couldn't fold. I couldn't give in and let him know that I loved him and wanted him back.

Spencer stood up from her stool and rubbed my back.

"Girl, you need to pull yourself together. Your makeup is a mess. Snot everywhere. People are looking over here. You look horrible. What is wrong with you? We have to get you into the bathroom and freshen you up. Makeover central, here we come."

I rose from the bar stool as Spencer grabbed our purses, looked over at Johnnie and said, "We'll be right back. Hold our seats."

Once we were in the bathroom, Spencer locked the door and I stood over the sink crying. My shoulders shook uncontrollably and I could hardly breathe.

"Rich, get yourself together and tell me what is wrong." She leaned on the counter, next to me.

I wiped my eyes. "I miss my man, Spencer. I miss him," I snorted. "Oh Jesus. I need him."

"Well, most people go to church, Rich. They don't do all this crying in the bar."

"I'm not talking about Jesus. I'm talking about my man!"

"Which one?"

"Who do you think?"

"Corey?" She frowned.

"No!" I screamed.

"Jonathan? I thought you swore you would never talk about that again. That was a drunken one-night stand!"

"No! Not Jonathan! Knox—" Tears continued to pour from my eyes.

"Knox?" Spencer said, clearly confused. "What the flim-flam-fluck? You have a lot of miles on that cootie-cat. You've laid around the world and back. Your legs have been up in Guatemala. Iceland. Turks and Caicos. Jamaica, Australia, Aspen—"

"That's enough, Spencer. I have changed my ways. And I am a one-man woman!"

"Wow, miss a minute, miss a lot. So when did you settle down and become Mrs. Knox? I thought maybe y'all were just kickin' it."

"Well, we were. But we weren't. And then we tried to make it work. And then, and then—" Tears caused my voice to tremble.

"Wait, Rich," Spencer said. "Just slow down and tell me from the beginning what happened."

I did all I could to keep my tears at bay and just as I went to tell my story, I noticed Spencer fluffing her hair and freshening up her makeup. At least London had the decency to give me eye contact. Spencer had no manners.

"Spencer, are you listening to me?"

"Yes, I'm listening. I just want you to get to the point. And I don't want lies. And no exaggeration. You didn't save the world. You didn't find weapons of mass destruction. If anything, you cheated on him or he has caught you in one of your lies. So what was it this time, Rich?"

"I would never cheat on Knox! And there were no lies. I really tried this time. He just couldn't accept me for who I was."

"And who was that, Rich? A hot mess? Party girl? Boom-bop-pop, running from the cameras? Everything was about you and nothing about him."

I paused. There she was, blaming me, just like Knox. "What are you two?" I asked. "Still best friends? I thought I broke that up in first grade."

"You did, but I still know Knox. And I know that he is a nice guy. And his only flaw is that he loves you. It just baf-

fles me. How he could be so in love with you and your vi-
cious ways? But he loves your dirty drawls."

I hated that Spencer made me laugh at my own ex-
pense. I wiped my eyes and said, "I love him. And I love
him more than words can say. He's in everything that I do.
All of my thoughts are about him. My life is crumbling,
Spencer." I broke down again. "And I keep fighting, and
fighting, and fighting my feelings, trying not to love him.
But ever since I was eight it won't go away."

"Huh?"

"What I'm saying is that Knox wants to control me!"

"Knox? Knox isn't like that—"

Knock, knock! cut across our conversation.

"I know no one's knocking at this door!" Spencer said
as she marched over to the door and snatched it open. A
woman attempted to step inside and Spencer blocked her
path and said, "Turn your bootie-bop right back out that
door unless you wanna be Maced."

All the color left the woman's face.

"And you look like a man anyway. Now go use the men's
room!" She pushed the woman back and slammed the
door in her face. "Now back to you, Rich. I don't want to
hear that sad, ridiculous mess you're trying to fool me
with. I'm not London. And I know you. And I know that
you were so busy trying to be in control that you lost the
only man you love who could love you. Why he loves you,
I have no idea and it's none of my business. But he does.
But what I do know is that you are going to lose a nice guy
if you keep your drama up. Now stop standing here crying
and telling me you love him and go tell *him*. Now wash
your face, freshen up that makeup, and go get your man!"

I didn't answer; instead I washed my face, touched up my makeup, and turned toward the door.

"Now what are you going to do?"

"I'm going to get another drink."

I walked out of the bathroom with Spencer hot on my heels, saying something about me making the biggest mistake of my love life. I couldn't take any more of her buzzing behind me so I whipped around and said, "Just be quiet about Knox, already!"

"Okay, I'll be quiet. Lips are sealed. And I want you to be quiet, too. Because see, all those tears and snot and carrying on I will only do with you once. Now if you want to drink and act like Knox doesn't exist then there's nothing else to cry about. Let's drink up and be merry."

"Exactly."

"Fine then. Next round's on me."

Our heels clicked back to our seats and a few moments later the lights went down and a smooth-sounding Jaheim-esque voice floated through the crowd. I closed my eyes and as soon as Knox appeared in my thoughts I quickly erased his vision by opening my eyes. A few moments later the stage lit up and there before me was Justice. Singing his heart out. Instantly our eyes locked.

He smiled.

My heart fluttered.

"Oh my God." Spencer leaned into me. "Wasn't he at London's? Isn't that the same boy?"

"Yes. That's the cutie who came when you stormed out of her room."

"Dangdropdownandgetchapopon. He's so fine I might need to change my panty liner. I feel moist."

I didn't even respond to that. I just kept my eyes locked

on his. Next to Knox he was the prettiest man I'd ever seen. I could easily get lost in his arms as he sang, "You have got to be the one for me/I've looked everywhere/I've been everywhere/And everything brought me back here to you…"

The crowd was going wild. But I sat silently, watching him watching me. He spoke into the mic and said, "How y'all doing tonight?"

"Fine!" the crowd chanted.

"I see y'all ready to feel good. Thought I'd tease you for a minute. I see a lot of beautiful ladies out there. My name is JB and I'm here for your pleasure."

"Yes. You. Are," Spencer purred. "Now take your clothes off!"

He continued. "I'm going to sing a few classics and a few that I've written myself. But I'm going to kick this set off with a little Erick Roberson. And I need a little help from the audience. Who wants to help me sing this song?"

Spencer hopped off the bar stool and said, "Rich, I'm going to sing real quick. I'll be right back." She took a step toward the stage. But was stopped in her tracks when he called my name.

"Rich, why don't you come up and sing this with me? I know you have skills. And if not, then your pretty face is enough."

"Fine as hell!" the guys in the club catcalled, while the girls all hated.

Spencer took a step back and said, "Looks like somebody has their eye on you. Too bad you have beer and hot wings on your breath."

I didn't respond to that either. I hesitated and blushed, waving no.

The crowd cheered and a few yelled, "Come on. Go on, girl!"

Spencer looked over at me and said, "You can do it. Go up there and then call me up to take your spot or we can tag-team him."

After hesitating a few seconds more, I swallowed my nerves and made my way onto the stage. I smoothed invisible wrinkles from my hips and shyly smiled at him. He nodded toward the mic and said, "Go ahead." I closed my eyes, and blessed the mic with a gift that very few knew that I had. My voice reminded those who knew I could sing of Jill Scott with a Mariah Carey range.

Usually I was too shy to sing before so many, but this time I felt a little different and I don't know what came over me. All I knew is that as I sang, the crowd yelled and Spencer screamed about how I was her friend. Then Justice stepped behind me, wrapped his arms around my waist, and sang his heart out.

This was perfect. I grooved my boom-bop and we swayed to the rhythms we created. And at that exact moment, no one else in the room mattered. It was me and him. JB and Rich. Together. Not even Knox could invade this moment. By the time the song ended we were engaged in an unexpected kiss with a whole bunch of tongue. And all I could hear were cameras chanting, *Click, click, click...*

17

Spencer

Caramel popcorn, check!
Twizzlers, check!
Mike and Ikes, check!
Two bottles of 5-hour Energy shots, check, check!
Night vision goggles, check!
Binoculars, check!
Rich in hotel with London's man, ho check!
London in parking lot, dumb-diggity check!
Phone call to Kitty's street team, juicy check!
Oh yes, oh yes...I can see the headlines now:
GUESS WHO GOT THE JUICE? SPENCER ELLINGTON DOES!
EX-RUNWAY MODEL RUNS NAKED FOR LOVE!
PSYCHO-SOCIALITE GOES CUCKOO FOR THE COCK-A-DOODLE
DO!
RATCHET, NASTY SUBWAY RAT LOSES EVERYTHING!
The thought of it was so juicy I had to lick my fingers. I
fell back in my seat cracking up, watching London through

my binoculars as she stormed out of the hotel lobby back to her car.

"Yeah, DogKeisha, I see you with your ghetto-tail self, pacing around looking all thirsty. I'm the one who sent that text to you, ho."

I giggled, pulling out my throwaway phone, then scrolled back through the text messages I had sent to her two hours earlier. Dumb hoes were delicious to watch!

Have you seen your man today?

London had texted back: Who is this?

Ur Fairy Ho Mother. And I come bearing gifts 4 u

Then I followed it up with a photo of Justice at the hotel desk with a caption that read: Kaboom! Guess who stepped in the room? Spotted: 6 feet tall, fine Panty Droppa with whore! And she isn't U

London replied: Who is this again?

It isn't Justice cause he's in a room gettin whacked off by a queen sleaze in the trap, queen sleaze in the trap

I giggled.

Poor little whore with nothing left to do. Whatcha gonna do when the cleanup woman comes after you?

I finger popped, feeling good. I should be a rapper. I could rap and Rich could sing my hooks. Then again, the way she likes to booty-pop-it up on stage, she could be one of my backup singers and dancers.

I got it, I got it. You gonna sit in the dark, watchin' ya man like a hawk... while he and his new boo make a fool outta you... break-a, break-a, one-time... dingaling-aling... sit back and wait for the alarm to ring... ya man got his tongue stuck in that thing-thing...

Heeheehee.

I picked up my binoculars and zoomed in on London's big face for a visual update. She was pacing back and forth in front of the car.

I should call the police on her for loitering.

Nah...I'd rather watch her kill herself when Justice comes out with Rich. Mmmph...hot scandal!

I laughed. "You can't even keep Justice. Mmmph...and you think you gonna keep Anderson? Not! He's gonna be with me. Think Rich is gonna be your best friend? Not! Right about now Hot Drawz is flipped upside down with the Panty Droppa! She's putting it on him so good he's calling out her grandmother's name, Rovina Sue 'Eat 'Em Up-Eat 'Em Up' Gatling. Yeah, she got him in there porn-starring it up! Toes curling, biting down on his bottom lip. Oooh, yes! I know Miss Freaks R Us is doing him right. 'Cause she's nasty like that. I raised her well. She is doing momma proud! Drop it on him, Rich! Drop down on him, boo!"

Ooooh, I was so dang amped!

I couldn't help but giggle again.

I stuffed my mouth with a handful of Mike and Ikes, then washed them down with a swig of my energy shot. Boom! Boom!

I was floating on sugar!

Higher than a lampshade!

Happier than Co-Co Ming being lost in Boys Town!

I cracked up, picking up my binoculars again.

"You're not the only trashy whore in town, Miss London. Miss I'm From New York. Miss Amazon Gone Wild. Miss This Is How We Do It. Miss Upper East Side Trick-A-Lot. Open your checkbook, ho. I bet you have more skid marks on your panty liners than you have zeroes in your bank accounts, Miss Brokeback Low-Money. I'm about to tear your playhouse all the way down."

I usually didn't munch on junk, but tonight was a special treat. I knew the minute I spotted Mr. Sexy Chocolate up on that stage and saw Rich hop her thick-in-the-hips, two-biscuits-and-a-shake booty up there with him that this was going to be a ringside moment. The circus was in session. The fat lady was about to sing. And the main attraction was loaded up on hot wings and beer about to start the freakfest. Whoooo-hoooooo! Ring the alarms, goshdarn it!

"Freak on the loose. And she's doing your man!" I screamed in laughter as I reached into my creep-creep kit and pulled out a pair of night goggles. I slipped them on and watched London all night.

It was already close to two in the morning.

Rich had stumbled up into the elevator with Sexy Chocolate around eleven thirty—how do I know? Because I was there. Duh—and I waited to see what floor it would stop on. Mmmph, the twenty-first floor. Then I sent London her first text at exactly eleven forty-three. I wanted to give Hot Drawz a chance to get stripped down first, before I reached out and touched a ho. That was my new community service project: the Reach a Ho, Teach a Ho project.

"Mmmph, just look at her. Pacing back and forth on them sausages she calls feet. I know them things gotta be fried down to the skin by now. Public works will probably have to come out in the morning to fill in the dents she done put in the road. Wasting taxpayer dollars on her dumbness!"

I decided to send her another text: U find ur man yet? oooh, oooh, U smell that? it's sex in the air. and it ain't with u!

London replied: Silly little girl. Tricks r 4 kids! My man is right here n my bed! So stop botherin' me. Get a life. Dumb whore!

Liar, liar. Whore on fire! u better try the next trick's bed. Ur man's nowhere near U. He don't even want u!

I zoomed in on her again. She swung open the car door, then threw her phone over into the passenger seat. Then the poor wretched stank-a-dank pressed her forehead up against the steering wheel. Her shoulders shook. Poor thing was crying over her boo. What a mess! She started banging the steering wheel, screaming with the windows rolled up. I took my phone and snapped pictures. Oh, this was priceless.

I laughed. *This slore is nuts! With her big-faced, big-hand self! She's just a big ole funky elephant!*

I watched her blow her snout, then wipe snot away. Ugh, nasty! Then out of nowhere the selfish tramp sped off, like a wild woman. I screamed, knocking over my box of Mike and Ikes and spilling my energy drink. "Wait! Where you going, ho? Wait, wait, wait for me. Your man's in the hotel! Twenty-first floor!"

I cranked up my engine and started following London. She was driving like she was a scorned bat fleeing hell. And now I saw why. Justice had sped out of the hotel's parking lot and she was following behind his car. I swung around the bend to catch up to her and sideswiped the *Dish the Dirt* news van. *My God...idiot, why don't you watch where you're going!* "You're supposed to be getting this trick's news, not hitting me!"

I was pissed. I had Kitty on board and this ho was running out on me. My phone rang. "Tell me I did not just waste time and money for some ho-chase gone wrong," Kitty sneered into the phone. "And then you're out there hitting my news van. I have an irate driver on the phone with his hot cup of coffee tossed in his lap because you don't seem to know how to drive. The man is shaken up."

I huffed, "Well, he should have been watching where he was pulling out!"

"Spencer, the van was parked!" she yelled into my ear.

I gasped. "Well, he must have road rage, then. Who would get in my way knowing I'm on a mission?"

"Whatever, Spencer. You get me my story, or else!" The line went dead.

"Oh, whatever, Kitty. Bite me. And bite me good!" I yelled, turning another corner and running up on a curb. I pressed down on the pedal to keep up with Hoesha.

"Lonnnnnnnnnnnndon, I'ma ram your pipes in!" I screamed, trying to keep a discreet distance behind her.

She ran a red light, then swerved over onto the other side of the road, turning down a one-way street, going the wrong way. Now I was getting pissed. This trick was trying to do me in.

Ohmysweetluckycharms... Trickamona is trying to get me killed!

"This idiot! This is why she can't keep a man. 'Cause she can't keep up with him! What are you doing, trick? He hooked a left on West Cota Street, you dumb Amazonian roach! This makes no sense burning up good gas! What the hell is wrong with you, London? I see why I can't stand you!"

I wonder if I speed up next to her and tap on her window and tell her which way he went she'd think that was strange, or would I have to Mace her down like a rabid dog? Mmmph. I'd probably have to twist her eyeballs out.

She merged onto Route 101 heading south back toward Hollywood. She drove like a fire-eating lunatic for almost ten miles before she finally swerved over onto the side of the highway, crying again.

I hit the lights and eased over a few hundred feet in back of her. Thank goodness it was still dark out, or my cover would have been blown.

I rolled my eyes. All those waterworks were burning a hole into my booty cheeks. Like who does that? Crying over a boy like that. I mean, really, strap on your big-girl lace thongs and get your mind right. Geesh.

My phone rang and it was Kitty calling back. I pressed Ignore, sending her straight to voice mail. I was not in the mood to curse her out for old and new Chanels 'cause I knew she couldn't see straight, calling me with her craziness.

This was getting ridiculous. I sat and I sat and I sat, waiting to see what Trickalicious was gonna do next. I screamed when I glanced at the clock and realized I had been sitting in the car for ninety gotdang minutes waiting for this cluckeroo to make her next move. I felt like calling Rich and telling her to get her bloodline of hoodboogas to come pull a carjacking and leave London in the middle of the street stripped down to her drawers. Then I'd ride by and ask her if she had a ride.

I giggled at the thought.

"Oooh, oooh, no, no... I know what I could do," I said to myself. "I can call animal control and report a wild mammal on the loose and have her harpooned. Yeah, that's it!"

Oh, how I cracked myself up, thinking about all the devilish ways to destroy Miss Low-Money London. Now I saw why she couldn't get her money up; she was just dumb and stupid. There was no dang way tire tracks shouldn't be running up Justice's back, but nooooooooo... we were stuck on a three-lane highway in Santa Barbara. Where were the police when you needed them? I felt like running up on London in a ski mask and wig and Macing the back of her retinas for being so dang pathetic.

Kitty rang my cell incessantly, like the world was on fire. I ignored her. A few minutes later I spotted her news van speeding by. I guess they had given up. But I hadn't. I was going to sit there until the sun came up and the last rooster crowed, if I had to. I'd eat up my snacks watching and waiting for this whore-heifer to pull it together.

"Ugh, you disgust me, you gutter rat," I snarled, chomping down on two Twizzlers, then popping a handful of Mike and Ikes into my mouth. I took a shot of my energy drink. I felt the sugar shoot through my veins. I was glucosed up and started to hallucinate.

Yes, that was it.

I had to be seeing things when I saw a stretch limo speed by, then pull over on the side of the highway behind London's car. I zoomed in on the target and screamed, crouching down in my seat. It was Anderson. Four thirty in the morning and he was out in his red cape playing Captain Save A Tramp.

What is he doing here?

Why would she be calling him?

That's my man!

Why didn't she call Panty Droppa?

London has this all the way jacked up, calling my boo

bear this time of the morning. There were only two things these late-night calls were good for: doughnuts and neck bobbing!

Ohmygod, Anderson better not be playing me. I pulled out my cell and dialed his number, but quickly disconnected when he pulled it out of his jacket. *Wait a minute! I have the game tied up. The game doesn't have me tied up. I run this. I'm no man's prisoner. I take prisoners.*

I took another shot to the head.

I torture them.

I bring them to their knees.

Oh, noooo...bees in the trap. They had me messed up!

Relax, Spencer. Pull it together. Keep it calm. Let's see what part of the game this may be...

I took several deep breaths.

Her window went down.

He leaned into the car. They were talking.

Oooh, I wish I knew what they were saying.

I already had my zoom lens on high and could see everything crisp and clear; everything except for what the heck they were saying. I couldn't read their lips for skunk piss, dangit!

Maybe this was a photo op or something.

I lifted up my night goggles and peered through my binoculars, hoping for a closer look. London handed Anderson her cell. I frowned as he scrolled through it. *What the sneezusjeezus does she think giving him her phone is gonna do?*

Anderson said something to her, shaking his head as he handed her phone back to her.

Oh God, more tears! Here she goes with her Queen of Pathetic role again, crying. Maybe Rich was right; this tramp was really stupid. And here I thought she was being her usual two-faced self, but Rich was right. This ho-dog was sniffing up the wrong tree with her dumb self.

Anderson couldn't care less about her. Poor, stupid London...sitting on the highway with her big hoofs pounding the pavement...but Anderson is about to come my way ...'cause I got that goodness...

I mean really, why would he want buffalo chips, when he could have a slim in the waist, pretty in the face cutie-boo on his arm? After all, I had beauty, body, and I gave good brain...I mean, I had brains, too. Heeheehee.

I got that wet-wet...slurp 'em up, slurp 'em up...got that bombness...bees in the trap...I'ma bring him to my...

Wait!

Why is he opening up the driver's-side door? And why is London getting out of the car? And, wait, wait...why is Anderson's driver pulling off?

Anderson walked London over to the passenger's side of her car, opened the door for her, then waited for her to slide her monkey-donkey self in before shutting the door.

My mouth dropped open when I saw his eyes drop down to her behind.

Why are his eyes stuck to her behind like that? I should ram into the back of her car!

Anderson slid behind the steering wheel, then shut the door. I waited with bated breath to see what happened next. And then...and then...

He stroked her chin.

He tucked her hair behind her ear.

And then he did the unthinkable.

He grabbed London by her gizzard chin, guided her to

him and planted...*ohsweetgorillaandduckpoo*...he kissed her!

That no-good, horny corndog kissed her on the lips! And he had the nerve to take his time kissing her, like the two of them were enjoying it.

Ohfortheloveofcleandrawersandmatchingbras! *How could he do this to me?!*

I screamed, gripping my binoculars with both hands as they kept kissing. I held them so tight that I could have easily snapped them in half as if they were Anderson's neck. It looked as if he was nibbling and sucking on her lips, too. I felt myself getting more agitated by the minute as I imagined Stink Bottom sitting there with her Under-oos sticking to her roach nest, getting all gooey-ooey in-side from the kisses that Anderson should have been giving to me! His tongue was supposed to be dancing with mine, moving with heated passion, twirling around mine, making my treasures wet. Not hers!

Ohgodohgodohgod...his hand moved from her face to the back of her neck. He pulled her in more. He wanted a deeper kiss. *Ohgodohgodohgoddangit!*

They kissed and kissed and kissed, then he slowly pulled away, staring into her eyes.

Finally, the trick turned from him. They both fastened their seat belts. Anderson started the engine, then slowly pulled out onto the highway, driving off and leaving me parked on the side of the road with my bottom lip hitting the steering wheel.

I screamed, "Anderson Ford! I am going to crush you into a meat grinder then feed you to the sharks for licking and kissing all over that foul-mouthed septic waste! You nasty buzzard!"

My cell rang. Without thinking, I answered. "Wh-wh-whaat?"

"Spencer, what the hell do you think you're doing?!" Kitty screamed into my ear. "Where are you?"

I blinked.

"What happened to the secret boo? What happened to the story? You had my men out all night chasing ghosts! I can't even count on you to get that right? This is a hot mess! You have wasted time and money! Spencer, Spencer... do you hear me talking to you?"

I blinked.

"He kissed her. He really kissed her. He's been lying to me..."

18

Rich

What did I just do?
It must've been an out-of-body experience.
It had to be...
I knew I was on that stage...
I knew I went up to his hotel suite...
I knew we started kissing at the door...
My body was pressed up against his...
His kisses traveled from my lips, down my neck, over my collarbone, leaving a wet, warm trail along the center of my body...
Stop thinking.
Just breathe.
I can't do that...
I had to get my mind right. My thoughts in order. I raced south down the freeway and I wasn't sure if I was outrunning the wee hours of the morning or my life...All I knew was that I had to get out of there.
I'm not a cheater...Maybe this wasn't cheating...

Yes, it was...

Why did I let him take me there?

He lifted me over the threshold and the hotel door closed behind us; the automatic locks clicked in place.

I knew then I should've run. But I didn't...I was trapped between a heated kiss, a warm body, and strong hands that placed me onto the bed. I knew then he was no boy. He was all man.

What happens now?

What happens next? How will I look my man in the face?

Maybe Knox doesn't have to know.

No. He doesn't need to know.

He will not know.

This is nothing that needed to be repeated.

This will be buried with my old, run-over Chanels with the broken heel and the hole in the bottom. Next to my dog, Fido, my bird named Elephant, and my diary that held all of my secrets.

I watched the sun fill the sky and instantly I could still feel the heat of Justice's fingertips. The way he pulled, and pinched, and tickled, and caressed parts of me that I didn't know existed. My body was completely alive for the first time in my life and it wasn't at the hands of my man.

This is a problem.

This is a big problem.

Maybe I don't need to sweat this.

Maybe I could pretend that this didn't exist.

But it did exist. And I was there in that hotel suite, lost in the rapture of Justice's body. Caught up in the moment of lust. And just when we were set for the moon I stopped him. And pulled the sheet over my nakedness. Thank God

I still had on my panties...even if the only reason I still had them on was because guilt wouldn't let me take them off. "I can't do this," I said in a husky whisper.

He didn't hear me at first. Instead he continued on, reaching for my panties. I grabbed his hands and said, "No. I can't."

"Yes, you can," he whispered. "Don't do me like this. I've been wanting you for a minute. I've been feelin' you. What happened to all of that good, sweet, sexiness you were talking to me?" Again he reached for my panties.

I let him slide them down over my hips and then I quickly pulled them back up. My heart skipped four beats. I knew I wanted it. I wanted him. He ran the tip of an index finger across the tattoo on my pubic bone that read Good Girl. He placed a soft kiss there. I closed my eyes and the memory of when Knox and I went for tattoos popped into my mind. Knox's tattoo was his Omega Psi Phi line name, The Regulator. And I thought it was apropos, especially since I knew that he knew that I knew he was the only one who could handle me...until now...

"What do you mean, stop?"

"I just can't do this," I said to Justice. I felt like crying, screaming, bolting out of there. Taking the rest of my clothes off. Putting them back on. All of the ingredients for a passionate night were all there: the five-star hotel suite, the balcony overlooking the ocean, the music on low, candles were lit, and I was on ten. Ready and about to go in, but I couldn't, because this was the wrong man.

And I needed my man. Superman. My Knox. I lifted Justice's face to mine, softly placed one last kiss on his lips and said, "I have a boyfriend."

He didn't say anything; he simply stared at me.

"And I know I shouldn't have let things get this far... and yeah, we've been having issues. And he's mad at me. But I love him. And I want him back. And I have to go and get him."

Justice let out a deep sigh and sat up. I knew for sure he was going to call me a tease... and maybe I was. "Rich"— he ran his hands through my hair—"you're so beautiful and I want nothing more than to spend this night making love to you. But, I'ma respect your wishes."

"I'm sorry." I reached for my clothes.

"Where are you going?" He took my clothes out of my hand. "It's too late for you to go out there like this, plus you've been drinking. Just chill. Wait until the morning and then you can bounce. I want you to be safe. Just let me hold you."

And I did. My back against his chest. And we drifted off to sleep.

I have to get to Knox. I can't go another minute. Idle time is truly the devil's playground for me.

I exited the freeway and pulled into San Diego University's off-campus apartment complex, where Knox lived. My heart sank to the bottom of my stomach, awakening the nervous butterflies that lived there.

I pulled down the vanity mirror and my eyes were red. I looked exactly how I felt. A mess. I pushed my hair back behind my ears and hopped out of my car. I raced to Knox's apartment. Out of breath. Fighting tears and praying they didn't sneak up on me and roll down my cheeks.

I have to get it together.

What am I going to say?

Just tell the truth... for once.

I felt desperate. It was six thirty in the morning and I didn't know if Knox or his roommate were up and I didn't give a damn. I had to end this standoff between my man and me right now. I couldn't go another day, another minute, another second, another moment without him. I couldn't breathe the way I needed to without him in my life. Because the more I tried to breathe the more my lungs burned. He was my oxygen. He was the only steady truth and true love in my life. And nothing, and no one, compared to him.

I rapped on the door with all my might, breathlessly, and no one answered. I pounded over and over and over again. Finally the door swung open and there stood Midnight, Knox's roommate, with crust in his eyes and dried drool along the sides of his mouth. "Yo, you runnin' up on us like you five-oh or somebody's baby mama. Are you serious? What? Did I forget to call you? My fault, ma. But you can't be runnin' up in here like this. Come back later. Shortie from last night is still here."

"Boy, move." I pushed him out of my way. "I'm not in the mood and I'm not here for your foolishness!"

"So does that mean you're still into Knox? I thought for sure I had a chance."

"Shut. Up. Get out of my face!" I rushed toward Knox's bedroom door and Midnight was on my heels.

"Yo"—he blocked my path—"You don't wanna go up in there! Didn't I just tell you about Shortie from last night?"

"What the hell!" Knox snatched his door open. "Yo, Midnight, what are you . . . doing . . . ? Rich, why are you here?"

A river filled my eyes.

"Do you know what time it is?" Knox asked, annoyed.

"I needed to see you," I said.

"For what?" He scowled and crossed his arms over his bare chest.

I looked him over from his beautiful face to his boxers, to his bare feet. All I wanted was to jump into his arms, but judging by the way he looked at me with disgust and disdain in his eyes, I knew running into his arms was not the move, so I said, "I'm a mess. And I'm an even bigger mess without you." I paused. Read his eyes. He wasn't impressed. He was still pissed.

"I messed up big time," I continued, wiping tears. I felt so guilty, but I was so happy to see Knox. I needed him. And I needed him to need me. I needed him to want me here. But I didn't know what to do or what to say that would sway him to want me again. To want to have me again. I'd messed up so many times, but this time would be different. Because if I got him back I would not be letting him go...

"Knox—" I took a step toward him and reached for his hand. He left me hanging.

"I'm not about to do this with you again," he said. "I'm not feelin' it and I don't have time to be playing games with you. Now what? Whatchu want?" he asked, still pissed.

"I want you, Knox." I took a step closer to him.

He didn't say anything.

I continued. "I have messed up so much. And I know I'm not perfect. I shut you out when I shouldn't have. When I should've let you love me."

"Rich, please. Enough with the violins. Get to the point. You're saying all of that to say what?"

"That I—"

"You know what, Rich. This back-and-forth is tired. Played. I love you, but I'm sick of you. And sick of your selfishness. You're self-centered. And I'm sick of the TV cameras that follow you. Those ridiculous blogs. The headlines. Everything is one-sided. Life is not all about you. Things that you do affect other people. You hurt me. You hurt us. Your recklessness is going to destroy us! You have something good, so why do you keep doing this to us? To you? I'm tired, Rich. And the way I feel now, I'm done with you. Last I saw you, you were pregnant and I haven't heard anything else about it. I've been calling you and calling you and you haven't answered one call. Now we don't have to be together and yeah, this is effed-up timing, but you need to talk to me about my baby. Because I will be taking care of my responsibilities regardless. So skip the drama and get to the point!"

My heart dropped to my stomach. *He wanted our baby... as much as I had. And here, at my mother's insistence, I'd left the fruits of our love in Arizona. Dammit!*

Tears continued to race along with my thoughts. That's when I knew what I had to do. And though I hated to do this, and I hated to lie, I had to. I had to pull this card from my desperate Rolodex and play it like a poker game's flush. I bit into my bottom lip. Tears slid from my eyes to the corners of my mouth and my voice trembled as I said, "I miscarried."

"What? When? What did you just say?" he stammered. His face was suddenly covered with worry.

My shoulders shook. "The night after you came to my house. After we had that argument I was so stressed and I just love you, and..." I couldn't talk anymore. Everything in me collapsed. My knees felt weak and I couldn't stop shaking. I was wracked with tears. I was enthralled in the moment. I was fighting for my life. My love. There was no turning back, because when all was said and done, I was determined to be Mrs. Superman.

He placed his arms around me.

Got him.

"Why didn't you call me?" He held me tightly.

I buried my head into his chest. He smelled like heaven and I knew then he was worth the fight. He was worth the love. And he was worth the lie.

"I love you," he said. "When you hurt, I hurt. I'm here for you. I ain't going nowhere. And we'll get it right this time."

I nodded.

He wiped my tears. "Stop crying."

"I love you so much."

"I know you do." He pressed his lips against mine. Our tongues danced and I knew that this was right. This was where I was supposed to be last night. Lost in Knox's arms.

"Damn," Midnight said, interrupting our moment. "Y'all got me crying. All choked up. I'm caught up in the moment like a mofo." He sniffed. "I ain't felt like this since *Stomp the Yard*. I need a hug."

Ignoring Midnight, Knox took me by the hand and led me to his room, and as he shut the door Midnight yelled, "Can I come in, too? We line brothers, man, we 'spose to share." He started barking, making frat calls.

"I'll never leave you again," I said to Knox.

"And I won't let you." He pulled me onto the bed.

The morning sun slipped in through the slits of the mini-blinds as I leaned in to continue our love groove and just as we were about to lose ourselves, Knox whispered, "Babe, why do you smell like hot wings and beer?"

19

London

Two weeks later

I was alone.
I was unhappy.

And I was hurting.

I still hadn't heard from Justice. And the more the moments passed, the sicker I became. Every inch of my body ached. I couldn't eat. I couldn't sleep. I couldn't think. No, I could think—only about Justice. He was consuming me. My every waking moment was cluttered with thoughts of him. Justice! Justice! Justice! I couldn't shake him.

I can't keep going through this craziness with him! Over and over and over again, the pain was killing me. The emptiness was eating away at me. All I kept thinking was that he was with someone else, giving her all of his good loving; giving her every part of him that belonged to me. I didn't want to ever be the other woman, but I loved Justice so much that I was almost willing to share him. Almost willing to drop down to the number-two slot in his life, and play the position of part-time fool.

Almost...

Just until I was able to put things in motion with Rich.

I had to get my man back. By any means necessary. So I was willing to give him his space, as much as it was destroying me, and be his friend—anything to be in his life—so that he could finally see that I was the one.

The only one...

I stood in front of my all-glass curio cabinet in my sitting room, staring at the assortment of crystal butterflies I had collected over the years. As beautiful as these exquisite pieces were, I felt like smashing every last one of them. My life was a shattered mess, so why shouldn't they be?

I glanced at my favorite Swarovski butterfly sitting on my end table, and sighed. "Have I not prayed faithfully to you?" I whispered, picking the crystal object up. I stared at it. "Have I not been specific about what I wanted, hoped for? Then why have you forsaken me? What have I done that's so horrible for you to keep me living in this hell without my man? Please. I beg of you, butterfly gods, bring Justice back to me."

I set it back down on the table, wiping a lone tear as it slid down my face.

After all of my praying and worshipping and wishing and talking to these butterflies, waiting for my dreams to come true and my wishes to be granted, I still didn't have one thing I wanted. I still didn't have Justice. I didn't have his heart, I didn't have his love. And I sure didn't have him in my bed, holding me in his arms as we made plans for our future. No, I had nothing but shards of emptiness that were cutting into me, gouging my heart and my spirit.

I was bleeding...to death! And Justice was nowhere around to save me.

"Good morning, my beautiful darling daughter," my mother sang out, cutting into my one-woman pity party as she whisked into my suite carrying her scale, leather-bound logbook, and Spartacus pen for our morning mother-daughter ritual.

I glanced over my shoulder at her, feeling a pang of jealousy.

She was gorgeous. Everything was in place. Her hair, her face, her beautiful mahogany skin...all perfect! Too perfect! She was everything I was not. Everything I envied, and hated!

She whisked in and kissed me on the cheek. Her signature hyacinth-, orchard-, and amber-scented fragrance swirled around the room. "Come. Let's get you weighed and measured."

I glanced at the crystal clock on the vanity and sighed: 5:30 A.M. I untied my robe, then let it slide off my shoulders as I stepped up on the scale.

"Fantistico!" she exclaimed in Italian, grabbing me excitedly. You've lost four more pounds. We just need to lose ten more pounds..."

We?

She rattled on about how proud she was of me as she wrapped her measuring tape around my waist, then hips, then breasts. I had lost two inches.

"Oh, my darling *Londra*! I can see it now. London, Paris, Rome. You will be the modeling sensation you were born to be in no time. It is your destiny, mi bella una..."

Beautiful one? Yeah, right. I didn't feel so beautiful. I swallowed. I was sick of everyone trying to control my life and tell me what was best for me. "But what if I don't want it to be? What if modeling isn't what I want for me?"

She tilted her head. "Then you *will* pretend that it is. You will smile for the cameras. Back straight, hips forward, one foot in front of the other, you will work the runway. You will own it. You will serve the fashion world—face, grace, and glamour. And you *will* love it, whether you want to or not. And will make your mother proud. Do you understand me?"

I clenched my lips together. There was no sense in arguing with her. I was in enough trouble with my parents. So I did what I did best, pasted on a tight smile and robotically said, "Yes, Mother. I understand."

"Good. Now go get dressed, dear. Anderson will be here for you in an hour to take you to school."

With that said, she kissed me on the cheek again, then gracefully waltzed out.

"London, you need to let that dude go," Anderson said as he drove me to school. "That bum doesn't give a damn about you."

What's it to you?

That was easier said than done. A part of me wished like hell it were that simple to toss Justice into the trash can of my memory and be done with him. But it wasn't. Truth is, I couldn't let go. I was afraid to let go. Justice was all I knew. He was the one who had given me my first taste of love. He was my first. He was my true love. And there wasn't anything I wouldn't do to keep him.

I was a total wreck without him. And I knew it.

"Look, don't call him that. He's not a bum. No one understands him like I do. And besides, maybe I'm not ready to get over him. So just leave it be. Let me handle my love life. And I'll let you handle yours. Besides, even if I wanted to,

I don't know how to do without him. And I don't think I wanna know."

He took his eyes off the road, glancing over at me. "Then let me help you learn how to do without him."

I eyed him. "And why would *you* want to do that—help me get over Justice?"

"Because I don't like how he treats you."

I frowned. "What's it to you? How Justice treats me is none of your business."

He shook his head, sighing. "Okay, London. You're right, it isn't. So, moving on. You want to go with me to this party my frat brothers are having Saturday night?"

I twisted my lips up. "Illll, gross! I know you're not trying to ask me out on a date."

He chuckled. "Oh, right, right. You don't do dates, do you? I forgot. Just like you don't do talking about that kiss we had, either."

I feigned ignorance. Yeah, I remembered it. How could I not? It was something I had been trying to block out of my head ever since it happened. That wasn't supposed to happen. Not with him. Anderson? Oh God, no way, no how!

"What kiss?"

"You can act like it didn't happen all you want. But you know, and I know, what happened that night. And it wasn't about the red carpet, or trying to look good for the press, or for our parents. It was you and me. And you enjoying my lips pressed against yours and my tongue twirling around yours, and my hands traveling up..."

The memory caused me to flush with embarrassment and guilt, and a tinge of...confusion. Anderson? Never!

I cut him off. "Trust me. It'll never happen again."

He took his eyes off the road again, eyeing me. "I thought

you didn't remember it. But, whatever. You're right. It definitely won't happen again. I don't do confusion. And I don't do nonsense. And I don't do rebounds. So, what's up? You want to go to this party with me, or what? You know it's the only way Mr. Phillips is letting you out of the house."

I rolled my eyes, annoyed that he was right. I was still being held against my will.

"Don't worry. I won't let your hormones get in the way. I'll keep your lips off of me."

I sucked my teeth. I couldn't help but feel my face flush. "Boy, shut up."

"Shut me up. Matter of fact, give me another kiss."

"Ugh. This is soooo not funny."

"Uh, yes, it is. And what's even funnier is you liked it."

"Boy, please. What*ever*!" I said as he pulled up to the front doors of the school. "You're delusional."

"Yeah, right," he said, chuckling. I eyed him as he got out of the car and came around to open the passenger-side door for me. *Justice would have never opened the door.* I quickly shook the thought as I slid out of the car. Anderson reached for my hand and helped me out. Then that fool had the audacity to kiss me on the cheek, and pat me on the behind. "Be a good girl today. No drama, no suspensions." He laughed.

I sucked my teeth. I hated that I liked it. "Mmm hmm, it figures you'd wanna grab my booty. So typical. You're such a booty bandit. I almost forgot you were addicted to that part of the anatomy."

I walked off, back straight, hips forward, one foot in front of the other, sashaying away as I felt the heat of Anderson's stare burning into me.

20

Heather

I was *soooo* tired of faking the funk.

Tired of pretending that I wanted to be drug free when I didn't.

And no, I wasn't professing to be a junkie. And yeah, I knew I pledged allegiance to the "I'm a junkie" flag in front of my counselor and in group. But that was more like politicking.

Like I'd said a million times before: I was. Not. A. Junkie.

Hell, I'd been forced to dry up in here for weeks on end and I survived. If I was a junkie I would've died. What I was, was a disrespected star. Hollywood's sweetheart who'd gotten a bad rap simply because I liked to have a good time and kick my party up a notch.

Unfortunately, I was completely misunderstood and no one ever wanted to hear anything I had to say. Instead, everyone listened to Camille's hatin' rants and her self-righteous speeches about being the best mother she could be.

Gag me.

Camille was such a liar. If she wasn't, she wouldn't have just told my counselor, Mr. Mills, that I never tried to kill myself—knowing that I'd attempted suicide twice.

Once at twelve, courtesy of a gleaming BIC razor blade that I sliced across my left wrist. The second time at thirteen, when I dumped an entire bottle of naproxen down my throat and chased it with a stiff glass of bourbon. And if I had to sit here a minute longer and continue listening to Camille's bad acting, I'd be bolting out of here, searching for the nearest California cliff, and my third suicide attempt would be jumping off of it.

"Now tell me, Ms. Cummings," Mr. Mills said, sitting upright in his olive-green leather chair, "is there any history of substance abuse in your family?"

Camille cleared her throat and swept the flying strands of her blond hair behind her ears—which were now beet red—and said, "Absolutely not."

Whaaaat?!

She continued, "My mother was very religious. And my father was a hard-working man. Neither of them believed in drugging or drinking, which is why outside of a glass of champagne and a little white wine here and there, I don't indulge."

Spoken like a true West Virginian drunk.

Mr. Mills scribbled Camille's bullshit in his notepad. He looked over at me, and for an unexpected moment our eyes locked and our gazes lingered. I wondered what he was thinking.

A few seconds too long into staring at my counselor, I thought about calling out Camille and her lies, but I didn't. Instead I dropped my head, crossed my legs, and picked at invisible dirt beneath my fingernails.

Mr. Mills refocused his attention on Camille. "Ms. Cummings, what about Heather's paternal family?"

I sat up at attention. Looked directly at Camille.

Camille paused. Swallowed. "What about them?"

"Do they have a history of drug abuse?"

Camille cleared her throat, reached in her purse and pulled out a cigarette.

"There's no smoking in here," Mr. Mills said, interrupting her from flicking the silver lighter she held in her hand.

"Fine." Camille sneered. "But I need a cigarette, so I'm thinking it's time for me to get out of here. I've told you enough. And I still don't understand what getting in my business has to do with Heather being addicted to drugs."

"You didn't answer his question," I snapped. Sucked my teeth and looked Camille dead in her eyes. "He asked you about my father's family."

Camille looked at my counselor and said, "I don't know what she wants from me. I've tried everything. I've done everything! When she was five she wanted to be a beauty queen, so I put her in pageants—"

"Psst, please," I spat. "I never told you I wanted to be a beauty queen! That was your idea—"

"It was not!"

"*It was!* And you know it. 'Sit up straight, Heather. Hold your back straight, Heather. Shoulders squared. Smile for the camera. Wipe those tears. No one cares. Do you want to be nothing for the rest of your life, Heather?'"

"That never happened!"

"It did and you know it! What five-year-old is up by four in the morning, made to walk from one end of the room to the next, practicing with tiaras, and capes, and high heels, and makeup—tons and tons of makeup—and those wigs. And let's not even talk about that isolated and stupid homeschooling!"

"I homeschooled you to spend time with you! You wanted to be a star and I made you one!"

"I never wanted to be a star! You made me a star because you had fallen off!"

"I most certainly did not! I gave up my career because I was your mother and I knew I had greatness on my hands. I was trying to groom you, you spoiled ingrate! You were destined for stardom. And I was determined as your mother to get you there by any means necessary. And if that meant getting you up at four in the morning, home-schooling you, and perfecting your posture, poise, and confidence, then so be it!"

"Yeah. And after all that I still didn't win even one pageant. Because, just like everything else you've ever done for me, Camille, it wasn't good enough! So you beat and berated me for nothing."

"Don't put that off on me, misseee. You were a selfish, self-centered brat, who lost on purpose! If I said left, you said right. If I said sing, you said rap. You were always defiant. Unruly. Looking down your nose at me! You didn't even like my family!"

"Your family. You mean the Southern drunks who you just said didn't have a history of substance abuse? Well, maybe what he should have asked you about was alcohol abuse!"

"They didn't abuse that either!"

"Oh, puhlease! Let me tell you about your family, Norma Marie. They were a buncha racist, nasty trailer park—"

"Don't you dare—"

"Trash! Who treated me like I had leprosy!"

"My mother loved you!"

"Yeah, in secret. When Big Daddy wasn't around to remind her of how you ran off to Hollywood, slept with the Rainbow Coalition, and messed up his Anglican blood!"

"How dare you! My mother died apologizing for the way my father treated you! She was a good woman!"

"She was a drunk! Just like you!"

Camille jumped out of her seat and the counselor said forcefully, "Ms. Cummings, you need to have a seat! I've explained the rules. And you cannot be jumping out of your seat with aggression. Heather has a right to feel what she feels."

"But she's lying!" Camille cried. "My mother was a good woman. My mother loved me and she loved Heather!"

"Lies!" I spat. "She pitied me. Wished that you had had a bisque baby instead of a brown one! I was never good enough for them and I've never been good enough for you!"

"You're just nasty! Ungrateful!"

"I wanna know who the HELL MY FATHER IS, CAMILLE!"

"Your father is a man who doesn't give a damn about you," she said coldly, as she collected her purse and tucked it beneath her right arm.

"Ms. Cummings," Mr. Mills said, "let's just calm down and talk this out."

"I'm done." Camille scowled.

"Just let her go. I don't care if I never see her again!" I

did all I could to push back tears, but failed. I didn't know what pissed me off more; that I let Camille see me cry or that I couldn't get up and choke her.

Mr. Mills stared at me again. For a moment I thought he would hand me a tissue until I remembered that he swore crying was an expression of emotion that didn't need to be stopped or dammed up with Kleenex. That tears were better left alone.

I took the backs of my hands and wiped my eyes. I could tell by the way Mr. Mills looked at me that he wanted to comfort me and give me a hug and a kiss on the forehead like he had at the last individual session—when his hand slid down the small of my back, and I leaned into his chest and cried. For a moment I wished that he would embrace me now. His arms were the only place I'd ever felt safe... and wanted.

Camille cleared her throat.

For a moment I thought she'd disappeared.

Wishful thinking...

Mr. Mills turned back toward Camille and said, "Ms. Cummings, let's get back to why we are all here. Heather's treatment. Now, is there a reason why you refuse to share with Heather about her father? Let's talk about that."

"There's nothing to talk about. He was married. I slept with him. I was supposed to have an abortion"—she glanced over at me—"and obviously I didn't! He didn't want her then—and his wife and their kids have not made him sensitive, moved him, or changed his mind about being interested in her now! End of discussion. Now let's get this straight, so you don't be fooled by those big button eyes or those boobs: she's not here because she doesn't know who her father is; she's here because she chose to use drugs!"

"I hate you!"

Camille chuckled. "You can hate me, Heather, because if you keep being disrespectful, the feeling will be mutual! Now I already told you the last time you had an attack, tore up my house, threatened to assault me, and tossed my bar over the balcony, to give up the fairy tale! And stop looking for love from a man who wants nothing to do with you. So you better get yourself together and understand that I pull the strings. And need I remind you that you are on probation until you are eighteen!"

"Ms. Cummings," Mr. Mills interjected. "You seem a little hostile. But underneath the aggression I can tell that you care about your daughter."

"Hostile! You don't know me or what I am. I am far from hostile. I'm just sick and tired that every time I turn around this girl is in a buncha mess!"

"Yeah, that's the only time you notice me."

"Then you are sicker than I thought! So you have turned to being a crackhead looking for attention—"

"Well, it's better than being a drunk who doesn't get any attention! And yeah, I want attention. And instead of you being jealous of me—"

Camille slammed her clutch on the table. "Jealous! Why in the hell would I be jealous of you?! I am an Oscar-winning—"

"Flop. Do I need to remind you? A drunk! What was the last script you read? The last casting call you had? You're mad because I'm at the height of my career."

Camille laughed and shook her head. "You are at the height of your career? Really? When's the last time you turned on your TV? You were fired, remember? Someone else has replaced you.

"You are no longer on top because you wanted to get high. Now don't blame me for your misery, Heather! You were in this business because of who I am. Not because of your talent. There are a million girls who can act and sing. And a million more who can do it better than you! So you better get yourself together while you have a chance!" She turned to Mr. Mills. "If you don't mind, I think I need a word alone with my daughter before I blow this place!"

Mr. Mills looked over at me. "How do you feel about that?"

I was a mix of embarrassed, confused, and mad as hell. This whole ordeal was for the birds. It was clearly not for me. I wished I could write Camille off as dead to me. But I needed her, because with me being on probation until I was eighteen, she was right; she pulled the strings. I shrugged and nodded.

"I'll be right outside if you need me." Mr. Mills got up from his seat and closed the door behind him.

"Camille—"

"Don't Camille me, Heather! Got this man thinking I'm the worst mother ever! I should slap your face!" She flipped her hair behind her shoulders. "Lil ho in training, struggling to make it in Hollywood. You better get your practice up on how to get out of tough situations and how to stay on top, starting with your counselor! And don't you dare open your mouth to cut me off either! Because I saw the looks that both of you were giving each other. Now I don't know what's going on here, but it's something. And whatever it is, you better kick it over the edge and stop worrying about me and my drinking! I might be a drunk, but I have the recipe for your success! And the difference between me and you is that I didn't have to start off at the bottom sleeping with drug counselors. I did movie directors. Politicians. And music producers! Shakers and movers.

"Not Mr. Twelve Steps. Somebody trying to clean up junkies and their thieving ways. Being a crack whore was never on my list of things to do and it was never a role I played. But you, my dear—this seems to be where you need to start. If you want out of here, as bad as I know you do, then you need to sleep your way out of here and get your womanhood on! And if you can pull that trick then I'll know that you are ready to make your return to Hollywood and maybe then I'll help you take it to the next level!

"But as long as you are sitting up in here like you are carrying the world on your shoulders and have a million problems, then these people will never let you out! Now do you want your life back or not?!" She paused. "Answer me!"

I nodded.

She leaned into my face and said, "Then do what you need to do to get out of here!" She grabbed her clutch and stepped out the door.

21

London

I pursed my gloss-coated lips as I approached my locker and saw Miss Rich standing there, waiting with a hand up on her hip. I flipped my hair. "Mmmph, funny seeing you here. I thought you were off somewhere playing hand games with your girl, SlowKeeta."

Rich tucked her hair behind her ears. "Oh, London, please. Spencer can't help herself for being stupid. She was born with that gene. That's just a part of her handicap. But once you're able to get over her being stupid and dumb and a whore, stealing everybody's boyfriends and being in everybody's business, she's really not that bad to stomach. I actually like her as long as she stays up off her knees. And you would, too, if..."

"I did crack," I said snidely as I opened my locker.

Rich balled over in laughter. "Bwaaaaaahhaaa, oh, you so wrong for calling her a crack whore. Bwaaaaaaaahhaaa."

"Yeah, a dumb crack whore at that."

"Yeah, Crackalicia, with her dizzy behind. Crack-crack-

crack-crack it up!" Rich snapped her fingers, then dropped down and booty-popped-it up. She shimmied it, then hip bumped me. "Let's crack-crack-crack it up."

I couldn't help but laugh. Rich was a mess, but she was my girl. Two-faced or not, I was glad to see she had come to her senses and realized who her true friend was. Not that nasty knee-dropping, man-guzzling trick, Spencer. As long as Rich was dogging her out, I knew we were back on track being bestie-boos.

"Girl, you are comical," I said, getting caught up in the moment. I was feeling good; despite Justice being MIA, I had my girl back. This was phase one of *My Boo Returns*.

I did like Rich, really. But Rich was two-faced. And I still couldn't get over how she had turned on me, dissing me for Spencer. That really hurt my feelings. But at the end of the day, I knew that Rich wasn't loyal to anyone except herself. She was selfish. And I also knew that if the tables were turned, she'd do the same thing to me. So there was no room for feeling bad about doing her first.

I smiled as I finger popped with her and did a two-step. Yes, we were back on track. "Crack, crack, crack is whack…"

"Aaaaaah," Rich snapped, jumping up and popping her booty. "Do it, boo! Work it, girl. Loosen up."

"I am loose. Crack, crack, crack is whack," I repeated as I shimmied my shoulders.

Rich started chanting and dancing. "There's some whores in this house, there's some whores in this house. Work that mofo…the roof is on fiiiiiiire…we don't need no whores, let 'em all burn…crack kills…burn, mofos, burn…"

She pulled me by the hands and started two-stepping with me, drawing attention over to us. Cameras clicked, as usual. And kids started finger popping and head bobbing to our impromptu moves.

Someone started making catcalls, and someone else started making human beat-box sounds. Then out of nowhere, Spencer appeared and dropped her diamond-encrusted Birkin bag and started pumping her pelvis up into Rich, doing some kind of giddy-up two-step, like a horse and cowgirl dance. She was practically riding Rich's back. She started singing and making gestures with her hand as if she were whipping a horse. "Eeeeehaaaaw, giddy-up, giddy-up, giddy-up...move them buffalo hips... when I hit the dance floor, I be doin' the Stanky Leg. Aaaaah Eeeeehaaaaw...get it, get it...It's time to make it twerk up in this mofo...I said it's time for the percolator"—she clapped her hands—"Giddy-up, goshdang it... booty-booty...cootie pop it...let me see you make it drop... to the left, to the left..." Spencer dropped it low then started winding it back up, then dropped down again, then bounced and rolled with it. "Now, shake ya Laffy Taffy..."

Rich started jumping up and down, "Wait, wait...I got some throwback hotness for you pimps 'n' pimpettes and hoes..." She reached into her bag and pulled out her iPhone, then pressed a button. Then "Cupid Shuffle" started playing "...C'mon my bottom beeeeyotch," she said as she pulled Spencer over to her. "Let's boom, bop, drop it...to the right, to the right, to the left, to the left... right kick, right kick..."

Hollywood High immediately went from a school for the elite to a performing arts school. What a mess! I didn't know what the hell they were doing, but they were doing it. And for a moment, I wanted to know how they did it.

Let go. And I wondered how it must feel to be Rich and Spencer.

Free.

As the beat kept playing, I found myself bouncing my shoulders, still a tinge of jealously sweeping through me watching Spencer and Rich laugh and dance like they were the best of friends. *Oh, that trick has to go. And now!*

I almost hit the floor, hard, when Rich bent over and grabbed her ankles and shook and bounced her rump-shaker up into Spencer. And I practically went into cardiac arrest when Spencer started smacking her on the booty.

Rich went straight skid row and started chanting, "Ride that horse, boo...smack it up, smack it up, smack it up..."

The boys went wild as Spencer started humping into Rich's behind. Ugh! I rolled my eyes in disgust and felt myself ready to throw up in the back of my mouth.

What kinda nasty tricks are these two freakazoids into?

Rich turned to Spencer, then slid one leg in between hers, and they both threw their hands up over their heads and danced hip to hip. I was too through!

OMG, what a buncha whores!

"All right, all right, break it up," boomed through the crowd. "Let's clear these halls!" Mr. Westwick yelled. His face was beet red. "I'm appalled at all of you! What kind of school do you think we're running here? The school for the Hippity Hop Homeless? Jeezus! If the board of directors were here, they'd have us shut down. I'd be carted off out of here. You want to dance, get to ballroom class. This is unacceptable. Now get a move on." He pulled out a hanky and started dabbing his wet forehead.

Kids started scattering and laughing.

"I'm not going back to the monastery," he screamed, waving his arms theatrically in the air.

Spencer snatched up her handbag. "Hi, Mr. Wessssst-wick," she said sweetly. "That London sure knows how to bring the ghetto out. Hoodlum City." She tossed her hair and strutted off.

Slut!

"Lonnnnndon?!" Mr. Sharp, Mr. Westwick's assistant, screamed. "I know you were behind this. This reeks of New York madness. Ever since you got here, there's been nothing but trouble here. If this is how you bop it, or drop it, or pop it, or whatever youse say in New York, that's not how we represent ourselves here. This is Hollywood High! We will not tolerate these kinds of shenanigans from you."

I blinked as Rich laughed, pulling me by the arm toward homeroom. "Girrrrrl, that was fiiiiiiiiiyah! That's how we gonna drop it at this party we're about to go to."

I frowned, looking at her like she was half-crazed. "We? What? Who's we?"

"Me and Christian and you and Louis, that's who."

"Rich, please. What are you talking about?"

Rich clapped her hands in my face, then snapped her fingers. "Get with the program, London. Snap, snap! Me and Christian Louboutin. And you and Louis Vuitton. Who else? Don't tell me you've had a designer freeze. Geesh. Wake up! Now there's a party that my boo's fraternity is giving and we will be the belles of the ball."

I batted my lashes. "Your boo? What boo?"

Rich let out an exaggerated sigh. "Get yo' mind right. Your thoughts in order. What is going on? Maybe you need

to do crack 'cause you messing up my hookah high. And I
don't do that. Who else would I be talking about?"

I shrugged. "Damon?"

Rich threw a hand up to her neck. "Clutching pearls!"
she hissed. "That was a one-night-way-too-late-at-the-bar
stand. You're tryna mess me up here. I told you about that
in secret. You know that boy stalked me for a week. Had
me hiding out in wigs. I had to be homeschooled for
weeks behind him. Noooo, uh-uh. Don't bring him up. We
don't talk about him. "

"Then who are you talking about? Last I knew you were
single. I thought you were home, moping and crying."

"Whaaaaaat? Moping and crying? I don't do that. My
middle name is Next. Next up! You got me confused, boo.
That's something you and Spencer would do. But, me...
Rich Gabrielle, I got it together. You don't see no mirror
over here. I'm not your reflection. I don't do that. Get all
worked up over no boys. Please. I'm too fly for that. Now,
I'm not taking no for an answer. I see you don't have your
head on straight. But we're going to my boo's party and
that's that."

"Well, who's your boo?"

"Knox. Didn't you hear a word I said? Don't get it confused. Always is, always will be. He can't live without me.
One day you'll grow up and be like me. Love 'em and
leave 'em and they chase you down, just to have you
again. See you at lunch." And with that said, she dipped
into her homeroom, leaving me standing there looking at
her like she was nuts.

I blinked. Rich was everything I was not and everything
I hoped never to be. But there were parts of her that I
wished I could be. I didn't want to be a whore. I wanted to

be a one-man woman. I didn't want to be inconsistent. I wanted to be consistent. The part of Rich that I wanted wholeheartedly was her freedom and her ability to move on. And if somewhere along the line she was faking the funk, I wanted that, too, because she was a good phony.

And for the next three periods, I couldn't shake myself. I hated it. I was miserable. All I could do was think about Justice. I was in my classes, but I wasn't there mentally. I didn't give a damn about these classes, or the fact that my grades were slipping. I just sat there, aimlessly—mind wandering, obsessing over Justice.

How could he do me like this?...

Brrrrrrrrring!

The sound of the bell jolted me out of my fog. And at that moment I made up my mind to try freedom on for size. *I'm going to try not to think about Justice. I'm going to focus on me and enjoy the rest of my day.*

I grabbed my books and handbag, then headed out the door.

As I walked into the café my cell vibrated, alerting me that I had a text. I quickly fished out my phone. *Please let this be Justice.* I glanced at the screen. It was a text from an unknown number. I opened it.

If Justice was ur boyfriend, he wasn't last week

I blinked. Felt my heart drop into my stomach. I texted back: who is this?

Unknown texted back: Wouldn't you like to know. LMAO

justice is this u? stop torturing me. Just let me talk to u

Unknown replied: London, OMG, ur so stupid. This is your worst nightmare

if u don't leave me alone I'm gonna report u 2 the police

Unknown texted back: do it!!!!!! I dare u, make my day ho! hahahaha no wonder justice dumped ur pathetic azz! madame beg a lot!

My knees buckled.

Who was this harassing me? I didn't know who was playing these sick games, but I wasn't feeling it one bit. Someone knew that Justice and I were involved. But who?

I gasped. *Anderson!* He was the only sneaky, sick bastard that would do something like this. No wonder he was being so nice. He wanted to torture me in unsuspecting ways.

I scrolled for his number and quickly texted: U dirty piece of nothing! 4 one sick moment, I almost thought u were human. But now I see u r from the planet creep. Get a life! And stay the hell out of mine, u punk sissy beeeeeeeeeoyotch!

I tossed my phone back into my bag, storming over to the table where Rich and Spencer were once again making love at the lunch table, cackling and carrying on. I felt like banging Spencer right in the middle of her forehead.

I threw my handbag up on the table, rattling the dishes. "It's about time," Rich huffed as she stuffed a sushi roll into her mouth. She talked as she chewed. "Oh no. Oh no. We don't do that. We don't do your attitude. And we don't do this last-year's handbag, either."

"Last year's handbag?" I snapped. "You had better check your fashion log. There's nothing last-year about my handbag. Now don't worry about my bags, worry about you being a worldwide freak."

"See. That's what I said," Spencer interjected. "Rich, I told you. You've been around the world. You've been in Milan, Paris, Hong Kong...I'm surprised you haven't brought back some kind of tropical disease."

"Whaaaat?!" Rich screeched. "Both of you better not be trying to bop it, drop it on me. Guzzle, guzzle, Spencer."

Spencer batted her eyes and licked her lips. "Yup, and good to the last drop." She licked her fingers and I almost threw up right there all over the table. Spencer was a whore and wore the title like a designer badge. She was proud and carefree. She continued, "At least I don't get pregnant. But how many does this make for you, Rich?"

"Don't you worry about my fallopian tubes. Worry about your tonsils. Now don't make us fall out, Spencer. We been doing good. But I will boom, bop it on you in a minute. Play with me if you want to."

Spencer gasped. "Play with you? You done gone too far now; just because I danced up on your booty this morning and we tag-teamed Raheem together last summer after one of his games, and booty popped it up in Ace Hood's Hustle Hard video, that doesn't mean I'm trying to play with you and that ran-over snatch patch of yours. You nasty freak!"

Rich hopped out of her seat. I leaned up in excitement, ready for her to knock Spencer's lights out. This was exactly what I hoped for. The two of them falling out.

Now bring it home, Rich. Bring it home...

"Ooooooooh, I almost forgot about that, girl. My name was Peaches. And your name was Cream. We was doin' it, boo. We were booty poppin' it, and they were making it rain."

Spencer hopped up and giggled, then stood up in her chair and wound her hips. "Hustle...hard...hustle, hard..."

I gagged. These tricks were into more than I imagined. I thought that was them in that video. Now I knew for sure they were freaks. And this was not going the way I had hoped.

I let out a disgusted sigh, slamming a hand down on the table. "Why can't the two of you stay focused? When are we going to start talking about this party?"

Rich's eyes popped open. "Uh, excuse you, Miss Mess. We were talking about it until you came over here with your funky-behind attitude. So, annnnnywaaaay...as Spencer and I were saying, we should do it up lovely. This masquerade ball has to be the party of all parties. It needs to be hotter than the invitation party was. I want them gagging when we step up in there, dropping dead at the door. Spencer is going to handle getting us the party planner and all we have to do is show up being fabulous."

"Works for me," I said, shifting in my seat. The last thing I cared about was some party.

"And make sure you leave that ole nasty frown at home. We don't need that kind of ugliness around us, messing up our aura. You need to get your chakra together."

Spencer blinked, blinked again. Tilting her head and staring at Rich real confused and crazy.

"What—what are you looking at me like that for?" Rich asked, frowning.

"I can't believe you were actually paying attention in spirituality class."

Rich blinked. "Spirituality, what? Who? Girl, please. I got that from a line in a movie."

Spencer gave Rich a blank stare. "Yeah, uh, anyway..."

Rich's phone started ringing. She pulled it out of her bag, then frowned at the screen. "Yeah, Fabulous here..." She got quiet, then her body stiffened. She looked nervous as she gathered her things from the table. "Uh, okay...

When?...I guess...no, no...that's not true..." Rich tossed her bag up over her shoulder and walked off, leaving me sitting there with Spencer, dumbfounded.

I blinked. "Oh no," I said, gathering my things. "I'm definitely not doing you."

"You're right you're not doing me, ho," Spencer spat, jumping up from the table as well. "I wouldn't do you even if I had two hairy buffalo balls." She stomped off, swinging her hips and bouncing her hair. "Rich, wait up."

Somehow, someway, I was going to make sure that that was the last time Spencer ran behind Rich. All I needed was a way to make it happen. And fast.

22

Rich

I can't believe I'm going through this...
Why am I struggling like hell to be good?
Faithful.
And committed...
I've always wanted to be Mrs. Knox.
Always.
And yeah, in the beginning, I fought like hell *not* to love him.
But I gave in.
Turned around.
And then fought like hell *to* love him.
Openly.
I professed my love in public.
To my parents.
And I didn't care who cared.
I just wanted my destiny unveiled so that I could be his girl.
And it was.

And I was.

And we kicked it.

Hard.

Our love was as sweet as brown sugar...Oh wait, it was sweeter than that.

He did more than make my heart skip beats. He made my entire circulatory system clap. Made the colorful butterflies in my stomach flutter. Placed a rhythmic African switch in my wide hips.

Made me share sweet drool with my eiderdown pillow as I dreamed of the endless possibilities called Us.

Christian Knox and Rich Montgomery were the It Couple. And no, he didn't want the press. But we got it. Owned it. And rocked it. My e-mail and my snail mail were full of fan letters wishing us well and telling me how cute my cutie was.

We were a whirlwind romance. A boom-boom-we-are-in-the room wicked fairy tale destined to be cherry-topped with a storybook ending.

For the first time ever, everything in *As the Rich World Turns* was perfect. Diamond studded and six-inch Manolo Blahniks perfect.

And no, I wasn't worried about karma coming around and the universe not keeping my tiny white miscarriage lie a secret. The Goddess of Desperation and I had an understanding: I had to do what I had to do.

And so I did. Which was how my man and I got back to love jonesin' again. Revamped our high and got lifted off our own romantic supply.

We made love every other night.

Went to movie screenings.

Killed the arcade.

Shut down campus parties.

Bowled.

Ate pizza.

Played dominos.

Spades.

We did things that made me feel free. That made us free. Knox was the only person who could love me like that. The only one I would let love me like that. And from the time I was uncomfortably chubby, wore glasses that were too thick to scream cuteness, had the worst acne, wore braces, and strutted around with fake self-esteem, Knox had loved me.

So why, oh why, oh why in the hell was I not following the commandments of a virtuous girlfriend? Why was I allowing myself to tiptoe and tightrope over to the wild side by kicking it to Justice Banks on the sly?

And yeah, Justice was fly.

He was fly.

And a good kisser...

A great kisser...

With the God-given hands of passion...

Geezus...

And yeah, I was a collector of finer things, and Justice was an exquisite piece of black art. But I already had one African statue. I didn't need two. Justice was supposed to be left at the club. Disposed of by way of a Dear John letter that simply read "Good-bye," and left to be a drunken memory that I'd blessed with two one-hundred-dollar bills, left on the hotel's nightstand for the heartbreaking inconvenience I'd caused him.

He was not supposed to be around long enough for me to bring the crazy.net out of him.

But he was.

He was downstairs, uninvited and unexpected. Getting his stalker on and squatting on me in the school's parking lot. And yeah, he'd texted me and told me that he needed to see me now...but still, that was so not the point...

I shook my head and tossed my dark brown, high-lighted infusion weave behind my shoulders. My iPhone vibrated with back-to-back text messages like crazy.

This dude was nutz!

I looked up and over toward where Spencer sat, hoping to get her attention. But, in true I'm-so-smart-that-I-must-pay-attention-to-every-godforsaken-word-the-teacher-says whack fashion, Spencer had her eyes glued to the teacher.

She was *sooooo* aggravating sometimes. Like who really listened to this dude? Duh, this was finance class. Something Hollywood High didn't even need, especially since everyone in here had an accountant. A How to Design Jewels class would've been much more beneficial to our needs.

Whatever.

I quickly wrote Spencer a note that instructed her to meet me in the girls' lounge. I folded it into a tiny square and passed it to the Rockefeller goth kid who sat next to me. He then passed the note up the underground railroad of note-passing; and once it landed on Spencer's desk, I eased out of the classroom and headed to the lounge.

A few seconds later Spencer walked in the door with her heels clicking and a worried look on her face. "Rich, are you okay? Is this a Mace day? Or a crampy, I-so-hate-my-period day?" She rummaged through her purse. "If so, I have...Mace and Midol."

"Mace? I don't do weapons in a can. And Midol?" I

frowned. "If I had cramps I'd be downstairs in the sauna or with the masseuse. I don't do Midol. How cheap and cheesy. That lil nasty pink package."

"Sweetbloodofaswampmonkey, what the heck am I here for?" She wiped her brow in exhaustion. "And please, please let it be worth me leaving class, missing the end of Mr. Donte's lecture, and not knowing what I had for homework!" She stomped her feet.

I know this chick didn't have an attitude. "Clutching pearls! Was that a tantrum, Miss Drama? Daaaang, it's only homework. Like, it's not that serious. And anyway, all you have to do is ask London for the assignment. She was sitting a few seats over from you looking all roach-eyed and crazy."

Spencer twisted her pink painted lips. "Yeah, real roachified."

"Bates Motel to the max," I snapped.

"Downright freakesque, coochie-burnin'-panty-liner nasty. And you expect me to talk to a weirdo like that? Really, Rich? Is that what you think of me? I don't speak the same language as freaks!"

"I never said that."

"Look, would you just get to the point? Why did you call me in here?"

I paused. And then gave Spencer the innocent Barbie-doll smile that always melted my daddy and worked wonders on Knox. "I need you on patrol."

"Patrol?"

I walked over to the windowsill and tapped it. "Posted right here."

Spencer's eyes popped open and she blinked rapidly. "Patrol? For what?"

"Remember Justice from the Kit-Kat Lounge?"

Spencer tooted her lips and tapped her right foot. "Yeah, what about him?"

"Well, long story cut down to two sentences. He's. Crazy."

"See, this is why you need to stay in class. Because what you just said made no sense. And I'm the dizzy one? I have no time for this. We have twenty minutes left before the day ends and if I leave now I can still catch Mr. Donte's recap of what we need to study over the weekend."

"OMG. Why are you so far up Mr. Donte's behind? Dang. Could you crawl out of his anus, please? You know what, I don't know why I called you anyway, Professor Do-Good who's too good to leave class and help your good-good friend out. I should've just passed the note to London."

Spencer's eyes narrowed. "Don't make me stab you, cut your tongue out, and then go back for your teeth and tonsils! Now nine-one-one, what is your emergency?"

"Nine-one-one, Justice has been sweatin' me for the past two weeks. I can't seem to shake him. Now he is downstairs waiting for me. He's crazy and I need you to make sure he doesn't try to kidnap me, force me in the car, and have his way with me."

"And why wouldn't you want that? Isn't that what you did with the twins? Called it role play. A way to spice things up."

Oh, she has lost her mind! "Clutching pearls! You must want your face slapped. I know you don't want to go there, Spencer. Because I will go Joey on you! Don't bring up the twins. They no longer exist. Now as I said, I need you on patrol."

"I don't do patrol."

"Oh, yes you do," I snapped.

"Umm, no, I don't. I have to get to class. So your hoein' will have to be put on layaway. You need Hoes Anonymous."

"You need to kill the hoes."

Spencer gasped and clutched the right side of her chest. "Kill the hoes? Rich, I can't believe you would suggest something like that! There are hoes that I love. Like you. Even Kitty."

I rolled my eyes toward the glass ceiling. *Dumb, dumb, dumb...* "Look, I don't ask you for much. And I really need you to do this for me."

Spencer sucked her teeth, walked over to the window, and looked down at Justice. "He is cute." She popped her lips. "Smooth chocolate." She licked her fingertips. "Nice and recyclable. But what about Knox? You told me you two were back together."

"We are. Which is why I have to tell Justice to step."

Spencer looked back out the window. "We might have to tag-team this one, Rich." She blew Justice a kiss. "So go on, get your ho on. I'll be here when you get back."

"Thanks, bestie-boo." I hurried out of the lounge, eased past security and into the parking lot where my eyes drank in Justice in full view.

He's sooo fine.

He leaned against the passenger-side door of his black Lexus coupe. The brim of his Yankees fitted fell down over his mesmerizing marble-brown eyes. He wore a dark blue pair of True Religion jeans and a crisp white Billionaire Boys Club T-shirt that highlighted and defined his hard, muscular pecs.

Oh father, he turned me on...

And on his myth-gratifying, long and big sexy feet were a pair of loosely tied Timbs that completed the sensual New York thug in him.

Goddamn...

His muscular arms were folded across his chest as I walked over to him and he boldly licked his lips.

Lips I wanted to lick...

I tried to hold back the words I felt were destined to leave my mouth, but I couldn't, they just fell out: "Umm hmm, lil daddy. Look at you drooling. You like what you see?" I twirled around, confident that my tailored black Dior shorts lay perfectly over my curvaceous hips, complimenting my shapely size-twelve thighs, and of course my boom-boom-that-brought-all-the-boys-to-the-room gluteus maximus spoke for itself.

After I twirled around so that he could appreciate me in full view, I gave him a standing pose. Face forward, hands on hips, fierce weave in check and dangling over my shoulders. I watched my reflection in his eyes as they dropped from my one-of-a-kind hot-pink Louis Vuitton blouse with the plunging neckline that dipped perfectly into my bubbling cleavage, to the Chanel belt that draped around my waist. His eyes dropped below the belt to my hips and legs, and landed on my six-inch open-toe black Manolos. All I could do was smile as his thoughts telepathically told me what I already knew: I was fiyah.

After taking inventory of me, Justice said, "Nah, yo. I more than like what I see. I want what I see." He gave me a lopsided smile and that's when it hit me that he resembled a twenty-year-old Idris Elba but taller; much taller.

Have Mercy.

We both bit into our bottom lips.

"C'mere," he said sexily. His deep voice danced chills over my spine. Nervously, I twirled the end of my hair.

Remember you have a man...

I swallowed and said, "You can want what you see, but you can't have me."

"Yeah, whatever, yo. That's what your mouth says. But the last time I held ya body it clearly told me somethin' different. So front if you want." He looked me over and I fought hard not to melt on the spot.

You have a man...

"Boy, please." I prayed he couldn't hear my heart skipping beats.

"Yeah, I got your boy, a'ight." He smirked and his biceps pumped with every word he spoke, seducing my eyes up the bulging veins that traveled along the sides of his arms and up his thick and kissable neck.

I needed somebody to pray for my sanity... 'cause I was about to go crazy...

He continued. "Yeah, just what I thought, yo. Now who's droolin'?" He walked over to me and stroked my cheeks. "Yo, why you playin' so hard to get?"

"I have a boyfriend."

"Oh, yeah, that's right. College boy. I almost forgot about that dude. But I'm sure you understand me forgettin' 'bout that cat. Especially since you never bring him up durin' our nightly conversations."

"We don't have nightly conversations."

"Yeah, a'ight. There you go frontin' again. But it's cool. So every other night."

"Like I said, I have a boyfriend. And I can't and won't be kicking it with you any longer. So you can leave now."

He laughed. *And oh, what a cute laugh.* "Yo, spare me, ma. All that ish you just spit out ya pretty lil' mouth, you don't even believe it."

I paused. Wondered for a moment if my conflicting feelings were that obvious or if he had a special gift that allowed him to see right through me. I continued. "Look. I don't do stalker and I def don't do uninvited guests. And it's creepy and rude that you would show up here without me asking you to."

"Yo, hol' up... Like I told you last night when we were s'posed to go on our lil' date, if you stood me up—which you did—that I was gon' come through and check for you. Now I'm a man of my word, fa real fa real. And you need to be a woman about yours and tell me what's really good."

"Dates? I don't do dates. I gotta man. I'm married."

Justice stepped closer into my personal space. He flicked my chin and whispered practically lip to lip. "Yeah, a'ight. You may have a man, but it's in title only, yo. So you may as well get rid of him, 'cause you know and I know ya man doesn't make you feel like I do. Remember when I—" He leaned in. Whispered dirty memories in my ear. Then he pressed his lips against mine and said, "And if you behave I'll do it all again." He gave me a soft peck and took a step back.

I closed my eyes. Drifted into the memory of our night in the hotel suite...

You got a man...

My eyes popped open and I took a step back. "All of that was a mistake." I took another step back. "And anyway, dude, what's wrong with you? You're acting real deprived right now. Real hood-bugger-anti-pimp-thirsty."

He frowned. "Thirsty?"

"Restraining-order thirsty. I don't do this. Creeping up on me. I didn't even drop no real big time on you. God forbid if I really dropped the boom bop, you'd be living on my doorstep. And by the way I don't do that either. Now go on back to skid row with Joey—"

"Joey?" He looked at me, confused.

"You heard me. I don't have a speech problem."

"Who is Joey? The last dude you left at the bar—?"

"You have me confused with one of your baby mamas."

"Baby mama? Yo, if anything I'm tryna make *you* my baby mama. But then again you probably have enough baby daddies."

I placed my hands on my hips. "You know what, I'm not doing this with you." I turned away from him and as I headed back toward the school he reached for my arm and gently pulled me into him. I knew I should've snatched away, but I didn't. And we were breasts to six-pack, and I was seconds from melting all over again. God, I needed to get away from him. "Let me go."

"You can walk away if you want." He raised his hands in the air.

But I didn't move.

Why didn't I move?

"Yeah, a'ight. Just what I thought."

I fought back a blush. "Look, I don't appreciate—"

"Yo, shut. Up. Enough. Let's just get outta here. You can come home wit' me. And you already know what it is wit' me. I don't kiss and tell."

"You are such a freak. And I don't do freaks."

He chuckled, looked over his shoulder and looked back at me. "Yeah, but I bet you do college boys. 'Cause he's right over there." Justice pointed across the parking lot. And my heart dropped into my heels. I quickly backed away from Justice, hoping that the scent of guilt didn't linger on me.

Get it together, Rich. You're not doing anything wrong. There's no harm in talking. You didn't kiss him and that stolen peck didn't count. And the other-other time in the hotel room…those kisses don't count either. Now dust your shoulders and smile.

"Hey, babe!" I rushed over to Knox, who was now only a few inches away. He didn't acknowledge me. He brushed past me and walked over to Justice.

Oh God, please be kind to me. This is not the time for a pissin' match… "Knox, I'm over here." I wedged my way in between him and Justice. Knox placed his hands on my waist and moved me to the side.

"Rich," Knox said, speaking to me but looking directly at Justice.

"Yes, baby."

"You wanna introduce me to your friend," he said, more like a statement than a question.

"Hell no." Pause. "Umm, I mean, umm." My heart raced like a running Clydesdale. "This is—this is, ummm… James, John—"

"Justice," Justice said, extending his hand toward Knox.

They gave each other dap and Justice looked back at me with a smirk. "Yo, Rich, I'll hollah at you later."

I can't believe he said that. Why would he say something like that? Oh, this dude was officially black history.

As Justice got into his car and disappeared into the distance I didn't know what to do. I didn't know whether to stand still or move. I looked over to Knox and he stared at me. Long. Hard. And the look on his face told me there were a million thoughts racing through his mind. All of which would require damage control. Before I could say anything and assess where his mind was, London bolted out the door in a panic, interrupting our troubled silence.

"Rich! What are you doing out here?" She looked up and over at Knox. "Is that—?"

I frowned. How rude—was she asking me twenty-twenty questions in front of my man and looking all crazy? I had enough explaining to do. I didn't need to explain why this crazed lunatic even knew my name. "Look, I'll talk to you later. I have to go." I flicked my hand bye and followed Knox to his truck. And instead of opening the door for me, like he usually did, he left me standing there, got in, and revved the engine.

I couldn't believe this.

He rolled down the passenger window. "You staying or you going?"

"Are you serious? So you're really not going to open the door for me?"

He clicked the locks. "The door's open. Get in or step. But I'm 'bout to roll."

Oh, he was trippin'. And I knew he felt some kinda way but still... I yanked the door open and said, "I don't do rudeness."

"I don't know what you'll do."

We rode an hour in pissed-filled silence. And I couldn't take it anymore. Knox had never been this mad with me. And yeah, I know me and Justice standing there may have looked funny, but I didn't do anything.

Noth. Thing.

And if Knox knew how hard I was fighting to keep our relationship honest and pure, he'd let go of this humbug, fall back and get his act together. For real-for real I didn't need this drama.

"Knox—"

Before I could finish the rest of my sentence he turned the radio up.

Oh, no he didn't!

Whatever.

Thirty more minutes of pissed-filled silence and I decided to try this again. "Knox—"

He pulled into the parking lot of his apartment complex, parked his truck, got out, and left me sitting there. And then to make matters worse he clicked the alarm.

Oh, hell no!

I rushed out of the truck before the alarm set and hurried up the stairs behind him. I was on his heels into his apartment, walked straight past Midnight and his dumb remarks, and followed Knox into his room and slammed the door. "Yo, what is your problem!" I didn't mean to scream, but I couldn't help it.

Knox removed his shirt, revealing his eight-pack. "You better lower your voice." He stepped out of his jeans and into a pair of basketball shorts.

"What is your problem?" I lowered my voice but kept the salt in my tone.

"I don't have a problem." He lay on his press bench and started lifting a hundred-pound weight, the way he always did when he was stressed or pissed, or both.

"Oh really?" I said. "You throw me mad shade on the

way up here. You don't talk to me, and then you leave me in the parking lot sitting in your truck and then you click the alarm like I wasn't even there! Who does that, like really! What's really good with you?"

He snapped, "Nah, the question is, what's really good with you? You knew I was coming up to your school to pick you up and bring you back to spend the weekend with me, and instead of waiting for me I walk up on you kicking it to some dude, like you don't even have a man! Now who does that?" He mocked me. "Like really."

"Knox—"

"Don't Knox me, Rich. That ish looked real crazy as hell! Now if for whatever reason you're feeling like you need to be free or if this relationship doesn't fit with the next headline you're trying to get into, then by all means, step."

My eyes and my mouth popped open. "What are you trying to say?!"

"I'm not trying to say anything. I said it."

My voice trembled. "You're breaking up with me?" A knot filled my chest.

"Nah, I'm checking you. And I'm letting you know that I don't do game. So you might be able to manipulate the press, and your fans, and some random dude up at your grand school. But you can't pull nothing on me because I have a degree in Rich-ology. And I know you." He dropped the weight back into its place, added on two twenty-pound discs, lay back down, and lifted it.

"Knox, why won't you let me explain! Why are you going to the left like this?"

"I'm not going to the left. I'm just letting you know that I know you."

"Are you going to let me explain?"

"Yeah. But make sure you think about the BS you say to me, and it better be the truth."

"You calling me a liar?!" I waved my hand in the air. "Wait a minute here. I know dang well you didn't call me a liar!"

"Rich, get to the point. Who was the dude that had you tongue-tied?"

"I wasn't tongue-tied. And that was a nobody from my finance class. I was outside waiting for you and he walked over to me and asked me would I tutor him."

"Tutor him? Don't play me, Rich. You don't even do your homework—your chef does."

Immediately I went on pause. I had no idea what to say next, but I had to say something before this argument went too far to come back...

Oh, sweet Goddess of Desperation, please tell me what to do here. I need you to answer me now or I'ma have a nervous breakdown. I can't lose my man...

"Oh, Rich, dear," the Goddess of Desperation spoke back to me, "you already know the golden rule. Do what you have to do..."

"Knox, just listen to me. You're right and I told him that the chef does my homework. And yeah, I'll admit he came on to me. But I told him I had a man. Who I loved."

"Uhmm hmm."

Dang, he was still on edge...

I walked over to him, straddled his lap, and ran my hands up his chest. He placed the weight on the hooks behind him. I planted a wet kiss on his neck and then down the center of his chest. "I told him I have a man who I wouldn't do wrong. For anything in the world."

"I love you, Rich. But I'm not stupid. And if I see that dude around you again and you're standing there and the situation looks crazy, we're done. No questions asked."

"Shhh." I kissed his lips. "It'll never happen again."

"It better not," he said, surrendering to my kisses.

23

London

Here it was a Friday night, and once again I was stuck on the antebellum plantation, being emotionally flogged. My masters—my mother and father—were abroad as usual. And my overseers, Genevieve and Daddy's security team, were somewhere scattered about the estate, watching everything I did, then reporting back to my parents, who called themselves keeping me on a tight leash. Everything was a mess!

I really didn't know how much more of being enslaved I could bear before I ended up being strapped to a gurney and carted off to a padded room somewhere. Then to add to my misery, there was some psycho-stalker out there who seemed invested in trying to take me to the edge of insanity, then pushing me over it. At first, I thought it was Anderson, but now I'm not so sure.

Still, whoever it was, they were really getting under my skin, peeling my nerves apart. And today was the final straw when I got that message that Justice was outside in the back parking lot of school. I snatched my books and bag, then darted out of the classroom, sprinting through the halls in my heels, trying to get outside to him. My heart raced with anticipation. I was finally going to see him. But when I burst through the back entrance, the only thing I saw was Rich standing outside with some very handsome guy who didn't look too happy about something.

Then Rich had the audacity to give me attitude when I asked her what she was doing out there. I was really getting sick of her! And I was still pissed at her for, once again, betraying me to the left with that slut-bucket, Spencer. That trick had the nerve to wave a folded note in my face as she slid out of our finance class, leaning into my ear and whispering, "You wanna know why you stay on the bottom, Bubbles? 'Cause you're a stupid ho, you hot trash stunt dummy."

When I craned my neck to get Rich's attention, she was gone! And Spencer walked out of the room with a triumphant smirk on her face. I don't know what I ever did to that conniving whore, but that chick hated everything about me. Jealousy was truly the root of her evil. And Spencer was green to her rotted core.

I was going to bring her down if it was the last thing I did.

My cell rang. I rolled my eyes as the ringtone, "You the Boss" blared out, letting me know it was Rich calling. I let it roll into voice mail. *Tramp, puhleeze! You diss me for Dizzy Lizzy, I don't think so!* A few seconds later, it rang again. I ignored it.

She called back-to-back-to-back. I finally answered after the twentieth time she called. "Yes, Rich," I said, my attitude on red.

"Pop, pop, get it-get it. I know you don't have no attitude, girl."

"Whatever. I didn't appreciate you leaving me in class to go off and have some secret rendezvous with Dumbzilla, while I had to sit and watch Mister Donte's bubble-butt sitting high up on his back and his pants all wedged up in his crack. That man needs to start wearing a girdle to hide all those craters in his behind. Every time he turns to write on the chalkboard I have to be subjected to that nastiness. And you left me sitting there counting his bullet holes. You know that man has a behind like a war victim."

"Whaaaat? Clutching pearls. Stop the press! You must have OCD. Who does that, counting craters in some man's behind? You need help, girl."

I huffed. "And what was that grandstanding stunt you pulled out in the parking lot this afternoon? I didn't appreciate that one bit."

"Hold up. Wait a minute. Why is drama meeting me at the door? Hello, Drama? Get off the phone and put London on 'cause I didn't call for you. You better get your life together. What's going on with you, girl? You have changed. And not for the good, but for the desperate!"

"Desperate? How dare you!"

"No. How dare you try to disrupt my get-right! Do you know how high I am right now? You don't give a damn about me, London. My man got that crack, girl."

"I don't give a damn what your man has. If you'd stop spending so much time on your back you'd see how crazy you are. You keep playing me to back of the bus, dismissing me like my name is Miss Whack To The Back. And I don't like it."

"Girrrrrrl, please. Not tonight. I'm not doin' this with

you. You are not screwing my good-time-party moment. My man and I just finished getting it in real, real good; not once, not twice, but three-and-a-half times...we're breaking world records up in here. My man might be over there knocked out, but I am fully charged. And you will not drain my battery. Not tonight, you won't.

"You sure know how to ruin a phone call of consideration. So I advise you not to open the get-it-crunked door, London, 'cause I'm telling you, I'm trying not to be annoyed. I'm trying to use my church voice on you, but you're about to have me forget my religion. I'm now the new member of the Sweet Holy Ghost of the Desperate Goddess congregation, so don't do me."

I pulled the phone from my ear, staring at it. This chick was bananas.

"So are you going to get your mind right, get dressed, and get down here so we can boom-boom the room on these college cuties? Let me know now 'cause if not, I got Spencer on speed dial."

I felt my nerves about to pop. I was sick and tired of her throwing Spencer up in my face. "You know what, Rich. Call Spencer. I don't give a damn. Now go boom-boom on that."

I disconnected the call.

Screw her! I don't need Rich.

I immediately thought about calling Justice again for the hundredth time, but just as I was about to place the call, Rich called back and said, "She didn't answer. So are you coming or what?"

"No, I'm not coming. I'm not doing anything with you, Miss Mile High. So go on back to your little sexathon with Captain Got That Crack. Obviously some of Spencer's dumbness is rubbing off on you if you think I'm playing second best to that ho. I'm tired of you being two-faced. And thinking it's all about you. Well, newsflash: it's not..."

Rich huffed. "See, there you go with your drama, again."

"Drama this—here's the next headline for you, Miss It Couple: We're done!"

"Done? How must you sound? This isn't the LGBT clique. I'm all for gay marriages and all, but we're not a couple. And I'm not interested. So there's no way we can be done when we never started. Boom! Now hit the floor with that!"

"Rich, delete my number."

"Done; it's deleted."

I ended the call. There was nothing else to say. I was through with her. She had me messed up. At this point, I didn't care if I never spoke to her again.

For the first time in a long time, I wished I was back in New York. I wondered what my old Upper East Side crew was doing right now. I glanced over at the Tiffany clock. It was already six thirty in the evening. *Probably getting ready to attend some gala at MetLife*. And here I am stuck in the center of my bed, looking out at the Pacific Ocean instead of the Hudson River. God, I missed New York. And I missed Justice even more.

I got up from my bed and lazily went into my bathroom, feeling the tears welling up in my eyes. I had to shake this loneliness; had to shake my thoughts of him. I decided a relaxing bubble bath was what I needed to release some of this tension. Well, what I really needed was Justice's hard, chiseled body pressed up against mine, but the Jacuzzi would have to do.

Maybe if I'm lucky I'll slide down into the water and get lost.

Forty minutes later, no luck. I stepped out into my bedroom, naked, feeling refreshed but still not relaxed. I almost fell out when I saw Anderson standing in the middle of my room with his arms folded across his chest. His designer tie hung loosely around his neck. And he wore a scowl on his face.

He shifted his eyes from my breasts as I threw my arms up over my chest. "Ohmygod! What are you doing in here?" I screamed, racing back into the bathroom to grab a robe to cover myself.

He was hot on my heels. "Let me tell you something. I don't know what you're going through. But don't you ever come out the side of your neck at me again, calling me some punk-sissy, cursing me out like I'm nothing."

I blinked, tying the belt of my robe around my waist. "Boy, don't be walking up on me like that." I pushed him out of the way as I walked back out into the bedroom.

"I mean it, London. Don't ever in your life call me that again."

"Don't ever call you what? A punk-sissy? Oh, puhleeze. That's exactly who you are—a fake, a phony, a front; the definition of down low. And I'm tired of you always in my face. But, don't worry, boo. I'm going to keep your little gay-bird secret."

His jaws tightened. "Guess what? I'm the same punk-sissy that picked you up at four in the morning on the side of the road, looking crazy. I'm the same punk-sissy who covers for you and lies to your parents whenever you wanna play the devoted fool to some idiot who doesn't give a damn about you. I'm the same punk-sissy who is constantly there for you. So you wanna keep secrets, then let's not forget about the one you have tucked away in Italy..."

I felt my knees buckle.

"...I'm the one who told you that Justice had not one, not two, but three baby mamas and you still stayed with him. You better hope that's all he has instead of some nasty disease. You have the effen nerve to text me some craziness, then wanna stand here and call me a fake, when you're the biggest phony there is, fronting. Trying to be everything you're not. You've never had any friends. And the only boy you've ever been with has run all through you, and all over you."

"You know what—"

"I'm not done speaking. That's your problem—you're disrespectful."

"You don't—"

He walked up on me, cutting me off. "I said I'm not done. I'm not going to keep playing this back-and-forth game with you. You've disrespected me for the last time. I'm done with you. You really have me confused. I don't need *you* to get my trust fund. The difference between you and me is I'm wealthy on my own. I don't need that money. I want it. And I deserve it. But I won't be putting up with you to get it. So you go run along and keep plotting to set up your little friend with your boy-toy, hoping for a miracle, because I'm done with you. And by the way, I have something to add to that secret you think you have on me. This punk-sissy's not gay."

I blinked. I couldn't believe that in a matter of thirty minutes I had been cursed out twice in two different ways.

I stood there with my mouth dropped open. I had never seen Anderson like that before. Pissed and hurt.

He walked out of the room. Before I could even get my thoughts together, I was walking out behind him, calling his name. "Anderson, wait."

He turned to me. "Oh, now I'm supposed to wait for you? Really? I'm sick of waiting for you. And watching you wait for Justice and cry over Justice. Your whole world is wrapped up in Justice. You need to pay attention to what's right in front of you. I'm feeling something for you. And I don't know what it is, or why it is; it just is. But it's not worth your level of disrespect. I've been more of a man to you than your so-called man has ever been to you. So if you wanna sling secrets, then how about you start with your own, 'cause this little arrangement we have, it's done."

And with that said, Anderson walked off, leaving me standing in the middle of the hall, feeling like I had been plowed over by a tanker. It took me a minute to collect myself and pick the pieces of my face up off the floor, before I was able to make it back to my room. I slammed the door, willing my tears at bay.

Rick Ross's "You the Boss" started blaring from my phone again. I sighed. "What do you want?!" I snapped.

"Umm, temper, temper, boo. I keep telling you, girl, you need anger management, quick."

"Whatever. I thought I told you to get rid of my number."

"I did. But I had to go in the trash and get it. Ummm, are you over yourself? You know we had already made these plans to get our boom-bop-drop on tonight, and here you go backing out on me at the last minute. I told Knox that I had my girl coming down here; now you have me down here looking like a fool. Who does that? And I thought we were bestie-boos. Now you can do whatever you want to me, but when it comes to my man, that's something you don't do. He didn't do a thing to you, London. And then you had the nerve to come outside this afternoon, talking some 'is that?' like it would be somebody else. You were trying to get me all messed up. Tryna get your hate-on on the low. I had to come back here and do a Spencer move on him and get my Becky on. And you know I don't do that.

"Now you know you're dead wrong for making these plans with me. But you know what? I'm gonna be the bigger woman here. And I'm gonna do something I've never done before, so I'm breaking a world record. I'm gonna go out on a limb here, and just apologize to you so you can get over your attitude."

I blinked. This girl was relentless. But the truth was, after the tongue-lashing Anderson gave me, I was happy she called back. I needed a distraction. "You know what? Okay, Rich. My God! Shut that mouth."

"Wait a minute. Drop the mic. Lower the volume. You don't yell in my ear. So now that we've got that straight, let's get it poppin'! So get the jewels out, leave the heels. Get the Chanel sneakers out. Don't come down here like you're about to hit the runway, 'cause you know and I know you haven't been on stage in a minute. And this isn't the place to practice."

"Wait a minute now. You don't tell me how to dress. We haven't been broken up that long. You know me better than that."

"What? Hold up, wait a minute. There you go again. What is your problem?!"

I sighed. There was no getting this girl to shut up. "Rich. Will you shut up!"

"I'm just saying, London. Is there something you want to tell me? Because I'm trying to figure out why you keep using terms like us breaking up. That's real gross. I don't do the rainbow. Now you can handle your scandal any way you want to, but there will be no lucky charms over here!"

"My God! Just be quiet. I said I would go!"

"You don't tell me to be quiet. You're not going to bully me. So you better get your mind right. Now, the driver is outside. And you are expected to get dressed and get in that car. Time is money. Money is time. Do you understand? I'll talk to you when you get here. Now bye."

As I went to hang up, I could hear Rich speaking to someone in the background. "Baby, I don't know what the hell is wrong with that London. But she tore my nerves all the way down to the floor with her craziness. Did you hear me trying to talk some sense into her? The girl's crazy. Now I see why no one likes her. But I kinda like her...but she is demanding. And real stuck on herself..."

I blinked in shock. I couldn't believe she was talking about *me*. How two-faced!

"Rich? Rich?"

"...And she's always running her mouth. She won't even give me five minutes to get a word in, without her cutting me off. Ohmygod she's so rude. So, yeah. We need to let Midnight do her right so she can wake up to a good morning. And I know he will rock that big boat of hers..."

I blinked again. "Rich? Rich?"

"Hello? Ooops. Girl, you still on the phone. I was just talking about you. I have a real cutie for you, girl. But anyway, you have thirty minutes to primp, pamper, and pounce out the door. I already have your weekend bag packed. I had my stylist hook you up. So, let's get it-get-it. Now chop, chop! We're going to set the roof on fire."

I blinked. "I hope you didn't mean that literally?"

Click.

An hour and a half later, the limo was pulling up in front of this huge two-story purple house with gold shutters. There were a slew of Ques all donned in their fraternity's paraphernalia hanging outside. Although I had never partied with any of them, I was familiar with the fraternity because of my father. He was a Que, too. But he wasn't a goon. These dudes standing out here were goons...

This has got to be a mistake.

I tapped on the glass partition. "Excuse me, driver. This must be the wrong address. There has to be a mistake."

"No, ma'am. This is where Miss Rich instructed me to bring you. Perhaps you should finish your glass of champagne to help you get through the night."

"Yeah, I think you're right," I said, lifting the flute and guzzling the bubbly down. I poured another drink, feeling like this was going to be a very long night. Just as I put the flute up to my lips, the limo door swung open, startling me.

"Girrrrl, let's go! Get out! I got your drink here! And your man over there"—she pointed in back of her—"and he's been hounding me all night about you."

I blinked. Rich snatched the flute from out of my hand, guzzled back the champagne, then tossed the empty glass into the limo, grabbed me by the arm and pulled me out.

She leaned into my ear and whispered, "Girl, I walked in on your new boo one night in the bathroom, coming out of the shower, and he has the Rock of Gibraltar. Whew! You

can swing with it, rock with it. But you don't have to call
him in the morning, girl. Two hundred dollars on the
nightstand and a Dear John letter is all you need."

"Rich, have you lost your mind? You must be drunk. I'm
not sleeping with none of these boys; and especially some
boy called *Monster*."

"His name is Mid. Night. Not Monster."

I twisted my lips. "Well, what*ever* his name is, I'm not
sleeping with him. I don't do random sex."

"Oh my...clutching pearls. You're not a virgin are you,
girl? I should have had the driver stop by the church first.
'Cause we're tossing all virtue out the window tonight,
girl. We're gonna get our sin on."

"Daaaaayum, Rich!" This tall, lanky, dark chocolate guy
said as he licked his lips. "You got that off real lovely, baby
girl." He gave Rich a pound, then turned to me and made
an hourglass shape with his hands. "Bam! You a glamazon
just like Rich said. Just how I like 'em."

I gave him a blank stare.

Rich smacked her lips, then popped her collar. "I told
you my girl was all that. Excuse her attitude, though, 'cause
she can get real stink sometimes. But she doesn't mean any
harm. But when your mother is a rigid top model and
your father got his pants up his behind and his tie knotted
all tight, what you expect? This is what they're going to
produce."

I blinked. *Here this ho goes again, disrespecting me.*

"Daayum, baby, you look good. They call me Midnight,
but you can call me all night. You a big, sweet, juicy jawn.
Juicy like...Roscoe's chicken and waffles; real juicy with
ribs and red Kool-Aid on the side and fluffy mashed pota-
toes. And your face"—he licked his lips—"is so beautiful,

like buttery cornbread. I just wanna lick all over your face with your sweet, tasty-looking self. And I promise not to leave any crumbs behind..."

OMG, this clown is comparing me to some chicken and rib platter, like I belong in some greasy-spoon diner!

He dragged his eyes up and down my body as if he were trying to undress me. "Baaaaby-boo, you're prettier than a batch of fried chicken fresh out the grease. Daayum, how tall are you, baby, like seven feet? You're like the Statue of Liberty. Tall and solid. I've wanted to climb all through the Statue of Liberty for a long time. I asked her to marry me last year, and she still hasn't answered me. I think she got mad when I told her that her last name couldn't be Liberty anymore. It was gonna be Johnson. Statue of Johnson. Now that's hot...That's gon' be yo' name."

I blinked. *My God...this fool must be related to Rich with his nonstop motormouth!*

"...Ya girl told me you're from New York. You know we're neighbors, right? I'm from Philly. You know, like the City of Brotherly Love, like Philly cheesesteak, like the Seventy-Sixers. I thought I was out here for an education, but after seeing you. Daayum...I know I'm out here to break yo' back in, and run my seeds all in you..."

My eyes popped open. "Rich, get this nasty fly out of my face before I go the hell off on his crusty azz."

He grinned, keeping his eyes on me. "Nah, baby. That's what I want. I want you to go off on me. I like it dirty. Mistreat me, you sexy biscuit. You gonna make me smear gravy all over them pretty lips, then suck it off. Talking dirty is a fetish of mine. As long as we end up in that bed, I don't give a damn what comes out ya mouth."

Rich huffed. "Damn, Midnight! See, you don't listen. I told you to go in easy on London. I told you she was a prude. You can't be talking to her all rough and dirty like that. Talking about some waffles, chickens, and ribs. And breaking her back in. And licking gravy off her lips. She's not trying to eat. She's gonna think you're ghetto."

Think? Oh no. Too late! He is *ghetto!*

"A'ight, a'ight, Rich. I got this. I'm just excited. She's so beautiful. I need me a bib to catch the drool. I'ma need me some wipes for the rock in my pocket, too." He jutted out his pelvis, then gyrated his hips. "Pow! Pow-pow-pow! I'ma take you home to meet my mother. She likes big 'n' tall girls, too."

Rich grabbed her neck. "*Whaaat?!* Clutching pearls. That's where I draw the line, Midnight. Your mother likes Amazons, too? That ain't cute. That's not a compliment. You think London wants to look like this? She's cute in the face and all. But that body. She doesn't want that body. And there ain't no diet for too much height. She's stuck with this for life."

"Wait a minute, Rich," I snapped, shifting my handbag from one hand to the other. "I've about had enough of you and your pet snake here. I don't need you taking up for me."

"Oh no. That's it. See, boy, you got my girl all upset. You make me sick, Midnight. Come on, London, before this boy tears your self-esteem up. Let him get his mind right, and his family tree together." She snatched me by the arm and started pulling me up the walkway as she swished her hips toward the house before I could resist.

"Ooowwwww," Rich said, popping her hips up the stairs.

"This is my girl right here, y'all. Smile for the cameras, London. I'm sure they're somewhere around."

All of the guys hanging out on the porch spoke; a few whistled and catcalled; others simply winked. But I ignored them and Rich paid them no mind as she dragged me into the house. I couldn't believe my eyes as we stepped into a sea of purple and gold, a crest of royal blue and white, waves of pink and green, crimson and cream, black and gold, all flooding the room under the glow of strobe lights and disco balls.

Combat boots were making drum beats against the wood floor. Competitive catcalls and dog barks floated into the music. The DJ was pumping a Waka Flocka Flame jam and had everybody on the floor. Dollar bills were being tossed up in the air like confetti. The energy was on high. And despite not really wanting to be there, the party felt free and exciting. Something I needed, but didn't know what to do with it.

"Girl, loosen up," Rich screamed in my ear. She dropped it to the floor, then made her booty clap, then snapped back up. "Owwww…" She dipped at the knees, then made it clap again. "Whatever is on your mind, boo, let it go. It doesn't exist in here. This is all that matters."

She reached for the hand of the same guy I had seen her with outside at school and I knew for sure it was Knox. She shook her booty and gyrated into his crotch, then dropped down and did a split. Rich was in rare form. She snapped back up, then grabbed her ankles. Knox held up a bottle of beer in his hand, while Rich threw her hands up in the air and shouted, "Look, ma, no hands!"

Everyone was having a good time. Everyone…except me! I scanned the packed room of partygoers. Sweat was dripping everywhere. My jaw dropped open when I spotted Anderson. Anderson!

OMG, this is the party he was talking about!

He held a magnum of champagne up in the air and was sandwiched between two brown-skinned chicks who wore matching pink and green T-shirts and short denim skirts. They did their sorority call, then switched positions. Anderson looked relaxed, like he didn't have a care in the world. Judging by the way he was laughing and jumping up in the air, and barking over the music, I could tell he was having a good time as the two girls pressed their bodies into his.

Wearing dark jeans, a purple wifebeater with his fraternity's symbols in big gold letters emblazoned across his chest, I had to admit Anderson looked...good. As hard as I tried not to look, I caught myself staring at his thick muscled biceps, trying to remember if he'd always had arms like that. Or if tonight was the first time that I had noticed them.

I shook the thought.

Geezus, I need a cosmo!

I'm not going to lie. I don't know why, but I couldn't keep my eyes off of him. Every time I shifted my eyes to take in the rest of the party, my eyes would land right back on him. I really screwed up, texting him those nasty things. Anderson was right. He was always there for me, even when I didn't want him to be. He really didn't deserve to be crapped on. I was connected to him whether I wanted to be or not. He knew a whole lot about who I was. And I really felt bad about hurting his feelings. Seemed like I was hurting everybody around me; most of all, myself.

I looked on amazed and amused as different girls danced their way up to Anderson, grabbing all over him. His body glistened from a mixture of oil and sweat. A pang of envy shot through me as four girls encircled him and started dancing around him, chanting, "Go, C-Smoove! Go, C-Smoove! Go, Smoove..."

Ohmygod, I had no idea that C-Smoove was his line name.

Well, obviously there are a lot of things you don't know about Anderson...

I'm not gay!

I looked over at Rich and Knox again. They were in their own love zone. I couldn't help but smile as Rich slid between Knox's legs, then tried to hump up on his butt. He turned around laughing, then pulled her into him and kissed her on the lips. They tongued each other down, then went back to dancing. Meek Mill's "House Party" started playing and the crowd started jumping up and down, singing, until the DJ eased in "Lean Wit' It"; then the crowd got wilder.

My eyes zoomed back over to Anderson. The four girls who had been dancing with him earlier had left and he was now dancing with this real cute girl with a sexy short haircut. She wore a crimson T-shirt with her sorority symbols in cream lettering. The two of them looked real cozy dancing together. Anderson started leaning and rocking with it, then pop-locking it. Then he did the Laffy Taffy, followed by the Tootsie Roll, then he kicked one leg up as if he was taking a piss and started humping into the air. The girl he danced with broke out in laughter when he started doing the Robot. I couldn't believe this was the uptight

Anderson I knew. He handed the chick the bottle he held in his hand. She took a swig, then handed it back to him.

Then the chick had the nerve to flick his chin. And he grinned. Then her arms flung up around his neck as she swayed to the beats. His hand dipped down to the small of her back as if he was pulling her deeper into him. Then he whispered something into her ear and the chick threw her head back and laughed. And for some reason, I was feeling some kind of way watching all of this unfold right before me. He wasn't really my man. And I had never looked at him like that. Still...

Rich danced up on me. Her sheer blouse stuck to her body. Her weave was sweated out. She slung her hair and beads of sweat splattered me in the face. I frowned as she spoke. "Look, boo. I see Midnight ain't work out. And you're real uptight in here. And I see you eyeing Doctor Corny over there. So I'm just gonna say this once. If you want Doctor Corny, go get him. 'Cause that chick's name is Nikki and she was all up on Knox one time. Don't worry, I got your back if she comes to you crazy. We'll clean her spine out like a dirty shrimp if she even thinks it. Now make it work, boo.

"And while you're at it, take it off those stilts. You can use those things as a weapon. Who does that, anyway, wear seven-inch heels to a college party? You in here floating above the room. Take it down, punkin-boo. Take it all the way down."

I couldn't help but laugh as I stepped out of my heels. Suddenly I realized that none of the females here had on shoes. They all had danced out of their footwear.

"That's right, boo. Drop down to eye level. Now go get Doctor Corny. 'Cause I can't stand here babysitting you all night. 'Cause you see that dude over there"—she pointed over at Knox, who grinned and winked at her—"was definitely worth fighting for, you hear me? Now you stand here looking crazy and let that tramp have your man, if you want to. And, trust me, she will have him 'cause I've seen her in action. Now I'm not trying..." She snapped her fingers as Rick Ross's "B.M.F." started playing. "Ooooh, this is my jam...!" She shimmied her way back over to Knox and the two of them started dancing again.

I couldn't take it anymore. Standing here, looking lost, wasn't it. Rich was right. I had to loosen up. I wanted to have fun, too! And I wanted to make up with Anderson.

I walked up on him and that Nikki girl dancing, then tapped her on the shoulder. "Excuse me, Nikki," I said, looking at Anderson. "I'm cutting in."

Anderson narrowed his eyes.

She gave me a confused look. I'm sure she was wondering how I knew her name. She looked at Anderson, who shrugged. She smiled and said, "Sure, go 'head." I stood in front of him in awkwardness, trying to decide if I should say something or just dance.

Anderson scowled. "Look, Little Miss Uptight. Before you can cut in, you need to apologize."

"You're right. I'm really sorry for what I said. I was wrong for that. And I hope you can forgive me."

"I'll think about it." I eyed the bottle of champagne he had in his hand. It was an expensive bottle of Perrier-Jouët. He took a swig, then handed it to me.

I took a sip. "So where do we go from here?" I asked, handing the magnum back to him.

He frowned. "I don't know what you're about to do. But I'm about to get my dance on. So if you're going to dance with me, then you need to put your back into it and dance like you mean it, or go on back over there in that lonely little corner and keep watching me from the distance, 'cause I'm here to get my party on. Now step with it, or step off it..."

I stared at him.

"I'm not playing with you, London. Dance hard or go home, mama."

Mama?

I blinked, then dropped my gaze down to his feet.

OMG, he has on a pair of gold spray-painted combat boots!

He gyrated his hips, pumped a leg up in the air, then started making barking noises. All of a sudden I spotted Knox, that critter Midnight, and a slew of other guys, cupping their hands over their mouths and barking. Chicks started making clicking sounds with their tongues and doing their own sorority calls.

"So what's it gonna be?"

"I'm gonna go hard," I said over the music.

"Then let's get it. If you wanna make up with me, then you need to let me see you make it twerk." When 2 Chainz's "No Lie" started playing, Anderson pulled me into him, and the two of us danced in sync to the beat. Two songs later, we were laughing and working up a sweat. When DJ Khaled's "Take It to the Head" started playing, I slid my arms around Anderson's neck, then looked up into his eyes and started singing.

He raised an eyebrow. "Ummm, I wouldn't do that if I were you."

"You wouldn't do what?"

"Sing. You just need to stay pretty."

"Mmmhmm," Rich said, popping up out of nowhere, getting all up in my business. "Yeah, 'cause that voice is tore up."

I rolled my eyes. "Rich..."

"Girl, don't mind me. Go on, get your love on. I just love love."

"Rich, baby," Knox said, grinning, "will you leave them alone and focus on me?"

Before Rich could open her mouth to start running it, Knox sealed her lips with a kiss. They looked so happy together. I looked back over at Anderson and said, "This is it."

"What?"

"This is exactly where I'm supposed to be." I cupped his face, then pressed my lips against his.

He grinned, then slowly licked his bottom lip. "Wow... I don't know what I'm gonna do with you."

I gazed into his eyes, taking my thumb and lightly brushing it across his lips. "I don't know either. But you can start by kissing me again."

And he did.

And for the first time ever, I let everything go. No Justice. No worries. Nothing but that moment. And for the rest of the night, I was truly Anderson's girl.

24

Rich

"Come on, man. Lil Bit'll be here any minute. And when she comes through the door, my girl gon' be ready to go. So, wassup? Can we chill wit' y'all?"

Hell to the no!

"She's coming all the way down from Baldwin Hills, man."

Eww...

"Come on now. And oh, a brothah needs a loan."

A what?

"Don't front, man. You already know my father is cheap as hell. Don't let his starting point-guard position on the Clippers fool you. That man will make a dollar hollah."

And...

"So you already know about the moolah situation."

And what is that?

"Raggedy."

O...M...G...Midnight's nonstop chatter drove me crazeeee...! It was not the voice I wanted, expected, or needed to hear early this morning. What I needed to hear was Knox whispering sweetness against my skin while sliding heated kisses down my body.

Nevertheless, Midnight's voice continued to rip through my fantasy. And. Tore. My. Nerves. Up. "So, me and Lil Bit gon' roll with you and wifey, right?"

Wrong! I jumped out of bed and quickly covered my nakedness with a sports bra, Knox's white T-shirt, and a pair of denim boy-shorts.

Evidently, Midnight had lost his mind and apparently Knox was too nice to tell him where to go and find it. But see—me, Rich Montgomery—I had no problem checkin' freaks at the door.

Snap. Snap.

"Look, Knox," Midnight begged—with his raunchy self. "Man, you know how Lil Bit do."

"Yeah, man, I do. And I don't know if she and Rich'll be a good mix. That's why I'm saying to you—"

"Hell. No," I said as I sashayed into the kitchen. I looked over at Knox, who stood near the stove with three eggs in his hand. "Knox, you need to start shuttin' creeps down...look at you." I paused. Then eased an index finger seductively into the right corner of my lips and inhaled my man in full view. His mahogany skin glistened, while his blue boxers hung loosely on his waist.

I love my man.

The single dimple in his right cheek deepened as Knox gave me a one-sided smile and asked, "Would you like an omelet?"

I blushed. "Yeah."

"And what would you like in it?"

"Don't ask me loaded questions."

His dimple deepened again. "Let me repeat that. What would you like in it?"

"Umm, let me see..." I walked over to him, placed my hands around his waist, and kissed him passionately.

I was almost lost in a whole other world until Midnight said, "All this for some eggs? I'd love to see what happens when he offers you bacon!"

I frowned and turned toward Midnight, who instantly made my stomach curdle. His nasty butt stood near the sink in too-tight long johns with one leg purple and one leg gold. Both of his hands were tucked in his waistband.

Gross!

"Ewwl, Midnight, clutching pearls." I frowned. "Your manners are all messed up. Straight up nasty. Take your hands out of your pants."

"Are my hands bothering you and your pearls? What? You want my hands in your pants? Well, I don't do that. My hands are fine right where they are. Now, Knox, what's good? Can me and Lil Bit hang with y'all today or not?"

"First of all, what's a Lil Bit?" I slammed my hands on my hips. "Is she a little broke? Or a lil bit ugly?"

Midnight had the audacity to look insulted. "Hold up, BJ."

"Pause." I held a hand up. "Midnight, who the hell is a BJ?"

"You."

"Excuse you?"

"It stands for big jawn. It's a Philly term for bigness, thickness, and in your case it stands for big and thick mouth, 'cause you talk too much."

"Knox, you better get him. 'Cause I know he didn't just try and disrespect me!"

"Don't worry about that, baby," Knox said, holding back

a snicker. "You don't talk that much. Only on Sunday, Monday, Tuesday—"

"Wednesday," Midnight added.

"Shut up!" I said. "I'm not thinking about either one of you. And, Midnight, don't call me a big jawn anymore."

Midnight smirked. "You should take that as a compliment. Being a big jawn is like being a dinner plate with a steak on it. That's sexy. But see, the difference between me and my boy is that I like a buffet. Steak ain't enough for me."

"Whatever." I rolled my eyes. *He makes me sick!*

"Anyway," Midnight continued, "like I was saying to my boy and not his girl—"

"And like I said"—I stopped him in his tracks—"No. Lil Bit can't go and neither can you! Tonight is couple's night and we are not going to the petting zoo. And we don't need freaks for security either. So my man and I, and my girl and her man, will be going out—without you and your Lil Bit. And anyway, where was this Lil Bit last night when you were so busy trying to lick up my girl's face? Talking about chicken crumbs and buttery biscuits. Running your seeds up in her! That was so gross and disrespectful."

"Your girl needs some seeds ran up in her; then maybe she'll loosen up."

"Whatever. But that'll be the last time I'll ever try and hook you up with decency! And if Lil Bit was so important then why wasn't she at the party?"

"Hold up, BJ! Knox, you better get ya girl. Lil Bit just came home last night. Six months ago she ran into a hand-to-the-gut situation at the Dairy Queen her father owns. She hand-hooked the cashier in the gut for rolling her eyes and sucking her teeth when my baby ordered four chocolate sundaes, six banana splits, three shakes, and two chicken-strips baskets. And then the cashier topped it off by saying, 'I know you not gon' eat all that.' And since my baby doesn't play when it comes to her food, she had to put down the smack down."

"She did what?" I was stunned.

"And after six months of being made to sit down, she's coming to see me so we can get our celebration on. So that's why Lil Bit wasn't at the party last night. Now shut up and let me finish my conversation with my roommate."

"Oh God, you are so annoying."

"Hold up, you in my crib...all the time."

"A'ight, y'all. Chill." Knox chuckled as he slid the omelet on a plate, then walked over to the table and took a seat. He called me over to sit on his lap. And of course I did.

Knox took his fork, cut into the omelet, and slid a piece into my mouth.

"This omelet is delicious." I leaned in to kiss him.

He smiled and said, "Just like my baby's kisses."

"Umm, excuse me." Midnight knocked on the table and tapped Knox on the shoulder. "Unless you're going to give me some and finally make this a threesome, y'all need to stop the kissing and answer me."

"Yo, man." Knox laughed. "Chill."

"For real," I snapped.

"Yo, you and your sew-in need to step. You might have my man all strung out, but I'm not trippin' off of you. You would never be my type. You're not big enough. So you can't shut me up. I'm not Knox. He's the one who can't see straight. Declaring an end to his playa-playa days. Ridiculous. And then to top things off he told me he loves

you like he's never loved anyone else before—and I kept
trying to figure out why. You too short, and you trying to
be thick, but you need to gain about fifty pounds because
you look anorexic to me. Like you need a sandwich. And
you know—"

"A'ight, man," Knox said. "You're running your mouth
too much now. Enough is enough."

Midnight looked at Knox, gave him a sympathetic look,
and whispered, "You know this chick got you strung out.
We s'pose to be wild dogs, not house pets." He paused
and said as if a lightbulb had just gone off, "You know
what, on second thought, I'ma keep Lil Bit home with me.
The last thing I need is for her to be around BJ and then
suddenly start thinking she's gon' put me on a leash, too."
He gave us the peace sign, walked into his room, and as
he went to close the door he said, "I'ma still need that
loan though, man."

O...M...G...

Once Midnight had finally removed himself from my
sight I looked at Knox and said, "He is so effen annoying."

"He's not annoying. He's a'ight. That's my boy."

"Umm hmm." I popped my lips. "So tell me. Did you
really say all of those things about me?"

Knox laughed and then he looked at me seriously. "You
know I love you, Rich. And at this moment I can't see being
with anyone other than you."

"I don't want anyone but you either. You're my best
friend."

He smiled and gave me a quick peck on the lips. "I know
I am, which is why I'm saying to you, don't play me."

Now that took me aback. "Play you?"

"I didn't forget about that dude."

Not this again... "Could we please drop that? He was a nobody. I promise."

"A'ight."

I smiled. "Now, before I forget, my mother invited you over for dinner. And she is finally going to love you as much as I do."

Knox grinned. "Now that's worth celebrating." He lifted me off of his lap, grabbed my hand, and led me back to his room.

The sultry sounds of Elle Varner singing about a refill, greeted us as we walked up the short Inglewood block and into a place called Muddy Moments. It was a hole-in-the-wall, a greasy spoon, or a breath of fresh air. A place where you could leave your celebrity at the door and the only thing that mattered was the music, the honey-dipped fried chicken, collard greens, and drinks.

The place was a one-room club that was packed with people everywhere. It felt like a beautiful step back in time—from the front door that was covered in red leather to the collection of black velvet paintings that hung behind the bar. There was a small wooden-plank stage that sat in the corner of the room, with wooden beads draped on both ends. And on the stage were a piano, two microphones, and a karaoke machine.

There were petite round tables covered with black-and-white checkered tablecloths placed sporadically around the room. And naked black bulbs, which hung over each table, contributed to the down-home and cozy mystique of the place. There were hand-painted signs littering the walls, with rules of how you were expected to party:

NO CREDIT. CASH IN HAND OR BUTT OUT THE DOOR.

LEAVE YOUR ATTITUDE ON THE SIDEWALK.

NO SWEARIN'.

NO CUSSIN'.

BELCHING IS FREE BUT PASSING GAS GETS YOU PUT OUT OF HERE.

FISH FRY ON FRIDAYS ONLY.

and ONLY GOOD TIMES ALLOWED.

And then there was us. My baby and I, both dressed in jeans, mine fitted and his slightly baggy. Knox wore a white tee and I wore a tight, fitted pink tee with the word *Queen* scribbled in Swarovski crystals on the front. He rocked a hot pair of customized High Pro FLOM Nikes and since I was one to never be outdone—not even by my man's four-thousand-dollar kicks—I opted for my customized pair of pink Nike Air Force Ones adorned with pink diamonds around the Nike symbol. My baby and I were killin' 'em. And we only had one problem—well, two: London and her boo—who'd just walked up in the place. Anderson spotted us immediately, but London was too busy clutching her bag to her chest and trying to avoid anyone brushing against her to see me standing directly in front of her.

Doctor Corny was dressed in a fly Armani suit—yes, a suit—with a loose tie around his neck. And his chick—OMG, seven-inch Jimmy Choos, ultra miniskirt, white silk camisole, and a Gucci blazer. Yes, a blazer. Both of them looked like yuppies gone wild.

My Gawd.

Anderson smiled at me and then he turned to Knox, gave him some dap and said. "Yo, man, we ran late as hell." He took off his loose tie, slid it in his pocket, and unbuttoned the top two buttons of his crisp white shirt. "My father called an unexpected board meeting this afternoon. And since I'm a major shareholder he wanted me there. By the time the meeting was done, I had to swing by and get London from my apartment. We came straight here. I had zero time to change."

"It's cool," Knox said. "Let's grab a beer."

"For real," Anderson said. "I need a cold one fa'sho."

"And I, umm"—London popped her lips and cleared her throat—"need to speak to you for a minute, Rich." She wiped invisible beads of sweat off of her forehead in disgust.

When I didn't answer her and instead said, "Knox, can you grab me a Heineken?" she looked at me like I had lost my mind, then she closed her eyes and tapped her heels three times, like Dorothy looking for a way home. This chick here...was trippin'.

London huffed as she repeated herself. "I *said*, I need to speak to you for a minute, Rich Gabrielle Montgomery."

No the hell she didn't! "Clutching pearls. Why are you calling me by my government? Who does that?" I looked from one side of the crowded room to the other. "And you gon' do that amongst mixed company, too. What is wrong with you, London? Maybe you need to go outside and come back in, because clearly you clicked your heels past the sign that read 'Leave your attitude on the sidewalk.'"

London frowned. And squinted her nose as someone walked by her and brushed up against her shoulder. "Ohmygod!" She shuddered. "I have been contaminated. I may need to be quarantined. What kind of lil rinky-dink place is this? This whole setup is hazardous." She flicked more invisible sweat from her forehead. "I feel like I'm in the midst of a drive-by. Rich Gabrielle, I'm serious! I must have a word with you."

"What in the boom-bop hell?! Here you go again. You don't follow instructions, do you? You just do what you wanna do. Always trying to be the boss! You really need to learn some respect and hear me when I say this—and this is gon' be the last time I check you politely—Don't call me by my government." I cocked my neck and bucked my eyes wide open. *I am about sick of her disrespecting me!*

"Well, what would you like me to call you?" She looked baffled.

"Oh, now you wanna play stupid." This chick knew how to send me straight to twenty! "You know my name is Rich, London. So that's all you need to call me. Rich. My government is off-limits!" I held up a hand and did a chop.

She gave me a blank stare.

I popped my lips and said, "Now pick your face up, punkin. And simply own the fact that you're wrong for that! I don't call you by your government. I don't call you London Elona Phillips! And why do you keep staring at me like I have three or four heads. What? Do I have a stain on me?"

London blinked about three times before she came out of her trance and said, "For two nights straight, you have had me partying hoodlum-style—like hood hoes are what we need to be. Now I don't know what you fantasize about or dream about at night, but my dreams don't involve guns, stolen cars, cheap drinks, or cheesy clubs! I don't party with these kinds of people. And I don't care if they all look young. It's weird. And I feel like an old head standing here! And just so you know, Rich *is* your government name!"

It took everything in me not to bust London dead in her throat. "Yo' azz is crazy!"

I turned toward my baby, who had just walked up and handed me my beer. Knox leaned in and kissed me on the lips. And Doctor Corny being the knockoff that he was, was of course trying too hard when he leaned over and desperately tried to get his C-Smoove on, trying to kiss Ms. Uptight Drawls on the lips.

Fail.

She played him. Took her left hand, held it up in his face, and instead of his lips landing on hers, they kissed her palm—leaving Doctor Corny with his face cracked.

I would've laughed had I not just remembered the very reason Miss Potpourri Panties would never keep a man. She was a virgin. Or at least that's the story she wanted me to believe. *What. Ever!*

Shaking my head . . .

Before Anderson could get his face together and London could get her mind right, a man walked onto the stage. He must've been the MC. He grabbed the mic and said, "Welcome to Muddy Moments couples karaoke night!"

The crowd clapped and cheered.

Karaoke was my thing! What-what! Hell, I could sing, but I could also bust a rhyme like no other. After all, my daddy was one of the original MCs. Okay!

Snap. Snap.

The MC continued, "So we hope y'all came here to have a good time!"

"I know I did!" I yelled and London looked at me with her eyes popped wide open.

"Tonight's grand prize is five hundred dollars in cash."

Instantly I felt deflated. *What kind of prize is that? A mess...*

"And a platter of honey-coated hot wings and a bucket of ribs, on the house!"

Oh, hell yeah! Just that fast I have my mojo back! Now that's what I'm talking about! I broke out into the running man. Did a Soulja Boy Superman move, mixed it with a booty bounce, and ended it with a pop-back-up-in-place. "Oooo, hot wings, that's right up my alley! Babe, you know we got this in the bag! You know this is ours! Hell, I'm so psyched that I might even save Midnight and his Lil Bit a rib!"

Knox laughed. "My baby is serious, huh? You on those wings!"

"Hell yeah, I feel like Lil Bit at the Dairy Queen. I might hand-hook somebody."

"Oh. My. God," London mumbled. "How soon we forget where we come from."

I blinked. Quickly thought about turning around to lay this chick down, but then changed my mind. "Knox," I said. "Hook it up, baby. Go on and put our names on the list. And tell them we gon' amp this party up a bit. We gon' put it down with "Money, Power and Respect." The remix. Now excuse me."

I turned around toward London, locked arms with hers, and before she could protest, I walked her swiftly to the bathroom—which was tight as hell with only two stalls and one pedestal sink. For a moment, I had to do a double take. This place was homey. Country. Cheap. And yeah, cheesy. And plagued with more hand-painted signs than a lil bit. There was even a sign on the bathroom window that read IT'S A BRICK WALL WITH NO EXIT OUT THERE, SO I SUGGEST YOU TURN AROUND, GO BACK, AND PAY FOR YOUR FOOD!

But whatever, I didn't have time to analyze the decor in the bathroom. I wanted to get my good time on, and my bestie-boo was wreckin' my fun-flow.

"What the hell is your problem here!" I slammed my hand on the sink. "Do you have multiple personalities? 'Cause who was she last night that was at the frat party? The one who had a good time? I need to see that chick again. 'Cause you are boring me to pieces. And I don't do boredom."

"And obviously you don't do class either!" she snapped. "Now all I know is that I need to get out of here. I need a shower!"

"Then bounce! Nobody is holding you hostage here. Pow. Pow. Pow. Bounce, baby, bounce." I held my arms out like I was riding a motorcycle and revved the engine. "Make it happen. 'Cause you and your dead weight are too much to carry. My man and I, and even Doctor-Corny-by-day-and-C-Smoove-by-night, are trying to have a good time, like we did last night. We tryna bring sexy back. And we will do it with or without you. Trust. 'Cause I will hook Doctor Corny up in two seconds flat. Now dare me. 'Cause you know Spencer will be up on him without hesitation!"

"That's a bit much!"

"No, you're a bit much. You're a prude. You're a snob. You're stuck up."

"I am not!"

"Yes. You. Are, Dryzilla! You need to look in the mirror.

Now, I don't know what's weighing you down, but you need to let that ish go. 'Cause it's ugly and it makes you ugly. It's definitely not cute. And ugly is another thing I don't do. And you wonder why I like to hang out with Spencer. Spencer knows how to have a good time. She may be dumb, but she is fun!"

London blinked.

"You can blink all you want. But you are clearly confused. Clutching your bag, all jeweled up. Who comes out to a hole-in-the-wall with diamonds, a Chanel clutch—and what happened to the stuff I packed for you? Right now you're supposed to have on a pair of neon-green hot shorts, white fishnets, a midriff and a tattoo reading Thugette Life wrapped around your waist. Oh, and red patent leather wedges!"

"You have nerve, Rich! Where are your fishnets?"

"Knox tore them off of me last night! 'Cause I am loose and free. I know how to have a good time and let myself go. But you, you wanna stand here and look stupid. Like people are trippin' off of you. These people here don't know you up in here. They're not even thinking about you. So you need to stop trippin' over yourself or go out there and summon you a limo.

"But I tell you what, if you leave up outta here you will never get another invite from me! I will be done with you and you'll be sitting on the sidelines and I'll be kicking it with Spencer! Boom! Now hit the floor with that! 'Cause I'm out!" I walked out and slammed the door behind me.

I had zero time for the foolishness. Plus I didn't do cold hot-wings, and judging by the music it was about time for me to bust a move!

I strutted out of the bathroom and the music was

bumpin'. I danced my way over to Knox and Anderson, who were drinking cold beers and laughing. I leaned against Knox, he handed me his beer, and I took a sip.

"Where's London?" Anderson asked.

"I'm right here," she said, standing behind him. Her smile was still fake, but it was better than that sourpuss frown she had on a few minutes ago. Now let's just hope she had that mind together.

I looked at Anderson and said, "Give her a sip. She needs a drink." And then I turned around toward my baby and we commenced to getting our party on.

The MC introduced the first couple on stage. The girl couldn't sing a lick, but her dude—when he opened his mouth the sound of angels came out. And I found myself lost in his voice, and then...I felt transformed and transported back to the Kit-Kat Lounge—back on stage, singing my heart out, and lost in Justice's arms. His kisses felt sweet, and heated, and they were melting me. It was like... like I could really feel them. They were lining the right side of my neck, moving up toward my earlobe. I knew it was wrong, but I had to kiss him. So I turned around and that's when it hit me: it was all a memory.

"You all right, baby?" Knox asked me.

"Yeah, yeah." I blinked. "I'm fine."

"Are you sure? You still wanna do this?"

"Yeah."

"So then what are you waiting on? They just called us up."

I blinked. "Okay." *Collect yourself.* "Then let's get it, baby!" I said in a forced excitement. Knox stared at me for a second and I wondered if he was back to reading my thoughts.

"A'ight," he said, "let's get it!"

I sashayed on stage and Knox playfully pimp-walked over to the other microphone. The bass line to The LOX's classic started playing and before we began our routine I said to the crowd, "I'm getting ready to bless y'all with my version of Lil' Kim. It's not gon' be trashy. My nose is real. I'm naturally thick. I love my chocolate skin. And nothing is pumped up over here!"

I ran my hands over my hourglass. "I'm gon' upgrade the East Coast's queen bee and show her how the West do it. Boom. Boom!" I threw my hands like loose guns in the air. "Drop it!" I spat lyrics from "Money, Power & Repect."

My baby and I were doing it. And he straight killed it, especially when he did a DMX bark and then rapped.

By the time we were done, we had everyone bumping, even London and Anderson.

I strutted offstage with confidence. I knew I would be taking the hot wings and the bucket of ribs home with me! And the five hundred dollars. Mmph, they could keep that.

I walked straight over to the yuppies gone wild and said, "I know you saw my work. And don't hate either." Knox and I gave each other some dap.

"Yeah, I saw you," Anderson said. "And you were a'ight." He wiggled his left hand. "But you don't have any work for C-Smoove."

I know he didn't just pop his collar. Oh, yes he did.

"Boy, please." I flicked a wrist. "You couldn't bring it if it was brought to you, or brought for you."

"Is that a challenge?" he asked, amped.

"Take it however you want. 'Cause me and my baby got the wings in the bag! All up in ya grill. Pow! You doing a whole lotta talking, but I don't see you movin'."

"You ain't said nothing but a word."

"Umm-hmm, and what you gon' do, C-Smoove? The "Y.M.C.A." or you gon' kick it up a notch and resurrect Slick Rick's career?"

"Nah, baby girl." He flicked my chin and for a moment I thought maybe he was kind of cute with some swag. Good thing I was faithful and anti-grimy; otherwise I may've turned him out and threw some action his way. "London and I are going to surprise you," he said.

"I'm not going up there." London sucked her teeth.

"Girl, you better go and stand by your man. Don't let him lose by himself. And while y'all are up there, Knox and I will look for the nearest exit for when you get laughed offstage!"

Anderson pulled London up to the stage. And reluctantly she walked up there, giving the crowd a small wave, and I yelled, "That's my girl over there!"

I didn't know what they were going to sing, but I knew it would be country. Which was exactly why my mouth hit the floor when Tupac's "Hit 'Em Up" dropped and Anderson and London brought the house down.

"You two cheated," I insisted, upon my return from the bathroom. I sat down and Anderson, who was just returning to his seat from the bar, said, "We didn't cheat." He set a pitcher of beer down on the table.

"Don't try to bribe me and my baby with drinks. Tell 'em, babe," I said, reaching for one of their wings.

Knox didn't respond, he simply sipped his beer and stared at me. Appearing to be lost in his thoughts.

Whatever. I reached for another one of their wings and said, "You two watched how we rocked it and you copied all of our moves." I paused. "Umm, dang, make it hot, make it pop, these freakin' wings are delicious!" I licked my fingers.

London laughed—a genuine laugh. "Girl, they are da bomb!" She reached for one and fed it to Anderson. He looked at her, smiled, and she kissed the barbecue sauce off of his lips.

"Awwl." I teased them. They looked so cute together. This was the London that I knew and loved. The one who liked to have fun. And as for the stuck-up one—well, she was always stuck up—but the stuck-up one with the extra-extra bourgeois-glam; thank Gawd that snotty heifer was abandoned in that cheesy, country bathroom.

Knox huffed—evidently he was pissed about something. I looked at him and asked, "Are you okay?"

"I'm cool. But I'll be even better when you answer your phone." He pointed to my iPhone that sat on the edge of the table.

"Phone?" I said, surprised. "I didn't even hear it ringing." I reached for the phone and Knox's eyes were glued to the screen that read *JB*.

I swallowed and I knew by the way Knox looked at me that he was suspicious.

"It's nobody," I said as low as I could, given the fact that we had company. "You can answer it if you want." *Please, oh please, refuse to answer.* My heart skipped three beats and I could've sworn it thundered louder than the music.

Knox slowly sipped his beer. Never responding to me. *Thank you, Jesus.*

I leaned over and kissed my sweetie. "You know you being jealous turns me on."

"I shouldn't have a reason to be jealous," he whispered against my lips.

"You don't."

"Tell me you love me."

"I love you to the moon and back."

"You better."

I could tell he was struggling to shake off his pang of jealousy. But he did it nonetheless. I snuggled next to him and slyly slipped my phone, which had started ringing again, on Silent.

"So, Doctor Corny—I mean, umm, Anderson," I said. "You kind of cool. I think I may like you."

"Me too." London brushed her thumb across Anderson's lips.

He smiled at her and said to us, "Excuse me." Anderson leaned over and whispered something in London's ear. She started to blush like crazy. She turned toward him and returned a whisper. He bit his bottom lip.

"All right now!" I snapped my fingers. "What, you two making plans to get it-get it?" I clapped my hands. "No more virgin for you, boo!" I got up from my seat, stood behind London, took my cell phone, and snapped a picture. "I wanted to get a pic with the world's oldest virgin."

She laughed. "Shut. Up."

I resumed my seat, leaned over in my baby's lap and took a picture of us. Then I sat up and texted the pic to him with the words, "I love you more."

Knox looked at me and snapped, "Your phone is vibrating again!"

"No, that's my phone," London said, lifting Anderson's arm from over her shoulders. "And I need to get this." She got up from the table and briskly walked toward the bathroom.

"My fault," Knox whispered to me, holding his phone

in his hand. "You know you're my favorite girl, right?" I slid my arms around his neck.

"And it better stay that way." And yeah, Doctor Corny was sitting there, but I didn't care; I still kissed my baby passionately.

"I can't wait to get you out of here," Knox said to me.

"Hopefully, that's right now," London said, rushing back over to the table, "because I have to go."

"What?" we all said simultaneously.

"What do you mean, you have to go? Like leave?" I frowned.

Anderson looked at London, perplexed. "Is everything all right? Are you okay?"

"I'm fine," she said, agitated. "And everything else is, too. I just have to get out of here."

I was confused. "Was that phone call an emergency?"

"Look. I don't have time for the twenty-twenty questions, okay. Now, Anderson, we need to leave. I need you to take me home. Now!"

He paused. Looked to be in thought and then he said, "Everything is fine, but suddenly you want to go home? Nah, I'm good right here. If you want to leave you should call car service."

"London," I said, pissed. "Did you go in the bathroom and pick up that extra-extra snotty chick that I specifically told you to leave in the bathroom?"

"Rich, I do not have time for this!" She dialed a number on her phone. "Yes. I need a car right away. I'm in the ghetto. I mean, Inglewood. Yeah, the corner of Century and Crenshaw. Thank you." She pressed the End button. "Rich, are you coming?"

"Absolutely not. We gon' sit and eat these wings."

"And there you have it," Anderson said. "Matter of fact, let's order another round."

"You haven't said nothing but a word." I rolled my eyes at London. *She may as well say bye to Doctor Corny because as soon as I get back to Hollywood High I will be hooking him up with Spencer.*

Believe that.

I looked at London, rolled my eyes, and sucked a hot wing down to the bone as she beat it out the door.

25

London

I burst into my bedroom, heaving and sweating from racing into the house and up the stairs to my room where
Justice had said he'd be when he texted me and told me to
come home because he missed me and wanted to see me,
now. So here I was running through my suite in search of
getting my life back. My eyes rapidly shifted around the
room from the rumpled bed to the Juliet balcony to my
walk-in closet. He was nowhere.

Dear God, I took too long!

I started hyperventilating.

I pounded my forehead with a fist, feeling myself about
to lose control as tears filled my eyes. I leaned my back up
against the wall, giving up my balance. And just as I was
about to slide down to the floor and crumple up and die,
there came my lifeline.

"Yo, baby, why you crying?"

"Because...I...thought...you...were gone..." I said
in between hiccups and tears. "And I can't...keep...going...

through this. If you're not going to be here and be real and be with me...and love me...then just leave...now. I don't even want you here. I can't do this anymore, Justice."

He slid down to the floor beside me and pulled me into him. "Yo, cut all that out. I ain't going nowhere, girl. Every time I do leave, where do I always come back to? You just make me so mad. I don't want to leave you. I love you."

"I haven't seen or heard from you in way too long. You ignored all of my calls. Why?"

" 'Cause you be buggin', yo. And I wasn't sure if you was still beat to make this work, yo. Real ish, yo. I got tired of tryin' to make somethin' pop wit' you when you ain't seem beat for it. I'm just tired of my dreams not bein' fulfilled, feel me? But, on e'erything, yo. I got mad love for you, London. That's why I'm here. Because you a part of my dream. I thought you believed me, yo. But now I'm not so sure." He lowered his head, then covered his face.

His shoulders shook.

My heart ached.

"Justice, what's wrong?"

He slowly lifted his head and looked at me. Tears were gliding down his beautiful face. "I'm so tired of runnin' behind nothin', baby. I'm tired of not knowin' what's happenin' with us. I need you, yo. And this plan with Rich, let's just dead it, a'ight? I don't even want it. It's caused too much beef wit' us. I'm gonna get a job. And my music, I'm just gonna have to give it up for now."

Seeing him all broken, hurt me like never before. I took him by the face and stared into his wet eyes. "Baby, you're too talented for that. I can't let you do that. While you were gone, I've been playing my part and still holding you down, doing what a girlfriend is supposed to be doing for her man. I've already put the plan in motion. I have to do this. I need to do this. You deserve this. Don't give up yet, baby. I promise you, everything you've ever wanted is about to be yours. But you can't cut me off. Us not talking is not good for me, or you. We are meant to be together forever, Justice. Nothing will ever come between us. All I need for you to do is believe in me, and hold on. I got you."

He sniffed. "Nah, baby...it's all good, yo. I can't let you do that. I know I was bein' mad selfish, not considerin' you. I know how much you dig Rich."

"But you mean more."

"But I don't want you jeopardizin' ya friendship with ya girl."

"The only thing that's important to me is you." I wiped his tears, then kissed him on the lips. "I've missed you so much."

He kissed me back. "I've missed you, too, baby. I've been so effed without you, yo. But I still don't want you riskin' anything..."

I placed a finger to his lips. "Sssssh...don't you worry about anything. I have it all under control. And I will make this happen."

I kissed him again and the heated passion that I had missed found its way home. The way he looked at me, the way my body erupted, I knew I would do whatever it took to stay in Justice's arms.

He looked me in the eyes. "Don't front on me, London. Are you really sure you wanna to go through wit' this? You told me yes once before, then flipped the script on me."

"But this time I mean it."

Monday afternoon

"Why didn't you meet me at my locker this morning?" I asked Rich, walking up to the table where—once again—she and Spencer were cackling like the besties I'd make sure they'd never be.

Rich scoffed. "You've got to be kidding me. I'm pissed with you."

"About what? What did I do to you? If anything, I should be mad at you. I asked you to leave with me, and you said no."

Rich turned to Spencer. "So, listen. We're kicking it this weekend, right? I have someone I want you to meet."

Spencer raised her eyebrows. "Uh-huh...Really?"

"Yeah, really. But anyway, we're having a good time, right? We went to this frat party. I tried to hook her up with the Rock of Gibraltar. But, of course, she has a man. And I accepted that. So whatever. Anyway, Doctor Corny...I mean Anderson, C-Smoove, isn't a bad guy after all. I was actually starting to like him. He really, really seems like a nice guy. And you should have seen the way he was looking at London, like she was some hot wings and a pitcher of beer..."

Spencer's eyebrows furrowed as she shifted in her seat. "Oh really? What could he possibly see in her?"

I blinked.

"Girl, I don't know. But he acted like she was the only girl in the room, like he was all in-love. He—"

"Wait a minute," I snapped, placing a hand up on my hip. "First of all, don't be sitting here talking about me as if I'm not standing here. Second of all, if you have a problem with me, Rich, then you address *me*. Don't effen sit there and discuss me or my business with her. I don't deal with her."

Spencer slammed a hand down on the table. "This *her* happens to have a name, trick. And it's Spencer. And you're right. You don't deal with her, Turkey Neck, so I know you don't want me to do your gizzards in, Miss Rooster. Looking like Yosemite Sam's grandmother on steroids. You oversized bird. You Fiona look-alike; matter of fact, that's an insult to Fiona, with your big he-man self."

I blinked.

Rich stretched out, laughing. "Bwaaahahahaha. Ohmygod, ohmygod, ohmygod...I can't breathe. Bwaaahahahaha...Okay, okay, let me stop." She glanced back over at me and started laughing again. "Bwaaahahahahaha. Spencer, you are so wrong for that."

She was laughing so hard tears were coming out of her eyes.

I frowned. "What the hell is so funny, Rich?" I snapped. "This dumb whore and her whack insults are a bore."

"And so is your face," Spencer spat. "But you don't see me yawning about that. I hate you. And everything you fall for."

"Good, because I hate you, too. So we're even."

Spencer swung her hair over her shoulder. "No, you undercover skank, we will never be even 'cause you're a billion dollars too short. You're broke. You don't even deserve to be at this lunch table. You're only here by default. We only agreed to let you in because Rich told us how pitiful you were. And she was right. But she said you had potential. And she was right about that, too. You have the potential to bring down the reputation of all of us, you scheming ho. What a horrible disappointment you've turned out to be."

Rich grabbed her neck. "Oh my...clutching pearls! Spencer, you shouldn't have said that. I told you that in confidence."

I narrowed my eyes at Rich. "So is that how you see me, Rich—pitiful?"

Rich rolled her eyes. "Look, don't drag me into this mess. Y'all two hyenas need to put your bickering on hold, and let me finish my story."

I frowned. "I don't think so. There's no story to tell."

"You're right." Rich sneered. "Then how about this. There's no story to finish, but there's an argument to be had between you and me. Why would you leave me and Knox sitting there like that with your man? Like who does that?"

"Wait. The two of you went out on a double date?" Spencer asked, shooting a look over at Rich.

"Uh, yeah. Snap, snap. Keep up, Spencer. And don't interrupt me again. Now like I was—"

Spencer scowled. "You don't snap, snap me, Man-eater."

Rich hopped up from her seat. "Take it down, Spencer. Or get dropped. And I do mean dropped...all the way *down* to the floor. Now I'm tryna be nice today, but you are really trying my nerves. So, anyway, back to you, Miss Rude. That boy really, really seems to like you. And he probably almost loves you, but now I can see why if he doesn't."

"What? Rich, I know you don't want me to get started on Knox."

Rich tooted her lips. "Uh-huh. You're right, 'cause you're

trying to live today, or else we'll be up in here scrapping 'cause you know I don't let anyone talk about my boo. So I know you don't want that pretty face beat up. Have me do you like I did that day when I threw you in the pond and beat you down. Don't take me there, girl."

Spencer laughed. "Splish, splash, she got beat down next to the birdbath."

Rich and I got silent. We both blinked at Spencer. Rich threw the palm of her hand up in Spencer's face. "Uh... not! You don't get up in our arguments. This isn't a three-lane highway so bust a U-turn, boo-boo, and go back the other way."

Spencer blinked, tilting her head. She bit into her celery stick and chewed.

Slut!

"Now, back to you, London," Rich continued as she stared me down. "What you did was dead wrong. What in the hell was so important that you had to storm out of the club like that? And you know you were about to lose your virginity!"

"I told you I had an emergency."

Spencer snickered. "Yeah, an emergency meeting doggie-style, with your hind legs up in the air, I bet. She is no virgin! She just doesn't know how to appreciate a good man, and she is not alone!" She eyed Rich and then looked back at me. "I wouldn't be surprised if this little sneaky witch didn't hop up on her broom to be with some other boy. Rich, I don't know what part of this you can't see. But the writing is scrawled out all over the bathroom walls. That chicken ran off to peck somebody else's pecker. She has her own nine-hundred number."

"What? You don't know me, slut."

"Sweetie. I don't have to know you. I know your kind. And it's nothing nice. You don't appreciate anything. You have a good man and you'd rather toss him to the side for some nothing in Timbs, who only wants you for what he can get. And once you're used up, he's done. And you ruin the good man for the next one. It's whores like you that have us all messed up. Have us getting tossed off boats, getting dismissed like we meant nothing, leaving us home crying. All over crap we didn't do. It was some ungrateful ratchet ho like you that ruined him."

"Oh my. Oh wow," Rich added.

I frowned. "Let me tell you some—"

"You can't tell me a thing," Spencer said, sneering and cutting me off. "So save it." She side-eyed Rich. "And you. You keep on hanging with chicks like her and you'll be stuck with the same nothing dressed in Timb boots, too. And, as you say, Rich, 'hit the floor with that.'"

Rich curled up her lips. "Ewww, now what is wrong with you?"

"It's jealousy," I said, eyeing Spencer. "'Cause I know chicks like you, too. And your kind is always digging through someone else's scraps. You'll always be second best because that's what you settle for. But then again... you were raised that way. No one has ever put you first. Not even your father. The jungles of Africa came before you. Not your mother. She can't stand you. All she loves is her ratings. You don't even have any friends. And you don't have a man. Well, not unless you have someone else's. And even then, he's still not yours. Now, as Rich would say, 'hit the floor with that!'"

Rich threw her hands up over her chest. "Oh no, oh no... clutching pearls! Leave me out of your mess!"

Spencer hopped up from her seat. "London, you want it with me? You can't afford to have it with me. You want to talk about parents, then let's start with yours. The only way your mother is ever going to love you is if you make it back up on the runway, and from where I stand you're still a few pounds too fat for that. And let's not talk about the miserable scandal that rocked your mother's beauty-queen career. Miss Eighteen And Posing For *Hustler* Magazine. And we won't even get started on your father and the affair that he's rumored to be having. God only knows whose mother is topping him off. Are you satisfied, London, or do you want some more?"

I blinked. "You don't know what the hell you're talking about."

"Oh, I know *exactly* what I'm talking about. The writing's scribbled all over the sidewalk. Turner Phillips is stuck in a loveless marriage to an uptight, uppity pillow princess who doesn't know how to keep her own man happy. And sounds like the fruit doesn't fall too far from the tree! Now go hopscotch on that."

I swallowed back tears. I couldn't believe that she was saying such slanderous things about my father. It was one thing to say nasty things about me or my mother, but to smear dirt on my father, now that was going way overboard.

"Now wait a minute, Spencer," Rich snapped. "That's enough. You've gone too far."

"Well, obviously not far enough because she's still here."

Rich shook her head. "No, that's enough. Let's just forget this. We all have said more than we should. Now let's get back on track and talk about the itinerary the party planner sent us over the weekend about the masquerade ball."

Spencer rolled her eyes and shifted in her seat. "How about this: screw the itinerary. Let's talk about where you were this weekend. And why you kept sending me to voice mail instead of telling me that you were with your bestie-boo over there."

I smirked. "So that's what this is really all about. You're jealous, just like I said you were. Poor little Spencer, lost her best friend again. Now she doesn't know what to do with herself because no one else likes her. Face it, Spencer. You're jealous, always have been; always will be. I'm everything you'll never be."

"Exactly. Something you finally got right. You're everything I would never want to be. You're lonely and miserable, sitting up in your big mansion feeling sorry for yourself."

"Oh, never that, sweetie. Feeling sorry for myself isn't what I do."

She laughed. "But lying is, I see."

I waved her on. "Whatever. Think what you like. Like I said, you're jealous."

"Jealous?!" Spencer screeched. "Of what? You? I don't think so."

"Oh, you think? Oh wow...I didn't know that. I had no idea you possessed thoughts. Amazing. You're a crazy, jealous mess, Spencer. It's mighty funny how you didn't have a problem waving that note in my face when you and Rich had your secret little meeting in the bathroom last Friday. And you thought it was all about you. Well, guess what? It's not. You don't own Rich. She can have more than one friend"—I leaned up in my seat—"and it is possible for her to have two. But guess what, sweetie. I'm number one, and you're number two. And that's how it will always be. Now live with it."

Spencer jumped up from her chair and lunged at me. I glanced around the café and spotted onlookers pulling out their phones to get up-close footage of what happened next.

"I'm sick of you trying to get in the middle of my friendship with Rich."

Rich frowned. "Ewww. Hold up. I know I'm the flyest of them all, but all this fighting over me isn't cute. Both of you are sickening. And, Spencer, I don't why you have to get all jealous and crazy. You act like you own me. You're not going to be invited to every party. That's just how it is. Don't you have other friends? I didn't say anything when you were chopping it up with Heather.

"It's only one of me. And you two can't be arguing over me. I keep telling y'all, you can't be fighting over me. Geesh. It's annoying. I mean, I know I'm the queen of the clique. But, my God...even a queen can't be split in two. There are four days out of the week I can give you, so the two of you can split that down the middle. You two work it out. From where I'm sitting, why can't we all get along? And stay on task."

Spencer slung her celery sticks across the table. "You know what, Rich, shut your fat trap. Enough of you and your selfish ways. I don't need to split anything other than your face. If you want to hang with this monster, then rah-rah...do you. I don't have to be your friend. Nobody has time to sweat you. I have more important things going on in my world, other than you. And if you were a friend you'd care. But you're nothing but a two-faced, chubby little slut who likes to hang around with monsters. And, no, Rich. You don't have two friends; only one. So both of you gnomes can kiss the pink insides of my Massengill garden!"

She grabbed her things and stormed off, leaving Rich with her mouth dropped open. And mine with a secret smile.

One plan down; and one to go...

26

Spencer

"**S**pencer, darling…wake up, my love…Rise and shine."
I heard the voice as the drapes opened, and snapped up in bed, yanking my eye mask off. It was Kitty.

Kitty!

Standing over me wearing an orange one-piece Dolce & Gabbana bodysuit that had a plunging neckline, she held a serving tray in her hands.

I blinked, trying to adjust my eyes to the sunlight flooding the room. The 18-carat floating Chopard diamonds dangling from her ears and wrapped around her wrist practically blinded me as I frowned, staring her down.

Warlockstewandwitch'sbrew…what in the hell is she doing here?

"I brought you breakfast, dear," she said, placing the tray in front of me. She lifted the lid. There was a piping-hot Belgian waffle smothered in strawberries, blueberries, and coconut shavings, lightly drizzled with warm honey;

one scrambled egg with cheddar cheese; two sausage patties; and a glass of orange juice.

Sausage patties?

I felt under par! One, because I was looking at Kitty first thing in the morning. Two, because I didn't like sausage; well, heehee...not sausage from a pig, cow, or any other four-legged animal. But that was beside the point. The point was, the smell of Kitty's Clive Christian perfume and that fried animal meat were making me sick. Then seeing the imprint of her puffy slice of yeast pie in that getup she had on was all I needed to toss my guts up right there on the spot. She was an old, horny, saber-toothed tiger who needed to be chained up in a cage.

I eyed her. "*You* cooked this?"

She waved me on. "Oh, don't be foolish, Spencer; of course not. I had this delivered from that darling little breakfast bistro you've always loved."

I rolled my eyes, shooting her a disgusted look. "I haven't eaten there since I was twelve, Mother. Remember, the year you shipped me off to Switzerland? And if you paid attention, you'd know I don't eat meat. I don't drink orange juice in the morning. And I only like hard-boiled egg whites. And what is all this mess slopped up on this waffle? You must think I'm some pig, hunting truffles." I shooed the plate away from me. "Yuck! Get this mess out of my sight. Now what are you doing here?"

Kitty huffed, snatching the tray from me. She walked over and set it up on the round marble table I have over in the corner. "Fine, Spencer. Be an ungrateful little snot this morning."

I folded my arms across my chest. "Mother, it's too early in the morning for your antics. I wanna know why you aren't in New York with your precious TV show, or swinging from the chandelier with your boy toy. Or have you tired of him already?"

She ran her fingers through her crinkly hair. Her sleek bob was growing out and was practically brushing her shoulders. "I came home late last night, darling. I couldn't bear being out on the East Coast another night, knowing what's been going on here with you. So I had Charlie gas my jet and bring me home. I'll work from my studio here in L.A. until I can figure out how to clean up this mess Vera's created."

I blinked.

No, no, no, no, no . . . noooooooooooooooooooo!!!!

"W-w-what exactly do you mean, Mother? Surely not that you'll be here . . . with me!"

I held my breath, feeling myself ready to burst into tears!

"Yes, my darling!" she exclaimed. "That's exactly what I mean. I told you when you had that godawful meltdown over that Anderson boy that I was going to selflessly put my life on hold to raise you the right way. So, here I am. Starting today, I'm going to whip you into shape."

"What?!" I shrieked, jumping out of bed. "Oh, no the ricketycrickety hell you won't! If you even think about putting your hands on me, I will do you in real good, Kitty. I will clean your lunch box. And I mean it! I'm sixteen, not six. And I'll be damned if you'll ever whip me and try to ruin my shape. What kind of hateful woman are you, wanting to whip me? I promise you, Mother. I will chop your hands off in your sleep if you dare!"

She stared at me with a blank look on her face.

"Don't look at me all crazy, like you don't understand a

word I'm saying. I don't want...no, I don't *need* you here.
I've been doing fine on my own. And I don't need you
coming up in here disrupting my life, trying to be something you don't know how to be. Now, where's Vera at?"

She walked up on me and grabbed my hands. "Oh,
Spencer, darling, don't be like that. Stop with all the
threats. Look at this as an opportunity for you and me to
renew our mother-daughter bond."

I snorted. "Renew? Ha! The only thing you can renew is
your passport to hell. Now I wanna know where Vera is."

"I fired her," she pushed out nonchalantly.

My heart leaped into my throat.

"You did *whaaat*?"

"You heard me. I fired her."

Right there on the spot, I died inside. Kitty had taken
her diamond blade and sawed it into my spirit. Once
again, that selfish joy-killer snatched away someone else
who I cared about and who cared about me. And in the
process she reopened an unhealed wound. The loss of my
first two caretakers, Esmeralda and Solenne.

My lips quivered. Then without warning, tears sprang
from my eyes.

I dropped down to my knees and wailed, "Whyyyyyyy?
How could you do this to me? Fortheloveofallthingssweet-
sourandsassy...Why, Kitty? Do you hate me that much?"

"I gave her rules and things I wanted instilled in you
and she failed. And when you fail to do your job, you are
dismissed. So cut the theatrics, Spencer. And get up off
your knees before they end up all black and rusty. I do
know how much you love being down on them, but now
is not the time for show-and-tell. Vera will be fine. I gave
her two-years' severance pay and told her that her services

were no longer needed. I'll give her a good reference and she can go ruin someone else's child's life, but her work here is done."

"You call Vera, and you hire her back!" I yelled, crawling over to my chaise and pulling myself up. "Right this instant!"

"I will most certainly not! You are stuck with me. And you better hope like hell that I enjoy mothering you; otherwise I am going to make your life a living hell."

I blinked, then narrowed my eyes at her.

"By the way," she added, tossing her hair. "Your father sold that little private island of his with all those wild birds on it in Hawaii for six-hundred million. He'll be transferring the money from the sale into another account for you."

"I don't care about his money! I hate you! I want Vera back!"

"Well, too bad! You should have thought about your precious Vera before you showed me what a weak little girl you are. You better woman up, Spencer, dear. If you want me out of your hair, then you had better get with the program. Be the cunning, conniving, backstabbing, fearless woman I know you can be. Get me a scandalous story, dear. And I'll give you back your life. But, until then...it's you and me. So you had better buckle up and get used to it. Now, do Mother a favor and tell me what grade you're in again so I can have cupcakes sent to the school."

I blinked.

"Oh, never mind," she said, heading toward the door. "I'll have my assistant call Hollywood High and find out for me. By the way, I'm having brunch with Camille this morning to discuss doing a feature story on her in *Dish the Dirt* magazine. It'll be titled: 'From Trash to Riches; The Rise and Fall of a Hollywood Star.' That country bumpkin has more skeletons in her backyard than a graveyard. And I want 'em dug up. In the meantime, it's time you make nice with that junkie daughter of hers. Toodles."

The minute my cell rang, I rolled my eyes up in my head. Somehow I knew Kitty was behind this call. God, how I hated that woman! I took a deep breath, sighed, then answered as if I were a recording. "I'm sorry. The number you have reached has been disconnected to drug addicts and freaks. Don't try this number again."

"Spencer, this is Heather..."

I blinked. *FortheloveofAlexanderGrahamBell...this trick really thinks I'm a voice mail. How stupid is that?*

My goodness...crack really kills!

"Heather? Heather? Are you that cracked out that you don't know the difference between a machine and a human being? You need to get your life together and get back in school. Seems like your brain cells are dying by the minute."

"Listen, don't hang up on me," Heather said, sounding frantic. "I just need to talk to you, please."

"Oh no, Miss Heather, I don't do Skittles parties. And I don't do you. And you do remember we're not friends, right? Never were; never will be. Your words, not mine. So why would I want to talk to you?"

"Spencer, you don't have to talk; just listen. Please."

"Well, I don't know if I want to listen to any more of your party rants. So you listen to me, Miss Crack City. Since you like to rap and all, let me tell you what brought

Heather down…schemin' on her friends…kickin' them down to the ground…you tried to play me…and I didn't like that…you ain't nuthin' but a bee in a trap…And, no, Heather, I'm not takin' you back… 'cause at the end of the day, you still wippity whack…"

"Spencer, why are you rapping?"

"Oh no, sweetie. You rang the bell for the battle when you rapped about me in your backyard. Threatened to have me tossed off property that you don't even own. You're *rent*ing, Heather. You don't own property, remember? You can't toss me anywhere. I should buy that bungalow and become your new landlord, then toss you off the property…"

"Spencer, are you ever gonna move past that?"

"What? Don't be trying to pack me up somewhere. Do you want your face clawed off? Obviously you need a good Mace-down to get your mind right, telling me to move past something. You haven't even apologized to me…"

"You won't give me a chance to. Every time I call you, you go off on me, then hang up. I've sent you flowers, I've written you. I even sent you a Chanel bag, and you know I don't really have money like that."

"Well, that's too bad, Miss Crack-A-Lot. If you really knew me, you'd know that Chanel does nothing for me. You meant to send that package to Rich. I have style and grace. I'm not some shallow trampette who drops down for the nearest handbag."

Heather chuckled. "First name Trampette; last name Man-eater."

I giggled at her filling in the blanks of my joke about Rich. She was the only one I had told that to. And we had laughed over drinks for hours, the one time that she had stayed at my house when Camille had thrown her out. That was a fun night.

I rolled my eyes. "That was funny. But, anyway, she's my best friend. And I don't laugh at my friends. Or throw crack-laced baby aspirin parties and curse them out on microphones, either."

"Spencer, *please*! The day that I hurt you was one of the worst days of my life. I messed up. I don't know any other way to keep saying I'm sorry. If you hate me that much, and don't want to be bothered with me, I will leave you alone."

"Look, Flatty Patty, I'm not trying to make you feel bad, but I just want to make you face reality by torturing you. Make you feel how you made me feel. All the other girls hated you. London talked about how dirty and trifling you were. Rich called you all kind of cheesy-baked booga-boos. Rich cursed you out like a dog. Like a gutter dog. And I was there for you. I took up for you. And you gave me your extra-plump booty bags to kiss. All I ever did that might have been wrong was Mace you. And that wasn't anything close to what you did to me..."

"Spencer, my eyes were swollen for a week."

"Oh, you wanna go there, Heather. You wanna bring that up. I thought we were supposed to move past all that. So you wanna get it skunked up again, huh?"

She giggled.

"Oh, you think this is funny?"

"No, I don't think it's funny. I miss you so much, Spencer. I messed up. All I want is my friend back. But if you don't wanna be my friend then I understand."

"That sorrow card doesn't work either, Heather. So get

your eyes up off the sparrow and look at the sunlight. And see your way out of jail first, before you try to make me feel sorry for you."

"I'm not in jail. I'm in rehab."

"Well, good for you, junkie. I'm impressed. Glad to see they cleaned up the streets. Now maybe they can collect Co-Co, too."

She sighed. "Spencer. I miss you. I really, really, really, really miss you. And if you give me another chance to be your friend, I'll never betray you again."

"Umm, you're five weeks late and a few thousand dollars short, because my life has changed, Heather. I've been going to church services with Rich. I've converted over to the Goddess of Desperation. So I'm saved now. And that's the only reason I'm thinking of having a forgiving heart toward you. But if I ever convert back to my old, nasty ways, I might turn on you, so you better watch your step."

Heather sighed. "Glad to hear you've changed your life. And I want more than anything to be *your* friend. But I can't stand Rich."

I gasped. "Now, Heather, I just told you to watch your step, and already you're high-stepping up the wrong path. Yeah, I used to hate Rich, too. Used to want to cut her belly fat out, but now she's lost a few pounds—not much, but enough so that her stomach isn't hanging over her designer belts—and we're friends again. Even if I had to set her straight yesterday!"

"Spencer, I've been away from Hollywood High for too long. And there are two things I don't miss. That bear, Rich. And that tyrannosaurus, London."

I cracked up. "Hahahahahaha. That was almost hilarious. Because only half of that was funny."

"Which part?"

"About that big-faced London. With her big-hoofed self."

Heather cracked up.

I popped my lips. "Mmmph. So, are you trying to get back in with the Pampered Princesses, or do you need to be replaced like they did you on *The WuWu Tanner Show*? Or are you tryna rock another lunch table across the room?"

"No, I want my old life back. And if that means I have to do tea at Jurassic Park with London and indulge on too many snacks with Rich, I'll do it. I just want my best friend back."

"Mmmph. And who's that? Who's your best friend, Heather? And say it like you mean it."

"You are, Spencer. Always have been; always will be."

"Now apologize to me for being so ratchet."

"I'm sorry."

"Now tell me you'll never do it again."

"Spencer, I swear to you I will never, ever do anything to hurt you, or our friendship, again."

"Now, say crack is whack, so we can pour the tea on what's been going on at Hollywood High."

Heather laughed. "See, this is what I miss about you; your sense of humor."

"Well, I tell you what, Heather. I'm going to give you one more chance. Don't ruin it 'cause you know I'm not vengeful. But I will get you back. So now tell me. What's going on at the prison yard? But wait. Let me catch up on this real quick. Rich is back with Knox. London is running around chasing some boy who doesn't want her. And you know who he wants?"

"Who? *You?*" Heather asked, sounding like she was drooling at the seams. "Are you creeping with him in the bathroom, too?"

"What? Oh, no you didn't even go there, Heather. See, this is why you can't forgive a crack whore. Don't do me, Heather. Bees in the trap! 'Cause I gets it done. I'll zig-zag your skull, then connect the dots all across your face."

"I didn't mean it like that, Spencer."

"Yes, you did, liar. Don't try to insult my intelligence, Heather. Yeah, I was in the bathroom with Coreeey. But I made a mistake. Although Corey was wrong 'cause he knew Rich was my friend. And as a crack whore, I would think you'd understand."

"Spencer, will you kill the whore. I didn't do crack. And I'm not a whore."

I rolled my eyes. "That's what they all say. Show me the receipts that prove you bought something other than crack. Until then, you are a crackhead. Now make that the last time you bring up something about me on my knees in a bathroom. I'm trying to be loving and kind to you. And you're already trying to get me to backslide, trying to do me, like I'm some low-end heathen."

"Spencer...shut up. Please. Finish telling me the gossip."

"Whatever, Heather. Anywaay...before I forget my religion, back to the bees in the trap. Rich and London are hot, sloppy messes."

"Yeah, sluts."

"Now, Heather. I would not consider Rich to be a slut. That's not nice. She is more like...like a ho. And I mean that in a good way. If I meant it in a bad way I'd call her a dirty ho, but calling her a slut is just going too far. Now, anyway...what's going on behind the barbed wire?"

"Spencer, please...for the last time, it's rehab. But anyway...I have to tell you something. And you can't tell anyone."

"What, girl? Are you planning an escape? Did you dig yourself a hole so you can crawl out and get your freedom on? I know you're not smuggling drugs in there, are you, Heather?"

"Spencer. No, no...listen."

"I'm listening."

"I um...I um...I slept with Shakeer..."

"Who? *Shakeer?* What in the world is a Shakeer? That sounds so hood; so deliciously ghetto. Is that some new designer drug you done got your hands on?"

"No...it's my counselor." She lowered her voice. "I had sex with him. And I don't know how to feel about that."

My mouth dropped open. "You did what? Where?"

"In his office."

Ugh! This nasty whore!

"Oh no. That nasty dog! I'm gonna have to report him. That doesn't sound right. It sounds nasty; real gutter-trash nasty. And how old is this nasty pervert, like forty? Yuck! Viagra on overload."

Oooh, yes, yes, yes! Heather, you whore!

"No, he's twenty-five."

Oh my...scandalous! I smiled. *I hit the Jack and the Beanstalk with this news! I'll be able to get Kitty out of my face, much sooner than later!*

"Well, did you want to be bent over with your booty cheeks up in the air?"

"Honestly...yes."

"Why, Heather? Why would you want to sleep with your counselor?"

"Because he's the only one who understands me. He makes me feel special. Camille was up here ragging on me. Telling a buncha lies. All I've ever asked of her is to tell me about my father. That woman hates me so much. How could a mother hate her own child like that?"

I thought about Kitty and rolled my eyes. *Mmmph, same thing I'd like to know!*

"Heather, she doesn't hate you. She's self-centered. And trust me. Kitty wrote the book on self-centered mothers. So don't even get me started on that. But, anyway, don't stress that foolery."

"That's easier said than done. No matter how hard I try, I still end up hurt and feeling alone. Why can't that woman just tell me who my father is?"

"Heather, I mean really. Get over it. If that man wanted to be a father to you, he would be. Look at my father. I don't know mine. He's always off somewhere chasing fountains of youth. But you don't see me running to Africa to bond with him."

"Yeah, but the difference is, you know who he is. I know nothing about mine. All I know is his first name is Richard."

I twirled the end of a curl, shifting in my seat. "And that's already too much information. Now let it go. And get on with your life. So, anyway, when are you going to ask me about my life? Or are you going to continue to be selfish and keep talking about yours? I have things I want to talk about, too." I glanced over at the clock. "'Cause in another hour I need to get ready for school, so we need to wrap your life up in about two seconds so we can get on to what's been going on in mine."

"And what could possibly be going on in your perfect life?"

I blinked. "Are you trying to get it skunked again? Is that a dig, Heather? 'Cause I'm the original grave digger. Now I'm warning you, don't do my nerves."

"No, it's not. I promise you, it wasn't. So tell me. What's been going on with you?"

I smacked my lips. "Well, since you asked...I've been thinking about committing murder, but I'm trying to figure out how I can get the charges downgraded to simple assault."

"What? What are you talking about?"

"I was seeing this guy who I liked...*a lot*. But I found out that he was lying to me..." I sighed, then paused and told Heather everything. From how I had met Anderson that day his driver stopped in the middle of the road and caused me to run into the back of his limo, to that night he cursed me out and tossed me off his yacht like seaweed, and how I cried because I didn't have any of my weapons with me to do him in right then. "Anderson hurt me, Heather," I continued, keeping my emotions in check and remembering Kitty's threat to stay here and torture me.

"Anderson? Wait. Anderson Ford? Better known as C-Smoove on his party nights?"

I blinked. "What did you say...?" I paused. Blinked again. "How do you know him? Please don't tell me he was doing you, too."

"No, he was doing Co-Co."

The line went dead.

27

Rich

After a weeks-long standoff and me holding my ground and my crown, the queen's mother finally came to her senses and saw the error of her ways.

Pow!

I knew I would win.

How?

Because I knew that my mother knew, that in ten, fifteen years tops, what side her old and stale bread would be buttered on.

Snap. Snap.

Logan Montgomery was a lot of things, but stupid wasn't one of them. And she understood that when she became old, decrepit, and could hardly move, and her life choices dwindled from diamonds and Dior to Polident, Bengay, Depends and orthopedic shoes—that her Richie-Poo would be the only one to take care of her.

Not Daddy.

And certainly not the prince, RJ, especially since he was

a selfish, self-serving bastard who didn't give a damn
about the value of a dollar. Talk about bringing the family's name down—hmph. Well, meet Mr. Draino.

Not to mention he was idiotically in love with Slow-
Aysha, better known as Spencer, and I would be damned if
those two dumb bunnies would run through my parents'
money and trick it all away.

Can you say hell-to-da-no!

But anyway, Logan Montgomery was back to having my
back. Like a mother should. And being the kind and con-
siderate diva that I am, I was willing to forgive her for turning on me...as long she remembered her place...and
didn't do it again.

"Whatcha thinking about, Richie-Poo?" drifted into my
thoughts.

I turned toward my mother, who lay on the spa table
next to me, a sparkling crystal chandelier overhead, enjoying a Tui na treatment. Her eyes rolled to the top of her
head in enjoyment as she turned and faced me. "Oh, this
is sooo relaxing. Mmm..." She shivered in excitement and
smiled. "Now tell me, Richie, what were you thinking?"

I smiled and it took everything in me—or out of me, de-
pending on how you looked at it—to keep a straight face.
"I was just thinking about how much I'm enjoying myself
with you. I'm so glad you came to your—" My mother's
eyebrows raised and I quickly caught myself. "I mean, I'm
so glad you had this idea."

"I am, too." My mother extended her left arm and
reached for my right hand. We locked fingers. "Rich, I love
you so much. And I..."

*Oh God...Please don't be selfish and get all religiously
lovey-dovey on me and ruin the day. This is not the time*

to interject your emotions. Because all I want to do at this moment is have a gold scrub and dip my hands and feet in paraffin.

My mother continued. "I know the past few weeks have been difficult between us."

Shoot me now...Here she goes with her classic "If my mother was still alive" speech...

"And if my mother was still alive..."

You would what, Logan? Be the best daughter you could be, of course.

"I'd be the best daughter I could be. And I would know that my mother only wanted what was best for me."

Of course she did, Logan. And I'm sure she would've somehow managed to stay alive if she had known you were destined to bore the hell outta me with this speech. Trust, the only thing you need to be thinking about is anti-aging cream. And Botox.

"And as your mother, all I've ever wanted and will ever want..."

Is what's best...

"Is what's best for you."

I know...I know...now will you shut. Up!

"Okay, ladies you're ready for the steam room now," one of the masseuses said to us as we rose from the table, wrapped our towels around us, and sauntered into the steam room, where beautiful clouds of light mist greeted us as we walked in. We lay back on the reclining teak chairs, side by side, with only a wet bar between us containing glasses of mineral and rose water. Yayue music filled the room with the lovely sounds of wind chimes and softly strummed guitars.

This was heaven.

I placed a damp Satsuma organic white cloth over my face and for once I decided that I wouldn't fight off the un-expected thoughts of Justice that danced through my mind. Instead, I would allow my mind to bathe in the heated memory of our taboo night.

I could feel the soft flesh of his lips...

His hands...

The weight of his body...

God, this was so wrong...

But oh, so right...

"You know, Rich, I've been thinking about you and Knox."

My eyes snapped open. I looked over to my mother who, thank God, had her face covered with a cloth and couldn't see the guilt consuming me.

She continued. "And I've been thinking that, although he's not who I would have chosen for you, he seems like a really nice guy who genuinely cares about you."

And your point...?

"And my point is that I hope you're being honest with him." She slid the cloth off of her face.

I felt myself about to get pissed. "And why wouldn't I be honest with him?" And yeah, I said it with an attitude. "Just so we're clear, I don't lie to Knox. Why would you even suggest that?"

"I know we're not giving attitudes, Rich." My mother eased up from her chair, taking it out of the reclining posi-tion. She looked directly at me and arched a brow. "Are we?"

"I'm just saying—"

"No, *I'm* just saying. I know you. And you know that I know you. Well. Quite well. And I'm giving you some advice that you ought to take—don't lie to him and don't play with his feelings."

Oops! Did she just cross the line or what? I don't do advice when it comes to my man. Who she needs to lecture is Mr. Multicultural. Mr. Thinks He's British Now— Richard Gabriel Montgomery the Third a.k.a RJ—and worry about the whores he's running through. Stay out of my affairs. My man and I are the It Couple. We got this.

I started to serve her, but since being disrespectful wasn't a part of my personality, I simply said, "Ma, thank you for your concern. But, umm, I'm cool over here. And I know how to take care of Knox. Trust. I finally have him, I will not do anything to hurt him, and we will be in love forever."

My mother pursed her lips and side-eyed me. "Rich Gabrielle, we are not going to ruin this day."

"And why would we do that? I just simply told you that I had my life in order. I'm situated. I'm not in Europe partying like a rock star."

My mother drank in a deep breath and released it in a loud and exaggerated huff. She reached for a glass of rose water and slowly took a sip. "Rich, I almost forgot you knew it all. You have all the answers and I'm so glad that you do. Forgive me for overstepping my boundaries. Besides, I don't know anything. And I especially don't know why a young man by the name of Justice called your phone a few days ago."

What?! "Clutching pearls! Why would you be answering my phone?! Who does that! And then you didn't give me the message. What kind of person springs this on someone in the steam room?!" I blinked my eyes, twice. "You can't be serious with this." *I need a drink and some hot wings.* I looked toward the door hoping to see someone who could take my order. This chick had wrecked my nerves.

"Like I said, I know you. Who doesn't know you, is Knox. Not as well as he thinks he does."

"Ma, I appreciate you looking out for my relationship with Christian Knox. But I—"

My mother snickered.

Did she really just laugh?

She sipped her drink. Then snickered even more.

Oh, I'm about to go straight to twenty! "And what's so funny, Mrs. Montgomery?"

"Oh, Richie, here I thought you knew me just as well as I knew you. But apparently you don't. Because if you think I really give a damn about you staying with Knox, clearly you're confused. Christian Knox was never, has never, and will never ever be my choice for you. I was simply shining a moment of mommy-kindness and womanly advice on you. But since you know everything. And you got this. Then I'm going to sit back and let you have it. Because now I don't have to think of creative ways to come between the two of you; I now know that you will do it for me."

"I don't believe you just said that!"

"Believe it," she said as she placed a damp cloth back over her face and reclined in her seat.

I stared at myself in my dressing room's full-length, diamond-encrusted mirror, doing my all not to let Logan's unsolicited advice haunt me. I hated that she always found a way to manipulate herself under my skin.

I couldn't imagine that a mother would be jealous of

her own daughter, but there was a part of me that wondered why she was so caught up in my life. Was she struggling to live vicariously through me or what? My God, I was sixteen. Old enough to make my own mistakes. I didn't need her jumping on the tracks and telling me a train wreck was coming. I could feel that.

I sighed. Looked down at my ringing cell phone with the name JB flashing across my screen. I wanted to answer and tell him to fluck off. Problem was, I wasn't convinced that if I answered I wouldn't close my eyes and be seduced by his voice and his constant requests for me to sing to him again.

I shook my shoulders. Flicked invisible dust from them and then shot myself a fake smile.

"Miss Rich." A soft knock interrupted at just the right moment.

"Yes."

"It's Chantel," my house manger said. "Mr. Knox is here."

"Okay. Thanks!" I said in excitement. Nervous butterflies sank to the bottom of my stomach. Why was I nervous? I wasn't sure. All I knew is that I hadn't felt like this since I was eight when I lured Knox into the pool house and taught him how to French kiss.

I gave myself a once-over and patted the sides of my size-twelve hourglass hips, which were covered with a sexy pair of hot pink, form-fitting Gucci jeans. I unbuttoned the top four buttons of my sleeveless soft pink, scoop-necked D & G blouse—complemented by a pink diamond brooch shaped like a flimsy bow, placed on my right shoulder. All in an effort to ensure that sneak peeks of my black lace bra were available to tease Knox. I stepped into my six-and-a-half-inch royal blue Louboutins. And *bam!* Just like that I was ready to greet my man.

My parents were smiling and chatting with Knox when I stepped out of the elevator and into the grand room. Knox was soooo freakin' cute that he was damn near pretty. Scratch that, he *was* pretty. Pretty fine.

Hollah.

My baby wore black True Religion jeans, a red and white checkered Polo button-up, and black Louis V. sneakers on his feet. My boo cleaned up hella well.

Boom—thought you knew!

I was all smiles as I walked over to Knox and my parents. He was telling my daddy that he was majoring in sports medicine. Logan was all ears. And for a moment I could've sworn that she was impressed.

"What happened to the love?" I said to Knox as I held my arms open for a hug.

Knox looked at me and something about his smile was off-kilter. His puppy brown eyes usually brightened up when he looked my way, but this time they didn't even twinkle.

WTH...

Knox walked into my embrace, kissed me on my forehead, and whispered, "We need to talk."

I swallowed. *Talk about what?* It was evident by the sound of his voice that something had jumped off.

Dear Jesus...You know I don't do well with drama... so please...

"Knox, how are your parents?" my mother asked him, giving me the don't-trip-and-think-I'm-pleased-with-you side eye.

"They're well; thanks for asking. They're out in Martha's Vineyard this week."

"Oh, I just love it up there. We just purchased Ted Kennedy's old property. So we will be getting there very soon. Perhaps this summer we'll invite you and your parents over to the East Coast so we can have a get-together."

"Yeah," Knox said with the fakest sincerity ever. "We'll have to do that. You know what, Rich"—he turned to me—"I need to speak to you for a moment."

I swallowed again. Sweat had gathered in my palms. *What does he want?* "Ok, we can chat after dinner."

"It can't wait that long. Excuse me, Mr. and Mrs. Montgomery, do you mind if Rich and I have a moment to talk?" He flashed my mother a smile and she smiled back.

"No, sweetie, that's fine," my mother said and then glanced over at me with a smug look that said *Umm-hmm, what'd you do now?*

"It's cool, man," Daddy said. "I understand wanting to hollah at your girl before you have dinner with her parents. But it's no need to be nervous. I already called your daddy and told him I was gon' press the hell outta you now, since you've moved from being my accountant's son to dating my daughter."

My mother chuckled. "Richard, behave. He will not. How about this, Richard? Why don't we go into the kitchen and tell the staff to move dinner to the terrace? It's a clear and cool night. Dinner there should be wonderful. I'll even tell them to get the outdoor fireplace roaring."

"Sounds cool." Knox smiled.

"Thanks," I said.

I watched my parents hold hands, and my daddy pulled

my mother into him. He kissed her on the side of the head. They were so in love. How sickening. They walked out of the room and as they got lost in the distance, I turned to Knox and reached for his hand. But instead of accepting my gesture he took a step back. "I don't need you to touch me right now."

"What?"

"Because every time you touch me I get off focus and there's something on my mind that I've been stewing on all weekend."

I frowned. My mouth was twisted to the side. *What does he mean, all weekend? We were laid up practically all weekend, so when did he have time to get this pissed?* "All weekend?" I arched my brow.

"Yeah, all weekend."

"So when were you going to say something?"

"I was trying to shake it because I didn't want to believe it. I still don't want to believe it. But it's eating at me because I need to know. I asked you before would you ever lie to me. And you told me no. And I'm hoping that's true."

Now I took a step back. "What do you mean, you're hoping?"

"Before you open your mouth with the boom-bop that I am in no mood to hear, you need to give it to me straight. Did you have an abortion?"

My heart and my nerves dropped to the bottom of my feet, forcing me to bite the inside of my cheek. I leaned from one stiletto to the next and quickly tried to figure out who would have told him such a thing.

Get it together. Stand up straight. Don't shift your eyes. Stop biting your cheek. Do not stutter and push out the very answer to set this straight. "No. I did not." I didn't blink an eye. I tilted my head and said, "So whoever told you that, needs to go back and get their facts straight. I told you what happened. I had a miscarriage from all the stress we were under. And furthermore, don't ever let somebody tell you something that has you questioning me!"

"Watch your tone," he said sternly. "'Cause it's not that I wanted to believe what I heard. It's that I know you. And I know that you only mentioned that miscarriage once, and then we made love—as usual—and you were good to go. Swag was in check. And I have not heard anything else about this so-called miscarriage."

"So you're really going to stand here and call me a liar, after everything we've been through? Oh, word? That's how we're dropping it now?"

"I'm not calling you anything. I'm simply saying that something that traumatic that supposedly happened to you doesn't seem to have affected you. That's all."

"Knox, I was affected by it! I was depressed for three days! I shut out you and everyone else around me. But I realized I had to get on with my life. I couldn't be stuck and remain depressed; it wasn't going to change anything!"

"Oh really . . . ? So what were you doing in Arizona?"

My knees buckled and I swayed just a bit. I prayed like hell he didn't notice it. But I felt like a tsunami was on its way. "I wanted our baby!"

"Is that so . . . ?"

"Yes! I wanted our baby more than anything. And I didn't want any sympathy from you. I didn't need that type of attention."

"Rich, you love attention. And that would've been the prime opportunity for you to gain attention and have more followers on Twitter and fans on Facebook. Gather more headlines, so you can have me twisted up in there with you."

"Why would you say something like that? Is that what you think of me? After all we've been through? I don't even believe in abortions."

"Rich, you just had one last summer."

Did I? I did...I forgot all about that...Oh well.

"Well, that doesn't mean I believe in them. But I believe in us. I believe in you and me."

"You know what, Rich, I wasn't there. And I would hate to believe that you would make up something like a miscarriage. But, I'ma tell you like this—you need to watch the company you keep, 'cause somebody is lying on you."

"I don't believe this!" Tears filled my eyes.

"No need to cry. We ain't beefin'. We're just having a talk."

"I just can't believe this is happening. Do you know how many people are jealous of us? And trying to ruin our relationship?!"

"Baby, the only person who's going to ruin us is you."

I blinked. Blinked four times. "And how am I going to ruin us? You have got to be kidding me! You, better than anybody, know how hard it's been to get my mother to accept you. And I'm not going to do a thing to mess this up. We are right where we need to be. And one thing I don't believe in is lying to my man."

"Yeah, I hope not. But—"

"We're still stuck on a *but*?"

"No, we're not still stuck on a *but*, 'cause I'ma give you

enough rope to hang yourself." He stepped into my space, stared me in the eyes, and gently kissed me on the lips. I slid my hands over his shoulders and slightly parted my mouth, hoping for some tongue. Instead he stepped back, breaking our embrace, and said, "Let's go eat."

I watched Knox walk out of the room and at that moment I knew that I was gon' have to cut a bitch...

28

London

"Wait 'til I find that dirty whore," Rich spat, punching her fist into the palm of her hand. "I'ma kick her as—"

I grinned inside. Spencer was finally going to get her just due. *Eff with me if you want!*

"Calm down, Rich. Keep it calm, and keep it cute. Tell me what has you so upset."

Rich punched a locker. "I wanna take my heels off and beat her in the head with 'em."

"Wait a minute. Who are you talking about?"

"That two-faced Spencer, that's who!"

"Rich, girl, calm down for a second, and tell me what she did. And start from the beginning. I'm sure we can work this out."

"There's nothing to work out except for my fist in her face, and my knee in her neck. She has crossed the line this time. Trying to disrupt my relationship with Knox! I don't give a damn who you are, that's grounds for a beat-down. I've fought too hard to get him, and I'll be damned if I'm about to let anyone come in between us and screw it up. There are three things I don't play with: my money, my man, and my hot wings. And I do mean in that order."

I blinked. *Hot wings? What is this cow talking about? Whatever!*

"Listen. You are going to have to calm down; otherwise you won't be able to get her the way you want to. Now what happened? Matter of fact, let's go into the lounge."

Tears sprang from Rich's eyes as I led her into the girls' lounge. "I have been nothing but good to that girl. And this is how she repays me? Stab me in the back while smiling all in my face. The whole time wanting to destroy me. You were right. That trick is jealous! I try to be nice to people. I'm so sick of it!"

She started pacing the length of the lounge area, her heels clicking against the tiles like angry drums.

"You're too nice. I keep trying to tell you that, Rich. People don't appreciate you."

"You're right. People are always trying to take my kindness for a weakness."

Yeah right.

"That's because you're too freakin' nice. Enough already."

"You're right. From now on, I'm going to start being a selfish, self-centered *beeeyotch* who treats people the exact way they treat me..."

Oh wow...what else is new?

"How could she betray me like that? Why would she tell Knox I had an abortion? All jokes aside, that's not something I play with. "

"She did what? Oh no, girl," I said, pacing back and

forth alongside of her. "Oh no she didn't. When? How did you find that out?"

"You heard me. She told Knox that I had an abortion. Can you believe that? I don't know when she told him because he wouldn't say. All I know is, he came at me with an attitude and told me I needed to watch the company I keep. And the only person who I told about that miscarriage and who knows Knox, is Spencer."

"You really think she would do that?"

"I know she would."

"Well, you know it couldn't have been me, 'cause I just met him."

"Exactly. Spencer is the only one who knows him like that. So I know it wasn't you. You'd never do me like that. You're not the one who's jealous of me; that whore Spencer is. You've been nothing but good to me. The more I think about it, the more I know it was her because that night we went out for drinks she had the nerve to tell me that Knox was too good for me..."

Oh well, that's what you get for not calling me. That'll teach you.

I stopped pacing, placing a hand up on my hip. "She did what?"

"Yes, girl. She told me that if I didn't watch myself I was going to lose him."

"See. And you should have cut her off right then."

"I know. I know. But I wanted to give her a chance. You know how I am."

I most certainly do. You're a two-faced whore just like your slutty friend Spencer...

"So, I know it was her. She wants my man! Stupid, delusional whore. A nothing."

I silently smirked.

"And it's a shame because you were really a good friend to her, Rich. She never deserved your friendship. You've given her so many chances, from sleeping with Corey to turning your brother against you and talking behind your back, you've done nothing but forgive her over and over again. I would have cut her off a long time ago. When is it going to stop? Enough is enough."

"I'm not like you, London. I have a heart."

I blinked.

Yeah, the heart of a rattlesnake!

"I know you do, Rich. And it's been crushed by someone you thought you could trust." I paused, eyeing her. "Please tell me Knox and you are still together."

Please say no...

I held my breath as she dabbed tears from her eyes.

"Yes. Thank God! But I had to go into damage control. That slore really tried to do me in; tried to make my life a living hell! She knows how much I love Knox. I've always loved him."

For once I have to agree with that crazy slut: you don't deserve him!

"Yeah, she knew. And she knew it would hurt you. And imagine the bad press it would have caused."

She sighed. "Oh, London, please. You're going overboard. There's no such thing as bad press. And besides, lucky for her, it didn't get that far 'cause the headline would have read: Dead Whore Found at Hollywood High."

I snickered. "Bottom line, she knew it would hurt you. Think about it. She never wanted you to have any friends other than her. She was always catching attitudes, always calling and checking in on you, and always questioning your whereabouts. She wanted to keep you all to herself. That's what jealous whores do. Been there, squashed that. And that's why she wasn't at lunch today or at her locker this morning because she knew what she did. But you had to see Spencer for yourself. That trick can't be trusted."

Rich's chest was heaving and her hands were balled up by her sides.

"And that's why I'm going to beat her face in. And give her the beating that her mother was too neglectful to give her."

"Now wait, Rich," I said, placing a hand on her shoulder, causing her to stop in her tracks. "Remember what happened the last time you went to beat someone up, *we* both ended up in jail. Let's play this one smart. You don't want to beat her down to where you end up being locked up and sued again. But she definitely needs to get it."

"And I'm going to give it to her."

"No, this is what you have to do—"

Rich cut me off. "I don't want to hear anything about keeping it calm and keeping it cute. That trick wasn't keeping it cute when she told Knox them lies on me."

Whore, the truth was told. You did have an abortion. You are so delusional . . .

We both paced the floor again.

"Girl, nothing but lies," I said, secretly grinning. "I'm so hurt that she would stoop so low and do you like this. Seeing you hurt, hurts me. She was dead wrong for doing that. And that's why I'm saying, enough of the niceness. Enough of being kind. You have to get at her without putting her on defense. Don't let your emotions get in the way, either. The best way to slay an enemy is with a smile. Get her away from that purse.

"Pretend to be real nice and sweet, then reel your hand

back when she least expects it and slide her face across the floor. Sling that slap from your gutter roots of Georgia. Leave your business card in her face. Then stare her down, and let her know. And don't be doing too much talking, preparing her for the smackdown. You step up to her face. Sling her with words. And then you strike!"

Rich stopped in her tracks, taking pause, then narrowed her eyes and pursed her lips. "You know what? That's *exactly* what I'll do."

I smiled as the bell rang, unlocked the lounge door and stepped out.

Get ready to rumble...

"Mmmhmm...there she goes right there," I whispered as Rich and I walked into our finance class. Spencer was sitting up in the front row of the class. "Remember the plan. Keep it cute. Not too many words. Strike from the guts of Georgia, and take her face off."

Rich didn't say a word. She kept her eyes locked in on her target.

"Excuse me, Spencer," Rich said, trying her best to stay calm. "Can I talk to you for a minute in back of the class?"

Spencer eyed Rich up and down. "No, we can talk right here because once Mister Donte starts class I'm not going to do any talking. The last time I slipped out of class with you, I missed out on all the information I needed, so how can I help you? What do you want?"

Rich batted her eyes, then gently swiped Spencer's bang over her forehead. "All I want to do is apologize. We've always been good friends, haven't we, Spencer?"

She turned her lips up. "Uh-huh...you're right. We sure were. Until London came along and you changed."

Rich tilted her head and lowered her voice. "Oh, wow...
so sorry you feel that way. But you're right. I have changed."
She gathered her weave into a ponytail. "I'm smarter. I'm
wiser. And I know who my real friends are."

Spencer batted her lashes. "Oh, isn't that special. So
you're finally coming to your senses now."

"I sure am. I'm finally able to see you for who you really
are. Nothing but a hating slut who likes to dig through
garbage, but then again...you are garbage."

"Wait a minute, Rich..."

"No, you wait a minute—"

I cut Rich off, clearing my throat and making slicing motions across my neck, gesturing for her to cut it short and
smack her way to the point. I sat on the edge of my seat,
waiting for the action to unfold.

Next thing I knew, Rich reared her hand back from the
guts of Georgia just like I told her, and slapped Spencer so
hard that spittle flew out of her mouth and she stumbled
out of the desk. And hit the floor.

Bam!

The classroom went on mute. Dead silence!

"Aaaaah!" Spencer screamed, clearly caught off guard.

Rich slipped out of one of her six-inch pencil heels and
held it over her head as she stood over Spencer. "Unless
you're looking to die, you will shut your mouth and leave
me and my man alone! Don't you *ever* as long as you
breathe cross me! Because the next time you do, I'll be
dancing on the dirt over your head. Every time I see you,
slut, it's on! Now hit the floor with that!"

As the cameras clicked, I smiled. "Well done. Now let's
get out of here. You've had enough for the day. Drinks
on me."

29

Spencer

"I just got word you were slapped down to the floor," Kitty said, barging into my room, disrupting my moment. I was lying back on my chocolate leather chaise with my eyes sealed shut from crying and a Wagyu steak pressed up against the side of my swollen and bruised face. I still couldn't believe Bearzilla had swung her paw at me. "Why in God's name do you have a steak up on your face?"

I lazily lifted one eyelid open, bringing Kitty into tear-clouded view. I was in no mood for her or her foolery. "Really, Mother?" I said with annoyance. "Because my face is black-and-blue, and steaks are supposed to heal the bruising faster. Why else do *you* think I'd have a steak on my face?"

She tilted her head. "A cooked steak, Spencer?"

I breathed out an aggravated sigh. I swear, with all of her billions, Kitty could be so dizzy at times. I frowned at her. "You can't possibly think I was going to put a raw steak on my face and end up with E. coli. I don't think so. I had Jean Paul broil it."

She blinked, then sauntered over toward me. "Okay, dear, if you say so. Now, up, up. Let's assess the damage done."

I opened my other eye and stared at her. "And why do you want to do that?"

"Why else, darling? I want to see what the next line of attack needs to be."

I huffed, removing the steak. Kitty tilted my head, taking in the paw print stamped in my face. She clapped her hands, her diamond bangles clanking to a beat of their own excitement. "Yes, darling, yes, yes, yes...that Rich Montgomery did you good and dirty. This is perfect! Being home is working out better than I thought."

"Whaaaat?!" I screeched. "How dare you take joy in seeing what that whore did to me? How can you stand there and say such a thing, Mother?" I slung the steak across the room, then screamed at her in French. *"Pourquoi avez-vous tant de haine pour moi, Mère?!* Why?"

"Nonsense, I do not take joy in what that child did to you..." She paused, walking over to the intercom and pressing a button.

"Yes, Missus Ellington?"

"Consuela, be a dear and bring me up an ice pack to Spencer's suite."

I rolled my eyes.

"Yes, ma'am."

Kitty turned back to me. "I, my darling, am rejoicing in all of the endless possibilities this little situation has created. Now if you wish for me to understand a word you just said to me in French, then you will need to speak to me in English, dear. Now what is it you were screaming about?"

Tears welled up in my eyes again. "I want to know why you have so much hate for me, Mother. Why? Everyone hates me. First Heather turned on me for her precious drugs. Now Rich has turned on me for that Upper East Side scallywag."

She scowled at me. "Hate you? Don't be foolish. And stop with the tears. Where in the world would you get such an idea that I hate you? I don't hate you. No, darling. I love you. But I am appalled that you want to sit here and cry because your feelings were hurt; because you were slapped and embarrassed. Darling, that is one of the best things that could have ever happened to you."

"What?! You can't be serious!"

Consuela knocked on the door, then entered when Kitty acknowledged for her to do so, handing her an ice pack. Consuela glanced over at me, then parted her lips in a slight smile; one of pity, I'm sure.

"Oh, Consuela, please fetch that steak that my darling daughter tossed over on the other side of the room." Kitty and I eyed her as she did what she was told, then waited for her to walk out, closing the door behind her. Kitty walked over and sat on the edge of the chaise, placing the ice pack on the side of my face.

I flinched.

"Thank goodness your face is only bruised and swollen. You'll be as good as new and gorgeous as ever in time for the masquerade ball. I already FedEx-ed the party planner the remaining balance you owed toward the party."

"Well, that's too bad because, after what Rich did to me, I'm not going to that stupid party."

"Oh, you most certainly will. Your dress is already being designed. And your mask is already being jeweled with the finest pieces. You will walk into that ballroom and make everyone's mouths drop with envy. Do you hear me?"

"But Rich hates me."

She shook me by the shoulders. "Spencer, have you not heard a word I've said? The best games are always played with your enemies."

Tears fell from my eyes.

"I don't want enemies. I want friends. I'm tired of this. I want to go back to Switzerland."

She huffed. "Oh, now you want to embarrass me further by being a runaway. Mmmph. Don't have me slap the other side of your face. Stop being so selfish and so hard-headed, Spencer! And for once do what I tell you. You keep making this more difficult than it has to be.

"Oh no, darling...like I said. You will go to that party. Psychological warfare is in full effect. You are amongst little girls, my dear, who want to go up against you. And they need to be taught well. They are all talk, smoke and mirrors. But you, my sweet, darling Spencer, are an Ellington. The daughter of Kitty Ellington, heir to a billion-dollar throne, and the one thing I did not give birth to is a failure, or someone who quits. And I'll be damned if you will shame me. Even in your worst moments you are expected to do your damned best. Do you understand me?"

"But Rich slapped me behind something that I know London told her. That whore has turned my best friend against me. And put her up to smacking me in front of the whole class. I've never been so humiliated in my entire life."

Kitty stared at me, then sighed. "Get over it. Once again,

have you not learned anything from me? I have raised you to be the Ace of Spades of messy. And look at you. Sitting here looking pathetic. All this crying is ridiculous. Have you really allowed them to take everything from you? Your dignity? Your self-respect? Have you no shame, Spencer? When she slapped you, you should have gotten up with a smile, shook her hand, and thanked her for declaring war. Those girls want to play dirty, then get dirty with them."

"I just want to be left alone."

Kitty dropped the ice pack in my lap. "You know what, Spencer? I'm getting real sick of your insolence. All those other girls are just like their mothers, cut from the same cloth. But you keep giving me a hard time. Listen to me. You think Rich Montgomery goes to school for an education? Absolutely not! Her wretched mother expects her to marry wealthy and become some miserable house trophy like her. And do you really think London Phillips is supposed to be at Hollywood High? No, dear. She's supposed to be on a Parisian runway, gracing the covers of fashion magazines like her mother. But that girl can't seem to shake off fifteen pounds of baby fat, *pun* intended."

I blinked, tilting my head.

She continued. "And Heather. Do you really think Camille has Heather on my show to make a difference? Of course not! It's about her being a star; about her continuing to be seen. It doesn't matter if she stays high on pills. All Camille cares about is that Heather becomes the next hottest actress in Hollywood. So you see. All of those girls know the rules. Even if they don't like them, they fall in line. But you, my darling daughter, keep giving me a hard time. And it's really starting to press on my nerves. I don't know what I'm going to do with you. You are gorgeous, smart, and witty, Spencer. And you have the world at your fingertips."

I tossed her an incredulous look. I sniffled.

"Yeah right..."

"Listen to me, Spencer." She leaned in. "Are you listening to me?"

"Yes."

"Good! Now pay attention and let your mother lead you to greatness. First thing, learn to keep your mouth shut. Never let your friends or your enemies know what you're thinking or planning to do. Do not give out more than what is needed. Learn to conceal your intentions. Then strike when they least expect it. Second, learn to use your enemies. An enemy can become your best ally..."

I blinked.

"Spencer, are you listening to me?"

"Yes."

"Good. Third, nobody ever gives you power or respect. And stabbing everyone in the back to get it is not how you do it. You want power, you want respect...you pretend to surrender, then you take it! Now here's your next move..."

"I'm so glad you came," Heather said, releasing me from a hug as we air-kissed. "I didn't think you would. It's really good to see you."

After what happened to me yesterday, I took what Kitty had said and decided to turn the battle into a full-fledged war. But first I had to come waving a white flag in Heather's face. Like Kitty said, I needed an ally.

Heather stepped back, and we took each other in. Her thick hair was pulled back into a wiry ponytail. And it looked like she had lost weight. Five, maybe ten pounds more than she could afford. Girlie was all boobs and no booty-bags. And she didn't even have on a coat of makeup. I had almost forgotten what she really looked like without all that war paint on her face. Even though she was skinny as sin and didn't have one swervy curve on her body, she was still a very pretty girl. She was just real ugly on the inside. Almost like a pretty wrapped present that gets opened and there's nothing but a bunch of poop inside. Still, there was something different about Heather. She looked...mature.

Maybe it's from grabbing her ankles, I thought, taking a seat across from her.

"Ohmygod," she gasped, covering her mouth with a hand. "What happened to your face?"

"That cow London set me up. Told Rich a bunch of lies, and the dumb whore believed her and attacked me in finance class. Then Rich had the nerve to stand over me and threaten my life. And you know I don't take kindly to threats. But not to worry. I'm gonna milk London's breadbox if it's the last thing I do."

Heather blinked, blinked again. "OMG, they stole on you?"

I frowned. "*Stole* on me? They didn't steal anything from me. You know I don't do thieves. Those two whores are a lot of things, but I don't think they're filchers. Even as broke as London is, I don't think she'd stoop that low to steal from me. So where you got that from is beyond me. I told you, Rich hit me."

Heather gave me a blank stare.

"Well, why didn't you spray her down when she hit you?"

"She caught me off guard. By the time I realized what

was happening I was already on the floor. And I had just put a fresh can of Mace in my bag, too. This is the second time they've ambushed me and caught me off guard. The last time London put Rich up to attacking me, I was trapped in a car down in that ditch. This time, they waited until I was in class and my handbag was tucked under my seat."

"Spencer, I think you're giving London way too much credit. I don't think Rich is that much of a follower."

"Oh no. Heather. You don't know Rich like I do. And I think you've been locked up too long. I don't give out credit. I'm cash only. And trust me, London has none. I know she put Rich up to it."

"Well, what did you do to her?"

I gave her a look of disbelief. "Heather, how dare you! I didn't do anything to that...that Jenny Craig fraud. That bone cleaner, Miss Hot Wings And Blue Cheese."

Heather gave me a confused look, then shrugged. "Well, how do you know it was London who was behind this?"

I snorted. "Ugh. Because she's a jealous lowlife who's miserable. She's nothing. Mad because she can't lose enough weight to hit the runway. The only thing she'll ever hit is a street corner. That pork roll has been nothing but problems ever since she stepped her big snout in Hollywood. She couldn't stand my friendship with Rich. Always flapping her jaws talking about me and *you*. And you never did anything to her, Heather. So the last thing you should be doing is underestimating her. Trust me. She hides her hate behind her oversized Chanels. That whore is a conniving, undercover snake who likes to grin in your face, then stab you in the back.

"And there's a video uploaded on the Internet. And of course, once again…I've gone viral. My phone has been ringing off the hook. My e-mail has been flooded with all kinds of nastiness saying I deserved it. That I got what my hand called for. And my hand can't even speak. How crazy is that? My hand didn't do a dang thing to her."

Heather looked away, then looked up at the ceiling as if she was looking for her thoughts there. Or maybe she wanted to count the cobwebs in the corner.

"It was all lies, Heather. I did nothing for her to turn on me like that."

"Spencer," she said, bringing her attention back to me, "that doesn't matter. People don't give a damn about that…" She paused. It looked as if she wanted to cry. She dabbed the corner of her eye with the end of her sleeve. "All they care about is what you did do. You can do a million things right and one thing wrong and you're finished. They'll only re-member that one indiscretion. Everything else that ever mattered to you no longer matters to them. You become marked." She took a deep breath, then blew it out, shak-ing her head. "One day I was in every teen magazine. I had dolls named after me. I had fans who adored me. I had everything. Hell, I even had books written about me. And a boomin' television show. And was about to have my own cartoon show. And now I only have tabloid attention. Why? Because I partied too hard? Is that really a crime? For Christ's sake, I did Adderall. Not crack. Not heroin. Not even weed. All I wanted was a little slice of heaven, just a pinch of good times; a notch up from a hookah."

I gave her a blank stare. Obviously, she meant she was a step away from being a hooker. But I felt too sorry and sad for her to bother correcting her.

Tears filled her eyes. "I'm miserable, Spencer. I want out of this place. I want my life back. It's been hell being away from the flashing lights." She looked around to see who was in earshot, then leaned in and whispered, "If it wasn't for my counselor helping me pass the time away in here, I'd probably lose my mind. No. I know I would. He has been the best thing that could have ever happened to me in here."

I smirked. "Mmmhmm...I bet he has."

"He has. But it's not enough."

"Yeah, but it's nasty."

"Well, maybe it is. But who are you to judge me? Desperate times call for desperate measures. So I had to do what I had to do. This isn't about you. It's about me. And there comes a time when you have to know the recipe for your own success and make it happen. I want out of here. And I will do whatever I need to do to make it happen. And if that means I have to kiss him a little bit, love him a little bit, and get my Becky on, then so be it. 'Cause, guess what? When it comes time to recommend me out of this hellhole, guess who is going to sign those papers without hesitation? Mister Mills. You know why? Because one hand always washes the other."

I sat back in my seat and crossed my ankles, impressed. Heather was growing up; doing momma proud. She was talking my kind of language. Using what you had to get what you needed.

Nothing was off-limits when it came to getting what you wanted.

I grinned. "Then let's wash hands."

She furrowed her eyebrows, giving me a confused look. "And how will we do that?"

"Well, one way is we can go into the bathroom to get soap. Another way is, you can tell me everything you know about Anderson Ford. And I do mean everything. And if you tell me the right thing that makes me tingle, when all is said and done, I'll have a surprise and a very big bonus treat for you. You know that little probation problem of yours you have until you're eighteen? Well, Kitty knows the head of the probation department very well. I mean Friday night after bingo, well, when his wife goes to bed, he slips out at two and three in the morning to get his West Hollywood stroll on down Santa Monica Boulevard. And let's just say he isn't out picking up groceries."

Heather's eyes popped open. "Oh my... prostitutes?"

I batted my eyes. "A special kind of prostitute."

"A mess," she said, shaking her head. "And what about the judge?"

I grinned. "All you need to know is he owes Kitty a few favors."

"But—"

"Not a word," I warned her, cutting her off. "All you need to do, Cinderella, to step back into your Hollywood heels—before the stroke of midnight catches you—is give me the goods on Anderson and... trust me... I will see to it that your carriage is trimmed in eighteen-karat gold for the royal ball. And you'll be back on top eating pumpkin seeds in no time."

Heather shifted back in her seat. Her eyes glimmered brightly. She licked her lips in anticipation. "So if I tell you everything I know, you'll have Kitty get me off probation?"

"Exactly."

"And I'll be free to do what I want? I can have my life back?"

"Yes."

She eyed me as if she wasn't sure if she could trust or believe me. "And I won't have to sell my soul to do it?"

Well, partmycheeksandspreadtheseas...Heather had no idea that she had already sold her soul the first time she snorted up those Skittles. And she sold it again when she bent over the devil's desk. Oh, bless her. Her soul was signed, sealed, delivered, and paid in full a long time ago. And there were no refunds.

I sweetly smiled. "Of course not, Heather. Your soul is right where it needs to be. Have I ever lied to you? I told you I was going to do you in. Didn't I keep my word? Aren't you here? Didn't you make the headlines? So obviously you know *I* know how to make it happen. And I know how to make it disappear. Now tell me about Anderson and Co-Co."

She glanced over her shoulder, then leaned in. "Well, this is what I know..."

I sat and stared in utter shock as Heather dished the dirt on how Co-Co had tossed back a whole bottle of pills and tried to kill himself over Anderson. That they had been lovers. That he was Co-Co's first. That all Anderson was doing was using London as a cover. That his parents never expected that he liked...boys. And Co-Co was okay with keeping their relationship a secret until he caught Anderson with another boy who Anderson left Co-Co for.

"I'm telling you, Spencer. Anderson Ford is a user. He toys with people's emotions, gets all up in their heads, then tosses them to the side like they're nothing. What that heartless bastard did to Co-Co and God knows who else is despicable."

I blinked.

Sweethairybuttcheeksandhandcreams...Now it all made sense to me. Anderson was one of those trisexual guys who wanted the cake, the frosting, and the crumbs, too. He was the worst kind of low-down queen there was.

All that fluckery about needing to be with London to get his inheritance was a bunch of hot lies. Him telling me that he wanted to wait until the time was right to make love to me...lies! Had me believing he really thought I was beautiful and sexy, and wanted to be with me. And the only thing he really wanted was to be *me*.

I was speechless.

And to think I invested all of that time on him, wasting good sexual energy trying to seduce him, thinking he was fresh, untouched, unspoiled man meat. Imagining all of the blue-ribbon things I could have taught him. How I wanted to open up the doors to the schoolyard and teach Buff Daddy how to play in my treasure chest, and all the while he was a sneaky little Puff Patty who had high heels and handbags on his mind. No wonder he didn't want to sleep with me! All that time he had me thinking there was something wrong with me because he didn't want to blaze my trail or butter my biscuits. And there wasn't one dang thing wrong with me. No, he was the problem! And he was trying to work me up to be the next cover because London was out of control.

He really made a fool out of me!

I swallowed back my anger.

"Do you have proof?"

Heather nodded. "Co-Co has pictures."

"Well, I need to see them."

She wagged a finger at me. "Ah, ah, ah...it's your turn."

I uncrossed my ankles, clasping my hands in front of

me. Kitty once told me before she shipped me off to boarding school that everything about Hollywood was intertwined in high drama, high fashion, and high stakes. Well, guess what? Now that I was loaded with this juicy piece of news, you had best believe they could add high casualties to the list, because Rich, London, and Anderson were all going to get shot down.

I leaned in and reached for Heather's hand, eyeing her. "I know who your father is..."

GET READY FOR WAR

Ni-Ni Simone
Amir Abrams

ABOUT THIS GUIDE

The following questions are intended to
enhance your group's reading of
GET READY FOR WAR.

Discussion Questions

1. Rich felt as if she was forced to have an abortion and she resented her mother for that. What did you think of that? Do you think Rich had a right to be upset? And if you were in a similar situation, how would you feel?

2. What did you think of London and Justice's relationship? Do you think it was a healthy relationship? Why do you think London was unable to let Justice go?

3. What do you think about Heather being in drug rehab? Do you think she will change? Or do you think she will become more vindictive and continue to use?

4. How do you think Heather's life will change when she finds out who her father is?

5. Spencer spent a lot of time getting revenge on London. Why do you think she hated London so much? Do you think the two of them could ever be friends?

Don't miss the first book in the series,
HOLLYWOOD HIGH.
Available wherever books are sold!

1

London

Listen up and weep. Let me tell you what sets me apart from the rest of these wannabe-fabulous broads.

I *am* fabulous.

From the beauty mole on the upper-left side of my pouty, seductive lips to my high cheekbones and big, brown sultry eyes, I'm that milk-chocolate dipped beauty with the slim waist, long sculpted legs, and triple-stacked booty that had all the cuties wishing their girl could be me. And somewhere in this world, there was a nation of gorilla-faced hood rats paying the price for all of this gorgeousness. *Boom*, thought you knew! Born in London—hint, hint. Cultured in Paris, and molded in New York, the big city of dreams. And now living here in La-La Land—the capital of fakes, flakes, and multiple plastic surgeries. Oh…and a bunch of smog!

Pampered, honey-waxed, and glowing from the UMO 24-karat gold facial I just had an hour ago, it was only right that I did what a diva does best—be diva-licious, of course.

So, I slowly pulled up to the entrance of Hollywood High, exactly three minutes and fifty-four seconds before the bell rang, in my brand-new customized chocolate brown Aston Martin Vantage Roadster with the hot pink interior. I had to have every upgrade possible to make sure I stayed two steps ahead of the rest of these West Coast hoes. By the time I was done, Daddy dropped a check for over a hundred-and-sixty grand. Please, that's how we do it. Write checks first, ask questions later. I had to bring it! Had to serve it! Especially since I heard that Rich—Hollywood High's princess of ghetto fabulousness—would be rolling up in the most expensive car on the planet.

Ghetto bird or not, I really couldn't hate on her. Three reasons: a) her father had the whole music industry on lock with his record label; b) she was West Coast royalty; and c) my daddy, Turner Phillips, Esquire, was her father's attorney. So there you have it. Oh, but don't get it twisted. From litigation to contract negotiations, with law offices in London, Beverly Hills, and New York, Daddy was the power-house go-to attorney for all the entertainment elite across the globe. So my budding friendship with Rich was not just out of a long history of business dealings between my Daddy and hers, but out of necessity.

Image was everything here. Who you knew and what you owned and where you lived all defined you. So sur-rounding myself around the Who's Who of Hollywood was the only way to do it, boo. And right now, Rich, Spencer, and Heather—like it or not—were Hollywood's "It Girls." And the minute I stepped through those glass doors, I was about to become the newest member.

Heads turned as I rolled up to valet with the world in the palm of my paraffin-smooth hands blaring Nicki Minaj's

"Moment 4 Life" out of my Bang & Olufsen BeoSound stereo. I needed to make sure that everyone saw my personalized tags: LONDON. Yep, that's me! London Phillips— fine, fly and forever fabulous. Oh, and did I mention... drop-dead gorgeous? That's right. My moment to shine happened the day I was born. And the limelight had shone on me ever since. From magazine ads and television commercials to the catwalks of Milan and Rome, I may have been new to Hollywood High, but I was *not* new to the world of glitz and glamour, or the clicking of flash bulbs in my face.

Grab a pad and pen. And take notes. I was taking the fashion world by storm and being groomed by the best in the industry long before any of these Hollywood hoes knew what Dior, Chanel, or Yves St. Laurent stood for— class, style, and sophistication. None of them could serve me, okay. Not when I had an international supermodel for a mother who kept me laced in all of the hottest wears (or as they say in France, *haute couture*) from Paris and Milan— Italy, that is.

For those who don't know. Yes, supermodel Jade Phillips was my mother. With her jet black hair and exotic features, she'd graced the covers of *Vogue, Marie Claire, L'Officiel*— a high-end fashion magazine in France and seventy other countries across the world—and she was also featured in *TIME*'s fashion magazine section for being one of the most sought-out models in the industry. And now she'd made it her life's mission to make sure I follow in her diamond-studded footsteps down the catwalk, no matter what. Hence the reason why I forced myself to drink down that god-awful seaweed smoothie, compliments of yet another one of her ridiculous diet plans to rid me of my dangerous curves so that I'd be runway ready, as she liked to call it. Translation: a protruding collarbone, flat-chest, narrow hips, and pancake-flat booty cheeks—a walking campaign ad for Feed the Hungry. *Ugh!*

I flipped down my visor to check my face and hair to make sure everything was in place, then stepped out of my car, leaving the door open and the engine running for the valet attendant. I handed him my pink canister filled with my mother's green gook. "Here. Toss this mess, then clean out my cup." He gave me a shocked look, clearly not used to being given orders. But he would learn today. "Umm, did I stutter?"

"No, ma'am."

"Good. And I want my car washed and waxed by three."

"Yes, ma'am. Welcome to Hollywood High."

"Whatever." I shook my naturally thick and wavy hair from side to side, pulled my Chanels down over my eyes to block the sparkling sun and the ungodly sight of a group of Chia Pets standing around gawking. Yeah, I knew they saw my work. Two-carat pink diamond studs bling-blinging in my ears. Twenty-thousand-dollar pink Hermès Birkin bag draped in the crook of my arm, six-inch Louis Vuitton stilettos on my feet, as I stood poised. Back straight. Hip forward. One foot in front of the other. Always ready for a photo shoot. Lights! Camera! High Fashion! Should I give you my autograph now or later? *Click, click!*

2

Rich

The scarlet-red bottoms of my six-inch Louboutins gleamed as the butterfly doors of my hot pink Bugatti inched into the air and I stepped out and into the spotlight of the California sun. The heated rays washed over me as I sashayed down the red carpet and toward the all-glass student entrance. I was minutes shy of the morning bell, of course.

Voilá, grand entrance.

An all-eyes-on-the-princess type of thing. Rewind that. Now replace princess with sixteen-year-old queen.

Yes, I was doin' it. Poppin' it in the press, rockin' it on all the blogs, and my face alone—no matter the headline—glamorized even the cheapest tabloid.

And yeah, I was an attention whore. And yeah, umm hmm, it was a dirty job. Scandalous. But somebody had to have it on lock.

Amen?

Amen.

Besides, starring in the media was an inherited jewel that came with being international royalty. Daughter of the legendary billionaire, hip-hop artist, and groundbreaking record executive, once known as M.C. Wickedness and now solely known as Richard G. Montgomery Sr., President and C.E.O. of the renowned Grand Records.

Think hotter than Jay-Z.

Signed more talent than Clive Davis.

More platinum records than Lady Gaga or her monsters could ever dream.

Think big, strong, strapping, chocolate, and handsome and you've got my daddy.

And yes, I'm a daddy's girl.

But bigger than that, I'm the exact design and manifestation of my mother's plan to get rich or die trying—hailing from the gutters of Watts, a cramped two-bedroom, concrete ranch, with black bars on the windows and a single palm tree in the front yard—to a sixty-two thousand square foot, fully staffed, and electronically gated, sixty acre piece of 90210 paradise. Needless to say my mother did the damn thing.

And yeah, once upon a time she was a groupie, but so what? We should all aspire to be upgraded. From dating the local hood rich thugs, to swooning her way into the hottest clubs, becoming a staple backstage at all the concerts, to finally clicking her Cinderella heels into the right place at the right time—my daddy's dressing room—and the rest is married-with-two-kids-and-smiling-all-the-way-to the-bank history.

And sure, there was a prenup, but again, so what? Like my mother, the one and only Logan Montgomery, said, giving birth to my brother and me let my daddy know it was cheaper to keep her.

Cha-ching!

So, with parents like mine my life added up to this: my social status was better and bigger than the porno tape that made Kim Trick-dashian relevant and hotter than the ex-con Paris Hilton's jail scandal. I was flyer than Beyoncé and wealthier than Blue Ivy. From the moment I was born, I had fans, wannabes, and frenemies secretly praying to God that they'd wake up and be me. Because along with being royalty I was the epitome of beauty: radiant chestnut skin, sparkling marble brown eyes, lashes that extended and curled perfectly at the ends, and a 5'6", brickhouse thick body that every chick in L.A. would tango with death and sell their last breath to the plastic surgeon to get.

Yeah, it was like that. Trust. My voluptuous milkshake owned the yard.

And it's not that my stuff didn't stink, it's just that my daddy had a PR team to ensure the scent faded away quickly.

Believe me, my biggest concern was my Parisian stylist making sure that I murdered the fashion scene.

I refreshed the pink gloss on my full lips and took a quick peek at my reflection in the mirrored entrance door. My blunt Chinese bob lay flush against my sharp jawline and swung with just the right bounce as I confirmed that my glowing eye shadow and blush was Barbie-doll perfect and complemented my catwalk-ready ensemble. Black diamond studded hoops, fitted red skinny leg jeans, a navy short-sleeve blazer with a Burberry crest on the right breast pocket, a blue and white striped camisole, four strands of sixty-inch pearls, and a signature Gucci tote dangled around my wrist.

A wide smile crept upon me.

Crèmedelacrème.com.

I stepped across the glass threshold and teens of all shapes and sizes lined the marble hallways and hung out in front of their mahogany lockers. There were a few newbies—better known as new-money—who stared at me and were in straight fan mode. I blessed them with a small fan of the fingers and then I continued on my way. I had zero interest in newbies especially since I knew that by this time next year, most of them would be broke and back in public school throwing up gang signs. Okay!

Soooo, moving right along.

I swayed my hips and worked the catwalk toward my locker, and just as I was about to break into a Naomi Campbell freeze, pose, and turn, for no other reason than being fabulous, the words, "Hi, Rich!" slapped me in the face and almost caused me to stumble.

What the . . .

I steadied my balance and blinked, not once but four times. It was Spencer, my ex-ex-ex-years ago-ex-bff, like first grade bff—who I only spoke to and continued to claim because she was good for my image and my mother made me do it.

And, yeah, I guess I'll admit I kind of liked her—sometimes—like one or two days out of the year, maybe. But every other day this chick worked my nerves. Why? Because she was el stupido, dumb, and loco all rolled up into one.

I lifted my eyes to the ceiling, slowly rolled them back down and then hit her with a smile. "Hey, girlfriend."

"Hiiiiii." She gave me a tight smile and clenched her teeth.

Gag me.

I hit her with a Miss America wave and double-cheeked air-kisses.

I guess that wasn't enough for her, because instead of rolling with the moment, this chick snatched a hug from me and I almost hurled. Ev'ver'ree. Where.

Spencer released me and I stood stunned. She carried on, "It's so great to see you! I just got back from the French Alps in Spain." She paused. Tapped her temple with her manicured index finger. "Or was that San Francisco? But anyway, I couldn't wait to get back to Hollywood High! I can't believe we're back in school already!"

I couldn't speak. I couldn't. And I didn't know what shocked me more: that she put her hands on me, or that she smelled like the perfume aisle at Walgreens.

OMG, my eyes were burning...

"Are you okay, Rich?"

Did she attack me?

I blinked.

Say something...

I blinked again.

Did I die...?

Say. Something.

"Umm, girl, yeah," I said coming to and pinching myself to confirm that I was still alive. "What are you wearing? You smell—"

"Delish?" She completed my sentence. "It's La-Voom, Heather's mother's new scent. She asked me to try it and being that I'm nice like that, I did." She spun around as if she were modeling new clothes. "You like?" She batted her button eyes.

Hell no. "I think it's fantast!" I cleared my throat. "But do tell, is she still secretly selling her line out of a storage shed? Or did the courts settle that class action lawsuit against her for that terrible skin rash she caused people?"

Spencer hesitated. "Skin rash?"

"Skin to the rash. And I really hope she's seen the error of her...ways..." My voice drifted. "Oh my...wow." I looked Spencer over, and my eyes blinked rapidly. "Dam'yum!" I said tight-lipped. "Have you been wandering skid row and doing homeless boys again—?"

"Homeless boys—?" She placed her hands on her hips.

"Don't act as if you've never been on the creep-creep with a busted boo and his cardboard box."

"How dare you!" Spencer's eyes narrowed.

"What did I do?!" I pointed at the bumpy alien on her neck. "I'm trying to help you and bring that nastiness to your attention. And if you haven't been entertaining busters then Heather's mother did it to you!"

"Did it to me?" Spencer's eyes bugged and her neck swerved. "I don't go that way! And for your information I have never wandered skid row. I knew exactly where I was going! And I didn't know Joey was homeless. He lied and told me that cardboard box was a science experiment. How dare you bring that up! I'm not some low-level hoochie. So get your zig-zag straight. Because I know you don't want me to talk about your secret visit in a blond wig to an STD clinic. Fire crotch. Queen of the itch, itch."

My chocolate skin turned flaming red, and the South Central in my genes was two seconds from waking up and doing a drive-by sling. I swallowed, drank in two deep breaths, and reloaded with an exhale. "Listen here, Bubbles, do you have Botox leaking from your lips or something? Certainly you already know talking nasty to me is not an option, because I will take my Gucci-covered wrist and beat you into a smart moment. I'm sooo not the one! So I advise you to back up." I pointed my finger into her face and squinted. "All the way up."

"You better—"

"The only commitment I have to the word better, is that I *better* stay rich and I *better* stay beautiful, anything other than that is optional. Now you on the other hand, what you *better* do is shut your mouth, take your compact out and look at the pimple-face bearrilla growing on your neck!"

She gasped.

And I waited for something else nasty to slip from her lips. I'd had enough. Over. It. Besides, my mother taught me that talking only went so far, and when you tired of the chatter, you were to slant your neck and click-click-boom your hater. But, never with the hands, that was so unlady like. Instead, one was to clip their nemesis with a threat that their dirtiest little secret was an e-mail away from being on tabloid blast. "Now, Spencer," I batted my lashes and said with a tinge of concern, "I'm hoping your silence means you've discovered that all of this ying-yang is not the move for you. So, may I suggest that you shut the hell up? Unless, of course, you want the world to uncover that freaky videotaped secret you and your mother hope like hell the Vatican will pray away."

All the color left her face and her lips clapped shut.

I smiled and mouthed, "Pow! Now hit the floor with that."

3

Spencer

I can't stand Rich! That bug-eyed beetle walked around here like she was Queen It when all she really was, was cheap and easy. Ready to give it up at the first hello. Trampette should've been her first name and Man-Eater her last! I should've pulled out my crystal nail file and slapped her big face with it. Who did she think she was?

I fanned my hand out over the front of my denim mini-dress, shifting the weight of my one-hundred-and-eighteen-pound frame from one six-inch, pink heeled foot to the other. Unlike Rich, who was one beef patty short of a Whopper, I was dancer toned and could wear anything and look fabulous in it. But I *chose* not to be over-the-top with it because unlike Rich and everyone else here at Hollywood High, *I* didn't have to impress anyone. I was naturally beautiful and knew it.

And yeah, she was cute and all. And, yeah, she dressed like no other. But Trampette forgot I knew who she was *before* Jenny Craig and *before* she had those crowded ass teeth shaved down and straightened out. I knew her when she was a chunky bucktooth Teletubby running around and losing her breath on the playground. So there was no way Miss Chipmunk wanted to roll down in the gutter with me 'cause I was the Ace of Spades when it came to messy!

I shook my shoulder-length curls out of my face, pulled out my compact, and then smacked my Chanel-glossed lips. I wanted to die but I couldn't let pie-face know that, so I said, "Umm, Rich, how about *you* shut *your* mouth. After all the morning-after pills you've popped in the last two years, I can't believe you'd stand here and wanna piss in my Crunch Berries. Oh, no Miss Plan B, *you* had better seal your own doors shut, *first*, before you start tryna walk through mine. You're the reason they invented Plan B in the first place."

I turned my neck from side to side and blinked my hazel eyes. *Sweet... merciful... kumquats!* Heather's mother's perfume had chewed my neck up. I wanted to scream!

Rich spat, "You wouldn't be trying to get anything crunked would you, Ditsy Doodle? You—"

"Ohmygod," London interrupted our argument. Her heels screeched against the floor as she said, "Here you are!" She air-kissed Rich, then eyed me, slowly.

Oh, no this hot-buttered beeswax snooty-booty didn't!

London continued, "I've been wandering around this monstrous place all morning—" She paused and twisted her perfectly painted lips. "What's that smell?" London frowned and waved her hand under her nose, and sniffed. "Is that, is that you, Spencer?"

"Umm hmm," Rich said. "She's wearing La-Voom, from the freak-nasty-rash collection. Doesn't it smell delish?"

"No. That mess stinks. It smells like cat piss."

Rich laughed. "Girrrrl, I didn't wanna be the one to say it, since Ms. Thang wears her feelings like a diamond bangle, but since you took it there, *meeeeeeeeow!*" The two of them cackled like two messy sea hens. Wait, hens aren't in the sea, right? No, of course not. Well, that's what they sounded like. So that's what they were.

"I can't believe you'd say that?!" I spat, snapping my compact shut, stuffing it back into my Louis Vuitton Tribute bag.

"Whaaaaatever," London said, waving me on like I was some second-class trash. "Do you, boo. And while you're at it. You might want to invest in some Valtrex for those nasty bumps around your neck."

I frowned. "*Valtrex?* Are you serious? For what?"

She snapped her fingers in my face. "Uh, helllllllo, Space Cadet. For that nastiness around your neck, what else? It looks like a bad case of herpes, boo."

Rich snickered.

I inhaled. Exhaled.

Batted my lashes.

Looked like I was going to have to *serve her, too.*

I swept a curl away from my face, tucking it behind my ear.

Counted to ten in my head. 'Cause in five…four… three…two…one, I was about to set it up—wait, wait, I meant set it off—up in this mother suckey-duckey, okay? I mean. It was one thing for Rich to try it. After all, we've *known* each other since my mother—media giant and billionaire Kitty Ellington, the famed TV producer and host of her internationally popular talk show, *Dish the Dirt*—along with Rich's dad, insisted we become friends for image's sake. And in the capital of plastics appearance *was* everything. So I put up with Rich's foolery because I had to. But, that chicken-foot broad London, who I only met over the summer through Rich, needed a reality check—and *quick*, before I brought the rain down on her.

Newsflash: I might not have been as braggadocious as the two of them phonies, but I came from just as much money as Rich's daddy and definitely more than London's family would ever have. So she had better back that thang-a-lang up on a grill 'cause I was seconds from frying her goose. "You know what, London, you better watch your panty liner!"

She wrinkled her nose and put a finger up. "Pause."

Did she just put her finger in my face?

"Pump, pump, pump it back," I snapped, shifting my handbag from one hand to the other, putting a hand up on my hip. My gold and diamond bangles clanked. "You don't *pause* me, Miss Snicker-Doodle-Doo. I'm no CD player! And before you start with your snot-ball comments get your facts straight, Miss Know It All. I don't own a cat. I'm allergic to them. So why would I wear cat piss? And I don't have herpes. Besides how would I get it around my neck? It's just a nasty rash from Mrs. Cummings' new perfume. So that goes to show you how much you know. And they call me confused. Go figure."

"You wait one damn minute, Dumbo," London hissed.

"*Dumbo?!* I'll have you know I have the highest GPA in this whole entire school." I shot a look over at Rich, who was laughing hysterically. "Unlike some of *you* hyenas who have to buy your grades, *I'm* not the one walking around here with the IQ of a Popsicle."

Rich raised her neatly arched brow.

London clapped her hands. "Good for you. Now . . . like I was saying, *Dumbo*, I don't know how you dizzy hoes do it here at Hollywood High, but I will floor you, girlfriend, okay. Don't do it to yourself."

I frowned and slammed my locker shut. "Oh . . . my . . . God! You've gone too far now, London. That may be how *you* hoes in New York do it. But we don't do that kind of perverted nastiness over here on the West Coast."

She frowned. "*Excuse* you?"

I huffed. "I didn't stutter, Miss Nasty. I *said* you went too damn far telling me not to do it to myself, like I go around playing in my goodie box or something."

Rich and London stared at each other, then burst into laughter.

I stomped off just as the homeroom bell rang. My curls bounced wildly as my stilettos jabbed the marbled floor beneath me. *Welcome to Hollywood High,* trick*! The first chance I get, I'm gonna knock Miss London's playhouse down right from underneath her nose.*

But first, I had more pressing issues to think about. I needed to get an emergency dermatologist appointment to handle this itchy, burning rash. My heels scurried as I made a left into the girls' lounge instead of a right into homeroom. I locked myself into the powder room. I had to get out of here!

OMG, there was a wildfire burning around my neck. *Ooooh, when I get back from the doctor's office, I'm gonna*

*jumpstart Heather's caboose for her mother trying to do
me in like this.*

I dialed 9-1-1.

The operator answered on the first ring, "Operator,
what's your emergency?" Immediately I screamed, "Camille
Cummings, the washed-up drunk, has set my neck on fire!"

4

Heather

My eyes were heavy.

Sinking.

And the more I struggled to keep them open the heavier they felt. I wasn't sure what time it was. I just knew that dull yellow rays had eased their way through the slits of my electronic blinds, so I guessed it was daylight.

Early morning, maybe?

Maybe...?

My head was splitting.

Pounding.

The room was spinning.

I tried to steady myself in bed, but I couldn't get my neck to hold up my head.

I needed to get it together.

I had something to do.

Think, think, think...what is it...

I don't know.

Damn.

I fell back against my pillow and a few small goose feathers floated into the air like dust mites.

I was messed up. Literally.

My mouth was dry. Chalky. And I could taste the stale Belvedere that had chased my way to space. No, no, it wasn't space. It was Heaven. It had chased my way to the side of Heaven that the crushed up street candy, Black Beauty, always took me to. A place where I loved to be…where I didn't need to snort Adderall to feel better, happier, alive. A place where I was always a star and never had to come off the set of my hit show, or step out of the character I played—Wu-Wu Tanner. The pop-lock-and-droppin'-it, fun, loving, exciting, animal-print wearing, suburban teenager with a pain in the butt little sister, an old dog, and parents who loved Wu-Wu and her crazy antics.

A place where I was nothing like myself—Heather Cummings. I was better than Heather. I was Wu-Wu. A star. Every day. All day.

I lay back on my king-sized wrought iron bed and giggled at the thought that I was two crushed pills away from returning to Heaven.

I closed my eyes and just as I envisioned Wu-Wu throwing a wild and crazy neighborhood party, "You better get up!" sliced its way through my thoughts. "And I mean right now!"

I didn't have to open my eyes or turn toward the door to know that was Camille, my mother.

The official high blower.

"I don't know if you think you're Madame Butterfly, Raven-Simoné, or Halle Berry!" she announced as she moseyed her way into my room and her matted mink slippers slapped against the wood floor. "But I can tell you this, the cockamamie bull you're trying to pull this morning—"

So it was morning.

She continued, "—Will not work. So if you know what's best for you, you'll get up and make your way to school!"

OMG! That's what I have to do! It's the first day of school.

My eyes popped open and immediately landed on my wall clock: 10:30 A.M. It was already third period.

I sat up and Camille stood at the foot of my bed with her daily uniform on: a long and silky white, spaghetti-strap, see-through nightgown, matted mink slippers, and a drink in her hand—judging from the color it was either brandy or Scotch. I looked into her ice-chipped blue eyes. It was Scotch for sure. She shook her glass and the ice rattled. She flipped her honey blond hair over her blotchy red shoulders and peered at me.

I shook my head. God, I hated that we resembled each other. I had her thin upper lip, the same small mole on my left eyelid, her high cheekbones, her height (5'6"), her shape (a busty 34D), her narrow hips and small butt.

Our differences: I looked Latin although I wasn't. I was somewhere in between my white mother and mysterious black father. My skin was Mexican bronze, or more like a white girl baked by the Caribbean sun. My hair was Sicilian thick and full of sandy brown coils. My chocolate eyes were shaped like an ancient Egyptian's. Slanted. Set in almonds. I didn't really look white and I definitely didn't look black. I just looked...different. Biracial—whatever that was. All I knew is that I hated it.

Which is why, up until the age of ten, every year for my

birthday I'd always blow out the candles with a wish that I could either look white like my mother or black like my father.

This in-between thing didn't work for me. I didn't want it. And I especially didn't like looking Spanish, when I wasn't Spanish. And the worst was when people asked me what was I? Where did I come from? Or someone would instantly speak Spanish to me! WTF! How about I only spoke English! And what was I? I was an American mutt who just wanted to belong somewhere, anywhere other than the lonely middle.

Damn.

"Heather Suzanne Cummings," Camille spat as she rattled her drink and caused some of it to spill over the rim. "I'm asking you not to try me this morning, because I am in no mood. Therefore I advise you to get up and make your way to school—"

"What, are you running for PTA president or something?" I snapped as I tossed the covers off of me and stood to the floor. "Or is there a parent-teachers' meeting you're finally going to show up to?"

Camille let out a sarcastic laugh and then she stopped abruptly. "Don't be offensive. Now shut up." She sipped her drink and tapped her foot. Her voice slurred a little. "I don't give a damn about those teachers' meetings or PETA, or PTTA, PTA or whatever it is. I care about my career, a career that you owe me."

"I don't owe you anything!" I walked into my closet and she followed behind me.

"You owe me everything!" she screamed. "I know you don't think you're hot because you have your own show, do you?" She snorted. "Well let me blow your high, missy—"

You already have....

She carried on. "You being the star of that show is only because of me. It's because of me and my career you were even offered the audition. I'm the star! Not you! Not Wu-Wu! But me, Camille Cummings, Oscar award-winning—"

"Drunk!" I spat. "You're the Oscar award-winning and washed up drunk! Whose career died three failed rehabs and a million bottles ago—!"

WHAP!!!!

Camille's hand crashed against my right cheek and forced my neck to whip to the left and get stuck there.

She downed the rest of her drink and took a step back. For a moment I thought she was preparing to assume a boxer's position. Instead she squinted her eyes and pointed at me. "If my career died, it's because I slept with the devil and gave birth to you! You ungrateful little witch. Now," she said through clenched teeth as she lowered her brow, "I suggest you get to school, be seen with that snotty-nose clique. And if the paparazzi happens to show up you better mention my name every chance you get!"

"I'm not—"

"You *will*. And *you will* like it. And *you will* be nice to those girls and act as if you like each and every one of them, and especially that pissy princess Rich!" She reached into her glass, popped a piece of ice into her mouth, and crunched on it. "The driver will be waiting. So hurry up!" She stormed out of my room and slammed the door behind her.

I stood frozen. I couldn't believe that she'd put her hands on me. I started to run out of the room after her, but quickly changed my mind. She wasn't worth chipping a nail, let alone attacking her and giving her the satisfaction of having me arrested again. The last time I did that it took forever for that story to die down and besides, the creators of my show told me that another arrest would surely get me fired and Wu-Wu Tanner would be no more.

That was not an option.

So, I held my back straight, proceeded to the shower, snorted two crushed Black Beauties, and once I made my way to Heaven and felt like a star, I dressed in a leopard cat suit, hot pink feather belt tied around my waist, chandelier earrings that rested on my shoulders, five-inch leopard wedged heels, and a chinchilla boa tossed loosely around my neck. I walked over to my full-length mirror and posed. "Mirror, mirror on the wall who's the boom-boom-flyest of 'em all?" I did a Beyoncé booty bounce, swept the floor, and sprang back up.

The mirror didn't respond but I knew for sure that if it had, it would've said, "You doin' it, Wu-Wu. You boom-bop-bustin'-it-fly!"

HAVEN'T HAD ENOUGH? CHECK OUT THESE GREAT SERIES FROM DAFINA BOOKS!

DRAMA HIGH

by L. Divine

Follow the adventures of a young sistah who's learning that life in the hood is nothing compared to life in high school.